THE BOOK

"The reader is bombarded with a surfeit of imaginative images, symbols, and events. And after putting down the novel and allowing some time to elapse, the characters, the kaleidoscope of events, assume a cohesive and even more meaningful form. . . . John Irving's achievement is astonishing."
—*The New York Times*

THE AUTHOR

"John Irving, it is abundantly clear, is a true artist. He is not afraid to take on great themes."
—*The Los Angeles Times*

THE ACCLAIM

"The novel flows with an undercurrent of whimsy that keeps a silly grin on the reader's face, and is punctuated by madcap twists that turn the grin into chair-shaking laughter."
—*Newsday*

Books by John Irving

The 158-Pound Marriage
Setting Free the Bears
The Water-Method Man
The World According to Garp

Published by POCKET BOOKS

John Irving

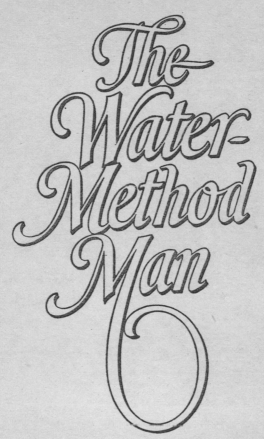

The Water-Method Man

PUBLISHED BY POCKET BOOKS NEW YORK

POCKET BOOKS, a Simon & Schuster division of
GULF & WESTERN CORPORATION
1230 Avenue of the Americas, New York, N.Y. 10020

ISBN: 0-671-82254-3

First Pocket Books printing November, 1978

10 9 8 7 6 5 4

POCKET and colophon are trademarks of Simon & Schuster.

Printed in the U.S.A.

ACKNOWLEDGMENTS

The author is grateful to the director Irvin Kershner for a valuable and exciting film experience in 1969 and 1970, and to the Rockefeller Foundation for their assistance in 1970 and 1971.

Especially, the author is indebted to Donald Harington. A vital passage in this book is his.

for Shyla

1: Yogurt & Lots of Water

Her gynecologist recommended him to me. Ironic: the best urologist in New York is French. Dr. Jean Claude Vigneron: ONLY BY APPOINTMENT. So I made one.

"You like New York better than Paris?" I asked.

"In Paris, I dared to keep a car."

"My father is a urologist, too."

"Then he must be a second-rate one," Vigneron said, "if he didn't know what was wrong with you."

"It's nonspecific," I said. I knew the history of my ailment well. "Sometimes it's nonspecific urethritis, once it was nonspecific prostatitis. Another time, I had the clap— but that's a different story. Once it was just a common germ. But always, nonspecific."

"It looks very specific to me," Vigneron said.

"No," I said. "Sometimes it responds to penicillin, sometimes sulfa does the trick. Once, Furadantin cured it."

"There, you see?" he said. "Urethritis and prostatitis don't respond to Furadantin."

"Well, there," I said, *"You see?* It was something else that time. Nonspecific."

"Specific," Vigneron said. "You can't get much more specific than the urinary tract."

He showed me. On his examination table I tried to be calm. He handed me a perfect plastic breast, as lovely a one as I've seen: realistic color and texture, and a fine, upstanding nipple.

"My God . . ."

"Just bite on it," he said. "Forget about me."

I clutched the rare boob, looking it straight in the eye. I'm sure that my father employs no such up-to-date devices. When you're erect, the nasty glass rod goes in a bit easier. I recall I pulled a muscle, trying not to cry.

"*Very* specific," said Jean Claude Vigneron, who responded in sly French when I told him it was at least unusual to hold a breast whose nipple one could bite without reserve.

Vigneron's diagnosis of my ailment is best understood with some historical perspective. Odd and painful peeing is not new to me.

Seven times in the last five years, I have suffered this unnamable disorder. Once it was the clap, but that's another story. Usually, the apparatus is simply stuck together in the morning. A careful pinch sets things right, or almost right. Urinating is often a challenge, the sensations always new and surprising. Also, it's time-consuming—your day spent in anticipation of the next time you'll have to pee. Sex, typically, is unmentionable. Orgasm is truly climactic. Coming is a slow experience—the long, astonishing journey of a rough and oversized ballbearing. In the past I had given up the act altogether. Which drives me to drink, which makes the pee burn: an unfriendly circle.

And *always* the nonspecific diagnosis. Terrifying new strains of possibly Asian venereal diseases are never substantiated. "Some kind of infection" is carefully not named. Different drugs are tried; one eventually works. *The Medical Encyclopedia of the Home* reveals vague and ominous symptoms of cancer of the prostate. But the doctors always tell me I'm too young. I always agree.

And now, Jean Claude Vigneron puts his glass rod on the problem. Specifically a birth defect. Not surprising—I have already suspected the existence of several.

"Your urinary tract is a narrow, winding road."

I took the news pretty well.

"Americans are so silly about sex," Vigneron said. From my own experience, I felt unfit to argue. "You think everything is washable, but the vagina remains the dirtiest thing in the world. Did you know that? Every unexposed orifice harbors hundreds of harmless bacteria, but the vagina is a superior hostess. I say "harmless"—but not to you. *Normal* penises flush them out."

"But not my narrow, winding road?" I said, thinking of

its odd crannies, where hundreds of bacteria could lead a secret life.

"You see?" said Vigneron. "Isn't that specific?"

"What's the recommended treatment?" I still held the plastic breast. A man with an invulnerable nipple can be brave.

"You have four alternatives," Vigneron said. "There are lots of drugs, and one will always work. Seven times in five years is not surprising, considering such a urinary tract as yours. And the pain isn't severe, is it? You can live with this periodic inconvenience to your peeing and your screwing, can't you?"

"I have a new life now," I said. "I want to change."

"Then stop screwing," Vigneron said. "Consider masturbation. You can wash your hand."

"I don't want to change *that* much."

"Remarkable!" Vigneron cried. He is a handsome man, big and cocksure; I gripped the plastic breast tightly. "Remarkable, remarkable . . . you are my tenth American patient to face these alternatives, and every one of you rejects the first two."

"So what's remarkable about that?" I said. "They're not very attractive alternatives."

"For *Americans!*" cried Vigneron. "Three of my patients in my Paris days chose to live with it. And one—and he wasn't an old man, either—gave up screwing."

"I haven't heard the other two alternatives," I said.

"I always pause here," said Dr. Vigneron. "I like to guess which one you'll choose. With Americans I've never guessed wrong. You are a predictable people. You always want to change your lives. You never accept what you're born with. And for you? For you, I can *sense* it. It's the water method for you!"

I found the doctor's tone offensive. With breast in hand, I was determined that the water method would *not* be for me.

"It is a fallible method, of course," Vigneron said. "A compromise, at best. Instead of seven times in five years, maybe one time in three years—healthier odds, that's all."

"I don't like it."

"But you haven't tried it," he said. "It's very simple. You drink lots of water before you screw. You drink lots

13

of water *after* you screw. And you go easy on the booze. Alcohol makes bacteria happy. In the French Army, we had an ingenious test-cure for the clap. Give them the normal dose of penicillin. Then give them three beers before bedtime when they tell you they think they're cured. If they have a discharge in the morning, more penicillin. You just need lots of water. With your curious tract, you need all the flushing you can get. After intercourse, just remember to get up and pee."

The breast in my hand was only plastic. I said, "You expect me to perform the sexual act on a full bladder? That's painful."

"It's different," Vigneron agreed. "But you'll have bigger erections. Did you know that?"

I asked him what the fourth alternative was, and he smiled.

"A simple operation," he said. "Minor surgery."

I sliced my thumbnail into the plastic nipple.

"We simply straighten you out," said Vigneron. "We widen the road. It doesn't take a minute. We put you to sleep, of course."

In my hand was an absurd synthetic mammary gland, an obvious fake. I put it down. "It must hurt a little," I said. "I mean, *after* the operation."

"For forty-eight hours or so." Vigneron shrugged; all pain appeared equally tolerable to him.

"Can you put me to sleep for forty-eight hours?" I asked.

"Ten out of ten!" Vigneron cried. "They always ask that!"

"Forty-eight hours?" I wondered. "How do I pee?"

"As fast as you can," he said, poking the upright nipple on the examination table as if it were a button summoning nurses and anesthetists—bringing him the polished scalpel for this surgical feat. I could imagine it. A slender version of a Roto-Rooter. A long, tubular razor, like a miniature of the mouth of a lamprey eel.

Dr. Jean Claude Vigneron eyed me as if I were a painting he was not quite finished with. "The water method?" he guessed.

"You're ten for ten," I said, just to please him. "Did any of your patients ever choose the operation?"

14

"Just one," said Vigneron, "and I knew he would, from the start. He was a practical, scientific, no-nonsense sort of man. On the examination table he was the only one who scorned the tit."

"A hard man," I said.

"A *secure* man," said Vigneron. He lit a foul, dark Gauloise and inhaled without fear.

Later, living with the water method, I thought about his four alternatives. I thought of a fifth: French urological surgeons are quacks, seek another opinion, seek lots of other opinions—any other opinion . . .

I had my hand on a real breast when I phoned Vigneron to tell him of this fifth alternative that he should offer his patients.

"Remarkable!" he cried.

"Don't tell me. You're ten for ten?"

"Ten out of ten!" he hollered. "And always about three days after the examination. You're right on time!"

I was quiet on my end of the phone. In my hand her breast felt like plastic. But only for this quiet moment; she came to life when Vigneron boomed at me.

"It's not a matter of another *opinion*. Don't kid yourself. The geography of your urinary tract is a *fact*. I could draw you a map, to scale . . ."

I hung up. "I've never liked the French," I told her. "Your gynecologist must have it in for me, recommending that sadist. He hates Americans, you know. I'm sure that's why he came here, with his goddamn glass rods . . ."

"Paranoia," she said, her eyes already closed. She's not a big talker, this one. "Words," she says, in her harumphing way. She has a gesture for what she thinks of words; she lifts one breast with the back of her hand. She has good, full breasts, but they need a bra. I'm very fond of her breasts; they make me wonder how that fake boob of Vigneron's had any effect on me. If I had it to do again, I wouldn't take the tit. Well, yes I would. *She* wouldn't ever need a device like that, though. She's a practical, no-nonsense, gut-level, secure person. Offer her those four alternatives and she'd take the operation. I know; I asked her.

"Surgery," she said. "If something *can* be fixed, then fix it."

15

"The water's not so bad," I said. "I *like* water. It's good for me too, in lots of ways. And I have bigger erections. Did you know that?"

She lifts the back of her hand and one breast stands up. I really like her very much.

Her name is Tulpen. That means tulips in German, but her parents didn't know it was German, or what it meant, when they named her. Her parents were Polish. They died peacefully in New York, but Tulpen was born in an R.A.F. hospital outside London during the blitz. There was a nice nurse whose name was Tulpen. They liked the nurse, they wanted to forget everything Polish, and they thought that the nurse was a Swede. Nobody found out what Tulpen meant until Tulpen took German in high school, in Brooklyn. She came home and told her parents, who were very surprised; it wasn't the cause of their death, or anything like that; it was just a fact. None of this is important; these are just facts. But that's when Tulpen talks: when there's a fact. And there aren't many.

Following her example, I began with a fact: my urinary tract is a narrow, winding road.

Facts are true. Tulpen is a very honest person. I am not so honest. I'm a pretty good liar, in fact. People who've really known me tend to believe me less and less. They tend to think I lie all the time. But I'm telling the truth now! Just remember: you don't know me.

When I talk like this, Tulpen lifts a breast with the back of her hand.

What in hell do we have in common? I'll stick to the facts. Names are facts. Tulpen and I have the carelessness of our names in common. Hers was a mistake, which doesn't matter to her. I have several; like hers, they're all pretty accidental. My father and mother named me Fred, and it never seemed to bother them that almost no one else ever called me that. Biggie called me Bogus. That was the invention of my oldest and dearest friend, Couth, who coined the name when he first caught me lying. The name stuck. Most of my old friends called me that, and Biggie knew me then. Merrill Overturf, who is still lost, called me Boggle. Like any name, there were vague reasons. Ralph Packer named me Thump-Thump, a name I despise. And Tulpen calls me by my surname, Trumper. I know why:

it's the closest to a fact that you can come to in a name. Male surnames don't often change. So most of the time I'm Fred "Bogus" Trumper. That's a fact.

Facts fall out of me slowly. So I don't get lost, I'll repeat them. Now there are two. One: My urinary tract is a narrow, winding road. Two: Tulpen and I have the carelessness of our names in common. And possibly not much else.

But wait! I am reaching for a third fact. Three: I believe in Rituals! I mean, there have always been things like the water method in my life; there have always been rituals. No particular ritual has ever lasted very long (I told Vigneron I have a new life, that I want to change, and this is true), but always I have moved from one ritual to another. Right now it's the water method. Some historical perspective on my rituals will take a little time, but the water method is clear. Also, Tulpen and I share an early morning ritual, of sorts. Although the water method has me getting up a little earlier—and a few times in the night—Tulpen and I have persisted in this routine. I get up and pee and brush my teeth and drink a lot of water. She starts coffee and puts on a stack of records. We meet back in bed for yogurt. Always yogurt. She has a red bowl, I have a blue one, but if we have different flavors we often trade the bowls back and forth. A flexible ritual is the best kind, and yogurt is a sensible, healthy food which is very kind to your mouth in the morning. We don't talk. This is nothing new for Tulpen, but even *I* don't talk. We listen to the records and eat our yogurt. I don't know Tulpen very well, but apparently she's always done this. An addition to her ritual was introduced by me: when the yogurt is all gone, we make love for a long time. After that, the coffee's ready and we have it. We don't talk as long as the records play. The only variation caused by the water method is minor, and falls somewhere after love and during coffee. I get up to pee and drink a lot of water.

I haven't lived with Tulpen for very long, but I've a feeling that if I'd lived with her for years and years, I wouldn't know her any better.

Tulpen and I are both twenty-eight, but she's really

17

older than I am; she has outgrown having to talk about herself.

It's Tulpen's apartment, and all the things in it are hers. I left my things. and my child, with my first and only wife.

I said to Dr. Jean Claude Vigneron that I have a new life, etc.; I said that some historical perspective on my rituals will take a little time; I also said that I'm not so honest. But Tulpen is. She helps me keep things straight by raising one breast with the back of her hand. In no time at all, I learned not to talk as long as the records play. I learned to say only what's essential (though people who've known me would tend to say that I am lying even now. Fuck them! I say, for such pessimism).

My urinary tract is a narrow, winding road, and right now there's yogurt and lots of water. I'm going to stick to the facts. I want to change.

2 : War-Built Things

Among his other kicks, Fred Bogus Trumper likes to remember Merrill Overturf, the diabetic. In Trumper's Iowa phase, his memories of Overturf are especially sweet. It helps, for accuracy, that some of Overturf is tape-recorded.

Such escapism. Listening to Merrill, in Vienna—while Trumper looks out his Iowa window, through a rusty screen and a fat katydid's wing; he sees a slow-moving, beshitted truck, brimming with hogs. Over the complaining pigs, Bogus listens to the ditty Merrill composed at the Prater—later used, Merrill claimed, to seduce Wanga Holthausen, a singing coach for the Vienna Boys' Choir. The background music is from the Prater go-kart track, where Merrill Overturf once held the 20-lap record. Possibly, he still holds it.

There are faint distortions on the tape; then Merrill is telling his swimming story, the one about there being a tank at the bottom of the Danube. "You can only see it in a full moon. You must block the moon with your back," says Merrill, "which cuts the reflection." Then, somehow, you arch out of the water and hold your face "approximately six inches above the surface—all the time keeping a land-sight on the dock at the Gelhafts Keller." Somehow you hold this position without stirring the water, "and if the wind doesn't make a single ripple, the tank's barrel swings up to where you think you could almost touch it, or it's perfectly aimed to blast you. And in a straight line off Gelhaft's dock, the tank's top hatch opens, or flutters in the water, or *seems* to open. But that's as long as I've ever been able to hold my face approximately six inches above the water surface . . ." Then, thinking diabetically, Merrill announces that this exertion always influences his blood sugar.

Bogus Trumper flips the switch that says REWIND. The hog truck is gone. but on the other side of the screen, the katydid still holds out its wings, more perfect and complicated than some Oriental silkscreen, and Trumper, squinting through this lovely mesh, sees Mr. Fitch, a retired neighbor, scratching his dry and overraked lawn. *Scritch-scritch* goes Mr. Fitch. urging the last ant out of his grass. Through a katydid's wing is the only way to make Fitch-watching bearable.

The car that now labors to the curb—the one that Mr. Fitch waves his rake at—carries Trumper's wife, Biggie, his son, Colm, and three spare tires. Trumper regards the car, wonders if three spare tires are enough. His face mashed to the window screen, he startles the katydid, whose sudden wing-whir startles Trumper—who lurches off balance, his head pushing the rotting screen free of the frame. Catching himself, Bogus jars the frame loose too, and what his startled wife sees is her husband's precarious dangle—his waist, the axis for his unexplained teetering on the window sill.

"What are you doing?" Biggie screams to him.

And Bogus finds the tape recorder with his foot, dragging it toward him like an anchor. He restores his balance by kneeling on the control panel. The recorder is confused; one knee says FULL SPEED FORWARD, the other says PLAY. In a high voice, Merrill Overturf blurts, ". . . off Gelhalft's dock the tank's top hatch opens, or flut—!"

"What?" says Biggie. "What are you doing?"

"I'm fixing the screen," Trumper says, and waves reassuringly to Mr. Fitch. who waves his rake. Not in the least distressed at window-dangling or odd shrieks, Fitch is used to various demonstrations of imbalance from this house.

"Well," says Biggie, with one hip cocked out, making a seat for Colm. "Well, the diapers aren't done. Someone will have to go back to the laundromat and take them out of the dryer."

"I'll go, Big," Bogus says, "just as soon as I fix this screen."

"That won't be easy!" hollers Mr. Fitch, leaning on his rake. "War-built!" he cries. "Damn war-built things!"

"The screens?" Bogus asks from his window.

"Your whole house!" Fitch shouts. "All these jiffy one-stories the university put up! War-built! Cheap materials! Woman labor! Junk!" But Mr. Fitch isn't really being unpleasant. Anything vaguely connected with the war effort sets him off. A bad time for Fitch; he was too old to go, even back then, so he fought the home front with the women.

At the see-through curtains of his front-porch window, Fitch's tiny wife is stirring nervously. *Do you want to have your fifth stroke, Fitch?*

When Trumper examines the rotten screen, he finds the accusation to be true. The wood feels like sponge; the mesh is rusted brittle.

"Bogus," says Biggie, straddling the sidewalk, *"I'll* fix the screen. You're terrible at that kind of thing."

Trumper slides back inside, moves the tape recorder to the safety of an upper bookshelf and watches Mrs. Fitch at her see-through curtain waving Mr. Fitch inside.

Later, Bogus goes to get the diapers. On his way home, his right headlight falls out and he drives over it. Changing his right front tire, he thinks he'd like to meet a man who thinks he's got a worse car. *I would trade with him in an instant.*

But what Trumper thinks he'd really like to know is whether there was anyone under the top hatch of that tank. Or if there really is a tank, at all; if Merrill Overturf really saw it; if, even, Merrill Overturf knows how to swim.

3: Old Tasks & Plumbing News

Bogus Trumper
918 Iowa Ave.
Iowa City, Iowa

Sept. 20, 1969

Mr. Cuthbert Bennett
Caretaker/ The Pillsbury Estate
Mad Indian Point
Georgetown, Maine

My Dear Couth:

How are you keeping the seventeen bathrooms, now that all the Pillsburys have left you with their plumbing? And have you decided in which master bedroom, with which sea-view, you will spend your winter?

Biggie and I appreciated your convincing the Pillsburys we were safe guests for the boathouse. That was a nice revival week for us, Couth—and a break to be able to leave my genitors.

It was a curious summer we had with my genitors. Great Boar's Head is the same summer scene as ever—a convalescent home for the dying, who seem to think that three months of wheezing in the salt air will preserve their lungs for another winter. My father's business thrives in the summer. He once told me something about old people: their bladders are the first to go. A urologist's heaven on the New Hampshire shore!

But it *was* something for the old boy to open his

basement to us for July and August. Since my disinheritance, Mother has obviously been feeling grandmotherly urges; their summer offer must have stemmed from Mom's desire to see Colm, not Biggie and me. And my father seemed to unbend his previous financial ultimatum—though the unbending was no more appealing to me than his cutting me off. Also, he charged me rent on the basement.

When we left to come back here, the good doctor orated, "Let's leave it like this, Fred. You're going on four years of doing it on your own, and I must tell you: I'm impressed. Let's see you tie down that Ph.D., and keep your grades, and I think Mom and I might be able to help you and Biggie and little Colm toward a nest egg. That Colm *is* a dandy."

And Mom kissed Biggie (when my father wasn't looking), and we all bundled back to Iowa City. Three tires and two fan belts later, we were back in our war-built one-story. The old man didn't give me so much as a dime for the tolls.

Which brings me to something important, Couth—if you could spare a little. The tolls alone ran us twenty bills, and I haven't even paid the credit-card companies for the trip east in July. And in Michigan City, Indiana, we had a Holiday Inn Experience which will probably mean the early retirement of my Gulf Card.

But! There is a thin shard of sunlight in this gloom. My thesis chairman, Dr. Wolfram Holster, has given me some of the Comparative Literature Kitty, as he insists on calling it. For my piece of the kitty, I run the tapes in the language lab for freshman German. My officemate, and fellow tape-runner in the lab, is a sly little pedant named Zanther, whose interpretation and "supra-literal" translation of Borgetz is being heralded in this month's issue of *The Linguist*. I showed Zanther the bulk of my summer's writing on my thesis; he read it all in one afternoon and told me he didn't think anyone would publish it. I asked him what the circulation of *The Linguist* was; we haven't spoken since. Following my period of proctorship in the language lab—when I know Zanther is coming on duty- I artfully misfile the tapes. He left me a note about it. "I know what you're doing," the note said; it was stuck in what he knew to be my favorite tape. I left him a note, too. It said: *"No one* knows what *you're* doing." Now communication is impossible between us.

Even so, it's a small kitty and I've got a small bite of it. Biggie's back with her old job at the hospital, bed-panning the elderly between 6 A.M. and noon, five days a week. Colm. therefore, is with me. The child gets up about the time Biggie leaves. I fight him off in bed until almost seven. Then his repeated news of what's wrong with the toilet prompts me to rise and call Krotz the plumber again.

We've seen quite enough of Krotz. I sublet the house this summer, you know, to three football players taking a summer make-up course in world culture. I knew football players might be rough types, that they might break a chair or split our bed; I was even prepared to find a raped and castaway girl; but I was sure they'd be *clean*. You know athletes—all that showering and deodering. I was sure they couldn't live in filth.

Well, the apartment was clean, all right, and there wasn't even a raped girl. There was a pair of Biggie's panties nailed to our door, and the more literate of the three had pinned a note to the panties, saying "Thanks." Biggie was a bit resentful; she'd packed all our clothes very neatly, and it disturbed her to imagine football players riffling through her underwear. But I felt enormously encouraged; the house had survived and the athletes' scholarships had paid their rent. Then the plumbing problems started, and Biggie concluded that the only reason the place looked so clean was because the football players had *flushed* all the crud away.

Krotz has sent his Roto-Rooter down our john four times. Among other things, he's retrieved six athletic socks, three whole potatoes, a crushed lampshade and a small girl's bra—clearly *not* Biggie's.

I phoned the Athletic Department and bitched. At first, they were very concerned. A man said, "Of course it doesn't do to have our boys getting a name for themselves with the local landlords." He said he'd take care of it. Then he asked me my name. and what property it was that I owned. I had to say that I didn't *own* it, really—that I rented it, and had sublet to the athletes for the summer. He said, "Oh, you're a *student?*" I should have seen the put-off coming, but I said, "Right—getting my Ph.D. in Comp. Lit." And he said, "Well, son, get your landlord to put the complaint in writing."

And since my landlord told me that I was responsible for any subletting, all bills from Krotz the plumber are mine. And believe me, Couth, Roto-Rootering is costly.

I'm afraid you know what I mean . . . if you've got some to spare.

I really think you've got the life, Couth. Better the caretaker than them who need to be cared for. Thanks be, though, it's the last damn year of this. My father says, "With your Ph.D. you'll have a profession that's dependable. But every professional man must suffer his training."

My father—as I'm sure he's told you before—didn't marry Mom until *after* college, *after* med school, *after* interning and *after* he'd established himself in Great Boar's Head, New Hampshire. The only urologist at Rockingham-by-the-Sea Hospital. After a six-year engagement to good old Mom—two thousand one hundred and ninety nights of masturbating ago—my father saw the time was ripe to marry.

I said to him this summer, "Well, look at Couth. He's set for life. A mansion to himself for nine months of the year, his expenses paid. And a mere three-month summer of fussing for the Pillsburys, tidying their ample grounds, caulking their boats and washing their cars; and they treat him like one of the family. Can you beat that?"

25

My father answered, "Couth doesn't have a profession, though."

Well, Biggie and I agree that you look quite professional to us.

Flush all seventeen of the johns once for me.

Love,

Bogus

4 : Iowa Evening Rituals

Since his father disinherited him, he had learned to hoard little injustices, wishing they might merge and leave him with one significant wound, for which he could guiltlessly martyr himself forever.

Bogus flips the record switch. "A keeper of petty injustices," he tells the microphone unconvincingly, "I was exposed to self-pity at a tender age."

"What?" says Biggie—a low, groggy voice down the hall.

"Nothing, Big," he calls to her, and notices he's recorded this too. Erasing, he tries to think: From what did he catch his self-pity? He can hear his father saying, "From a virus." But Bogus is sure he invented the whole thing himself. "I made it all myself," he says, with surprising conviction, then notices that he's failed to record it.

"You made *what* all yourself?" Biggie asks, suddenly alert in the bedroom.

"Nothing, Big." But her astonishment at the possibility of his doing something himself is painful.

Blowing hair off the control panel, he gingerly fingers his forehead; for some time he has suspected that his hairline will one day recede far enough to expose his brain. But would that be a significant humiliation?

Into the microphone he records: "There's a danger in dwelling on small emotional things."

But when he attempts to play this back, he discovers that he's jammed the announcement too close to one of his father's hospital reports—recorded in the good doctor's den at Great Boar's Head, with a live audience of Biggie and his mother listening to a description of an honest

27

day's fortune. Bogus is sure he's erased this once, but apparently he missed a bit of it. Or perhaps certain parts of his father's speeches are capable of reproducing themselves. Bogus is not beyond believing this.

"There's a danger in dwelling on small emotional ... *bladders which can be easily infected, though the major key is some kidney complication.*"

STOP. REWIND. ERASE.

With a brief titter, Bogus records: "I resolve to be more careful how I pee."

It's well past midnight when Bogus sees a light go on in Fitch's house, and Mr. Fitch minces down a hallway in broad-striped pajamas. His bladder, Trumper thinks. But Fitch appears on the front porch, gray-faced from the nearest streetlight. *Fitch can't leave his lawn alone! He's worried that a leaf has crashed in the night!*

But Mr. Fitch just stands on his porch, his face lifted, his mind beyond his lawn. Before he goes back inside, he looks up at the lighted window, where Bogus sits frozen. Then they wave to each other, and Fitch stealthily sidles into his eerie hallway and kills the light.

These night encounters. Bogus remembers Colm, sprouting a new tooth at Great Boar's Head. Colm was always a miserable teether; he kept Biggie and Bogus's mother up half the night. Once, when Bogus relieved them, he slipped off for a walk on the beach, passing each dark cottage until he smelled the pot in front of Elsbeth Malkas's porch. *Elsbeth is turning her parents on!* A childhood friend, he had grown up with her (once, in her hammock). Now she is a lady college instructor, referred to as the poetess at Bennington, where she returned to teach, three years after graduating.

"It's incestuous, really," she once told Biggie.

And Biggie had said, "I wouldn't know anything about it, really."

The mark of a child's acceptance these days, Trumper thought, is to be so successful that you can turn your parents on. He tried to imagine his own luck with that. In doctoral robes, he delivers the commencement address, then forces a joint on his father!

Bogus crept up to see this generational wonder, but the

28

Malkases' house was dark and Elsbeth, spotting Trumper's crouching silhouette against the lighter background of the sea, sat up in her porch hammock. Elsbeth Malkas had a chunky, oily body, nude and damp in her hammock gasping grass.

From the safe distance of a ledge beyond the porch, Bogus discussed Colm's habit of breaking new teeth in the night. There was a moment, later, when he could have discreetly left—when she went into the house to get her diaphragm. But the old-fashioned charm of this device touched him; he imagined the diaphragm crammed with erasers, pencils and postage stamps—tools of this poetess, who needed a deskful of receptacles—and he was too fascinated to leave.

He wondered, vaguely, if he would catch from Elsbeth what he'd caught from her long ago. But in the hammock he only expressed his disappointment that the diaphragm had been inserted while Elsbeth was inside her house. "Why did you want to *see* it?" she asked.

He couldn't very well mention the erasers, pencils and postage stamps, or even perhaps a torn, tiny scrap of an unfinished poem. After all, with a poetess, one might make fertile her very words.

But he had never liked Elsbeth's poetry, and afterward he walked almost a mile along the beach before he plunged in the ocean, to make sure she wouldn't hear his splash and feel insulted.

Bogus informs the tape recorder: "I resolve to go a fair bit out of my way to be polite."

Some dawn light falls on Fitch's manicured lawn, and Bogus sees the old man pad restlessly out on his porch again, just looking. What future is there for me, Trumper thinks, if Fitch, at his age, is still an insomniac?

5: A Dream to Me Now

I am not an insomniac any more. Tulpen has seen to that. She knows better than to leave me to my own devices. We go to bed at a reasonable hour, we make love, we sleep. If she catches me awake, we make love again. Despite lots of water, I sleep very well. It's in the daytime that I look for things to do.

I used to be very busy. Yes, I was a graduate student, getting my Ph.D. in comparative literature. My thesis chairman and my father were in agreement about specialization. Once, when Colm was sick, my father wouldn't write him a prescription. "Is a urologist a pediatrician?" Well, who could argue? "See a pediatrician. You're in graduate school, aren't you? Surely you know the importance of specialization."

Indeed I knew it. My thesis chairman, Dr. Wolfram Holster, admitted that he'd never been exposed to such specialization as mine.

I had a rare thesis topic, I confess. My thesis was going to be an original translation of *Akthelt and Gunnel*, a ballad in Old Low Norse; in fact, it was going to be the *only* translation. Old Low Norse is not well known. It's referred to, scornfully, in some satirical poems in Old East Norse and Old West Norse. Old East Norse is a dead language, North Germanic, which grew into Icelandic and Faroese. Old West Norse is also dead, and also North Germanic. It grew into Swedish and Danish. Norwegian evolved out of something between Old East Norse and Old West Norse. But the deadest of them all, old Old Low Norse, came to nothing. In fact, it's such a crude dialect that only one thing ever was actually written in it: *Akthelt and Gunnel*.

I was going to include in my translation a sort of etymological dictionary of Old Low Norse. That means a dictionary of the origins of Old Low Norse. Dr. Holster was very interested in such a dictionary; he felt it would be of some etymological use. That was why he approved the thesis topic; he actually thought *Akthelt and Gunnel* was junk, though he was hard pressed to prove it. Dr. Holster didn't know any Old Low Norse at all.

At first, I found the dictionary part very hard. Old Low Norse is pretty damn old, and the origins are rather obscure. It was actually easier to look *ahead*, at Swedish and Danish and Norwegian, to see what those Old Low Norse words would *become*. Mainly, I discovered, they were just bad pronunciations of Old West Norse and Old East Norse.

Then I found a way to make the dictionary part easy. Since no one knew anything about Old Low Norse, I could make things up. I made up a lot of origins. This made the translation of *Akthelt and Gunnel* easier too. I started making up a lot of words. It's very hard to tell real Old Low Norse from made-up Old Low Norse.

Dr. Wolfram Holster never knew the difference.

But I had some difficulty finishing the thesis. I would like to say that I stopped out of reverence for the main characters. It was a very personal love story and no one knew what it meant. I would like to say that I stopped because I felt Akthelt and Gunnel should be allowed to keep their privacy. But anyone who knows me at all would say that was a shameless lie. They would say I stopped simply because I hated *Akthelt and Gunnel*, or because I was bored, or because I was lazy, or because I had made up so much phony Old Low Norse that I could no longer keep the story straight.

There are elements of truth in what they would say, but it's also true that I was deeply moved by *Akthelt and Gunnel*. To be sure, it is an awful ballad. It's impossible to imagine anyone singing it, for example; for one thing, it's much too long. Also, I once characterized its metrics and rhyme scheme as "multiple and flexible." Actually, it has no rhyme scheme; it tries to rhyme when it can. And met-

31

rics were simply not known to its anonymous Old Low Norse author. (I imagine that author, by the way, as a peasant housewife.)

There is a false assumption usually made about the ballads of this period: that since the subjects were always kings and queens and princes and princesses, the authors were always royalty too. But peasants wrote about those kings and queens. The royalty was not alone in thinking that kings and queens were somehow better; part of being a peasant was thinking that kings and queens were better. I suspect that a fair portion of the population still thinks that way.

But Akthelt and Gunnel *were* better. They were in love; they were two against the world; they were formidable. And so was the world. I thought I knew the story.

I started out being faithful to the original. My translation is literal through the first fifty-one stanzas. Then I followed the text of the story fairly closely, just using my own details, until stanza one hundred and twenty. Then I translated pretty loosely for another hundred and fifty stanzas or so. I stopped at stanza two hundred and eighty and tried a literal translation again, just to see if I'd lost the hang of it.

> *Gunnel uppvaktat att titta Akthelt.*
> *Hanz kniv af slik lang.*

> *Uden hun kende inde hunz hjert*
> *Den varld af ogsa mektig.*

> Gunnel loved to look at Akthelt.
> His knife was so long.

> But she knew in her heart
> The world was too strong.

I stopped reading with this wretched stanza and gave up on *Akthelt and Gunnel*. Dr. Holster *laughed* at this stanza. So did Biggie. But *I* didn't laugh. The world *is* too strong—I saw it all coming!—the author was trying to foreshadow the inevitable doom! Clearly Akthelt and Gunnel were headed for grief. I knew, and I simply didn't want to see it out.

Lies! they would be shouting at me, those who knew me then. Old Bogus's mush-minded ability to read his own sentimentality into everything around him! The world was too strong—for *him!* He saw *himself* headed for grief—the only one we knew who could see a lousy movie and love it, read a rotten book and weep, if it had a flicker or a jot to do with *him!* Muck in his mind! Goo in his heart! What do you think he's called Bogus for? For *truth?*

Never mind them, the heartless *schlubs*. I live in another *varld* now.

When I showed Tulpen stanza two hundred and eighty she reacted in her solemn fashion. She put her head down to my heart and listened. Then she made me listen to hers. She does this when she recognizes a vulnerable situation; there are no sarcastic breast-flips when she's moved.

"Strong?" she said. I was listening to her heart; I nodded.

"Mektig," I said.

"Mektig?" She liked the sound; she went off playing with the word. Playing with the words was one of the things I really liked about Old Low Norse.

So there. Yogurt and lots of water, and a certain sympathy when sympathy matters. I'm all right. Things are straightening out. There is the matter of my urinary tract, of course, but in general things are straightening out.

6 : Prelude to the Last Stand

Bogus Trumper
918 Iowa Ave.
Iowa City, Iowa

Oct. 2, 1969

Mr. Cuthbert Bennett
Caretaker / The Pillsbury Estate
Mad Indian Point
Georgetown, Maine

My Dear Couth:

Am in receipt of your fine encouragements and most generous check. They have Biggie and me down and under at Iowa State Bank & Trust; I relish the feeling of plunking your check on them. If Biggie and I are ever in the chips, you'll be our honorary caretaker. In fact, we'd love to take care of you, Couth—to see that you eat enough during your long, alone winters; that you brush your mane forty strokes before sleep; and to provide a fine young fire for your sea-drafty bed. In fact, I know just the fine young fire for you! Her name is Lydia Kindle. Really.

I met her in the language lab. She takes freshman German, but little else has touched her. She approached me yesterday, chirping, "Mr. Trumper, are there no tapes with *songs?* I mean, I *know* the conversation. Aren't there any German ballads, or even opera?"

I stalled her; I browsed through the files with her bemoaning the lack of music in the language lab, and life in general. She's as shy as a cat underfoot; she fears her skirt might brush against your knee.

Lydia Kindle wants German ballads whispered in her ear. Or even *opera,* Couth!

I harbor no such musical illusion for my new job, my most degrading employment to date. I sell buttons and pennants and cowbells at the Iowa football games. I lug a large plywood board from gate to gate around the stadium. The board is wide and tippy with an easel-type stand; the wind blows it down; tiny gold footballs are scratched, buttons chip, pennants wrinkle and smudge. I get a commission: 10% of what I sell.

"Just one dollar for this Hawkeye pennant! A bell for two bucks! Big badges only seventy-five cents! It's a dollar, madam, for the pins with the little gold footballs attached. The kids love them; the footballs are just small enough for the wee ones to swallow. No, sir, this bell is *not* broken! It is simply a little bent. These bells are unbreakable. They'll dong forever."

I get to see the game for free, but I hate football. And I have to wear this bright-yellow apron with a fat change-pocket. A large, shiny badge on my coat says: HAWKEYE ENTERPRISES—GO HAWKS! Every badge is numbered too; we communicate around the stadium by numbers. Competition is fierce for the best stand. On Saturday Number 368 said to me, "This is my post, 501. Lug off, will you?" He wore a tie with red footballs on it; he sold many more pennants and buttons and cowbells than I did. I cleared just enough for a three-month packet of birth-control pills for Biggie.

Root for Iowa, Couth. Next game I might clear enough to have myself sterilized.

I was told that if Iowa ever won a football game, we would all sell many more things. The psychology of the fans was outlined to us in our Warm-Up Meeting by the concession sales head of Hawkeye Enterprises, Mr. Fred Paff, who told us that Iowans were proud folks, in need of a winner before they'd adorn their aerials and sprout badges and pins on their

35

coats. "Nobody likes to be associated with a loser," Paff said, and to *me* he said, "Well, we're both Freds, you know. How about that?"

"I know another Fred in Spokane, Washington," I told him. "Perhaps we should try to get something going."

"A sense of humor!" Fred Paff cried. "You'll do well here. A sense of humor is essential with the fans."

Let it be known, Couth, that you have more loyal and constant fans than these Iowans. Biggie and I appreciated your photographs almost as much as your money. Biggie especially liked your "Self-Portrait w/ Seaweed." I frankly suspect it's illegal to send such photographs through the mail, and I don't mean to insult your body, but I preferred "Dead Gull No. 8."

Please dip into your darkroom and print one like that for me; in fact, make it *of* me. Make me prone and sort of sallow; fold my hands in the appropriate fashion and place the ready coffin near my figure; crack the casket's lid ajar, waiting for Fred Bogus Trumper, who at any moment now could easily be tempted by that plush velvet liner. Destroy the negative. Print only one 8 × 10. Superimposed, include the faces of my family: Biggie solid with grief, but not bitter, and Colm at play with the casket's ornate handle. Please underexpose my father and mother. Move my father's mouth; in fact, *blur* it. He orates over the dead. The caption reads: "A professional man must suffer his training . . ." Then seal it in a black matboard and mail the whole thing to the University of Iowa Business Office, with a curt note of apology for the failure of the deceased to pay his tuition. Which has been raised again, by vote of the trustees, to include an additional recreation fee. To pay, no doubt, for new gold football cleats and a Homecoming Day parade float: millions of yellow roses, shaped to form a giant ear of corn.

You're lucky to have a darkroom, Couth. I see you naked in your eerie safelight, awash in chemicals, developing, enlarging; you print yourself on a clean white sheet. Sometime, if there ever is time, you must teach me photography. The control of it amazes me. I remember watching you bathe your prints; I saw the images emerging and defining underwater; it was more than I could stand! As if so many ameboid things swam into place and made a man.

I think of this while translating the eighty-third stanza of *Akthelt and Gunnel*. It's the last word that bothers me: *Klegwoerum*. My thesis chairman thinks it should be "fertile." I say "fecund." My friend Ralph Packer suggests "rank." And Biggie says it doesn't really matter. There is a hurtful ton of truth in Biggie.

I think she's cracking, though. It's not like her, but she's taking it personally that some octogenarian in the hospital gooses her when she empties his bedpan. But do you know, Biggie never cries. Do you know what she does do, though? She finds a hangnail and tugs it slowly down her finger; I've seen her tease one past the first joint. Biggie bleeds, but she never cries.

Couth, I have felt close to you ever since I caught your clap from Elsbeth Malkas. Or we both caught and shared what Elsbeth had to start with. The details of who began it have never seemed to me essential for our friendship.

Once more, flush all seventeen of the johns for me. It would do my heart good to know that somewhere there are toilets which are not clogged with jockstraps. Choose a foggy night, open all the windows— sound bounces best off water in the fog—and flush away! I will hear you and rejoice.

Biggie sends her love. She's in the kitchen peeling her fingers. She's pretty busy, otherwise I'd ask her for a hangnail to enclose, a shred of her Trumpering fortitude boldly traveling from Iowa to Maine.

Love,

Bogus

7 : Ralph Packer Films, Inc.
109 Christopher Street
New York, New York 10014

Tulpen and me at work. She does the editing; actually, Ralph is his own editor, but Tulpen assists him. She also does some darkroom work, but Ralph is his own developer too. I don't know anything about developing and not much about editing. I'm the sound tracker; I tape in the music; if there's sync-sound, I get it right; if there's a voice-over, I lay it in; if there's offstage noise, I make some; when there's a narrator, I often do the talking. I have a nice big voice.

The film is nearly finished by the time it's brought to me, with most of the unusable footage cut out, and the sequence of shots pretty much the way Ralph wants it, at least rough-spliced—more or less the way Ralph will finally edit it. Ralph is very close to a one-man band, with some technical help from Tulpen and me. It's always Ralph's script and his camera-work; it's *his* movie. But Tulpen and I have great technique, and there's a Ralph Packer Fan Club kid named Kent who runs errands.

Tulpen and I are not members in The Ralph Packer Fan Club. The kid named Kent is a one-man band at that. I don't mean to suggest that Ralph Packer's films are unknown. His first film, *The Group Thing*, won first prize in the National Student Film Festival. My nice big voice is in that film; Ralph made it when he was a graduate student in the Cinematography Workshop at Iowa.

I met him in the language lab. In a lull between lab-sections, I was editing tapes for freshman German when this shuffling man of hair came in. Possibly twenty, or forty; possibly student, or faculty, Trotskyite or Amish farmer, human or animal; a thief lumbering out of a camera shop, laden with lenses and light meters; a bear who after a terrible and violent struggle ate a photographer. This beast approached me.

I was still doing my translation of *Akthelt and Gunnel* then. I felt myself confronted by Akthelt's father, Old Thak. As he came closer a musk moved with him. One hundred glints of fluorescent light, off his lenses, buckles and polished parts.

"You Trumper?" he said.

A wise man, I thought, would confess it all now. Admit the translation was a fraud. Hope Old Thak goes back to the grave.

"Vroog etz?" I asked, just testing him.

"Good," he grumbled; he understood! He was Old Thak! But all he said was "Ralph Packer," freeing a white hand from an arctic mitten, pushing this toward me out of the cuff of his Eskimo parka. "You speak German, right? And you know tapes?"

"Right," I said cautiously.

"Ever done any dubbing?" he asked. "I'm making a film." A *pervert,* I thought; wants me in his blue movie. "I need a German voice," he said. "Some kind of clever German slipping in and out of the English narration."

I knew those film-making students. Passing by Benny's and seeing through the window a terrible fight, a girl with her bra torn off, holding her tits. I rush inside to this lady's aid, only to spill a cameraman from his dolly, tangle my feet in extension cords, jar a man with his hands full of microphones. And the girl says tiredly, *"Easy,* hey. It's just a goddamn *movie."* She gives you a look to say: Because of nuts like you, I'm on my fourth bra today.

". . . well, if you like playing with tapes and recorders," Ralph Packer was saying, "jamming voices, jumbling time. You know, sound montage. There's just a couple of things I want done, then you can play with it—you know, do what you want. Maybe give me some ideas . . ."

It was such a shock at the time: to be a football-pennant salesman, and here's someone suggesting I might even have *ideas!*

"Hey," said Ralph Packer, looking at me. "You speak English too, don't you?"

"What do you pay?" I asked, and he whomped his arctic mitten down on my tape stack, sending one reel flopping like a stunned fish.

"Pay *you!*" he shouted. A great shrug of his shoulders sent a zoom lens around his neck swinging. Scenes of Old Thak in a rage sprang to mind.

> Though well into his dotage, and weak
> With the arrow sunk deep in his chest,
> Which was wider than Gurk's wine cask,
> Old Thak strode up to the assassin-archer
> And strangled him with his own bowstring.
>
> Then, with his great palm, hardened
> By holding the reins for a hundred horses,
> Thak drove the arrow through his own chest
> And drew it out his back, groaning mightily.
>
> With the shaft still slimy with the old one's gore,
> Thak slew the treacherous Gurk—a disemboweling
> Thrust! Then did the Great Thak thank Gwolph
> And blessed the banquet laid before him bloodily.

Thus did Ralph Packer storm about the listening booths of the language lab, and a frightened gathering of freshman German students cowered in the door while he ranted on.

"Sweet fuck! I should *pay* you? For an *experience?* And an *opportunity!* Look, Thumper"—a titter from my disloyal students—"you should pay me for giving you the chance! I'm just getting started, I don't even pay *myself!* I sold fifteen hundred fucking football pennants for one wide-angle lens, and you want to be paid for your education!"

"Wait! Packer!" I cried; he was heading out the door, the students scampering.

"Fuck you, Thump-Thump," he said. And turning fiercely on the freshman Germans: "Fuck him, I say!" For a moment, sensing their blind dread, I feared the lot of them would rush me and impulsively obey his command. But I ran after him. I found him watering himself with deep, greedy draughts at the drinking fountain in the hall.

"I didn't know you sold football pennants," I said.

Later, when he was pleased with my sound-tracking games, Packer told me he'd be able to pay me one day. "When I'm able to pay myself, Thump-Thump, there will be work for you."

So Ralph Packer was true to his word. *The Group Thing* was a mild success. That part where the "Horst Wessel Song" is played over a beery crowd at Benny's? That was my idea. And the part with the Math department meeting at the University of Iowa, with German dubbed in and the subtitles reading: *"First* you arrest them with the proper court order, *then* you start arresting so many that group trials become acceptable, *then* you've got them so worried about the detention camps that they don't bother you about having to have a court order any more, so then . . ."

It was a kind of propaganda film. The evil was the innate hostility directed at the individual by groups. It was not a political film, however; all groups were equally misrepresented. The enemy was any unified crowd. Even a classroom with nodding heads: "Yes, yes, I see, I agree, *jawohl!"*

Everyone thought that *The Group Thing* was "innovative." Only one major complaint was ever leveled against it, and it came to Ralph in the form of a letter from the German-American Society of Columbus, Ohio. They said the film was anti-German; it "raked over a lot of old coals," they said. There wasn't anything especially *German* about groups, they said, and there wasn't anything wrong with groups, either. Ralph was referred to as a "nut." The letter was not actually signed by anybody, by any real person. It was stamped, with one of those ink stampers: THE GERMAN AMERICAN SOCIETY.

"Another fucking group," said Ralph. "Over five hundred people wrote that letter. And shit, Thump-Thump, I didn't really *mean* anything. I mean, I don't *know* what I meant . . ."

This is still true of Ralph; it has been the major criti-

cism of his films. They are nearly always called "innovative," often "unpretentious," usually "truthful." But *The
New York Times,* for example, notes "a certain lack of
resolution . . . he fails to commit himself to a point of
view." *The Village Voice* finds that "the visions are always
striving to be personal, authentic and fresh, yet Packer
fails to really deal with the issues . . . a simple portrait of
the action seems to satisfy him." I think it satisfies me too.

"Shit," says Ralph. "They're just *pictures,* Thump-
Thump."

In fact, their lack of "meaning" I find especially refreshing.

The Group Thing was his only propaganda film; it was
the only one to win a prize, too. His next two films, I
wasn't in on; I was leaving my wife and mind behind.

Ralph went on a long lam, from Iowa to New York.
Soft Dirt was about a rock group. Ralph just followed
them around when Soft Dirt was on a concert tour. Interviews with their girls, shots of the guys cutting each
other's hair, shots of the leg-wrestling competition organized among the girls, shots of what the winners won. The
high point of the film comes when the leader's dog gets
accidentally electrocuted by an amplifier. The group
canceled a week of concerts; out of sympathy, fans do-
nated about fifty dogs. "They're all very nice dogs," said
the leader, "but they're just not like old Soft Dirt." That
had been the name of the dog too.

The third film was about a small traveling circus, which
Ralph followed through an endless series of one-night
stands. There's a lot of footage of the tent going up and
coming down, and interviews with the trapeze girls.

"Is the circus dead?"

"God . . . why would you ever think that?"

And a very long vignette about the elephant keeper who
lost three fingers on his right hand when the elephant
stepped on him.

"Do you still like elephants?"

"Sure, I love elephants."

"Even this particular elephant who stepped on your
hand?"

"Especially this particular elephant. He didn't *mean* to
step on my hand. He didn't even know what he was step-

ping on. I just put my hand where he was stepping; he would have stepped there anyway. And he really felt awful about it."

"The elephant felt awful? He *knew* he'd stepped on your hand?"

"Christ, of course he knew. I yelled, 'You're stepping on my fucking hand!' Sure, he knew all right, and he just felt terrible."

Then there follows an episodic series of shots of the elephant, trying to convey how sorry he was. It was Ralph's worst film, I think. I can't ever remember the title.

But now that I'm back as his sound tracker, his films should improve—soundwise, at least. We're working on one now called *Down on the Farm*. It's about a hippie commune called the Free Farm. The Free Farmers want everybody to use the land—any land. They think private property is bullshit. The land should be free to them who'd *use* it. They run into a little trouble, from some real farmers up in Vermont. The real farmers think private property is okay. The Free Farmers try to tell the real farmers how badly they're being screwed by not having any free land. They appear to be headed toward a confrontation. A small liberal arts college in the area lends a certain intellectual confusion to the situation. Ralph goes up to Vermont every weekend to see if the confrontation has occurred yet. He comes back with reels and reels, tapes and tapes. "It's still building," he says.

"When the winter comes along," I tell him, "maybe the kids will get cold and hungry and just walk off the land."

"Then we'll film that," he says.

"Maybe there won't be any confrontation," I suggest.

"Maybe there won't," Ralph says, and Tulpen tips her tit with the back of her hand.

This irks Ralph. Tulpen was already working for Ralph when I came to New York; Ralph gave her the job because she was sleeping with him. Oh, long ago. Tulpen didn't know anything about editing film, but Ralph showed her. When she learned to do it very well, she stopped sleeping with him. Ralph didn't fire her because she's a fantastic editor, but sometimes Ralph gets mad about it. "You only slept with me to get this job," he tells her.

"You only gave me the job because I slept with you,"

43

Tulpen tells him, unperturbed. "Don't you like my work?" she asks him. "I like the job."

There is this understanding stalemate between them.

The kid named Kent, who runs errands, is another story.

Tulpen and me in the darkroom, sipping coffee, wondering where the doughnuts are. Tulpen is trimming some of Ralph's stills, hot off the dryer, cropping them in the big paper cutter. *Chomp!* And it's been two weeks since I've heard a word from that damn Biggie. Are the other kids kind to Colm in school? Does he still bite?

"Anything wrong?" Tulpen asks.

"My prick," I say. "I think it's getting gummed up again. Wretched water method . . ."

"See your doctor, Trumper," she says casually. "Have the operation."

Chomp! goes the terrible paper cutter; visions of Vigneron blood-fill my mind.

In comes Kent. "Hey!" *Hey yourself, Kent.* "Hey, you seen the new footage? He's really got it now."

"Got what, Kent?"

"Great *light* in the new stuff. It's getting cold up there now. Even the weather's closing in on them. Somebody's going to make a move. I mean, the fucking camera is *anticipating* it."

"That doesn't mean it has to happen, Kent."

Ralph comes in with a huff-puff of cold air. Sealskin boots, arctic mittens, Eskimo parka, though it's only fall. Trying to imagine Ralph alive in a tropical climate presents a problem: he would have to change his fur image. He could wear wicker and straw and reeds wrapped around him: a giant basket!

"Hey!" Kent says to him. "I saw *White Knees* last night."

"Whose?" says Ralph. We all know Kent doesn't get much.

"You know, hey. *White Knees,*" Kent insists. "It's the new Grontz film."

"Oh yeah, yeah," says Ralph, unmittening, debooting, emerging from his wool.

"Well, it's just another lousy one," Kent says. "More of the same, like his earlier shit. Heavy, you know?"

44

"Yeah, yeah," says Ralph, unmuffled, looking around. Something is missing.

"I looked at your new footage this morning," Kent tells him. Ralph is thinking, What's missing? "It's just great, Ralph," Kent tells him. "Even the fucking weather—"

"Kent?" Ralph says. "Where are the doughnuts?"

"I was just waiting for you to get here," Kent says, flushing.

"Two jellies, one cream puff," Ralph says. "Tulpen?"

"Two cream puffs."

"Thump-Thump?"

"A cruller."

"Two cream puffs, two jellies and one cruller, Kent," Ralph says.

When Kent leaves on his mission, Ralph asks us, "Who in hell is Grontz?"

"Search me," says Tulpen.

"White Knees," I say. "God knows . . ."

"Does Kent smoke?" Ralph asks. No one has any idea. "Well if he doesn't," Ralph says, "he should try some. And if he does, he should stop."

Back comes Kent, a mine of mystery and information.

"Two jellies, two cream puffs, one cruller."

"Thank you."

"Thank you."

"Thank you, Kent."

"Wardell's new one opens Friday night, at the Beppo," Kent informs.

"It won't last a week," I tell him, then look at Tulpen: Who is Wardell? Her look back at me says, Where is the Beppo?

"Right, right," says Ralph.

We watch Kent cramming the coffeepot. "Don't make it waterproof, Kent," says Tulpen.

Ralph is visibly upset with his two jellies. *"Red* jelly," he says, prodding with a cautious finger. "I like the purple."

"Grape, Ralph," I say.

"Yeah, grape," he says. "This red shit is uneatable."

Kent is worried. "I heard that Marco is out on the Coast," he tells us, "doing the riots."

"How's the cruller, Thump-Thump?"

"An excellent cruller, Ralph."

45

"Two crullers, Kent," says Ralph. "Can you eat another one, Thump-Thump?"

"No," Tulpen says. "He's getting fat."

"*Three* more crullers, Kent," says Ralph, poking the foul red jelly.

"You're *already* fat," Tulpen tells him. "Trumper can still be saved."

"Three crullers, Kent," says Ralph.

A static friction in the room escapes when Kent opens the door. Ralph listens for Kent's cloddy walking sounds out on the sidewalk. Something conspiratorial and special is being saved for our ears alone; we can always tell. Ralph goes a fair bit out of his way to avoid anything too personal with Kent. A kind of professional self-protection, I assume.

"Boy, Thump-Thump," he says; his broad arms draw Tulpen and me together. "*Boy*, you should have seen the tail I met last night . . ." But he is watching Tulpen, waiting for her to raise one breast with the back of her hand. She's subtle with him; she turns away. Moving toward the door, her elbow lifts a little behind her.

"I saw that!" Ralph shouts. But she's gone; the door to the editing room closes, and I am left alone with Ralph Packer, who—in spite of (perhaps, *because* of) never knowing what he means—is a vanguard in underground film.

We are waiting for crullers.

8 :   Other Old Mail

Fred Trumper
918 Iowa Ave.
Iowa City, Iowa

Oct. 3, 1969

Humble Oil & Rehning Co.
Box 790
Tulsa, Oklahoma

Dear Sirs:

I am in receipt of your reminder. Regarding that, I *do* consider my credit with you as a "privilege," and I have every intention of avoiding the "embarrassment" you speak of.

Enclosed is my check for $3.00. My Balance Due is thereby reduced to $44.56, which of course I shall be forwarding to you shortly.

You see, my son has been very sick.

Gratefully,

Fred Trumper
(Esso card # 657-679-896-22)

Fred Trumper
918 Iowa Ave.
Iowa City, Iowa

Oct. 3, 1969

Mr. Harry Estes
Dept. of Collection
Sinclair Refining Co.
Box 1333
Chicago, Illinois

Dear Mr. Estes:

You will find my check for $15.00 enclosed. And although this may be, in your eyes, "another drop in the bucket," it constitutes a considerable effort for me. And despite the fact that my Balance Due, still outstanding, is $94.67—and I *can* "appreciate" your concern—it is also with great effort that I control myself from responding as I would like to your rude note.

We are both aware that your company is perhaps not so well known as some. Perhaps you might be advised by my long and good experience with other credit-card companies, who demonstrate a degree of cheerfulness and tolerance that your own company would do well to imitate. Perhaps you don't know what it is that makes a well-known company so well known? Well, I'll tell you. It's *patience*.

Alas, if more of the values we esteem in individuals would be incorporated into our business values, I'm sure each of us would be more pleased with one another.

I had the highest hopes for your organization when you first came out with that big warm friendly green dinosaur. I retain the highest hopes that you will eventually live up to your image.

Respectfully,

Fred Trumper
(Sinclair card # 555-546-215-91)

_____

Fred Trumper
918 Iowa Ave.
Iowa City, Iowa

Oct. 3, 1969

48

Iowa-Illinois Gas & Electric
520 Jefferson St.
Iowa City, Iowa

Dear Sirs:
Enclosed is $10.00 to reduce my Balance Due; the remainder, I realize, is enough to warrant your assessing me with an extra service charge. I will responsibly assume this charge, but I sincerely hope that you recognize the seriousness of my intentions to settle this balance, and that you will not discontinue my service.

Speaking for that service, I will say, in all sincerity, that Iowa-Illinois has provided the best electricity my wife and I have ever known. Seriously, we once lived in a part of the world where the lights were *always* going out.

We've also appreciated your policy of giving small children lollipops, if accompanied by their parents, at your downtown office and appliance center.

Thankfully,

Fred Trumper

Fred Trumper
918 Iowa Ave.
Iowa City, Iowa

Oct. 3, 1969

Northwestern Bell Telephone Co.
302 South Linn St.
Iowa City, Iowa

Dear Sirs:
In regard to my present Balance Due of $35.17: I will not pay one penny of this until you delete from my bill the sum of $16.75, and the corresponding tax—for a call I never made to Georgetown, Maine. I don't know anybody in Georgetown, Maine, and to my knowledge no one in Georgetown, Maine, knows me.

This has happened before, if you remember, on a previous bill. I was charged for talking one hour and forty-five minutes to Vienna, Austria—which you finally acknowledged was an error, a foul-up involving the other half of my two-party line. About the other half of my two-party line, I could write you another letter, but your previous explanation of "Oversea Cable Operator Confusion" is not especially satisfying. In any case, it should not be my responsibility to tell you what I owe you.

Frankly,

Fred Trumper
(tel. 338-1536)

_____

Fred Trumper
918 Iowa Ave.
Iowa City, Iowa

Oct. 3, 1969

Mr. Milo Kubik
Peoples Market
660 Dodge St.
Iowa City, Iowa

Dear Mr. Kubik:

Your meats are a taste of the big city, a breath of the best kitchen wind! You're the only place in Iowa City for a decent kidney, tongue, blood sausage and a good heart. And all the little foreign jars, the exotic little tins of food in translation! We are especially fond of the Ragout of Wild Boar in Médoc Sauce. My wife and I, Mr. Kubik, can make a meal of your hors d'oeuvre counter.

I hope you'll forgive us for overindulging ourselves with your quality items this month. I am able to make this $10.00 deposit (enclosed) but the remaining balance of $23.09 I will have to leave outstanding for just a short time.

Next month we will more carefully budget ourselves against your fine temptations, you can rest assured.

Honestly,

Fred & Sue Trumper

Fred Trumper
918 Iowa Ave.
Iowa City, Iowa

Oct. 3, 1969

Mr. Merlin Shumway
President / Iowa State Bank & Trust Co.
400 Clinton St.
Iowa City, Iowa

Mr. Shumway:
    Enclosed is Mr. Cuthbert Bennett's check to me, for $250.00, endorsed to the bank, for deposit in my account (checking: 9 51 348). This should amply cover my minus balance.
    I am really appalled that the bank saw fit to bounce my wife's check back to the clothier, Sumner Temple. Had you covered this check, my account would have been delinquent by no more than $3.80 plus Service Charge. This small gesture of courtesy would have spared my poor wife an unpleasantry with Mr. Temple over the phone; a needless embarrassment for such a piddling sum.
    I can only suppose that you are holding the matter of my educational loan against me. But whatever your reasoning, I am tempted to move my account across the street to the Iowa First National. I will certainly do so if you continue to treat me with such suspicion. I simply had no idea I was overdrawn. As you see, I had in hand the available income to cover the deficit immediately.

Sincerely,

Fred Trumper

Fred Trumper
918 Iowa Ave.
Iowa City, Iowa

Oct. 3, 1969

Sears, Roebuck & Co.
Central States Office
1st Ave. & Kalona St.
Cedar Rapids, Iowa

Dear Sears:

Last June I purchased for my wife one Model X-100, Standard-Plus vacuum cleaner, which, at the suggestion of your sales office in Iowa City, I elected to pay for under the terms of the Sears Easy-Payment Installment Plan.

At this time, there is no need for me to go into my shock at the rather steep service rates under this "boon" of a plan. At the moment I only want to know *how many* payments you have recorded for me, and why it is that you don't include my current Balance Due in this month's Easy-Packet Payment Envelope. Each month I receive this handy envelope from you, and the enclosed note simply says, PAYMENT DUE: $5.00.

But it seems I have been paying out $5.00 for an awfully long time. How much further do I have to go? Understandably, I am not about to pay this next installment until I receive some notice from you concerning how much I still owe.

I would offer you this piece of advice, so that you will not sully your great reputation among humble folk everywhere. Be forewarned: it would be a shame if Sears, because of its bigness and far-reaching tendrils into the homes and minds of young masses, forgot, or tramped on, the simple needs of the "little person." After all, isn't it us "little people" who make Sears so big?

A Concerned Little Person,

Fred Trumper
(Easy-Payment-Installment Invoice No. 314-312-54-6)

Fred Trumper
918 Iowa Ave.
Iowa City, Iowa

Oct. 3, 1969

Consumers Union
Edt. Offices of *Consumer Reports*
Mr. Vernon, New York

Dearest Sirs:

From one nonprofit organization to another, let me
tell you that you are noble and good and a great conso-
lation in the face of creeping capitalism everywhere!

Where experience permits me an opinion, let me say
that I am in complete agreement with your 1968 uncov-
erings concerning false advertisement all around us.
You are to be congratulated. Keep giving them hell!
Don't ever be bought!

However, I beg to differ with you in regard to Sears,
Roebuck & Co. Most of your listings for their products
and service range from "fair" to "good." I have great
faith in your research, and I'm willing to admit that
your sphere of sources is far greater than my own. But
I feel I should add to your findings this consumer's
reaction to a certain Model X-100 Standard-Plus vacuum cleaner. Have you ever looked into *that* mechanical wonder? Well, go pick one up under Sears Easy
Payment Installment Plan.

You do such healthful, splendid work that I would
hate to see this oversight hurt your reputation.

Yours in nonprofit,

Fred Trumper

Fred Trumper
918 Iowa Ave.
Iowa City, Iowa

Oct. 3, 1969

The Business Office
University of Iowa
Iowa City, Iowa

Dear Business:
I'm afraid that this month I'll be forced to assume
the $5.00 Penalty Charge for late payment of tuition.
However, although I accept this $5.00 charge, I will
deduct $5.00 from my tuition bill as a refusal to pay
the newly added Recreation Fee (also $5.00), a school
expense for which I am *not* willing to assume responsibility.
I am a graduate student. I am twenty-six years old. I
am married and I have a son. I am not at the University of Iowa for "recreation" of any kind. Let them who
recreate pay for their own fun. I'm not having any fun
at all.
The only reason I'm telling you this is that I thought
there might be some misunderstanding on your part
when you eventually receive my payment of tuition.
You see, it might look as if I have ignored the Penalty
Charge for late payment. *That* $5.00 I will pay; it is the
other $5.00 that will not be included in my check.
(Which I will get to you soon.)
It *is* confusing, there being several $5.00 figures in-
volved, but I hope I have made myself clear.

Seriously,

Fred Trumper
(student ID 23 345 G)

Fred Trumper
918 Iowa Ave.
Iowa City, Iowa

Oct. 3, 1969

University of Iowa Educational Placement Service
Student Union Bldg.
University of Iowa

Iowa City, Iowa
Atten. Mrs. Florence Marsh

Dear Mrs. Marsh:
Having paid my Service Fee to you some time ago, I expected that your services would be at least reasonable. Your current enclosure for "Available Positions" does not strike me as reasonable in any way. I specified to you—in an endless form, filled out in triplicate—my capabilities, my field of interest, my degrees, and where (in what region of this country) I sought a teaching position.

In regard to your current information, I do *not* want to meet an interviewer from Carother's Community College of Carother's, Arkansas, "offering a position at their Maple Bliss campus, for five sections of freshman rhetoric at $5,000 per annum." Do you think I am utterly mad?

I told you: New England, Colorado or Northern California; at a college where I'd have some opportunity to teach more than freshman-level courses, for a salary of at least $6,500, plus moving expenses.

Some service you offer, I must say.

                                   Dismally,

                                   Fred Trumper

_____

                                   Fred Trumper
                                   918 Iowa Ave.
                                   Iowa City, Iowa

                                   Oct. 3, 1969

Shive & Hupp
Loan Associates, Farm & Town
U.S. Route 69, West
Marengo, Iowa

Dear Mr. Shive & Mr. Hupp:
Sirs, I repeat: I am unable at this time to make my

interest-due payment to you. Please refrain from sending me further form letters about your famous Rising Rate Scale, and your awkwardly veiled threats of "constables."

Just do what you have to do. That's all *I'm* doing.

Truthfully,

Fred   Trumper

Fred Trumper
918 Iowa Ave.
Iowa City, Iowa

Oct. 3, 1969

Addison & Halsey Collection Agency
456 Davenport St.
Des Moines, Iowa
Atten. Mr. Robert Addison

Dear Bobby,
  Cram it.

Best,

Fred

9 : Mice, Turtles & Fish First!

Tulpen takes care of the bills now. I don't even see the checkbook. I contribute, of course, and every week or so I ask her how our money is.

"Are you hungry?" she says. "Do you have enough to drink?"

"Well, sure, I have enough . . ."

"Well, is there something you need?"

"Well, no . . ."

"Well, the money's just fine, then," she says. "*I* don't need any more."

"*I'm* fine," I tell her.

"Was there something you wanted to buy?" Tulpen asks.

"No, no, Tulpen—really, everything's fine with me."

"Well, everything's fine with *me*," she insists, and I try to force myself never to bring it up again.

But I just can't believe it! "How much do we have?" I ask her. "I mean, just to get an idea of some rough figure . . ."

"Does Biggie need money?"

"No, Biggie doesn't need a thing, Tulpen."

"You want to send something to Colm—a truck, a boat or something?"

"A truck or a boat?"

"Well, some special toy, is that it?"

"Jesus, never mind," I say. "I was just wondering, that's all . . ."

"Well, honestly, Trumper, you should say what you mean."

Indeed, I should stick to the facts. That's what she means.

But I honestly think my avoidance of the facts has as much to do with my distrusting the relevance of them as it has to do with my lying a lot. I don't think the statistics in my life have ever meant very much.

When my mother used to write me, she'd ask about the stuff we had. She was concerned about whether we had a toidy pot for Colm. If we had one, we were all right. My father also suggested snow tires; with snow tires, we'd be happy all winter. I imagined their friends asking them how we were; my father would mention our winter driving, and my mother would bring up the toidy pot. How else could they have answered?

Most recently, in a terse phone conversation with my father, I was asked how I paid my bills. "With checks," I told him. (I guess that's how Tulpen does it.) "You shouldn't send cash through the mails." But he asked me as if that was all he needed to know—and knowing that, he would know about me.

Rituals are more revealing than facts!

For example, I once kept a tape recorder who was my friend. Also, I wrote letters to my wife; I mean, I wrote to Biggie while I was still living with her. Of course I never gave these letters to her; they weren't really letters, then; it was the ritual of writing them that mattered.

I showed one to Tulpen.

Iowa City
Oct. 5, 1969

Thinking of you, Colm—my only child. And you too, Biggie—those hospital smocks don't become you.

The way you arise at six: your fine, firm, muscular lunge for the alarm; your warm collapse back against me.

"Another day, Big," I mumble.

"Oh, Bogus," you say. "Remember how we used to wake up in Kaprun?"

"All the snow piled against the window," I mumble, by rote. "Some of it blown under the sash, a little puff of it on the sill . . ."

58

"And the breakfast smells!" you cry. "And all the skis and boots in the downstairs hall . . ."

"Talk softer, Big," I say. "You'll wake up Colm . . ." who just then begins his cooing down the hall from our room.

"Don't shout at him when I'm gone," you say, Big—and you're out of bed, tucking me back in. Prancing over the cold floor, your large, upstanding boobs peek at the dawn; they point across the hall to the kitchen window (what symbol intended by that direction, I cannot guess).

Then your bra, Big, seizes you like the bit shocks the horse. That damn hospital smock crinkles coldly down over you, and my Biggie is gone, anesthetized, sanitized; you're garbed as shapeless as a dextrose jug, which you'll see later this morning, upended, and dripping down its sugary strength to the elderly.

You grab a bite at the hospital cafeteria, chatting with the other nurses' helpers. They talk about what time their men came home last night, and I know you tell them, "My Bogus is in bed with our Colm. And last night he slept with me."

But last night, Big, you said, "Your father's a prick."

And I've never once heard you use the word quite like that. I agreed with you, of course, and you said, "What is it he wants you to prove to him?"

I said, "That I'm capable of falling flat on my face."

"Well, that's where you are," you said, Big. "What more does he want?"

"He must be waiting," I said, "for me to tell him he was right all along. He wants me to crawl across the floor and kiss his powdered doctor's shoes. Then I am to say, 'Father, I want to be a professional man.'"

"It's not funny, Bogus," you said. And I'd thought I could always count on a laugh from you, Biggie.

"It's the last year, Big," I told you. "We'll go back to Europe. You can ski again."

But all you said was, "Fuck." I've never once heard you use the word quite like that.

Then you just flounced in bed alongside me, leafing backward through a ski magazine, though I must have told you a hundred times that it's a poor way to read.

When you read, Big, you set your chin on your high chest; your thick, honey, shoulder-cut hair juts forward, covering your cheeks, and all I can see is the tip of your sharp nose peeking out of your hair.

But it's always a ski magazine, isn't it, Biggie? Nothing mean intended, perhaps, but just a reminder to me of what I've robbed you of, isn't it? When you find the inevitable Alpine scene, you say, "Oh look, Bogus. Weren't we there? Wasn't that near Zell, or—no! Maria Zell, isn't it? Just look at them piling out of that train. God, look at the *mountains*, Bogus . . ."

"Well, we're in Iowa now, Big," I remind you. "We'll take a drive tomorrow out in the corn. We'll look for a slight hill. We might more easily find a hog with a sloped back. We could coat him with mud, I could prop up his snout and you could ski between his ears, down to his tail. Not much of a run, but . . ."

"I didn't *mean* anything, Bogus," you say. "I just wanted you to look at the picture."

But why can't I leave you alone?

I keep at you: "I could tow you behind the car, Big. You could slalom through the cornstalks, routing pheasants! Tomorrow I'll simply install four-wheel-drive in the Corvair."

"Come on," you say; you sound tired. Our bedside lamp blinks, crackles, goes out, and in the dark you whisper, "Did you pay the electric bill, Bogus?"

"It's just a fuse," I tell you, and leaving the warm groove you put in our bed, I pad down to the basement. It's just as well I'm here, because I've not been down in the basement today to spring the mousetrap that you insist on setting for the mouse I don't want to catch. So I spare the mouse once more and re-

60

place the fuse—the same one that always blows, for no reason.

Upstairs, Biggie, you shout down to me, "That's it! It's on again! You got it!" As if some marvel has been performed. And when I come back up to you, you've got your strong, blond arms folded and you're kicking your feet under the sheets. "No more reading now," you say, a fierce twinkle about your eyes, and those heavy feet swishing.

Oh, I know you mean only the best for me, Big, but I know too that the thing with the feet is an old skier's exercise, good for the ankles. You don't fool me.

I tell you, "I'll be right there, Big. Just let me check on Colm."

I always watch him sleep for a while. What I mind about children is that they're so vulnerable, so fragile-looking. Colm: I get up in the night to make sure your breathing hasn't stopped.

"Honestly, Bogus, he's a very healthy child."

"Oh, I'm sure he is, Big. But he just seems so *small*."

"He's good-sized for his age, Bogus."

"Oh, I know, Big. That's not exactly what I mean . . ."

"Well, please don't wake him up, with your damn checking on him."

And some nights, I cry out, "Look Big! He's *dead!*"

"He's *sleeping*, for Christ's sake . . ."

"But look how he's just lying there," I insist. *"His neck is broken!"*

"You sleep like that yourself, Bogus . . ."

Well, like father, like son; I'm sure I'm wholly capable of breaking my neck in my sleep.

"Come back to bed, Bogus." I hear you calling me to your groove.

It's not really that I'm reluctant to go there. But I have to check the stove; the pilot light is always going out. And that furnace sounds funny; one day we will wake up baked. Then check the lock on the door. There's more than hogs and corn in Iowa—or there *might* be.

"Will you ever come to bed?" you shout.

"I'm coming! I'm on my way, Big!" I promise.

Bogus Trumper was just checking and double-checking. You may call him improvident, but never blasé.

Tulpen was unimpressed with my letter for no one. "God, you haven't changed at all," she said.

"I've a new life," I said. "I'm a different man."

"Once you worried about a mouse," she said. "Now it's turtles and fish."

She sort of had me there. My silence made her smile and lift, just slightly, a breast with the back of her hand. Sometimes I could really whap her when she does that!

But it's true. I *do* worry about the turtles and fish. Not in the same way that I once worried about the mouse, though. That mouse lived in constant peril; it was my responsibility to keep him out of Biggie's trap. But Tulpen was already taking care of these fish and turtles when I moved in. Her bed is framed on three sides by bookcases, waist-high; we are walled in by words. And all along the tops of the cases, in a watery U around us, these gurgling aquariums sit. They bubble all night long. She keeps them lit with underwater neon rays. I'll admit that it helps when I have to get up to pee.

But the aura around the bed takes getting used to. In a half-sleep, you actually *feel* underwater, in spooky color, turtles and fish circling you.

She feeds the turtles with a single chunk of steak tied on a string; all night they gnash at the dangling meat; in the morning, the chunk is gray, like a dead thing, and Tulpen removes it. Thank God she feeds them only once a week.

And once I imagined that the man in the apartment above us was building a bomb. (He does something electrical at night; odd hums and crackles are heard, and the lights in the aquariums dim.) If that man's bomb blew up, there's enough water in those aquariums to drown us in our sleep.

One night, with such a thought, I considered calling Dr.

Jean Claude Vigneron. For one thing, I have a complaint: the water method isn't quite working out. But more important, I just wanted to hear the voice of a confident man. And maybe I'd ask him how he got to be so cocksure. I think it would have pleased me more, though, to find a way to shock him, to fluster that confidence of his. I thought of calling him very late. "Dr. Vigneron?" I would say. "My prick just fell off." Just to see what he'd say.

I told Tulpen my plan. "You know what he'd say?" she said. "He'd say, 'Put it in the refrigerator and make an appointment with my secretary in the morning.' "

Even though I suspect she's right, I was glad she didn't doff her boob to me then. She's more sensitive than that. That once, she turned out the aquarium lights.

10 : Let's Not Lose Track of Certain Statistics

It grieves him to remember lovely little Lydia Kindle, enraptured with freshman German, wanting ballads, or even opera, hummed to her in the *Muttersprache*. He obliged her; he made a tape for her of her very own. Deep-throated Bogus Trumper lulling her senseless with his favorite songs. It was to be a surprise.

He gave her the tape one afternoon in the language lab.

"Just for you, Miss Kindle. Some lieder I knew of . . ."

"Oh, Mr. Trumper!" she said, and scurried off to her earphones. He watched her big-eyed little face concentrating over the rim of the listening booth. At first she seemed so eager; then she scrunched up her pretty face critically; she stopped the tape—broke his rhythms!—played it back, stopped it again. She took notes. He went over to ask what was wrong.

"That's wrong, isn't it?" she asked, pointing to her elfin scribbles. "It's not *mude*, it's *müde*. But the singer missed the umlaut sound, every time."

"I'm the singer," he said in pain. It's so hard to be criticized by the young. And he added quickly, "German isn't my best foreign tongue. I'm really involved more in the Scandinavian languages—you know, Old Low Norse? I'm afraid my German is a bit rusty. I only thought you'd like the *songs*." He was bitter with the heartless child.

But she said, then, so high and birdlike, as if her throat were pinched, or being kissed, "Oh, Mr. Trumper. It's a *beautiful* tape. You only missed *müde*. And I just *loved* the songs. You've such a nice big voice." And he thought: A *big* voice?

But all he said was, "You may have the tape. To keep." And retreated, leaving her stunned in the listening booth. Under the earphones now she dreamed.

When he closed the lab for suppertime, she skipped after him—careful, though, that she didn't touch him with her silky little clothes.

"Going to the Union?" she chirped.

"No."

"I'm not going there either," she said, and he thought: She eats her supper in birdfeeders, hopping from one to the other all over town.

But all he said was, "Where *are* you going?"

"Oh, anywhere, nowhere," she said, and tossed her light, fine, nervous hair. When he said nothing, she coaxed him: "Tell me. What's Old Low Norse like?"

He said some words for her. *"Klegwoerum, vroognaven, okthelm, abthur, uxt."* She shivered, he thought. Her shimmery little dress hugged her snug for a moment, then breezed loose again. He hoped she was sincere.

Being so frequently insincere himself, Trumper suspected the motives of others. His own motives struck him as bottomless. To be diddling this farm child in his mind while his own wife—Lady Burden, the Mistress of Cope— suffers more banal encounters.

Biggie waiting in line at the A & P, in the check-out aisle marked. EIGHT ITEMS OR LESS. She has less than eight items; she couldn't afford more. She lolls over the sparse cart, feels something old and athletic stirring her: an urge for the giant slalom. She puts her feet close together, one slightly ahead of the other, and shifts her weight to the downhill ski and bends her knees into a springy lock position. Still leaning on the market cart, she wedels ahead in line. Behind her, a soft and shapeless housewife glowers indignantly at Biggie's broad waggling; through Biggie's stretch pants, her rump is round and taut. The housewife's husband tries not to look, pretends he's outraged, too. Inside Biggie's cart, Colm has already opened a box of Cheerios.

Now the confrontation with the check-out girl, tired

and sweaty with this Friday-night rush to consume. She almost doesn't notice Biggie's check, but the name is a hard one to forget. Trumper is one of the suspicious ones. The girl checks an ominous list and says, "Hang on a second, will you, ma'am."

Bring on the manager, now, in a short-sleeved, drip-dry summer shirt, the kind so thinly materialed that a few of the pubic-like hairs on his chest are poking through the loose weave. "I got your name on my list, lady," he says.

Biggie wedels. "Huh?" she says.

"Got your name on this list," says the manager. "Your check's no good here. Better empty that cart . . ."

"Of course my check's good here," Biggie tells him. "Come on. You're keeping all these people waiting." But they don't mind waiting in line now; something ugly is being revealed. Perhaps the staring housewife and her husband are somehow feeling vindicated. That shapeless lady is probably thinking Maybe my ass is running down my legs, but my checks are good.

"Please empty your cart, Mrs. Trumper," the manager says. "You're welcome to shop here—with cash."

"Well, then, cash my check," says Biggie, who never grasps things right off.

"Now, look, lady," says the manager, encouraged; he feels the line of shoppers is on his side. Colm pours the Cheerios on the floor. "Have you got the cash to pay for that cereal?" the manager asks Biggie.

And Biggie says, "Now look, you, yourself . . . I've got a good check . . ." But the manager elbows himself up next to her and starts emptying her cart. When he separates Colm from the Cheerios, the child starts to howl, and Biggie—a good two inches taller than the manager— grabs the bossy bastard by his short-sleeved, drip-dry summer shirt, probably tugging the crispy hairs on his chest. Biggie shoves him hard against the counter, shovels Colm out of the cart and mounts him sidesaddle on her good high hip; with one hand free, she takes back the Cheerios.

"Last time I shop in this dump," she says, and snatches her checkbook away from the check-out girl.

"Now get out of here," the manager whispers, but he's addressing himself to Colm, not Biggie.

Who speaks: "Get out of my way, then . . ." which the

manager tries to do, pressing himself against the counter while Biggie squeezes past him, grinding her hip against him. You'd rarely see the person who could fit with Biggie in one of those skinny aisles.

And she holds her dignity very well, out the hissing, electric doors—swaggering through the parking lot, a wake of Cheerios behind her. If she's thinking at all, it goes like this: If I were on my old skis, I would execute a tight kick-turn in that aisle. My edges, I keep sharp. Through his drip-dry shirt, one outside edge would cut that nasty fucker's nipples off.

But all she does is inform Bogus of her opinion about the root of the money problem: "It's your father, the prick . . ."

. . . and I can't help but agree when we're all home together, Colm groveling in the Cheerios. The light down the hall in our bedroom crackles, blinks and goes out. Biggie doesn't seem to notice that it's the *only* light that's gone out; the others have stayed on. "They've shut us off!" she cries. "Oh, my God, Bogus, you'd think they'd wait until morning, wouldn't you?"

"It's probably just the bulb, Big," I tell her. "Or that damn fuse." And in my bumbling fashion I try to wrestle with her a moment to make her happy, but it's then that she seems to notice the mess poor Colm and the Cheerios are in. She shoves me off and I'm left to investigate the nightly basement alone.

Down the damp stone stairs, remembering I must spring the trap so the mouse won't be guillotined. And calling up again to Biggie. "A smart mouse we got, Big. He's sprung it again without getting caught."

But this time I notice he's actually sprung it himself— sneaked in and snatched the cheese without leaving his soft little head behind. It makes me sweat to think of him taking such chances. I whisper to the musty basement, "Look here, Mouse, I'm here to help you. Be patient; let *me* spring the trap. Don't take such a risk, you've got everything to lose."

"What?" says Biggie from upstairs.

"Nothing, Big," I call up. "I was just swearing at that damn mouse! He's done it again! He got away!"

For a long time, then, I huddle by the fuse box, long after the fuse is replaced and Biggie has shouted down to me that I've got it, that the light's on again. I can hear the electric meter ticking through the outside wall. I think I hear the mouse, his little heart beating. He's thinking, God, what are the great awful trappers up to now? So I whisper into the darkness, "Don't be frightened. I'm on *your* side." After which the mouse's heartbeat seems to stop. I'm on the verge of crying out, frightened almost the way I'm frightened when I think Colm's breathing has stopped in his sleep.

Biggie shouts, "What are you *doing* down there, Bogus?"

"Oh nothing, Big."

"What a long time to be doing nothing," Biggie says.

And I catch myself thinking, What a long time indeed! With nothing you could ever call real hardship or suffering. In fact, it's been quite a light pain, and sometimes fun. It's just the nightly things—all little—that seem not to have amounted to something very *big*, or finally serious, so much as they have simply turned my life around to attending almost solely to them. A constant, if petty, irritation.

"Bogus!" Biggie shouts. "What are you doing?"

"Nothing, Big!" I call up again, meaning it this time. Or seeing, a little more clearly, what it is like to be doing nothing.

"You must be doing *something!*" Biggie hollers.

"No, Big," I call up. "I'm really doing nothing at all. Honest!" Bogus Trumper isn't lying now.

"Liar!" Biggie shouts. "You're playing with that damn mouse!"

Mouse? I think. Are you still here? I hope you haven't gone upstairs, thinking it was your big chance. Because you're better off in the basement, Risky Mouse. There's nothing petty down here.

That's it! What I object to is that my upstairs life is so cluttered with *little* things——errors of judgment, but never crimes. I don't face anything very severe; I don't live with anything that's as basic to avoid or as final to lose to as that mousetrap.

"Bogus!" Biggie screams; I hear her flounce in bed.

"I've got it!" I call up. "I'm coming now!"

"The mouse?" says Biggie.

"The mouse?"

"You've got the mouse?"

"No, Jesus, not the mouse," I say.

"Well, Jesus, *what* then?" says Biggie. "What have you got that's taken you all this time?"

"Nothing, Big," I say. "I've got nothing, really ..."

... and so another night puts Trumper at his window for the witching hour, which seems to lure old Fitch, the lawn-watcher, out of his bed for his brief front-porch constitutionals. Perhaps he's bothered by another Iowa fall; all that ominous dying going on.

But this night Mr. Fitch doesn't get up. Gently pushing his ear to the war-built screen, Trumper hears a sudden dry rush of leaves, and in the yellowing streetlight sees a small scattering of dead autumnal rubble flicker upward in the wind around Fitch's house. Mr. Fitch has died in his sleep! His soul momentarily rebels, once more raking over his lawn!

Bogus wonders if he should ring up the Fitches just to see who answers.

"Mr. Fitch just died," Trumper says aloud. But Biggie has learned to sleep through his voice at night. Poor Fitch, thinks Bogus, genuinely moved. When asked, Fitch had said he used to work for the Bureau of Statistics. *Now have you at last become one, Mr. Fitch?*

Trumper tries to imagine some excitement in Fitch's long career in the Bureau of Statistics. Poised over the microphone, he thinks that the bureau would want him to be brief and objective. Vowing to limit himself to only the most vital statistics, he flips the RECORD switch and begins:

"Fred 'Bogus' Trumper: born March 2, 1942, Rockingham-by-the-Sea Hospital, Portsmouth, New Hampshire; delivered by his father, Dr. Edmund Trumper, a urologist and substitute obstetrician.

"Fred 'Bogus' Trumper was graduated from Exeter Academy, 1960; Vice President of Der Unterschied (the school's German-language film society); Poetry Editor for the *Pudendum* (the school's underground literary magazine); he lettered in track (pole-vaulter) and in wrestling (a problem with his concentration span: he would be beating his opponent, and well ahead on points, when he would find himself inexplicably pinned). Trumper's grades and College Board scores? Undistinguished.

"He attended the University of Pittsburgh on an athletic scholarship (for wrestling); his potential was considered 'vast,' but he must learn to conquer his regrettable concentration span. His scholarship was revoked at the end of the academic year when he left Pittsburgh. His wrestling performance? Undistinguished.

"He attended the University of New Hampshire. Major? Undeclared. He left at the end of the academic year.

"He attended the University of Vienna, Austria. Field of concentration? German. Span of concentration? Well, he met Merrill Overturf.

"He reattended the University of New Hampshire and was graduated with a B.A. in German. His aptitude for foreign languages was referred to as 'vast.'

"He was accepted at the State University of Iowa, in the Graduate School of Comparative Literature. He was granted full academic credit for a research-absence, in Austria, January through September 1964. He was to discover and prove that the dialect ballads and folk tales of Salzburgerland and the Tyrol were descendants, via an early North Germanic tribal movement, of Old Low Norse. He found no such thing to be true. He made further contact with Merrill Overturf, however, and in a village in the Austrian Alps called Kaprun, he met and impregnated a member of the U.S. ski team. Her name was Sue 'Biggie' Kunft, of East Gunnery, Vermont.

"He returned to America and presented this large pregnant athlete to his father at Great Boar's Head; father fond of referring to Sue 'Biggie' Kunft as 'that great blond German ship'; father unrelenting, even when told that Biggie's father was a German Vermonter.

"Fred 'Bogus' Trumper was cut off by his father, 'until such a time as responsibility toward the future is demonstrable.'

"Married in East Gunnery, Vermont, September 1964. Sue 'Biggie' Kunft was forced to split her mother's (and her mother's mother's) wedding gown with a razor and insert a flap of suitable material, expandable, to conceal some months of gestation. Biggie's father was only upset that a skiing career was wasted. Biggie's mother thought that girls shouldn't ski anyway, but she was upset about the dress.

"Trumper returned to the State University of Iowa with an acceptable M.A. thesis on the connection between the dialect ballads and folk tales of Salzburgerland and the Tyrol with Old Low Norse. He received permission to return to Austria to follow up this interesting information. He did so, after the shocking birth of his first child (he was treated at the State University of Iowa hospital in March of 1965 for a fainting spell, following the first look at his gory, swaddled son. 'It's a boy!' the nurse, fresh and dripping from the delivery room, informed him. 'Will it live?' asked Trumper, sliding gelatinous to the floor).

"He actually returned to Austria to relive his romance with his wife and to find his old friend Merrill Overturf. Failing both, he returned to Iowa and announced that he had disproved his M.A. thesis and would select a new topic for his Ph.D. He thus began the translation of *Akthelt and Gunnel* from Old Low Norse. He has been doing this for almost four years . . .

"He still seeks reconciliation with his father's income. He still wonders if his child will live. And he considers the advisability of being married to a former professional athlete who can do more sit-ups than he can. He is, for example, afraid to wrestle her, for fear that he will be handily beating her and suddenly find himself inexplicably pinned. And when he told her that he used to be a polevaulter, she told him she had tried that once too. He is afraid to ask for comparative heights . . ."

. . . at which point, dramatically, the tape whips to an end, whirs and frays off the empty spool, *tzikity tzikity tzikity tzat!*

"Bogus?" Biggie groans from the bedroom.

"Nothing, Big."

He lets the sleep come back to her, and then quietly replays his recorded statistics. He finds them lacking in objectivity, brevity, honesty and sense, and he realizes that Mr. Fitch and the Bureau of Statistics will reject all information concerning this fraudulent Trumper, and make no entry of his name. Looking out his window at Fitch's

71

dark house, he recalls that Fitch is dead. Strangely relieved, he goes to bed. But in the morning, with Colm bouncing on his chest, he turns his head on the pillow and squints out his bedroom window. Seeing the ghostly vision of Fitch at work on his lawn, Trumper lets his child bounce on the floor.

"My God, Bogus," Biggie says, stooping down to the wailing child.

"Mr. Fitch died last night," Bogus tells her.

Looking blandly out the window, Biggie says, "Well, he looks better this morning." So it's morning, Trumper decides, trying to wake up; he watches Biggie lie back down on the bed with Colm.

And if Biggie isn't at the hospital, he thinks, then it's Saturday. And if it's Saturday, then I sell football pennants, pins, buttons and cowbells. And if Iowa loses again, I'll change to a school with a winning team . . .

There is a sudden thrashing and general upheaval of child and wife on the bed beside him; Biggie is getting up again. He turns to nuzzle her breast before she can go, but it's her elbow.

He opens his eyes. Nothing is as it seems. How could there be a God? He tries to remember the last time he thought there was one. In Europe? Surely God gets to travel more than that. It wasn't in Europe, anyway; at least there was no God in Europe when Biggie was with me.

Then he remembers Merrill Overturf. That was the last time God was around, he thinks. Therefore, believing in God went wherever Merrill went.

11: Notre Dame 52, Iowa 10

God *may* be dead, for all I know, but Our Lady's Eleven seemed to have some twelfth and ominous player on the field, making things fall their way. I could sense some Holy Power believing in them, even before the game. I sold two Notre Dame pennants to every Iowa one—a sure sign that some faith was abroad in the land. Or else some pessimism, a defensiveness on the part of the hometown rooters; fearing the worst, they were not going to be further humiliated by being seen with an Iowa pennant. They filed empty-handed into the stadium, a subtle green tie here and green socks there: if Iowa lost, they could always claim to be Irish. and there would be no Hawkeye button or cowbell to incriminate them.

Oh yes, you could tell by the concession sales: The Fighting Irish—Mary's Team, the Pontiff's Maulers—had something special going for them.

But I missed the game; I was spared that pain. I had a disaster of my own.

With my awkward plywood board (a weak hasp holds an easel stand behind it, but the whole thing is too unsteady to resist the wind), I am hawking my wares by the end-zone gate. And since only students and last-minute ticket-buyers get end-zone seats, it is not the concession stand available to the upper crust of pennant, button and cowbell buyers.

I am selling my sixth Notre Dame pennant when I see little Lydia Kindle, swaying along with an utter *Glork* of a boyfriend. I swear the fierce wind died for a second, heavy with the scent of her hair! And I stop my insane clamoring with a cowbell; I cease chanting, "Pennants!

Buttons! Cowbells! Satisfying stadium cushions! Rain hats! Say it for Iowa or Notre Dame!"

I watch Lydia flutter along; her boyfriend scuffs beside her; the wind buffets her against him, and they're laughing. It would be more than I could stand if she should see me blue-cold and huddled by my garish showboard, hawking junk in loutish English, without a lilting trace of Old Low Norse on my tongue.

I dart behind my showboard, crouched with my back against the thing; the wind performs alarming unbalancing feats. Just in case, I unpin my hideous Hawkeye Enterprise button, No. 501, and cram it, with my yellow change apron, into the side-pouch of my parka. Then I lurk quietly behind the board. As her *Glork* announces, "Hey, whattaya know, Lid? Nobody watching the old board here. Have a button." And I hear her giggle.

But *Glork* doesn't quite have the knack for removing a pin from the cloth strips that swaddle the board, and he must be anxious to do his deed and run, for I can feel him tugging and wrenching so hard that I have to hug the easel stand to keep the whole apparatus from falling. Then I hear one of the cloth strips rip, and out the corner of my eye I see a string of Iowa buttons flap in the wind. Yes, the wind, or the combination of the wind and Lydia Kindle's boyfriend's last hard yank: I feel my balance lost, my dignity in motion. The showboard is falling.

"Look out!" cries my bright-voiced Lydia. "It's coming over on you!" But the *Glork* doesn't quite step back in time, not before he's trapped by the descending, seven-foot rectangle of what he suspects is only light plywood. He puts up a casual hand to catch it; he doesn't know I'm riding it down on him, like a 180-pound raft. And when it pins him to the cement, he lets out a terrible yell; the board, I feel, is splitting along my spine; I can feel him weakly scratching through the wood under me. But paying him no mind, I simply look up to Lydia.

"Klegwoerum," I tell her. *"Vroognaven okthelm abthur, awf?"*

She gawks while the board struggles under me. I change my language and garble German up to Lydia: *"Wie gehts dir heute? Hoffentlich gut."*

A muffled grunt under the board. I sit up slowly, with a

74

lofty air about me, and say a little overseriously, as if rudely awakened, "What's going on here. Lydia?"

Immediately defensive, she says, "The board fell over." As if I didn't know. I stand up, and the *Glork* scuttles out from under my fallen wares looking like a little crushed crab.

"What in hell are you doing there?" I ask him, just to put him on the defensive.

"Suffering shit!" he cries. "I was just taking one mucking pin!"

Fatherly, almost, I take Lydia's arm, pronouncing over the kneeling *Glork,* "Watch your language, kid . . ."

"What?" he hoots. "Is this *your* board?"

"Mr. Trumper runs my language lab," Lydia tells him icily—as if this makes impossible any connection I might have with these cheap wares.

But the *Glork* isn't convinced. He straightens up, visibly in pain, and says, "Well, what were you doing behind this damn board?"

"Why . . . the vender . . ." I say, "the vender had to leave it here a moment. Passing by, I offered to watch it for him while he was gone." And attempting to divert this conversation from scrutiny, I point out to the *Glork* that this vender would surely be upset at the condition of his board. Didn't the *Glork* think he should make amends?

A momentous moment. Worshipful Lydia Kindle, adoring me—a man of my talents and tastes, big and unsnobbish enough to stoop to help the most lowly vender. A humanist comes into young Lydia's life! At this peak of glory, I am even not above lifting the showboard upright while the *Glork* fumes beside it, fumbling the button out of his pocket, murmuring, "Come on, Lid, we'll miss the game."

Then I see Fred Paff, hawkish concession sales head for Hawkeye Enterprises, cruising the end-zone gate. Seeing how things are selling, no doubt. And he spots me and my mauled board. And I'm not wearing my proper identification pin, and I am not girdled in my stunning yellow change apron.

"I say, your boy's right, you know," I tell Lydia quickly. "Better get going or you'll miss the kickoff."

But her adoration is too great; she just gapes at me.

"Go *on!*" I beg them, and the *Glork* takes Lydia's elbow.

But it's too late; Fred Paff is upon us. I smell his approaching tweeds nearby; I hear his jowls flapping in the wind; he is athletically deodorized and powdered, sucking big-winded breaths beside me, robust, on the prowl.

He booms, "Trumper! So where's your Hawkeye pin, boy? Where's your change apron? And what in filthy hell has happened to your *board?*" I can't look at him as he flicks at the string of buttons trailing on the ground. He draws in his scented breath at the sight of that fine cloth strip that's been ripped. I simply can't talk. Fred Paff clomps on my shoulder. "Trumper?" he says, almost brotherly. It's more than I can bear; he's fondling me like a wounded dog. He gropes in my parka pouch, pulls out the awful evidence—my yellow change apron and my ID badge, No. 501. "Fred?" he says gently. "Fred, what's *wrong* with you, boy?"

"Ha!" cries the *Glork*. *"He's* the vender!"

And Paff asks, "Fred? Do these people want to buy something? Aren't you selling today, Fred?"

If only Lydia Kindle had hoo-roared at me too I could have stood it. If only she'd been the true compatriot of her *Glork*, I could somehow have borne up to this. But I felt her there, a sympathetic shiver beside me.

She said, "Oh, Mr. Trumper. You shouldn't be *ashamed.* Some people have to work, you know, and I think it's very strong of you, really!"

It's such stupid and innocent pity that hurts me.

Paff says, "My God, Fred, get hold of yourself." Even Paff! That he should care about what's wrong. (In our orientation meeting he told us he looked out for all his "boys," but I never believed he *meant* it!) It's too much.

They're around me, Paff and Lydia, and out in front of my board is that leering *Glork*. Him I can understand! And behind him, I swear, is a gathering throng. Seeing this drama before the game, better than a half-time show. The crowd is thinking, after a crowd's fashion, Now if they would only put on something like this during the half. If only they displayed the venders, fed them to Iowa hogs, let them humbly try to defend themselves with their goofy showboards—*that* would be genuine half-time entertainment!

I bolt.

I tackle my tray of wares and batter myself and the board into and over the wailing *Glork*. Off into the vile crowd, then; I shift the board, carrying it like a broad knife through the masses. I shift again; I bear it on my back, stooped and pitched forward; my shield protects me from rear attack. I see terror-struck faces loom up ahead of me, veer out of my charging path; insults are hurled after me. Sometimes my shield is struck or, more often, *picked* at. I am being picked clean from behind! I feel them like predatory birds, snaring a button here, a pennant there. There is a terrible jangle: all my cowbells are gone in a swoop.

Rounding the last edge of the end-zone gate, I see—too late to avoid him—an awestruck campus cop. I can only lower my head, I hear his breath sucked right out of him, and I watch his blue face dipping away from me, floating down between my pumping knees. Somehow I avoid stepping on his chest badge. Running on, I wait for his bullet to pierce my shield and shatter my spine. But I'm safely at the home-team gate and nothing happens. Perhaps, I think with dread, my board decapitated him; perhaps, when I saw his head falling, it was falling unattached.

I batter into the stadium concession room, sagging to my knees under the board. Someone is kind enough to lift it off me. It's No. 368, wearing his football tie. "God! 501!" he says, looking at my bare board. "You really cleaned up! Where was your stand?"

Others mill around me. The head counter starts to tally up my board, determining sales and percentage. I'm too weak to explain. He discovers I've "sold" all but one pennant, all but four of the big GO HAWKS! buttons, every one of the little Iowa pins with the little gold footballs attached, and all my cowbells. He announces, then, that I've "sold" more than three hundred dollars' worth of wares. He's tallying up the mathematical wonder which is to be my "commission" when I hand over my actual earnings: $12.75.

"I was picked clean," I confess. "They got me."

"They?" says 368, shocked.

"The mob," I groan, and struggle off my knees. "Mad fans," I tell them. They steady me; their concern destroys me.

"501," says 368, "you mean they *took* all your things?" And I weakly gesture to my ragged board, and to my tattered, gravel-embedded knees.

But feeling my wind return, I realize I should be moving along. Fred Paff will no doubt be here in a jiffy. There's a roar above me: kickoff time. Most of the other venders scatter; even 368, an avid fan, is tempted to leave me. In fact, I gesture that I'm all right, that he needn't stay to support me.

"We've got to *do* something about this," he mumbles, but his mind is really on the kickoff return. If I weren't so weary, I'd tell him that we must unionize all hawkers. I'd speak to him about profit sharing and the victimization of the proletariat. Give a primer to the man in the football tie! Freshman Marx! Hawkers of the world, unite!

But at this moment, five yards deep in his own end zone, the Notre Dame kickoff and punt-return specialist—fleet No. 25—receives the ball like a solid touch from a magic wand. And 368 says, "We should have two men with every board."

"Then you'd have to split the commission," says the head counter.

"Hell, no," says 368. "You'd *double* the commission. Don't tell me someone's not making any money off this junk ..." No doubt 368 is a business major who picked up his football tie dirt-cheap.

But this speculation is cut off. The stadium above us gives off an animal din. No. 25 of Notre Dame has burst up the middle, over his own 40, a very solid and gold-helmeted patron saint blocking in front of him. And our own 368 takes off down the sidelines of the stadium underground, heading for the nearest ramp, while the head counter dashes to a dungeonlike portal in the back of the concession room.

Wishing I had the speed of 25 of Notre Dame, I make my timely escape. This time the traffic is heavier. The masses who've missed the kickoff are flooding the gates. A cross-body block on a soft man swaddled in blankets squirts me loose from the underground panic, out the press-box gate, as free as No. 25 of Notre Dame who now finds himself all alone, across midfield, one Iowa lineman lagging behind and nothing but the Iowa end zone in front of him. The hometown roar stifles to a death rattle and a shrill fringe cheer goes up from the rabid Catholics in the stands. The Fighting Irish Band sends out a bright green note.

I simply run away, down toward the other end zone—away from where No. 25 is drawing first blood, away from where I suspect the campus cop lies headless, and where an army of R.O.T.C. volunteers is mustering to rout me out. I cross the intramural soccer field sucessfully, except for whacking my knees on the bumpers of all the parked cars and having to avoid the stare of the R.O.T.C. car-parker, wearing his suspicious eyes low, barely showing under his white M.P. helmet. Why do they wear M.P. just to park a car?

Then I'm weaving through the deserted upper campus, wending down to the Iowa River, past the appallingly quiet university hospitals. In front of the Children's Hospital entrance, several farmers sprawl on the hoods and front fenders of their pickups, waiting for their wives and kids who've gone inside for this social service the university offers. Treating pigbite and miscarriages and countless strange animal diseases that somehow are communicated to the farmers and their families.

I run blindly for an instant, struck with an awful, senseless image of Colm mauled by one of those demented sows who gobble up their own piglets.

Past the quadrangle of boys' dorms now. I hear only one phonograph in operation, playing a Scarlatti harpsichord piece defiantly—harsher and more religious than shattered stained glass. Obviously not a football fan. There's no one to see me atop and listen, or see me take up my pace again when I hear steps behind me.

They're scuffed steps, all tired out. Perhaps the upended campus cop, with his precarious head held by a sinew. Even so, he couldn't be as tired as I am. I stop. I wait for the steps coming up behind me and when a hand lights gently on my arm, I kneel; I touch my forehead to the sun-warmed cement in the dorm quadrangle and feel the Scarlatti play up and down my spine—as this hand does, too. I see one fine, fragile pair of legs. When the legs see that I'm looking at them, they draw together; two knees come down, like the bright cheeks of a baby's fine bottom. A weak hand tries to lift my head; I help. I lay my gravel-pocked chin in the hem of her skirt.

And Lydia Kindle says, "Oh, Mr. Trumper," in a sad little voice. And brightening her tone, she adds. *"Wie gehts dir jetzt? Hoffentlich gut ..."*

But I can hardly match her songster German. I revert to Old Low Norse. *"Klegwoerum,"* I tell her thickly. She slips her cold, brittle hand under the collar of my parka, down the back of my neck, and squeezes as best as she can.

Then, from the towering, near-empty dorms around us, I hear the harpsichord cut off. The last chord hangs above me so long that I half expect it to crash on both of us. I help myself and Lydia up, and hold her flush against me; there's so little thickness to her that I can feel her heartbeat at her spine. She lifts her young, wet face to me: such a fine-boned face. If I had a face that angular, I'd be afraid to roll over in my sleep, fearing I'd break off a piece. Yet she lifts her vulnerable face to me.

My mustache doesn't bear such close scrutiny, so I kiss her quickly. She can't keep her lips still, so I back off, keeping her hand. When I start to walk her along, I pull her closer beside me. Down the boardwalk to the river, I feel her slight, sharp hip jab me; she tries to fit her angles and her springy step to my bearlike swaying. Over the river and into town; after wordless practice, we finally walk well together.

I see our reflection in the storefront windows. We are superimposed over a mannequin with flowered panties and a matching bra, a purse on her arm. Then our image changes. See the next frame: we are superimposed, over the face of a sullen beer drinker, over the pale neon of a flashing pinball machine, over the heaving back of the pinball player, who appears to be furiously mounting the machine. Next frame: we are superimposed over nothing at all—over a dark and vacant storefront window, with only a sign in the bottom corner of our image. The sign says: TO LET. I've read it twice before I realize I've stopped walking and am aiming our faces at this storefront glass.

80

Her face and mine, close together. She looks surprised at herself, but happy.

But see me! My hair is wild, my eyes are mad, my mouth is uncontrollably grinning; my face is a grimace, as tight-skinned and as blotchy as a clenched fist. Behind our faces a small crowd slows and gathers, pausing just long enough to squint into this storefront, to see what's caught our eyes; they hurry on as soon as they see our unmatched faces—practically bolting away, as if my askew features scare them.

"I can see you anytime," says Lydia Kindle, speaking down to the sidewalk. "Just you tell me when."

"I'll call you."

"Or you can give me a note," she says, ". . . in the language lab."

"Sure, a note," I say, thinking: Jesus! *Notes in the language lab?*

"Or anything."

"Sure, anything," I say, and she fidgets a moment, waiting for me to take her hand again.

But I don't. I manage a smile—a dissected face in the storefront, with a grin as convincing as a skeleton's. Then I watch her swish off the curb, dally to the crosswalk, turning to give me a wave; I watch the window glass and see me raise my arm stiffly, from the elbow, as if the wires which help me to bend are somehow overwound or crossed.

Then I dally along behind her, pretending aloofness to the proud flick of her rump. But I notice people staring at my knees, and when I stoop to wipe off the tatters, the blood and gravel, I lose sight of Lydia.

Oh, sympathy and comfort. It's a queer thing that when you're given a little, you only want a lot.

Because I went home to Biggie and caught her stooped in the hall outside the bathroom door, flopping braless in one of my T-shirts, crammed into a pair of my Levis, so tight on her that she couldn't do up the fly. Colm played in the hallway between us, intent on smashing together two trucks. And Biggie, rolling a pail of ammonia cleanser out the bathroom door, caught me looking at her as if her *strength* at that moment had overcome me and left me gaping at her as if she were some animal, ugly and scary and able to eat me whole.

"What are you gawking at?" she asked.

"Nothing, Big," I said. But I was aware of the vision of myself in the storefront window and couldn't meet her eyes.

"Well, I'm sorry if I don't look *pretty* enough for you," she said, and I winced. She advanced on me, down the hall, prodding the ammonia pail along with her foot, having to bend her body to do this and sending one of her boobs askew—one swung out at her side while the other rode high and straight at me. As if I wasn't already intimidated enough.

She said "Bogus? What's wrong with you, anyway? Did they call off the game?" She lifted my face up with her broad hand.

Then I saw her mouth go slack, and at first I thought it was the sight of my storefront face that shocked her. Not recognizing, at first, that it was an angry look she gave me, and not tasting—until just that moment, with my tongue licking over my dry lips—Lydia Kindle's pale-orange lipstick at the corners of my mouth and on the bristles of my mustache: tangerine love.

"You bastard!" said Biggie, and brought up from the pail a soggy cleaning rag, first swatting my face with it, then wiping it smarting across my mouth. Perhaps it was the ammonia that started my eyes watering, with those fumes so strong under my nose.

I blubbered, "I lost my job, Big." She gaped at me, and I repeated, "I lost my *job*, Big I lost that fucking job ..." And I felt myself dropping down to my raw knees, brought to them I felt, too many times in just one day.

Biggie started to brush by me, but I caught her around the hips and hugged her, repeating over and over, "I lost the job, the job!" But she snapped her knees up and caught my chin: I bit my tongue and felt the sweet blood trickle down my throat. I grabbed for her again, looking for her face and found her suddenly close to me, down on her knees too, and saying in her quiet, calm way, her *other* way. "Bogus? What was the job to you, Bogus? I mean, it was a bad job, wasn't it? And it was never bringing in enough so that we'll notice it's gone . . . Right, Bogus?"

But that ammonia is strong stuff. I was beyond the hope

82

of talk; I could only grab the waist of Biggie's T-shirt to dab my gory mouth. Biggie pressed me against her; she's so solid I hardly made a dent, but I found my usual spot, hugged snug between bosom and thigh. I let Biggie croon to me there in her low, flat-sung voice, "It's all right, Bogus. Now, really, it's okay. It's all right . . ."

Perhaps I would have contested the point with her if I hadn't seen Colm, all through with bashing his trucks and coming our way—quite curious to know what sort of helpless creature his mother was mothering now. I hid my face against Biggie and felt Colm lightly poking my back and ears and feet to try to find exactly where I must have hurt myself. For the life of me, I can't say for sure where it was.

"I've got a present for you . . ." Biggie's rich voice drifts down the hall, comes back, sinks in. She hands it over. *A job-losing present for the oddly unfaithful!* Colm paws at the label while I translate the Hungarian. From Milo Kubik's Peoples Market one precious eight-ounce tin of my favorite Ragout of Wild Boar in Médoc Sauce. Milo Kubik, the refugee gourmet. He escaped from Budapest with memories, and actual tins of this and other ragouts. Thank God he made it, I say. I know that if I had been in Budapest—a bottle of boar-marinade in my pocket, a snifter of paprika in my crotch—I would have been *caught.*

12 : Do You Want to Have a Baby?

Tulpen went home early, but Bogus and Ralph Packer stayed late at the Christopher Street studio, playing with the sound track of *Down on the Farm*.

The hippie commune called the Free Farm had taken over about four acres of undeveloped land belonging to a local liberal arts college. They planted a garden and invited real farmers in the area to come share their harvest and plant gardens of their own. The college had several hundred acres of undeveloped land. The college authorities asked the Free Farmers to leave, but the Free Farmers said they were simply using unused land. Unused land was a crime against humanity; all over Vermont there are farmers without enough land. The Free Farmers would stay on the college land until the pigs threw them off.

Ralph screened some new shots of the latest developments; Bogus played with the sound.

(Medium shot; no sync sound; interior, day; general store. The Free Farmers are shopping, fanning out through the store aisles picking up things and putting them back, as if these foodstuffs and hardware were rare gifts)

NARRATOR *(Bogus, voice over):* The Free Farmers buy wheat germ, honey, brown rice, milk, oranges, apple wine, cigarette paper, corncob pipes, Camels, Marlboros, Winstons, Luckies, Salems . . .

(Medium shot; sync sound; exterior, day; general store. The Free Farmers mill around their psychedelic Volkswagen panel truck parked outside the store. The boy

holding the grocery bag has long hair tied back in a ponytail; he wears a pair of farmer's overalls. He is pawing around in the bag, pulling things out)

BOY: Whose Salems? *(He holds up the pack)* Come on! Who got the Salems?

Then they view the scene with the president of the local college. The president is useful to the movie because he blatantly foreshadows what's going to happen.

(Medium shot, moving; no sync sound; exterior, day; college campus. We follow the college president across the parking lot, up a path through the campus mall. He is sharply dressed; he nods graciously to several passing students)

NARRATOR *(Dogus, voice over):* The president is forty-three, once-divorced, now remarried, D.S., M S, Ph.D. in botany, Yale. He has four children of his own. He is the chairman of the State Democratic Committee ...

(The president follows a group of students into a building; the students walk on in, but the president stops to wipe his feet)

NARRATOR [v.o.]: He is opposed to having the police on campus; although he believes firmly in private property and has repeatedly asked the Free Farmers to leave, he will not call in the police ...

(Medium close-up; sync sound; interior, day; president's office. The president speaks directly into camera)

PRESIDENT: Why call in the police? The real farmers around here will take care of it ...

The bulk of the new footage has to do with the leader of the Free Farm, a character named Morris. One night a lot of real farmers come to the Free Farm and maul Morris. The police interview the nameless girlfriend of Morris, a witness to the mauling.

(Medium shot; sync sound; interior, night police station. Morris's girl wears farm overalls over a great soft pair of breasts in an old T-shirt that we've previously seen Morris wearing. The girl is talking to a police sergeant in the station, and a police secretary is taking notes)

GIRL:. . . then I couldn't tell what they were doing to Morris, 'cause one of them knocked me down—you know talking dirty to me. And one of them reached under me I was lying on my stomach—and he pinched me in the tit *(She lifts her breast to display the part pinched)* It's clear it's what they really want from us, of course Just fucking! that's really all. They pretend they hate us, but they really want our asses, man Oh sure, they hit me, knocked me down and all, but what they were really after was a cheap feel. You know, their wives with bras and girdles on all the time, and their hair in curlers—it's natural for them to go around wanting it all the time. But they just feel so threatened by us—at least they responded that way to Morris . . .

POLICE SERGEANT: Exactly how did they respond to Morris?

GIRL: They just beat the shit out of him, man.

POLICE SERGEANT: Did Morris provoke them?

GIRL: Morris? You've got to be kidding! Morris asked them to turn on with him! Morris just doesn't know how to fucking provoke anybody . . .

There follows a lot of dismal footage of the mauled, hospitalized Morris in traction. Finally, the rest of the Free Farmers have to get police protection because the real farmers raid them again and shotgun all the tomato plants. "Police protection" entails the police removing all the Free Farmers from the Free Farm.

86

When Morris is released from the hospital, he goes around the village conducting a kind of autopsy on the deserted Free Farm. He asks all the town farmers whether they really would have shot anybody, or whether in time they might have grown to tolerate the Free Farm. This is all pointless, since there is no more Free Farm, but apparently it is important for Morris to get the answers.

(Medium shot—fade in, from dissolve; no sync sound, music over; exterior, day; village firehouse. Morris, on crutches, is with his girl. They are talking with the fire chief, but there is no sync sound. The music is Neil Young's "After the Goldrush." Although Morris is doing all the talking, the fire chief keeps looking at Morris's girl. Medium shot; no sync sound, music over; exterior, day; farmer's house. Morris and the girl are talking with one of the real farmers, possibly involved in the mauling. The girl holds up her breast, probably referring to the pinch. Morris is friendly; the farmer is cautious. Medium shot; no sync sound, music over; exterior day; general store. Morris and his girl sit on the steps of the general store. They are drinking Pepsi; Morris talks enthusiastically, but the girl seems fed up with him. Another angle—to include the kids' psychedelic Volkswagen panel truck; sync sound, music fades. Morris and his girl, about to depart. They are getting into the truck. Morris talks directly into camera; his girl holds his crutches for him)

MORRIS: They wouldn't have shot us. Maybe they would've beaten us up again, but they absolutely would not have shot us. I feel we're much closer to them now; there's some communication happening. *(He turns to his girl)* You can just feel it, can't you?

GIRL: They would have blown your goddamn head off, Morris . . .

The plan of the film is to close with the college president's comment.

(Medium shot, moving; sync sound; exterior, day; Parents' Day picnic. Through a formal picnic spread, past many

87

neatly attired parents, all smiling, nodding hello, the president moves like a Pope bestowing blessings. He is eating fried chicken, and manages to do so in an unmessy way. The camera moves closer to him, coming in over his shoulder. He suddenly turns and faces camera. At first he is startled; then he turns on the charm, speaking seriously, as if renewing an old, tireless subject)

PRESIDENT: Do you know what really encourages me, even with such things going on all around us? Well, I'll tell you something about these kids ... and it's very encouraging, really. They live and learn, that's what they do. They really do ... and that's what encourages me. They just live and learn, like all kids, anywhere, anytime ...

Then Kent came in with the beer and cheese. He'd been cameraman for a lot of the new footage and was eager to see how he'd done.

"Did you show it already?" he asked.

"It stinks," Ralph said. "The whole thing. It's just awful."

"It isn't very good," Trumper agreed.

Kent unwrapped the cheese as if it were his failing heart. "The *camera* was bad, huh?" he said.

"The whole thing is terrible," said Ralph.

They sat there, wondering what went wrong.

"It was the fucking camera, wasn't it?" said Kent.

"It's the entire concept," Ralph said.

"The *people* are awful," Trumper said. "They're so obvious."

"They're simple," said Ralph. "There's nothing complex about the people."

"How about the girl with her tit-thing, though?" said Kent. "That was great, wasn't it?"

"It's the politics and the cuteness and the rotten humor that make it awful in every way," Ralph said. "At least that's *part* of it."

"Can I see the footage, please?" Kent said. "At least I should see the damn stuff."

"*You* won't even like your camerawork, Kent," Ralph said.

"You didn't like it, Ralph?"

"I didn't like *anything*," Ralph said.

"How's the editing?" Kent asked.

"No fair talking about editing when Tulpen isn't here," Trumper said.

"It hadn't really been edited yet, anyway, Kent," Ralph said.

"Yeah, *Jesus*, Kent," Trumper said.

"Okay, Thump-Thump," Kent said. "How's the *sound?*"

"Adequate," said Ralph. "Thump-Thump gets better and better, technically speaking."

"Right," said Trumper. "It's my imagination that goes nowhere."

"Right," said Ralph.

"Look," Kent said. "Can I please just see the fucking footage for myself?"

So they left him rewinding reels in the studio and walked out onto Christopher Street, headed for coffee at the New Deal.

"All I want to do in a film is describe something worthwhile," Ralph said. "I hate conclusions."

"I don't believe in endings," Trumper said.

"Right, right," said Ralph. "Just good description. But it has to be *personal* description. Everything else is journalism."

"If the New Deal is closed," Trumper said, "I will absolutely shit."

But it was open; they sat with two mugs of black espresso with lemon peel and rum.

"Let's scrap the film, Thump-Thump," Ralph said. "It's the same old thing. Everything I've done is extroverted, and I need to make an introverted film."

"Well, it's up to you, Ralph," Trumper said.

"You're a bundle of opinions, Thump-Thump. That's what's so exciting about you."

"It's your movie."

"But suppose *you* did the next one, Thump-Thump. What would it be?"

"I have no plans," Trumper said, observing the lemon peel in his coffee.

"But what do you *feel*, Thump?" Ralph asked him.

Trumper cupped his coffee mug with his hands. "Heat," he said. "At the moment, I feel heat."

What *do* I feel? he asked himself later, groping through Tulpen's dark apartment, encountering her clothes with his bare feet.

A bra, I feel a bra under my left foot there. And pain? Yes, pain; my right shin goes *ker-crack* against the bedroom chair: that's pain.

"Trumper?" from Tulpen, turning over in bed. He crawled in beside her, reached out for her, held on.

"A breast," he said aloud. *I feel a breast.*

"Correct," Tulpen told him, wrapping herself around him now. "What else do you know?" she whispered. *Pain?* Well, yes, her teeth nipping his belly; her kiss rough enough to turn his navel inside out. "I missed you," he told her. They usually left work together.

But she didn't answer him; her mouth shut on his sleepy life; her teeth worried him, and her thighs suddenly seized his head so tight that in his temples he felt his pulse pick up. His tongue touched her, and in her mouth he reached for her brain.

Then they lay lapped by the cold neon lights from the aquariums. Odd fish darted past them; slow turtles surfaced, keeled over and sank sideways. Trumper lay trying to imagine other ways to live.

He saw a tiny, translucent, turquoise eel, its inner organs visible and somehow functioning. One organ looked like a little plumber's helper; it plunged down, sucked up, and the eel's mouth opened to belch a tiny bubble. As the bubble rose to the surface, other fish investigated it, nudged it, sometimes broke it. A form of speech? Trumper wondered. Was a bubble a word or a whole sentence? Perhaps a paragraph! A tiny, translucent, turquoise *poet* reading beautifully to his world! Trumper was about to ask Tulpen about this odd eel, but she spoke first.

"Biggie called you tonight," she said.

Trumper wished he could send up a perfectly lovely bubble. "What did she want?" he asked, envying the eel's easy communication.

"To speak to you."

"She didn't leave a message? There's nothing wrong with Colm, is there?"

"She said they were going off for the weekend," Tulpen told him. "So if you called and no one was there, not to worry."

"Well, that's what she called for, then," Trumper said. "She didn't say anything was wrong with Colm."

"She said you usually called on the weekend," Tulpen said. "I didn't know that."

"Well, I call from the studio," Trumper said. "Just to talk to Colm. I thought you'd just as soon not hear ..."

"You miss Colm, Trumper?"

"Yes."

"But not her?"

"Biggie?"

"Yes."

"No," Trumper said. "I don't miss Biggie."

Silence. He scanned the aquarium for the verbose eel, but couldn't find him. Change the topic of the bubbles, he thought. Quick.

"Ralph wants to scrap the film," he said, but she was staring at him. "You know, *Down on the Farm?*" he said. "The new footage was awful. The whole idea is so simple-minded ..."

Tulpen said, "I know."

"He talked to you already?" Trumper asked.

"He wants to do a *personal* film," she said. "Right?"

"Right," he said; he touched her breast, but she moved away, turned her back to him, tucked into a ball.

"Something complex," Tulpen said. "Introverted and non-political. Something more *private*, right?"

"Right," Trumper said, worried. "I guess he told you more about it than he told me."

"He wants to make a film about you," Tulpen said.

"Me?" he said. "What *about* me?"

"Something personal," she mumbled into the pillow.

"What?" Trumper cried. He sat up and roughly rolled her over into his lap.

"About how your marriage busted up," Tulpen said. "You know, good description? And about how we're getting along ... now," she said. "And interviews with Biggie,

91

how's *she* living with it, you know? And interviews with *me*," Tulpen said. "About what I think . . ."

"Well, what *do* you think?" he shouted; he was furious.

"I think it sounds like a good idea."

"For whom?" he said nastily. "For me? Like some kind of therapy? Like going to a fucking shrink?"

"That might not be a bad idea, either," she said; she sat up beside him and touched his thigh. "We've got enough money for it, Trumper . . ."

"Christ!"

"Trumper?" she said. "If you really don't miss her, what's going to hurt about it?"

"It's got nothing to do with hurting," he said. "I've got a new life now. Why go back?"

"What sort of new life?" she asked. "Are you happy, Trumper? Are you going anywhere? Or are you happy where you are?"

"I've got you."

"Do you love me?" she asked. And he thought of the turquoise eel's bubble for that!—a terrible whirlpool rising, the other fish getting out of its way.

"There's no one else I'd rather be with," he said.

"But you miss Colm. You miss your son."

"Yes."

"Well, you can have another one, you know," she said angrily. "Do you want a baby, Trumper? I mean, I *could* produce one, you know . . ."

He looked at her, shocked. "You want a baby?"

"Do *you?*" she yelled at him. "I can give you that, Trumper, but you've got to really *want* one. You've got to let me know what you want of me, Trumper. You can't just live here if I don't even know you!"

"I didn't know you wanted a baby."

"That's not exactly what I said, Trumper."

"I mean," he said, "you seemed sort of aloof, kind of independent—like you didn't want me too close."

"Which is how you want it, isn't it?"

"Well, no, it's got nothing to do with how I want *you* to be."

"But how *do* you want me?" Tulpen said.

"Well . . ." he said, fumbling, a bubble too heavy to rise. "Well, just like you want to be, Tulpen."

92

But she turned away from him. "You want things cool, right?" she said. "Sort of detached, not committed, free . . ."

"Goddamn!" he said. "Do you really want a baby?"

"You first," she said. "I'm not putting out something for nothing. I could put out, Trumper. I *can* get involved," she said, looking up at him. "But can you?"

Trumper got up and walked around the aquariums, looking through the tanks at her. A fish darted down her cleavage, algae moved in her lap.

"You're not *doing* anything," Tulpen said to him. "You've got no direction, there's not a plan in your life. There's no plot to it, even."

"Well, I'd make a bad movie then, wouldn't I?" he said. He was looking for the turquoise eel and couldn't find him.

"Trumper, I'm not at all interested in what kind of movie you'd make. I don't care about the damn movie, Trumper." Looking at him staring at her through a fish tank, she snatched the sheet around herself angrily. "Stop looking at my crotch when I'm trying to talk to you!" she screamed.

He bobbed up above the tank, peering down at her. He was genuinely surprised; he'd just been looking for the eel. "I wasn't looking at your crotch," he said, and she fell back on the bed as if she were finally exhausted from sitting up.

"You haven't wanted to go away for a weekend," she said. "People just don't live in New York without at least wanting to go somewhere."

"You know that little see-through eel?" he said, poking around in one of the tanks. "The turquoise one, the very small one?" She popped up from under the sheet and stared at him. "Well, I can't find him," he said to her. "I think he was talking . . . I wanted to show you . . ." But her stare cut him off. "He talked in bubbles," Trumper told her.

Tulpen just shook her head. "Jesus," she whispered. He went over to the bed and sat down beside her. "You know what Ralph says about you, Trumper?" she asked him.

"No," he said, angry. "Tell me what fucking old Ralph says."

"He says you don't come across, Trumper."

"Come across?"

"No one knows you, Trumper! You don't *convey* anything. You don't do much, either. Things just sort of happen to you, and they don't even add up to anything. You don't make anything of what happens to you. Ralph says you must be very complicated, Trumper. He thinks you must have a mysterious core under the surface."

Trumper stared into the fish tank. *Where is the talking eel?*

"And what do *you* think, Tulpen?" he asked her. "What do you think's under the surface?"

"Another surface," she said, and he stared at her. "Or maybe just that one surface," she said, "with nothing under it." He was angry, then, but he stood up lightly and shook his head and laughed. She kept watching him, though.

"Well, you know what *I* think?" he said, and he peered into the tank, wondering what he really did think. "I think," he said, "that the tiny turquoise eel is gone." He grinned at Tulpen, then, but she was not amused and turned away.

"Then that's the second one I've lost," she said coldly.

"Lost?" he said.

"Well, I put the first one in another tank and he disappeared."

"Disappeared?" Trumper said; he looked around at the other tanks.

"Well, something ate him, obviously," Tulpen said. "So I put the second one in a different tank so he wouldn't be eaten by whatever ate the first one. And, obviously, something else ate this one."

Trumper put his hand in the tank, groping all around. "So they *ate* him!" he shouted. He looked and looked, but there wasn't a shred of turquoise, not even a dollop of the strange plumber's helper which had inspired the little eel's poetry. Trumper slapped his hand hard on the water surface; the other fish bolted, fled in terror, collided with each other and glanced off the glass walls. "You bastards!" Trumper screamed. "Which one of you did it?" He stared fiercely at them—the lean yellow one with a blue fin, the evil-red round one. He stabbed into the tank with a pencil.

"Stop it!" Tulpen yelled at him. But he stabbed and

stabbed, trying to lance one of them against the glass. They had killed the poet! The eel had been pleading with them—bubbles for mercy! And they had eaten him, the fuckers.

Tulpen grabbed Trumper around his middle and pulled him over on the bed. He thrashed out at her and snatched the alarm clock off the night table, flinging it at the murderous fish tank. The aquarium was thick-walled; it cracked and began to leak, but it didn't shatter. As the water ran out, the smaller fish were pulled up against the crack by the current.

Tulpen lay still under Trumper, watching the water level fall. "Trumper?" she said softly, but he wouldn't look at her. He held her still until the tank had emptied over the bookcase and the killer-fish lay flopping on the dry aquarium floor.

"Trumper, for God's sake," she said, but she didn't struggle. "Let me move them to another tank, please."

He let her up and watched her gently scoop them into another aquarium. In the turtle tank, a bright blue-headed turtle ate the thin yellow fish immediately, but left the evil-red round one alone.

"Shit," said Tulpen. "I never know who's going to eat whom."

"Please tell me why you want a baby," Trumper asked her very quietly, but when she turned to face him, she was calm, her arms folded over her breasts. She coolly blew a lock of her hair out of her eyes and sat down beside him on the bed; she casually crossed her legs; she watched the survivor-fish.

"I guess I *don't* want a baby," she said.

13 : Remember Merrill Overturf?

Learning to ski, I quickly realized Merrill Overturf's failure as a coach. Merrill is not a deft skier, though he has mastered the stop. At the children's slope in Saarbrücken, I assaulted the backbreaking rope tow. Aside from the children, it was fortunately unpopulated; most adults were at the races in Zell am See to see the women's downhill and giant slalom.

I mastered the bindings with only three cut knuckles. Merrill flayed a path through the children, leading me to the awesome rope tow; the rope slithered uphill a mere foot above the ground, the proper, comfortable height for five-year-olds and other three-foot dwarfs skiing there. But my knickers did not bend well at the knees, and I could barely stoop to reach the tow, then scoot uphill in the painful position of a coolie bearing a trunk. Holding the rope behind me, Merrill shouted encouragements during the endless journey. If it's this hard going up, I thought, what will it be like going down?

I liked the mountains, all right, and I thrilled to the giant cable-cars carrying you way up where the big skiers go; also, I liked the cable-cars going down—empty, with all the window space to yourself, excepting the leering lift operator who always remarked on the absence of your skis.

"We're almost there, Boggle!" Merrill lied. "Bend your knees!" I watched the bouncy children dancing on the rope in front of me while I carried the mountain on my back—the rope bunching my frozen mittens, my chin hitting my knees as my skis skated uncontrollably in and out of the ruts. I knew I had to straighten up or never use my spine again.

"Bend, Boggle!" Merrill hollered, but I straightened up. All that grief off my back for one lovely moment; I lifted the rope chest-high and leaned back. Above me I saw the little children, their skis completely off the ground, hanging from the rope, swinging like little puppets. Some dropped off, littering the path in front of me; it was clear that they wouldn't struggle out of my way in time.

At the top of the hill, a befurred lift attendant shouted unkindly at me. Below us, the gentle thud of mothers stamping their boots. "Let go of the rope, Boggle!" Merrill shouted. I watched the approaching tangle of children in the path, skis and poles clashing; stuck to the ascending rope were several of their tiny bright and frozen mittens. The lift attendant suddenly dashed for the control house, perhaps thinking the mittens were hands.

I was surprised at how cleverly I kept my balance as I skied over my first child. "Let go, Boggle!" said Merrill; I shot a quick look over my shoulder at the child I'd just trampled and watched him groggily rise up and catch Merrill in the solar plexus with his junior crash helmet. Merrill let go of the rope. Then I was surrounded by the tiny creatures, jabbing with their poles and yelping German for God and their mothers. In the midst of them, I felt the rope jerk to a stop in my hands, and I sprawled into a milling nest of them.

"Es tut mir leid."

"Gott! Hilfe! Mutti, Mutti . . ."

Merrill steered me out of the rope-tow ruts and onto the slope which had looked so slight and gentle from below.

"Please, Merrill, I want to *walk*."

"Boggle, you'd make holes for the other skiers . . ."

"I'd like to make one big hole for all the other skiers, Merrill."

But I let Merrill Overturf guide me to center slope and aim me in the general direction of the bottom, where the children appeared to be further dwarfed and the cars way below in the parking lot looked like the children's toys. Overturf demonstrated the snowplow stop, then showed off a wobbly stem-turn. Larkish little children flew by us,

97

poling and zigzagging and falling as lightly and safely as little wads of wool.

My skis felt like long, heavy ladders on my feet: my poles were stilts.

"I'll follow you," said Merrill, "in case you fall."

I began slowly enough; children passed by me with obvious scorn. Then I noted I was picking up speed. "Lean forward," called Merrill, and I went a little faster, my skis clicking together, swaying apart. What if one ski crosses the other? I thought.

Then I passed the first wave of surprised children as if they were standing still. That'll show the little bastards. "Bend your knees, Boggle!" came Merrill's voice from miles behind me. But my knees seemed locked, ramrod stiff. I came up on a bright-capped little blond girl and hipped her neatly out of the way, like sideswiping a squirrel with a train. *"Es tut mir leid,"* I said, but the words were blown down my throat; my eyes watered. *"Snowplow,* Boggle!" Merrill was screaming. Oh, yes, that stopping device. But I didn't dare move my skis. I attempted to *will* them apart; they resisted me; my hat flew off. Ahead of me, a gaggle of children poled and veered and terror-scampered; an avalanche was after them! Not wanting to gore anyone, I dropped my poles and bludgeoned through them. By the tow shelter at the bottom, an attendant came caterwauling out with a shovel; he had been packing down the tow ruts, but I suspected he would not hesitate to swat me. The lift line broke up; spectators and skiers burst for cover. I imagined an air raid, from the point of view of the bomb.

There was a flat shelf at the base of the slope; surely, I thought, this would slow me down. If not, there was an enormous bulldozed mound of snow piled up to prevent skiers from zipping down into the parking lot. I tried to think of the mound as soft.

"Use your edges!" Merrill screamed. Edges? "Bend your fucking knees!" Knees? "Boggle, for God's sake, fall down!" In front of the children? Never.

I remembered the man at the rent-a-ski place, telling me about the safety bindings. If they were so safe, why didn't they *do* anything?

I hit the flattened shelf off balance and felt my weight

98

fling me back on my heels; the tips of my skis were raised like the bow of a boat. The looming snowbank which protected the parking lot from the likes of me came up awfully suddenly. I saw myself drilled into it like a rifle grenade; they would dig for hours, then decide to blast me out.

The surprise has rarely been equaled: to discover that skis can *climb*. I vaulted the bank. I was launched into the parking lot. Below me, during my descent, I saw a family of sturdy Germans getting out of their Mercedes. Father Round in stout lederhosen knickers and a feathered Tyrolean hat; Mother Heft in hiking boots and swinging a walking stick with an ice-ax point; children: Dumpling, Dumpier and Dollop, with a baffling armload of rucksacks, snowshoes and ski poles. The opened trunk of their Mercedes waited for me to come down. A great whale's maw waiting for the flying fish to fall. Into the jaws of Death!

But sturdy Father Round, the German, precisely closed his trunk.

... after which I'm forced to rely on Merrill Overturf's description. I remember only a surprisingly soft landing, the result of my warm, fleshy collision with Mother Heft, wedged between my chest and the taillights of the Mercedes. Her sweet words were hot in my ear: "Aaarp!" and "Hee-urmff!" And the mixed reactions of the children; Child Dumpling's wordless gape, Child Dumpier's sudden avalanche of his belongings on Child Dollop, whose ear-splitting wail was shrilly clear from under the rucksacks, snowshoes and ski poles where he lay cringing.

Father Round, said Merrill, quickly scanned the skies, no doubt looking for the *Luftwaffe*. Merrill came clambering down the snowbank to where I lay dazed. Mother Heft's great wind had returned and she prodded me with the ice-ax tip of her walking stick.

"Boggle! Boggle! Boggle!" Merrill ran shouting. While on the lip of the bank above the parking lot, a crowd of those who'd survived me came to see if *I'd* survived. They are reported to have cheered when Merrill held up one of my broken skis and failed to find the other. My safety bindings had released. From the bank the lift attendant savagely hurled my ski poles into the parking lot, across which Merrill gingerly supported me. Insane applause and jeering from the snowbank, to see that I was somewhat marred.

It was then, Merrill claims, that the American couple drove up in their new Porsche. They were apparently lost; they thought they had come to the races in Zell. The man, a frightened one, rolled down his window and stared with considerable insecurity at the yelling crowd on the bank. With pity he smiled at Merrill helping the injured skier away. But the man's wife, big and fortyish, with a jutting chin, slammed her door and strode around to her husband's side of the car.

"Well, dammit," she said to him, forcing him to roll down his window. "You and your rotten German and your lousy sense of directions. We're late. We've missed the first event."

"Madam," Merrill said to her as he dragged me past them. "Be glad that the first event missed *you*."

But I have to take Merrill's word for this, and Merrill is suspect. By the time we were back at the Gasthaus Tauernhof in Kaprun, Merrill was in worse shape than I was. He was having an insulin reaction; his blood sugar was down to zilch. I had to help him to the bar and explain his exploring eyes to Herr Halling, the bartender.

"He's a diabetic, Herr Halling. Give him an orange juice, or something else with lots of sugar."

"No, no," Halling said. "Diabetics aren't supposed to have any sugar."

"But he's had too much insulin," I told Halling. "He's used up *too much* sugar." And as if to demonstrate my point, Merrill fumbled a cigarette in front of us, lit the filter end, disliked the taste and ground it out on the back of his own hand. I knocked it away from him and Merrill stared with some puzzlement at what might have been a dull pain coming from the burn. *Do you suppose that's my hand?* With his other hand, he picked it up and waved it to Herr Halling and me as if it were a flag.

"*Ja*, orange juice, immediately," Herr Halling said.

I propped Merrill up against me, but he skidded dizzily off his bar stool.

When he recovered, we watched a rerun of the women's races at Zell on television. The Austrian, Heidi Schatzl, won the downhill as expected, but there was an upset in the giant slalom. The first American girl to win an international race beat out Heidi Schatzl and the French star, Marguerite Delacroix. The video tapes were beautiful. Delacroix missed a gate in her second run and was disqualified, and Heidi Schatzl caught an edge and fell. The Austrians in the Gasthaus Tauernhof were glum, but Merrill and I cheered loudly, in the interests of international hostility.

Then they showed the tape of the American girl who'd won. She was nineteen, blond and very strong. She came through the upper gates smoothly, but a little slow. When she hit the mid-mark, her time was a bit long and she knew it; she bore down on those lower gates like a skidding bus, skating off one ski and then the other, dropping her shoulder and cutting so close to the flags that she left every one flapping. At the last gate, she performed a ballet on that ice-hard, overpacked snow: she lost her balance and managed to hold her cut with one ski off the ground, like a wing out beside her at her waist. Then she righted herself, touched that wild ski down as soft as a kiss, threw her great ass back over her heels and sat on the backs of her skis down the straightaway across the finish line, snapping herself out of that deep squat as soon as she crossed the line. She cut a wide, soft, snow-throwing turn just in front of the safety rope and the crowd. It was very clear that she knew she'd won it.

They had an interview with her on television. She had a smooth, handsome face with a mouth as wide as her cheekbones. No make-up, just the white stickum of Chap Stick on her lips; she kept licking them, laughing all out of breath and bold-faced, clowning into the camera. She wore a one-piece stretch-suit as sleek and tight on her as skin; it had a big gold zipper running from her chin to her crotch, and she'd let it open down to her cleavage, where her big, high, round breasts pushed out her soft velour pullover. She shared the winner's circle with second-place finisher Dubois of France—a petite, darting, ratlike lady with snap-out eyes; and third-place finisher Thalhammer of Austria, a dark, glowering, shapeless, hulking wonderwoman whose chromosomes, you can bet, were half male. The American was a head taller than either of them and an inch above the interviewer, who was as impressed with her bosom as he was with her skiing.

His English was awful. "You haf a Cherman name," he said to her. "Vy?"

"My grandfather was Austrian," the girl said, and the locals in the Gasthaus Tauernhof cheered up a little.

"Then you speak Cherman?" the interviewer asked her, hopefully.

"Only with my father," the girl said.

"Not just a little wit me?" the interviewer teased.

"Nein," said the girl, whose face now betrayed a certain tough irritability; she must have been thinking, Why don't you ask me about my *skiing,* twerp? A bouncy American teammate popped up over her shoulder and held out an unwrapped stick of gum. The big girl stuck it in her mouth and started to soften it up.

"Vy do all Americans jew cum?" the interviewer asked her.

"All Americans *don't* 'jew cum,' " the girl said. Merrill and I cheered. The interviewer knew he wasn't getting anywhere with her, so he tried to get snotty.

"Itz too bat," he said, "dis is the last race uf dis season, dough it mus be an honor to be the *erst* American to vin vun."

"We'll 'vin' lots more," the girl told him, chewing with little savage snaps.

"Nex year, maybe," the interviewer said. "Vill you ski nex year?"

"I'll see," the girl said. Then the video tape was cut and jumped out of sequence, causing Merrill and me to boo loudly. When the picture was clear again, the interviewer was trying to keep up with the girl, who was striding away from him, carrying her skis lightly on her shoulder. The camera was hand-held and unsteady, the sound track crunched with snow.

"Did it take anyting avay from you fictory," he was asking her, "to vin because Heidi Schatzl fell town?"

The girl turned to him, almost clipping his head with her skis. She didn't say a word, and he added a little nervously: ". . . or to vin because Marguerite Delacroix mist a gate?"

"I'd have won anyway," the girl said. "I was just better

102

than they were today," and she started off again. He had to duck under the backswing of her long skis and jog to catch up to her, his legs getting tangled in the microphone cord.

"*Zu 'Biggie' Kunft,*" the interviewer mumbled after her, stumbling along. "*Die Amerikanerin aus Fermont, U.S.A.,*" he said. He caught up with her, and this time remembered to crouch low under her skis when she turned to him. "Wit the conditions today," he said, "wit the snow zo iczy and fast, do you tink your veight helpt you?" He waited smugly for her reply.

"What about my weight?" she asked him; she was embarrassed.

"Does it help you?"

"It doesn't *hurt* me," she said defensively, and Merrill and I felt angry. "You got great weight!" Merrill shouted. "Every pound of it!" I said.

"Vy do they call you 'Biggie'?" the interviewer asked her. She was upset, you could tell, but she moved right up close to him, heaving out her breasts and cracking her broad mouth into a smile. She looked down on him; she seemed to be trying to push him backward with her tits.

" 'Vy' do you 'tink' so?" she asked.

The bastard interviewer looked away from her and beckoned the camera closer, beaming into the lens and rolling out his sly German, "*Mit mir hier ist die junge Amerikanerin, Zu 'Biggie' Kunft . . .*" he was announcing as she turned away from him suddenly and caught him beautifully in the back of his head with her swinging skis. He dropped out of frame and the camera attempted to trot after her, putting her in and out of focus and finally losing her in the crowd. But her voice, offstage, came back to us, angry and hurt: "Please leave me the fuck alone," she said, "*Please . . .*" The announcer didn't bother to translate this.

Then did Overturf and I loudly praise the virtues of this skier, Sue 'Biggie' Kunft, fending off the strongly nationalist arguments of several Austrians drinking with us in the Tauernhof.

"A rare girl, Merrill."

"An athletic lay, Boggle."

"No, Merrill. She's clearly a virgin."

"Or a man, Boggle."

"Oh, never, Merrill. Her glands are quite unmistakable."

"I'll drink to that," said Merrill, who was under great pressure from the limitations of his diabetic diet; not a well-disciplined person, he frequently substituted booze for food. "Did I eat my dinner tonight, Boggle?"

"No," I told him. "You missed dinner because you were in a trance."

"Good," he said, and ordered another slivowitz.

With TV-skiing over, the local Tauernhof clientele returned to their usual peasant savagery. The regular Hungarian group from Eisenstadt performed: an accordion, a tortured zither and a violin to make the mighty cringe.

With the great privacy afforded us by speaking English in a German-speaking tavern, Merrill and I discussed international sports; Hieronymus Bosch; the function of the American embassy in Vienna; the neutrality of Austria; Tito's remarkable success; the shocking rise of the bourgeoisie; the boredom of televised golf; the source of Herr Halling's halitosis; why the waitress wore a bra, were her armpits shaved or shaggy, and who would ask her; the advisability of chasing slivowitz with beer; the price of Semperit radial tires in Boston, of bourbon in Europe in general, of hashish in Vienna in particular; possible causes of the scar on the face of the man who sat by the door; what a worthless instrument a zither was; whether the Czechs were more creative than the Hungarians; what a stupid, backward language Old Low Norse was; the inadequacies of the two-party system in the United States; the challenge of inventing a new religion; the small differences between clerical fascism and Nazism; the incurability of cancer; the inevitableness of war; the general and overall stupidity of man; the pain in the ass of diabetes. And the best way to introduce yourself to girls. One way, Merrill claimed, was the "boob loop." "You hold the ski pole thus," said Merrill, holding it upside down, his fingers meshed in the basket weave, the point against the heel of his hand. He raised the end with the wrist-thong and waved it like a wand; the wrist-thong made a loop. "That's where the boob goes," Merrill said. He was watching the waitress clear the table next to ours.

"No, Merrill."

"A mere demonstration?"

"I think not here, Merrill."

"Perhaps you're right," he said, letting his weapon hang innocently. "The secret to the boob loop lies, in part, in the boob. The lack of a bra is a must. Also, a proper angle. I usually go over the shoulder; that way, they never see it coming. Under the arm, from the side, is good too, but that takes rare positioning."

"Merrill, have you ever done this before?"

"No. I just brought it up, Boggle, because I thought it would make a great introduction. Reel them in, then introduce yourself."

"They might think you forward."

"Aggressiveness is essential these days."

The waitress eyed Merrill's dangling loop with suspicion, but she offered a small target, at best. Also, Herr Halling, at the bar, could fairly have been termed "moralistic." Merrill forgot about his boob loop, swooned in his slivowitz, revived with beer and considered the possible need of checking his blood sugar by doing his usual urine test. But his test tubes and little vials of sugar-sensitive solutions were three floors up in the Tauernhof, and the men's room would be crowded this time of night; he would be forced to pee in the sink, a habit he knew I despised. Therefore, he went *off*, in his own peculiar fashion, sitting right where he was. He was simply away somewhere. As long as he wasn't hurting himself, I always left his trances alone. He was smiling. Once he said, "What?" "Nothing," I told him, and he nodded. Agreed: there had been nothing.

Then you walked in, Biggie. I recognized Sue 'Biggie' Kunft right away. I elbowed Merrill; he didn't feel a thing. I pinched a tight roll of flesh on his belly and gave him a hard, painful twist under the table.

"Nurse ..." Merrill said, "it's starting again." Then he looked over my shoulder at the sharp little faces and tiny antlers of the chamois trophies along the wall. "Hi! Sit down," he told them. "Shit, it's good to see you."

Sue "Biggie" Kunft had not yet decided to stay. She kept her parka on, though she unzipped it. She wasn't alone; two other girls were with her, obviously teammates. They all wore those parkas with the Olympic insignia and little U.S.A. stickers on the sleeve. Stunning Biggie Kunft, with two unattractive teammates, had shunned the hip and sporty crowds in Zell am See; had they come for local color—for local men, with whom they might remain anonymous?

One of the girls with Biggie Kunft announced that the Gasthaus Tauernhof was "quaint."

Her friend said, "There's no one under forty here."

"Well, there's *that* one," said Sue "Biggie" Kunft, meaning me. She couldn't see Merrill, who'd laid himself down on the far end of the long bench at our table.

"Nurse?" he asked me. I stuffed a ski hat under his head, trying to make him more comfortable. "I don't mind the sleeping pill, nurse," he said in a groggy voice, "but I refuse to have another enema."

The girls were making up their minds while Herr Halling and a few others took turns recognizing this great-boobed blonde. Should they take a table alone or sit at the far end of mine?

"He looks a little drunk," one girl told Biggie.

"What a funny body he has!" said the other.

"I think it's an interesting body," Biggie said, and she slipped her parka off her shoulders and tossed her thick, shoulder-bobbed hair; she bore down on my table with a self-sure swagger, a way of walking which was almost male. A big strong girl, she knew that the grace she had was an athletic sort; she didn't try to fake a kind of femininity she knew she didn't have. Knee-high, big fur boots and dark-brown jersey stretch pants, very snug; she wore a deep-orange velour V-neck, and the white of her throat and cleavage was a shock under her tanned face. Those two outstanding orange breasts were floating down on me, like some drunken double vision of a sunset. I lifted Merrill's head by his ear and bounced him lightly on the ski hat, then harder, on the bench.

"Aggressiveness is essential, nurse," he said. His eyes were open; he was winking at all the chamois on the wall.

"Ist dieser Tisch noch frei?" asked Sue "Biggie" Kunft, who on television had said she spoke German only with her father.

"Bitte, Sie sollen hier setzen," I mumbled for them to sit down. That good big one right across from me; the

other two hanging back, awkward jocks trying to look lithe and bouncy and girlish. They sat on her side of the table too, across from where Merrill Overturf lay unnoticed; no need, I felt, to make them uncomfortable by calling him to their attention. No need, either, to stand up politely and let Sue Kunft see that she had an inch on me; sitting down, we were equally tall. I've a fine torso; only my legs fall short.

"Was möchten Sie zum trinken?" I asked her, and ordered cider for the two nowhere girls and a beer for Biggie. Watching Herr Halling navigate the dark Keller, announcing over the girls' shoulders, *"Zwei Apfelsaft, ein Bier ..."* His mind took a long drink down the cleavage of the winner of the women's giant slalom.

I continued a distant German prattle with the champion across from me, while the tragic girls at the cold end of the table did fussy things with their hands and mewed together. "Biggie" spoke a sort of homemade German, learned and heard from only one parent, who had given her a perfect accent and no regard for grammar. She could tell I wasn't from around Kaprun or Zell because I didn't use the dialect, but she never guessed I was American, and I saw no reason to speak English; it would have allowed the girls at the end of the table to join in.

However, I wanted Merrill to join in. I reached out to slap his face, but his head was gone.

"You're not from around here?" Biggie asked me.

"Nein."

Merrill's head was not on the bench any more. I groped around for the rest of him under the table with my foot, behind the bench with my hand, smiling and nodding all the while.

"You like skiing here?" she asked.

"Nein, I didn't come to ski. I don't ski at all ..."

"Why are you in the mountains if you don't ski?"

"I used to be a pole-vaulter," I told her, watching her repeat the German softly to herself, then nodding; she understands. Now I watch her thinking of the relationship between being in the mountains and having been a pole-vaulter. Did he imply he came to the mountains because he used to pole-vault? She thinks this was implied. How will she handle this, I'm wondering. Also: Where the hell is Merrill?

"A pole-vaulter?" she said, in her cautious German. *"Sie springen mit einem Pol?"*

"I used to, yes," I told her. "But not now, of course."

Of course? you could see her thinking. But all she said was, "Wait. You used to be a pole-vaulter, but not any more, right?"

"Of course," I said, to which she shook her head and went right on.

". . . and you're here in the mountains *because* you used to be a pole-vaulter?"

She was admirable; I did love her perseverance. In such casual circumstances, most people would have given up trying to understand.

"Why?" she said insistently. "I mean, what does having been a pole-vaulter have to do with coming here to the mountains?"

"I don't know," I said innocently, as if *she* had proposed such a notion all by herself. She looked utterly confused. "What possible relationship could there be between mountains and pole-vaulting?" I asked her then. She was lost; she must have thought it was a problem with her German.

"You like heights?" she tried.

"Oh yes, the higher the better." And I smiled.

She must have sensed the nonsense in this talk, because she smiled too and said, "You bring your poles with you?"

"My pole-vaulting poles?"

"Of course."

"Of course I bring them with me."

"To the mountains . . ."

"Of course."

"You just sort of lug them around, huh?" She was having fun now.

"Just one at a time."

"Oh, of course."

"It beats waiting in lift lines," I said.

"You just vault right up?"

"It's harder coming down."

"What do you *do?*" she asked. "I mean, *really.*"

"I'm still making up my mind," I said. "Really." I was being serious.

"So am I," she said. She was serious too, so I dropped the German and went straight into English.

"But there's no one thing I can do," I told her, "as well as you can ski."

Her two friends looked up surprised. "He's American," said one.

"He's a pole-vaulter," Biggie told them, smiling.

"I used to be," I said.

"He's been putting us on," one of the uglies said, with a hurtful look at Biggie.

"He's got a nice sense of humor, though," Biggie told the girl, and then—to me, in German so they wouldn't know—"I miss a sense of humor, skiing. There isn't anything humorous about it."

"You haven't seen *me* ski," I told her.

"Why are you here?" she said.

"I'm taking care of a friend," I said, and gave a guilty look around for Merrill. "He's drunk and he's got diabetes, and right now he's lost. I really ought to try and find him."

"Why haven't you, then?"

I kept on, privately, in German, "Because you came in, and I didn't want to be away for that event."

She smiled, but looked away; her friends seemed angry with her for speaking in German, but she continued. "It's a funny place to pick up girls in," she said. "You couldn't have been trying very hard or you wouldn't be in a place like this."

"That's true," I said. "There's no chance of picking up girls in here."

"No, there *isn't*," she said, with a look to say she meant it. But she smiled. "Go find your friend," she said. "I won't go away yet."

And I was just about to do that, wondering where to look first. Under the darker Keller tables, where poor Merrill might be lurking insane or lying in a diabetic coma? Upstairs in the Tauernhof, conducting a drunken urine test, botching his test tubes over the sink?

Then I noticed how quiet the table behind the girls was—how some men sat intent on some intrigue. The sil-

109

houette of a large dog crept up behind the girls, approaching our table. Herr Halling, poised at the bar with his finger to his lips, about to spitshine a shot glass, was pretending not to notice anything. Then, into the dull light, at a level with our table, a dark shadow of a ski pole extended slowly, the wrist-thong end dipping like a wand toward the space between the elbow (on the table) and the breast of the winner of the women's giant slalom.

"This friend," I said shakily to Biggie Kunft, "is not himself."

"*Find* him, then," she said, truly worried.

"I hope you have a nice sense of humor too," I told her.

"Oh, I do," she said, smiling very warmly. And she leaned a little closer to me across the table, and touched the back of my hand a little awkwardly. Conscious of what big hands she had, she usually kept them folded. "Please go make sure that your friend's all right," she said. Then, into the exaggerated gap between her breast and her elbow, the wrist-thong of a ski pole came dancing; leaning forward, as she was, her breast pushed tight against the velour, she was a target only a fool could miss.

"I hope you'll forgive me," I said, and touched her hand.

"Of course I will," she laughed, as the snare seized her and the wrist-thong tugged her breast up into her armpit, oddly askew, and Merrill Overturf, behind her, weaved up to his knees, his ski pole bending like a fishing rod with a heavy catch, his eyes all glazed and terrible.

"Boob loop!" he screamed.

Then the girl athlete from Vermont demonstrated her catlike coordination and wonder-mother strength. Biggie slipped her breast free of the wrist-thong and seized the end of the pole, swinging her legs out from under the table and across the bench top, where her heavy thighs jarred Merrill Overturf off balance and dropped him on his rump. She was up on her feet, then, and obviously experienced at handling a ski pole, which she thrust repeatedly at Merrill who writhed on the floor, trying to free his twisted fingers from the pole's basket, trying to fend off the gouging pole point with the bleeding heel of his hand.

"Oh *blood*, Boggle! I've been stabbed!"—while Biggie fi-

110

nally pinned him, one of her tall fur boots resting heavily on Merrill's chest, the point of the pole puckering Merrill's belly.

"It's a game, it's a game!" Merrill shrieked at her. "Did I *hurt* you? Did I? Not on your life, I didn't. No, I did *not* hurt you . . . no, no, *no!*" But Sue "Biggie" Kunft poised over him, with just enough weight on the pole to keep Merrill pinned and threatened with disemboweling, while she flashed me an angry, betrayed look. *"Talk* to her, Boggle," Merrill pleaded. "We saw you on TV," he told her. "We *loved* you."

"We hated the interviewer," I told her.

"You were simply beautiful," Merrill said. "They tried to make your winning sound just lucky, but you were clearly above that bullshit." She stared at him, amazed.

"It's his blood sugar," I told her. "He's all mixed up."

"He wrote a poem about you," Merrill lied, and Biggie looked at me, touched. "It's a nice poem," Merrill said. "He's a real poet."

". . . who used to be a pole-vaulter," Biggie said suspiciously.

"He used to be a wrestler too," Merrill said suddenly, crazily, "and if you hurt me with that ski pole, he'll break your goddamn neck!"

"He doesn't know what he's saying," I told Biggie, who was watching Merrill holding up his bloody hand.

"I may die," said Merrill. "There's no telling what that pole's been stuck in."

"Pole him a good one and let's get out of here," one of Biggie's skimates told her.

"And keep the pole," the other one said, glowering at me.

"There are vital organs just under the belly lining," Merrill said. "Oh, God . . ."

"I'm not aiming for your belly," Biggie told him.

"When you were being mocked, we loved you," Merrill told her. "In that ugly, self-serious, competitive world, you had dignity and humor."

"What happened to your humor?" I asked her. She looked at me, stung. She was tender about that; it seemed to matter a lot.

111

" 'Vy' do they call you 'Biggie'?" Merrill asked her boldly. " 'Vy' do you 'tink' so?" he asked me.

"It must be her *heart*," I told him. Then I reached out and took the pole from her. She was smiling, and she blushed a hue resembling that deep-orange of her V-neck velour. *I suspect you are velour all over!*

Then Merrill Overturf stood up too fast. What remained of his consciousness had been used to a prone position. When he bounded to his feet like that, I think he left his brain lying down. We saw only the whites of his eyes, though he smiled at everyone. His hands dialed telephones in the air.

"Gob, Doggle," he said.

I noticed he was standing on his ankles just before he fell, like wet snow.

14 : Fighting the Good Fight

In my married phase, at 918 Iowa Avenue, optimism was reserved for Risky Mouse. For five nights running, he made his own daring thefts of the baited trap. I warned him again about it. I brought him a fatty portion of Biggie's steamed brisket, which I displayed in an alluring fashion, not in the trap itself, but several feet away. Making it clear that I'd take care of him. He needn't risk his furry, finger-sized neck in Biggie's overlarge trap designed for weasels, woodchucks, wombats and mammoth rats.

I never knew exactly what it was that Biggie had against the rodent. She only saw him once—surprised him on the cellar landing when she went to fetch her skis one night. Perhaps she thought he was getting too bold, that he had intentions of invading the upstairs. Or that he meant to gnaw her skis, which she moved to the bedroom closet. Occasionally, they fell on me in my morning-grope period. Their evil-sharp edges could gash you up good. It was one of the sources of friction between Biggie and me.

So one night Risky Mouse was given brisket, about which I had my doubts. Do mice eat meat?

Then I took a bath with Colm. He was so slippery in the tub that I had to keep my thumbs in his armpits or else he'd giggle under. Baths with Colm relaxed me, except that Biggie always came in and watched.

And with genuine concern, she'd always ask, "Will Colm have as much hair as you do?" Implying, How soon will the horrible growth start ruining him for life?

With some irritation I'd always say, "Would you prefer me hairless, Big?"

113

She'd back down, saying, "It's not that, exactly. It's more that I wouldn't want Colm to be as hairy as you."

"Relatively, Big, I'm not so hairy as most men."

"Well, *men*," she'd say, as if the only thing about me that bothered her was that I was one.

I knew what was on her mind, though: skiers. Blond and somewhat male (or if not blond, at least tanned); no tobacco stains on their teeth; hairless, linen-white muscles under their down underwear; smooth all over, from too much time in sleeping bags. The only repulsive part of skiers is their feet. I think skiers only sweat through their hot, cramped, layered feet. All those thick crusty socks! That's their only health gap.

I was the first and only nonskier Biggie ever laid. It must have been the novelty that impressed her. But now she wonders. Remembering all that snowbound cleanliness.

Is it my fault that I never had the silky chafe of down underwear to rub off all my hair? My pores are too big for skiing; the wind gets inside me. Is it my fault if I'm given to excess oil? Can I help it if baths don't quite work for me? I can step glowing from a tub, powder my groin, anoint my pits, slaver my fresh-shaved face with some scented astringent, and ten minutes later I start to sweat. I sort of gloss over. Sometimes, when I'm talking to a person, I see them start to stare; they're uneasy about something. I've figured out what it is. They suddenly see my pores opening, or maybe their attention is fixed on just *one* pore, opening in slow motion and sort of peeking at them. I've experienced the sensation myself, in mirrors, and I can sympathize with the observer; it's unnerving.

But you'd expect your wife not to ogle when your metabolism shows, especially in troubled times. Instead, she dispenses suggestions to improve my funny hair. "Get rid of your mustache, Bogus. It's really pubic."

But I know better. I need all the hair I can grow. Without hair, what would cover my terrible pores? Biggie never understood that; she doesn't *have* any pores. Her skin is as sleek as Colm's bum. What she hoped for, I knew, was that Colm would have her pores—or, rather, her lack of pores. Naturally, this hurt me. But I thought of the child. Frankly, I wouldn't wish my pores on anyone.

Even so, those bathtub confrontations grieved me.

I took a walk to Benny's, thinking that Ralph Packer, the polemicist, might be holding court there or otherwise formulating maxims. But Benny's was unusually empty, and I made use of the silence by making a mindless phone call to Flora Mackey Hall for Women.

"Which floor?" someone wanted to know, and I pondered which floor Lydia Kindle would live on. High up, close to the eaves, where the birds nest?

Different extensions were tried. A girl with a suspicious voice said, "Yes?"

"Lydia Kindle, please," I said.

"Who's calling, please?" the voice wanted to know. "This is her floor sister."

A floor sister? Hanging up, I imagined wall brothers, door fathers, window mothers, and I wrote on the plaster above Benny's urinal, FLORA MACKEY WAS A VIRGIN TO THE END.

In the crapper stall, someone seemed to be in trouble. Under the door peeked thonged sandals, purple socks, a pair of fallen bell-bottoms and obvious grief.

Whoever he was, he was crying.

Well, I know how it can hurt to pee, so I could sympathize. At the same time, I didn't wish to look further into this. Perhaps I could buy a beer from the bar, slip it to him under the door, tell him it's on me and quickly leave.

The urinal flushed—Benny's famous self-flushing urinal. To save the strain on the water pump, it is rumored to be electrically timed to flush semiannually. To think that I was on hand for the rare event!

But in the crapper stall, he heard it too; he felt someone was there; he stopped crying. I tried to tiptoe to the door.

His voice came weakly from the stall, "Please tell mo, is it dark out yet?"

"Yes."

"Oh, God," he said. "Can I leave now? Have they gone?"

A sudden fear was upon me! I looked around for *them. Who?* Peering under the urinal for strange, wet men lurking there. "Who's they?" I asked.

The stall door opened and he came out, hitching his bell-bottoms up. It was the thin, dark boy who is a poet and tends to wear lavender clothes; a student who works in Root's Bookstore, he is alternately assumed to be a great lover or a fag, or both.

"God, have they gone?" he said. "Oh, *thank* you. They told me not to leave until it was dark, but there aren't any windows in here."

A closer look at him revealed the savage beating he had taken. They had jumped him in the men's room and told him he belonged in the lady's room instead. They proceeded to roll him in the urinal; they scoured his nose with the deodorant cake, which graveled up his face and left him smarting, as if he'd been rubbed with a pee-soaked pumice stone. A terrible confusion of odors clung to him; in his pocket, a bottle of Leopardess toilet water had smashed. If perfume were poured in a privy, it could not smell worse.

"Jesus," he said. "They happen to have been right. I *am* a fag—but I might *not* have been. I mean, they had no way of knowing I was. I was just taking a leak. That's normal enough, isn't it? I mean, I don't hustle guys in men's rooms. I get all I want."

"What about the toilet water?"

"They didn't even know I had it," he said. "And it's not for *me,* for Christ's sake. It's for a girl—my sister. I live with her. She called me at work and asked me to pick up some for her on my way home."

He had trouble walking—they'd really stomped him around—so I said I'd help him out of there.

"I live right around here," he said. "You don't have to come with me. They might think *you're* one."

But I walked him out of Benny's on my arm, past two leering couples in a booth by the door. See the boyfriends! One of whom drank a bottle of perfume and then pissed his pants.

Benny himself posed with his shining beer steins at the bar in studied, cultivated ignorance of everything.

"Your urinal flushed itself, Benny," I said. "Mark the calendar."

"Goodnight, boys," said Benny, and a wispy artist at the

116

corner table sank his nose into the head of his beer to drown our passing odor.

"I knew Iowa would be awful," the fag told me, "but I never knew it would be *this* awful."

We were outside his walk-up on downtown Clinton Street. "You've been very nice," he said. "I'd ask you in, but . . . I'm very attached, you understand. I've never been so faithful before, really, but *this* one . . . well, you know. He's just very special."

"I'm not like you," I told him. "I mean, I might have been, but you happen to be wrong."

He took my hand. "It's all right," he said. "I know. Some other time, we'll see. What's your name?"

"Forget it," I said; I was walking off, trying to leave his reek behind. There on that shabby street in his bright clothes, he looked like some gay knight just entering a town wiped out by the plague: brave, silly and doomed.

"Don't be too proud!" he shouted after me. "Don't ever plead, but don't be too proud."

Rare advice from the strangest of seers! Down dark Iowa Avenue, a horde of fag maulers lurked in every shadow. Would they leave me alone if I showed them I was straight? If I meet a girl, should I rape her? Watch me! I'm normal!

Or I could have left the curtains open when I came home to Biggie, my great tawny lioness, propped in our well-grooved bed, lying on and under a wealth of magazines and little pillows with stitched-on Alpine scenes.

"My God, smell you!" said Biggie, staring at me. And the horror of an explanation struck me then as strong as the lush steam of perfumed urine wafting off me from my contact with the Root's Bookstore employee. I was a diluted version of his fragrance.

"What's that all over you?" said Biggie. *"Who's* that? You prick . . ."

"I just went to Benny's," I said. "There was a fairy in the men's room. The one who works at Root's, you know?" But Biggie came bounding off the bed, sniffing me all over, catching up my hands to her nose. "Really, Big," I said, and tried to nip her cheek, but she stiff-armed me away from her.

117

"Oh, you prick, you bastard, Bogus . . ."

"I haven't been illicit, Big, I swear . . ."

"God!" she cried. "You even bring her smell back to my own house!"

"Biggie, it was this damn fag in the men's room. He got rolled in the urinal, broke some toilet water he had in his pocket . . ." *Shit*, I thought. That doesn't even sound possible, not to mention, true. I said with hopeless calm, "It was very strong-smelling, it rubbed off . . ."

"I'll *bet* she's strong-smelling!" Biggie screamed. "Like some bitch in heat, she's got her damn scent all over you!"

"I didn't do anything, Big—"

"Something exotic, I'll bet," said Biggie. "One of those Hindus in robes, with their twitchy things. And smelling like a whole harem! Oh, I know you, Bogus! You always went for that, didn't you? Always ogling the blacks and those kinky Orientals and swarthy Jewesses! Goddamn you, I've seen you!"

"For Christ's sake, Big—"

"It's true, Bogus!" she yelled. "You really go for that, I know. Hairy ones and whorish ones . . . fucking gaudy dirt!"

"Jesus, Big!"

"You always wanted me different," she said; she bit her fist. "Look what you buy me for clothes. You buy me terrible things. I tell you, I'm not like that! My thighs are too big. 'Don't wear a bra,' you tell me. 'You got great boobs, Big,' you say. And if I don't wear a bra, I flop like a cow! 'Looks great, Big,' you say. Jesus, I know what I look like. My *nipples* are bigger than some girls' tits!"

"That's true, Big. They are. And I love your nipples, Biggie—"

"You don't!" she cried. "And you're always saying how you don't like blondes. 'I don't like blondes, as a rule,' you say, and then you pat me some place rude. 'As a rule,' you say, with your little nudges, giving me a feel—"

"I'll give you a little feel right now," I said, "if you don't shut up."

But she stepped back and put the bed between us. "Don't you touch me, goddamn you," she said.

"I haven't done anything, Big."

"You reek!" she screamed. "You must have done it in a *barn!* Wallowed with some sow in . . . in mulch!"

I tore off my shirt and bellowed at her. *"Smell* me, damn you, Biggie! It's just my hands that stink——"

"Just your hands, Bogus?" she said with icy calm. "In the barn," she said slowly, "did you finger-fuck a goat on the side?" I could see this was beyond reason, so I jerked off my boots, yanked down my pants and hopped at her, trying to get my underwear unsnaggled from my ankles.

"You animal!" she yelled. "You keep your thing away from me, Bogus! Oooogh! There's no telling what you've caught! I won't have any, thank you just the same." She dodged to the foot of the bed as I lunged at her, catching the bottom hem of her absurd, ballooning nightie—that wretched cotton-flannel one—ripping the thing up to the seam running around her neck and spinning her back on the bed. I had her almost strait-jacketed in the thing when she landed a high, skier-strong kick to my chest, leaving me holding the tatters of her nightie as she sprinted for the hall. I caught her from behind in the doorway, but she reached over my shoulder with one hand sunk in my hair; between her legs with her other hand, she gouged toward my vitals. I worked a neat back-heel trip—a better one, surely, than in my entire wrestling career. I was sure she'd be stunned, but she slashed an elbow back into my throat and bucked up to her hands and knees under me. With Biggie, you've got to control her legs. I tried a late body-scissors as she came up to her feet, but she bore me on her back across the room, tottering toward the dresser, in front of which she expertly tucked and rolled, driving my head and shoulders into the lingerie drawer.

I saw stars then, and tasted my tongue, which, despite half biting off in every wrestling match I ever had, I've never learned to keep inside my mouth. I clung to her hip as she strode away from the dresser, deftly blocking her fierce uppercut with my forehead, and while she raged over the pain in her hand, I pivoted behind her knee and dropped her with a side-leg dive—this time scissoring her near leg and barring her far arm in my tightest cross-body ride (a desperate, hang-on maneuver I often used in my career). She thrashed well, groping with her free hand for

119

something to hurt. I seized this moment to press my advantage and barred both her arms, spinning out at a right angle to her body and jacking her up on the back of her neck. Her fearsome legs crashed all around me, though she was stacked up good; in fact, I had her pinned, but there was no referee to slap the mat and call us quits. The double arm-bar hurt her, I knew, so I slithered my pale stomach up alongside her head, laying my navel against her hot cheek, watchful for her bite. I was careful not to lose my hold; it was at peak moments like these that I had developed the habit of getting myself inexplicably pinned. I inched my vulnerable part up close to her wild eye, ever mindful of her good teeth, just out of reach.

"I'll bite that damn thing off, I swear it," Biggie grunted, and she heaved against my double arm-bar which held her like a vise.

"Be kind enough to smell it first, Big," I said, brushing my belly on her smooth cheek; her heavy knees sailed around my ducked head and thumped my back. "Just smell me, please," I told her, "and give me your honest impression of the scent. Whether my important part has any *foreign* odor, any reek of harems, Big. Or whether what you smell is strictly me." Her knees pumped slower; I saw her nose wrinkle. "In your estimation, Biggie," I said, "in your wealth of experience in this matter of my odor would you say that you detect the faintest presence of anything unusual? Would you venture a guess as to whether this belly has slid against some other belly and taken on a different reek?" I could feel her cringe—a disarming shiver against the double arm-bar—and I let her turn her face a little and slide her nose where she would; my frightened part rested on her cheek now. *He put his life on the line to save his marriage.*

"What do you smell, Big?" I asked her softly. "Is there a stench of old stale sex?" She shook her head. My nervous part lay under her nose, across her upper lip.

"But your hands . . ." Her voice had a thin crack in it.

"I touched a poor beat-up fag all covered with pee and perfume, Big. I walked him home. We shook hands."

I had to sit her up against me before I could unlock the double arm-bar and plant a bloody kiss on her neck, my

120

tongue still bleeding sweetly down my throat. Above my left ear, my scalp stretched tightly over the swelling knot where the dresser had clouted me. I imagined the damage to the lingerie drawer. Were the panties shaken up by the blow—unfolded and flung into the deepest corner of the drawer, where they lay worried? Wondering, Whatever it is out there, I hope it doesn't want to wear *me*.

Later, in a gentler battle on our bed, Biggie said, "Move your arm, quick. No, there . . . no, not there. Yes, there . . ." And making us both comfortable, she began to glide under me in a way she has that always makes me feel she's going to get away. But she never does, and she doesn't mean to. It's almost as if she's rowing us somewhere, and I'm just pacing myself to the easy strength of her stroke. The secret is in her tireless, driving legs.

"This must be good for skiers," I told her.

"You know, I have some muscles," said Biggie, rocking easily, like a broad boat moored on a choppy sea.

"I love your muscles, Big," I said.

"Oh come on, not *that* muscle. I mean, that's not even a muscle, really," she said. "I mean, I've got a lot of muscles for a girl."

"You're all muscle, Big."

"Well, not *all* muscle . . . No, come on, *that's* not a muscle, you know damn well."

"It's better than muscle, Big."

"I'm sure you think so, Bogus."

"And this is better for you than skiing, Big. And more fun too . . ."

"Well, I'd hate to have to choose," she said, and I gouged her for that.

Heavy as she is, Biggie can roll with momentum, like a boat caught and borne along by a breaker. I floated her—a slow ride. Apparently we weighed nothing at all. Then the sea shifted and pitched us suddenly ashore, where our weightlessness went out of us and I lay as beached and leaden as a log under sand, and Biggie lay under me as calm as a pond.

Later she said, "Oh, bye-bye for a while. Bye-bye." But she didn't move.

"Bye," I said. "Where are you going?"

But all she said was, "Oh, Bogus, you're not such a bad person, really."

"Why, no, I'm not, Big," I said, intending to sound flippant. But it came out all hoarse and thick, as if I hadn't spoken for a long time. *Oh, the slow, furry voice of the successfully laid. I remember how I met you, Biggie* . . .

15: Remember Being
in Love with Biggie?

Through the quaint gloom of the Tauernhof Keller, I carried the swooned Overturf toward the stairs. I wasn't worried about Merrill. The mismanagement of his diabetes had him frequently fading out, and in again—his system alternately empty and too full of sugar.

"Too much alcohol," Herr Halling said sympathetically.

"Too much insulin, or too little," I said.

"He must be crazy," Biggie said, though she was concerned. She followed us upstairs, ignoring the harping from her ugly teammates.

"We should go now," one said.

"It's not our car," the other told me. "It's the team's car."

Crossing the landing with Biggie alongside me, I was conscious of her seeing how short I was. She looked a little down on me. To compensate, I pretended Merrill was no strain to carry; I tossed him around like groceries and took the next stair flight two at a time, letting Biggie see: he is not tall, but he is strong.

Marching Merrill into his room, I cracked his head on the doorjamb, which I had veered into thanks to blind spots induced by breathlessness. Biggie winced, but all Merrill said was, "Not now, please." He opened his eyes when I dumped him on his bed and he stared at the overhead light as if it were the ultra-high beam over an operating table where he lay rigid, awaiting surgery.

"I have no feeling, no feeling," he told the anesthetist; then he went limp and sleepy and closed his eyes. "If

123

you're going to take everything out of that suitcase," he grumbled, "You're going to put it all back, too."

While I got out all the sugar-sampling vials and set up the test-tube rack above the sink, Biggie whispered with the harpies in the doorway, about the fact that the racing season was over, that there was no curfew, that the team's car had been lent in good faith, that it must be returned.

"Merrill has a car . . ." I told Biggie in German, "if you would like to stay."

"Why would I like to do that?" she asked.

Recalling Merrill's lie, I said, "I'll show you my poem about you."

"I'm sorry, Boggle," Merrill murmured, "but they were such great boobs—Jesus, such a target—I just had to take a crack at them." But he was sound asleep, out of the fray.

"The car . . ." said one of the uglies. *"Really,* Biggie . . ."

"We've simply got to take it back," the other one told her. Biggie looked around Merrill's room, looked *me* over too, with a cool, questioning gaze. Where does the former pole-vaulter keep his pole?

"No, not now, please," Merrill announced to everyone. "I have to pee, oh, yes."

Juggling the vials and tubes for his urine test, I turned to the girls in the doorway, repeating to Biggie in German: "He has to pee." And I added hopefully to her, "You could wait outside . . ." *You warm solid hunk of velour!*

Then I was shut off from their mumbles in the hall outside Merrill's door, where I could hear only the harsh whisperings of the unwanted teammates and Biggie's quiet, solid indifference.

"You *know* there's a breakfast meeting . . ."

"So who's missing breakfast?"

"They'll ask about you tonight . . ."

"Biggie, what about Bill?"

Bill? I wondered, as I led Merrill unsteadily to the sink, his arms flopping in the wild take-off motions of some weak, ungainly bird.

"What *about* Bill?" Biggie hissed in the hall.

Right! Tell old Bill she's taken up with a pole-vaulter!

But Merrill's precarious stance at the sink needed all

124

my attention. On the glass shelf where the toothpaste goes was the test-tube rack with the gay-colored solutions for testing sugar in urine. Overturf gazed at these in the way I'd seen him ogle the bright bottles behind a bar, and I had to keep his elbows from slipping on the sink while I aimed his floppy prod into his special pee mug, a beer stein he'd stolen in Vienna; he liked it because it had a lid and held almost a quart.

"Okay, Merrill," I told him. "Let it come." But he just gawked at his test-tube rack as if he'd never seen it before. "Wake up, baby," I told him. "Fill 'er up!" But Merrill was squinting through the test-tube rack at his own death-gray face reflected in the mirror. Over his shoulder he saw me looming behind him—pressed evilly close to him, struggling to hold him up. He stared at my reflection with great hostility; he didn't know me at all. "Let go of my prick, you," he told the mirror.

"Merrill, shut up and pee."

"Is that all you ever think about?" Biggie hissed at her friends in the hall.

"Well, what are we going to tell Bill?" a harpy asked her. "I mean, I'm not going to lie—if he asks me, I'm going to tell him."

I opened the door, then, holding Merrill around the waist, pointing his pecker down into the pee mug. "Why don't you tell him even if he doesn't ask you?" I said to the appalled harpies. Then I closed the door again and steered Merrill back toward the sink. Somewhere along the way, he began to pee. Biggie's sharp laugh must have touched some nervous part of him, for he twitched, loosening my thumb's grip on the stein's lid, and found himself clamped in the pee mug. Wrestling away, he peed all over my knee. I caught up with him at the foot of his bed, where he spun about, still peeing in a high arch, his face with a child's look of bewildered pain. I stiff-armed him over the footboard and he landed limp on the bed, peed a final burst straight up in the air, then threw up on his pillow. I set the pee mug down, washed off his face, turned his pillow over and covered him with a heavy puff, but he lay rigid in the bed with his eyes like fuses. I washed the pee off me and used the medicine dropper to take pee from the pee mug and plunk it into the different

125

test tubes: red, green, blue, yellow. Then I realized that I didn't know where the color chart was. I didn't know what color the red was supposed to change to, or what color was dangerous for the blue to change to, and whether the green was supposed to stay clear or get cloudy, and what yellow was for. I'd only watched Merrill test himself, because he'd always come around in time to interpret the colors. I went over to the bed where he now seemed to be sleeping and hit him a good one in the face; he clenched his teeth together, grunted and went right on sleeping, so I tagged him a really solid blow in his stomach. But it just went *thok!* Merrill didn't flinch.

So I started tearing through his rucksack until I found all his syringes, needles, injector-bottles of insulin, bags of candy, his hash pipe and, at the bottom, the color chart. It said it was okay if the red got orange, if the green and blue became the same, and if the yellow got cloudy-crimson; it was not okay for the red to change "too quickly" to cloudy-crimson, or for the green and blue to behave differently, or for the yellow to turn orange and stay clear.

But when I turned back to the test-tube rack, the colors had already changed, and I realized that I had forgotten which ones were which colors to begin with. Then I read the color chart to find out what to do if you estimated your blood sugar to be dangerously high or low. You were supposed to get in touch with a doctor, of course.

There was silence from the hall outside the door, and I grieved that Biggie had gone away while I was in here fumbling with Merrill's pecker. Then I got a little worried about him, so I sat him upright by hauling him up by his hair; then I held his head and delivered a good roundhouse slap to his gray cheek, and then another and another, until his eyes rolled open and he pulled his chin down on his chest. He spoke to the closet, or to some spot over my shoulder: a high-spirited, defiant holler in the face of pain. "Fuck you!" Merrill shouted. "Fuck you to death!"

Then he called me Boggle in a perfectly normal voice and said he was terribly thirsty. So I gave him water, lots of it, and poured all the crimson, blue-green, orange pee-colors down the sink and rinsed the test tubes out so that
126

if he woke up in the night, berserk, he couldn't drink those too.

When I finished cleaning up, he was asleep, and because I was furious with him I wrung the washcloth out in his ear. But he never moved, and I dried his ear for him, turned out the light and listened in the dark to his breathing, just to be sure he was all right.

He was the great illusion of my life. That such a self-destroying fool could be so indestructible. And though I was sad to have lost that big girl, I liked Merrill Overturf a lot. "Goodnight, Merrill," I whispered in the dark.

As I eased myself out in the hall and latched his door behind me, he said, "Thank you, Boggle."

And there in the hall, all alone, was Biggie.

She had her parka zipped up; there was no heat in the upstairs of the Tauernhof. She stood a little stiffly, putting one foot on top of the other, shuffling; she looked a little bit angry and a little bit shy.

"Let me see the poem," she said.

"It's not finished yet," I told her, and she looked at me aggressively.

"Finish it, then," she said. "I'll wait . . ." Meaning she'd been waiting all this time, with a look to tell me I had some good work ahead of me to salvage this.

In my room, next door to Merrill's, she sat on the bed like an uncomfortable bear. Little crannies and confined places took her grace away. She felt too big for that room and that bed, and yet she was cold; she kept the parka zipped up and wrapped herself in the puff while I goofed around by the night table, pretending to be scribbling a poem on a piece of paper with words already on it. But they were German words, left by the last guest in this room, so I crossed them out as if I were revising my own work.

Merrill thumped his head against the wall between our rooms; his muffled hoot came through to us, "Oh, he can't ski, but he's sharp with his pole!"

On the bed, without a change of expression, the large girl awaited her poem. So I tried one.

> She is all muscle and velour
> crammed in a vinyl sheath;

> her feet, set in plastic,
> clamped to her slashing skis;
> under her helmet, her hair
> stays soft and hot . . .

Hot? No, not hot, I thought, aware of her there on the bed, watching me. No more hot hair!

> The woman racer is not quite soft.
> She is as heavy and firm as fruit.
> Her skin is as sleek as an apple's,
> and as tough as a banana's. But
> inside, she's all mush and seeds.

Ugh! Can bad poetry improve? By my bed, she'd found my tape recorder, was shuffling the reels, fondling the earphones. Put them on, I indicated, then dreaded what she might hear. Expressionless, she punched buttons and changed reels. *On with the poem!*

> See! How she holds her poles!

No, good God . . .

> When she cuts the mountain, she's
> packed like a suitcase, neat and hard.
> Contained, her metal leather plastic
> parts perform; her grace is strong.

Her legs are long? God no!

> But just open her, out of the cold.
> Unbuckle, -zip, -strap and unpack her!
> Her contents are loose and strewn
> things, stray things and warm things,
> soft and round things—surprising
> unknown things!

Be careful. She was playing through the reels of my life, divining it, rewinding it, stopping it, playing it back. Hearing the ditties. dirty stories, conversations, polemics and dead languages on my tapes, she was probably deciding to

128

ᴵᵉᵃᵛᵉ. Suddenly she turned the volume down, wincing. At least I knew which tape she was on: Merrill Overturf revving the engine of his '54 Zorn-Witwer. *For God's sake, hurry with the poem before it's too late!* But then she took the earphones off—had she reached the part where Merrill and I reminisce on our shared knowledge of the waitress in the Tiergarten Café?

"Let me see that poem," she said.

All muscle and velour, she shared the puff and read it sitting up straight—jacketed, panted, booted, wrapped and occupying the bed like a large trunk you'd have to deal with before you could go to sleep. She read seriously, her lips shaping the words.

"All mush and seeds?" she read aloud, with a stern look of disgust for the poet. In the cold room her breath smoked.

"It gets better," I said, not at all sure that it did. "At least, it doesn't get any worse."

Her grace is strong. The puff was a difficult size to share; she became aware that it was, at best, a three-quarter bed. Removing her boots, she tucked her feet under her and begrudged more of the puff to me. She tore apart a stick of gum, gave me the bigger half; our mutual, wet smacking disturbed the quiet room. There wasn't enough heat in the room even to frost the windows; we had a third-floor view of the blue snow under the moon, and of the tiny lights strung out on the glacier—way off to the lift-station huts where, I imagined, rough and big-lunged men were getting laid. Their windows were frosted.

Her contents are ". . . loose and strewn things?" she read. "What's this strewn shit? My mind, you mean? Like scatter brained?"

"Oh, no . . ."

"Stray things and warm things . . ." she read.

"It's just part of the suitcase image," I said. "Sort of a forced metaphor."

"Soft and round things . . ." she read. "Well, I suppose . . ."

"It's a pretty bad poem," I admitted.

"It's not that bad," she said. "I don't mind it." She took off her parka, and I hunched a little closer to her, my hip to hers. "I'm just taking off my parka," she said.

129

"I was just getting more of the puff," I said, and she smiled at me.

"It always gets so weighty," she said.

"Puffs?"

"No, sex," she said. "Why does it have to be so serious? You have to start pretending I'm so special to you, and you don't really know if I am."

"I think you are," I said.

"Don't lie," she said. "Don't get serious. It *isn't* serious. I mean, you're not special to me at all. I'm just curious about you. But I don't want to have to pretend that I'm impressed or anything."

"I want to sleep with you," I said.

"Well, I know that," she said. "Of course you do, but I like you better when you're funny."

"I'll be hilarious," I said, standing up with the puff like a cape around me and walking unsteadily on the bed. "I promise," I said, "to perform comic stunts and make you laugh all night!"

"You're trying too hard," she said, grinning. So I sat down at the foot of the bed and covered myself completely in the puff.

"Tell me when you're cold," I said, my voice muffled under the puff, hearing her gum snap and her short laugh. "I'm not looking," I said. "Don't you think this is the perfect opportunity for you to undress?"

"You first," she said, so I began, secretly under the puff, handing items out to her, one by one. She was silent out there, and I imagined her readying herself to bash me with a chair.

I passed out my turtleneck, my fishnet shirt, a wad of knee socks and my lederhosen knickers.

"My God, what heavy pants," she said.

"Keeps me in shape," I said, peeking out at her.

She sat fully clothed by the headboard, looking at my things. When she saw me, she said, "You're not undressed yet."

I went back under the puff and struggled with my long underwear. When I got it off, held it in my lap a while, then delicately handed it out: a rare gift. I felt her moving on the bed then, and waited in my tent as tense as a tree.

"Don't look," she said. "If you look, it's all over."

Unbuckle, -zip, -strap, and unpack her! Or better, let her do it herself. But why is she doing this?

"Who's Bill?" I asked.

"Search me," she said, then peeked into the puff. "Who *are you?*" she said, sitting knee to knee with me, Indian style. She snatched half the puff around herself, shading her tawny body from the light. She still had her socks on.

"My feet get cold," she said, willing my eyes to stay on her eyes and look nowhere else. But I took her socks off for her. Big broad feet and strong peasant ankles. I tucked her feet in the hollows of my knees, pinched them with my calfs and held her ankles with my hands.

"You have a name?" she asked.

"Bogus."

"No, really . . ."

"Really, it's Bogus."

"That what your parents called you?"

"No, they said Fred."

"Oh, *Fred.*" The way she said it, you could see it was a word for her like *tura.*

"That's why it's Bogus," I said.

"A nickname?"

"A truth," I admitted.

"Like Biggie," she said, and smiled self-consciously; she looked down to her golden lap. "Boy, I'm big, all right," she said.

"Yes you are," I said, with an appreciative run of my hand up her long thigh; a muscle tightened there.

"I was always big," she said. "People were always fixing me up with giants. Basketball and football players, great big awkward sorts of boys. Like it was necessary we be matched or something. 'Got to find someone large enough for Biggie.' Like they were finding a *meal* for me. People always fed me too much, too; they just assumed I was hungry all the time. Actually, I have a really small appetite. People just seem to think it means something if you're big—like being rich, you know? They think if you're rich, you only like things that cost a lot of money. And if you're big, you're supposed to have some special attraction to big things."

I let her talk. I touched her breast, thinking of other big things, and she ran on, not meeting my eyes now, but

131

watching my hand with a sort of nervous curiosity. What will it touch next?

"___n in cars," she said. "You're in the back seat with three other people, and they don't ask the smaller ___ if she has enough room; they always ask if you have enough room. I mean, if three or four people get stuffed into a car seat, nobody has enough room, right? But they seem to think you're some sort of expert at not having enough room."

She stopped and caught my hand where it moved across her belly, holding it there. "You should say something, don't you think?" she said. "I mean, I think you should say something to me. I'm not a whore, you know. I don't do this every day."

"I never thought you did."

"Well, you don't know me at all," she said.

"I want to know you, seriously," I told her. "But you didn't want me to be serious. You wanted me to be funny." She smiled, and then she let my hand move up to her breast and rest under it.

"Well, it's okay to be a little more serious than you're being now," she said. "You have to at least talk to me a little. I mean, you must wonder why I'm doing this."

"I *do*, I *do*," I said, and she laughed at that.

"Well, I don't know, really," she said.

"*I* know," I said. "You don't like big people." She blushed, but now she let me hold both her breasts; her hands, light on my wrists, took my pulse.

"You're not that small," she said.

"But I'm shorter than you are.

"Well, yes, but that's not so small."

"I don't mind being smaller."

"God, I don't either," she said, and ran one hand along my leg, where I had her feet trapped. "You've certainly got a lot of hair," she said. "I'd never have guessed it."

"I'm sorry."

"Oh, it's all right."

"Am I your first nonskier?" I asked.

"I haven't been to bed a lot, you know."

"I know."

"No, you don't," she said. "Don't say you know when
132

you don't. I mean, I once knew someone who wasn't a skier."

"A hockey player?"

"No," she laughed. "A football player."

"He was still big, though."

"You're right," she said. "I don't like big people."

"I'm awfully glad I'm small."

"You play things, don't you?" she asked. It was a serious question. "Those tapes. There's really nothing on them, is there? You don't do any one thing, you said."

"I'm your first nobody," I said, and fearing she might take me too seriously, I leaned forward and kissed her—her mouth dry, her teeth shut, her tongue lost. When I kissed her breasts, her fingers found my hair; they hurt me a little—she seemed to be pulling me away.

"What's wrong?"

"My gum."

"Your what?"

"My gum," she said. "It's stuck in your hair." Nestling eye to eye with her nipple, I realized I must have swallowed mine.

"I swallowed mine," I said.

"Swallowed it?"

"Well, I swallowed something," I said. "Maybe your nipple."

She laughed, lifting her breasts up to cup my face. "No, it's still there," she said. "Both of them."

"You have two?"

Then she stretched out on her stomach, across the bed, reaching for the ashtray on the night table, where she deposited the gum and a wad of my hair. I bore the puff over my shoulders like a cloak and stretched out over her. Pumpkin Rump! It was impossible to lie flat on her.

She turned so that we could tangle sideways, and when I kissed her, her teeth were parted. In the blue light that glowed off the snow, we pressed down under the canopied puff and told each other stories of our vague education and more vague experience with books, friends, sports, plans, politics, preferences, religion and orgasm.

And under the hot puff (one, two, three times) the drone of a low, coming airplane seemed to carry us loudly beyond that frosted room, *wung* us out over those blue

133

miles of glacier, where we exploded, and our burnt, melted pieces were flung far apart, snuffed out like matchheads in the snow. We lay separate and barely touching, the puff kicked back, until the bed seemed to cool and harden like a slab of the glacier itself. Then we bundled against the perishing dark and lay scheming under the puff as the first shot of sun glanced off the glacier. Gradually its bright, metallic glint cut slow rivulets through the frost on the windowpane.

Also there, in the harsh sunlight, looming beside our bed in a puff of his own, Merrill Overturf stood shaking and swaying, his face the color of city snow, his hand holding aloft a frail phallus—his hypodermic syringe, with 3 cc's of cloudy insulin to clear his bad chemistry.

"Boggle . . ." he began, and in an ice-thin voice gave a fearsome account of his ill sleep; in a hot dream he had thrown aside his puff and lay naked and uncovered through the cold night, wetting his bed and waking to find his hip fastened to the bedsheet with frozen pee. And when he filled his morning hypo with insulin his hands were shaking too much to give himself the shot.

I sighted down the needle to a spot on his blue thigh and took a gingerly poke, which glanced off. But he never felt it, so I cocked back my arm and flicked my wrist like a dart thrower the way I'd seen doctors do it, and drove the needle in a bit too deep.

"Jesus, you got a muscle," Merrill said, and not wanting to hurt him any longer than necessary, I snapped my thumb down on the plunger to get the stuff into him quick. But it resisted force, and the murky fluid seemed to move into him like a wad of dough. He appeared to swoon and attempted to sit down before I could pull the needle out, and the syringe separated from the needle, leaving the needle in him. He lay across the bed moaning while I found the needle and removed it. Then I looked him all over for frostbite while he looked at Biggie, actually seeing her for the first time; in German, forgetting she spoke it too, he said, "You got her, Boggle. Good work, good work."

But I just smiled at Biggie. "She got me too, Merrill."

"Congratulations to both of you," he said, which made Biggie smile. He seemed so frozen and vulnerable that we
134

stuffed him under the puff with us, letting the warm musky air trapped in there waft over him and pressing him between us as he shivered fiercely. We held him until he began to sweat and make obvious wriggling movements and suggest that he would feel better if he could be facing Biggie instead of me.

"I'm sure you would, Merrill," I told him. "But I believe you're better now."

"His *hands* are all better," Biggie said. "I can tell you that."

Later, his hands were occupied with the steering wheel. While Biggie and I fed him oranges from the back seat, Overturf drove the sputtering Zorn-Witwer, '54, through the crunching main street of Kaprun. No one else was about except a postman walking, for warmth, beside his mail sled, coaxing the furry horse, whose breath steamed like diesel exhaust. Higher up, the sun was thawing the crust on the glacier, but all the valley villages would stay frozen until midmorning, a layer of silver dust over everything, and the air sharp enough to breathe only in careful bits. Kaprun seemed seized in such a brittle cold that if we'd blown our horn a building would have cracked.

Outside the skiers' inn in Zell, Merrill and I waited for Biggie to finish her business, watching a growing number of the men's team forming on the steps of the hotel, looking us over. Which one is Bill? They all looked the same.

"You better get some air," Merrill said.

"Why?"

"You smell," said Merrill. Yes! Biggie's rich wild-honey scent was on me! "The car smells," Merrill complained. "Jesus, everything smells like it just got laid."

On the steps, the skiers looked at Merrill, thinking he was the one.

"If they attack us," Merrill said, "don't think I'm going to take the credit for something I didn't do." But they just looked us over; some of the women's team came out on the steps and milled around too. Then a clean, natty man, older than the others, came out and stared at the '54 Zorn-Witwer as if it were an enemy tank.

"That's the coach," I said as he came down the steps and walked around to Merrill's window, a plastic flap

135

which snapped together like a baby's rubber pants. Merrill unflapped it and the coach poked his head inside the car.

Always of the opinion that no one spoke that language but himself, Merrill spoke German. "Welcome to the vagina," he said, but the coach appeared to have missed it.

"What kind of car is this?" he asked. He had a face like the football players on those old bubble-gum cards. They all wore their helmets, and their head-shapes were all alike, or maybe their heads *were* helmets. "A Zorn-Witwer, fifty-four," said Merrill.

The coach showed no recognition. "You don't see many of them around any more," he said.

"You didn't see so many around in fifty-four, either," Merrill said.

Biggie was coming down the steps with an airline flight bag, a U.S. Ski Team bag and an enormous duffel. A member of the men's team carried her skis. I got out to open the Zorn-Witwer's trunk. The bearer of her long skis: Was this Bill?

"This is Robert," Biggie said.

"Hello, Robert."

"What kind of car is this?" Robert asked.

The coach came over to the trunk. "What a big trunk," he said. "They don't make them like that any more."

"Nope."

Robert was trying to figure out how to put Biggie's skis on the roof rack. "I've never seen a ski rack like this before," he said.

"It's *not* a ski rack, you idiot," the coach told him, surprisingly loud.

Robert looked hurt and Biggie went up to the coach. "Please don't worry, Bill," she said. *The coach was Bill.*

"I'm not worried at all," he said, and he started back to the hotel. "You have a copy of the *Summer Exercise Manual?*" he asked her.

"Of course."

"I should write to your parents," he said.

"I can do that," Biggie said.

Bill stopped and turned back to us. "I didn't know there were two of them," he said. "Which one is him?"

Biggie pointed to me. "Hello," I said.

"Goodbye," said Coach Bill.

Biggie and I got into the car. "I've got to stop at the Hotel Forellen," she said, "where the French team is staying."

"*Au revoir?*" said Merrill.

"There's a girl on the French team I was going to stay with," she said. "In France, you know—she was going to take me home with her for a visit."

"And what a marvelous opportunity to learn the language." Merrill bubbled. "Culture shock . . ."

"Shut up, Merrill," I said.

Biggie looked sad. "It's all right," she said. "I didn't really like the girl anyway. I think it would have been awful."

So we waited outside the Forellen for Biggie, and observed the similar milling habits of the French men's team. They all kissed Biggie when she went into the hotel, and now they scrutinized the Zorn-Witwer.

"How do you say 'What kind of car is this?' in French?" Merrill asked me, but none of them approached us, and when Biggie came out of the hotel, they all kissed her again.

When we were under way, Merrill asked Biggie, "How about the Italian team? Let's go say goodbye to them. I've always liked Italians." But Biggie was glum and I kicked the back of Merrill's seat. He was quiet, then, through Salzburg and out on the Autobahn to Vienna, the old Zorn-Witwer skittering along like a spider over glass.

Biggie let me take her hand, but she whispered to me, "You smell funny."

"That's *you*," I whispered.

"I know," she said. But we hadn't whispered soft enough.

"Well, I think it's disgusting," Merrill said. "Expecting an old car like this to endure such an odor." When we didn't respond raucously to this, he was silent until Amstetten. "Well," he said, "I hope to see you guys around in Vienna. Maybe we can make the Opera one night, if you have the time . . ."

I caught his face in the rear-view mirror, just enough of a glance to see that he was serious. "Don't be absurd, Merrill. Of course you'll see us around. Every day." But he looked sullen and unconvinced.

Seeing him in a slump, Biggie came out of hers. She was always good that way. "If you ever wet your bed again, Merrill," she said, "you can always come get warm with us."

"Speaking of smells," I said.

"Sure," said Merrill, driving on.

"When you freeze in your pee, we'll thaw you out, Merrill," I said.

I saw him catch Biggie's eye in the mirror. "If I thought that," he said, "I'd wet my bed every night."

"Do you two live together?" Biggie asked us.

"We used to," Merrill said. "But it's a small place, so I'll go out every night and leave you two alone."

"We don't want to be that alone," said Biggie, leaning forward, touching his shoulder. And she looked back at me, a little frightened, as if she meant this. We should only go out in crowds; being alone was too serious.

"You're not any fun to be with," Merrill told me. "You're in love, you know," he said. "And that's no fun at all . . ."

"No, he's not in love," said Biggie. "We're not in love at all." She looked at me for reassurance, as if to say, We're not, are we?

"Certainly not," I said, but I was nervous.

"You certainly are," said Merrill, "you poor stupid bastard . . ." Biggie looked at him, shocked. "Jesus, you too," he told her. "You're both in love. I don't want anything to do with either of you."

And he had sweet little to do with either of us, by God; we hardly ever saw him in Vienna. We were too vulnerable to his humor; he made us aware how our casualness was faked. Then he drove the Witwer down to Italy for an early spring and sent us each a postcard. "Have an affair," the cards said. "Both of you. With someone else." But Biggie was already pregnant then.

"I thought you had a fucking intrauterine device," I said. "An I.U.D., right?"

"I.U.D." she said. "IBM, NBC, CBS . . ."

"N.C.A.A.," I said.

"U.S.A.," she said. "Well, sure, I had one, dammit. But it was just a device, like any other . . ."

"Did it fall out?" I asked. "They can't break, can they?"

138

"I don't even know how they work," she said.

"Obviously they *don't* work."

"Well, it used to."

"Maybe it fell in," I said.

"God . . ."

"The baby's probably got it in his teeth," I said.

"It's probably in my lungs," she said.

But later she said, "It couldn't *hurt* the baby, could it?"

"I don't know."

"Maybe it's inside the baby," she said. And we tried to imagine it: a plastic, unfunctioning organ next to a tiny heart. Biggie started to cry.

"Well, maybe the baby won't get pregnant," I coaxed. "Maybe the damn thing will work for the baby." But she was not amused; she was furious with me. "I'm just trying to cheer you up," I said, "It's just something Merrill would say."

"It's got nothing to do with Merrill now," she said. "It's us, in fucking love, and a baby." Then she looked at me. "Okay," she said. "It's me in love, anyway. And a baby . . ."

"Of course I love you."

"Don't say that," she said. "You just don't know yet."

Which was true enough. Though at the time, her long body was a blotter of my pain. And though we left before Merrill got back from Italy—if that's really where he was—we did not escape his influence. His example— maybe all examples—of surviving your own self-abuse. That impressed us, and we convinced ourselves that we wanted the baby.

"What will we call it?" Biggie asked.

"Aerial Bombardment?" I said, the shock of it settling upon me. "Or something simpler? Like Megaton? Or Shrapnel?" But Biggie frowned. "Flak?" I said.

But after my father disinherited me, I thought of another name, a family name. My father's brother, Uncle Colm, had been the only Trumper to take pride in being a Scot; he put the "Mac" back in front of his name. If he came for Thanksgiving, he wore a kilt. Wild Colm Mac-Trumper. He farted proudly after dinner and suggested that grave psychological insecurities had compelled my father to specialize in urology. He always asked my mother if there were any advantages in sleeping with such a specialist, and then always answered his own question: No.

My father's first name was Edmund, but Uncle Colm called him Mac. My father hated Uncle Colm. By the time my son was born, I couldn't think of a better name.

Biggie liked the name too. "It's like a sound you'd want to make in bed," she said.

"Colm?" I said, smiling.

"Mmmmmm," she said.

At the time I was assuming that someday we would be seeing a lot more of Merrill Overturf. If I'd known otherwise, I'd have called our baby Merrill.

16 : Fathers & Sons (Two Kinds),
Unwanted Daughters-In-Law
& Fatherless Friends

918 Iowa Ave.
Iowa City, Iowa

Nov. 1, 1969

Dr. Edmund Trumper
2 Beach Lane
Great Boar's Head, New Hampshire

Dearest Dad & Doctor:
I have noticed in myself lately all the forbidding symptoms of terminal *Weltschmerz*, and I wonder would you send me some penicillin? I still have some of the old penicillin you gave me, although I understand that it increases its strength with age and requires refrigeration, and would by now be unsafe to use.
Do you remember when you gave it to me?

When Couth and Fred were fifteen, Elsbeth Malkas went to Europe and brought back the world in her crotch. Their older, former playmate had outgrown them; it was their first notion that summers at Great Boar's Head were changing. They looked forward to starting prep school in the fall, while Elsbeth prepared for college.
Couth and Fred were not prepared for the way Elsbeth's crinkly black hair affected their toes; it made

141

them curl. Occasionally, they'd notice too that the pads of their fingertips tapped on their palms. It was enough to convince them of evolution, this surely being a primate sort of instinct—derived, they guessed, from the stage when monkeys curled their parts to grip the boughs of trees. It was an instinct concerning balance, and whenever they saw Elsbeth Malkas, they felt they were going to fall out of a tree.

Elsbeth brought new and strange habits home from Europe. No tanning on the beach during the day, no dates at the casino by night. She spent the day in the hot garret of her parent's beach cottage, writing. Poems about Europe, she said. And painting. Couth and Fred could see her garret window from the waterfront; usually, they were throwing a football in the surf. In her window, Elsbeth stood motionless, a long brush in one hand.

"I'll bet she just paints the walls of that dumb room," Fred said.

Couth heaved the football out to sea and plunged through the waves after it, calling back, "I bet not!" Fred saw Elsbeth at her window, looking out. *Is she watching Couth or me?*

At night, they watched *her*. They lay in the sand, halfway between her house and the waterfront, to be ready when she'd come out all white and heated from the garret, wearing a paint-blobbed blue denim workshirt that hung to midthigh; until she bent over to snatch up a stone to throw, you didn't know there was nothing underneath. At the water's edge she'd throw the shirt off and plunge in; her great black hair floating behind her had as much of a life of its own as the tangled kelp abob in the surf. When she slipped the workshirt back on it would cling to her; she never bothered to button it as she walked back to the house.

"You still can't really see it very good," Couth would complain.

"A flashlight!" said Fred. "We could shine it on her up close."

"She'd just cover herself with the shirt," Couth said.

"Yeah, the damn shirt," Fred said. "Shit."

So one night they took the shirt. They ran down to the wet sand and snatched it up while she was out in the surf,

142

but they were back-lit by the cottage lights and she saw that they'd run behind the hedges near her porch, so she just walked right up to them. Rather than look at her, they attempted to conceal themselves under the shirt.

"Freddy Trumper and Cuthbert Bennett," she said. "You horny little bastards." She walked right past them onto her porch, and they heard the screen door slam. Then she called out to them, "You're going to be in a lot of trouble if you don't bring my shirt in here quick!" Imagining her naked in the living room, where her parents sat reading, Couth and Fred clumped up the porch and peered in the screen door. She was naked, but alone, and when they gave her the shirt back, she didn't even put it on. They didn't dare look at her.

"It was just a joke, Elsbeth," Fred said.

"Look!" she said, making a pirouette in front of them. "You wanted to look, so *look!*" They looked, then looked away.

"Actually," Couth said, "we wanted to see what you were painting." When Elsbeth laughed, they both laughed with her and stepped inside. Fred promptly bumped into a standing lamp, knocking off the shade and stepping on it when he tried to pick it up. Which made Couth hysterical. But Elsbeth tossed her shirt lightly over her shoulder and took Couth's hand and pulled him upstairs.

"Well, you must come see the paintings, Cuthbert," she said, and when Fred started up after them, she said, "You wait down here, please, Fred." Couth looked back over his shoulder, frightened and clowning and stumbling upstairs after her.

When Couth returned, Fred had completely ruined the lampshade with his reshaping efforts and was cramming it in a wastebasket under the desk.

"Here, let me fix it," Couth said, and pawed the mangled shade out of the wastebasket. Fred stood watching him, but Couth nervously shoved him upstairs. "Jesus, go *on,*" he said. "I'll wait for you."

So Fred climbed to the garret, unknotting the drawstring of his bathing suit as he went, critically sniffing his armpits and smelling his breath hugged into his cupped palms. But Elsbeth Malkas didn't seem to care about any of that. In a cot in her garret, she stripped his bathing suit off and told him that when she used to baby-sit for him, he would peek when she used the bathroom. Did he remember that? No.

"Well, please remember not to tell," she said, and then laid him so fast he scarcely noticed that every canvas in her room was white, all white; that any stroke or color put upon those canvases had been painted over white. The walls were white too. And when he joined Couth down in the living room, he noticed that the lampshade had been stuck back on the lamp all scrunched up and crushed, so that the light bulb was burning brown a part of the shade which touched it; the whole crazy lamp looked like a man whose head had been driven down between his shoulders, and in an effort to tug up the head, his glowing brain had been exposed.

Out on the blowy beach, Couth asked, "Did she tell you the bit about peeking at her in the bathroom when she used to baby-sit for me?"

"She used to baby-sit for me," Fred said, "but she's wrong; I never did that."

"Well, *I* did it," Couth said. "Boy, did I ever . . ."

"Where were her parents?" Fred asked.

"Well, they weren't home," Couth said, and they walked down to the sea and swam naked, then walked along the wet sand until they were opposite Couth's cottage.

Tiptoeing into Couth's hall, they were surprised to hear the murmurs of a lot of people in the kitchen, and Couth's mother crying. Peeking, they saw Elsbeth's parents and Fred's mother consoling Couth's weeping mother, and Dr. Trumper, Fred's father, seeming to be waiting for them at the door. *Their sin already discovered! She had told them, said she was raped or pregnant! She would marry them both!*

But Fred's father pulled him quietly aside and whispered, "Couth's father died, a stroke . . ." Then he stepped quickly after Couth, intercepting him before he got to his mother.

Fred couldn't look Couth in the eye, for fear that Couth might see how relieved he looked.

No such relief, however, did he see in his bathroom mirror on the morning there was no hole to pee out of. At first, a little pinch would open it. Then it began open-

144

ing and closing all by itself; he seemed to have no influence over it. He took aspirin and rationed his water.

But on the morning he shyly shared the bathroom with his father (turned away from his father's looming lathered presence shaving at the mirror), Fred straddled the hopper and peed what felt like razor blades, bent bobbypins and ground glass. His scream opened a messy gash on his father's chin, and before he could hide the evidence, his father shouted, "Let me see that!"

"What?" said Fred, clutching what he was sure was only a remnant of his former part.

"What you're holding," his father said, "that's what."

But Fred wouldn't let go, fearing it would fall at his feet; he knew that if he let go, they would never be able to put it back. He held on fiercely while his father raged around him.

"Stuck together, is it?" the good doctor roared. "A little discharge now and then? Something like nails in the way of your passing water?"

Nails! So that's what he'd felt! My God!

"What have you been into lately?" his father bellowed. "Sweet Jesus! Just fourteen and you've been into it already!"

"I'm fifteen," Fred said; he felt more nails wanting to come out.

"Liar!" boomed his father.

Down the hall, his mother called, "Edmund? He *is* fifteen! What a lot of shouting over such a silly issue!"

"You don't know what he's been into!" his father shrieked at her.

"What?" she asked. They could hear her coming toward the bathroom. "What have you been into, Fred?"

But this made his father conspiratorial. He locked the bathroom door and called to his wife, "Nothing, dear." Then, all pink-foamed, his shaving cut bleeding through his lather, he bent over Fred. "What was it?" he whispered grimly, and the way he said it made Fred want to say, A sheep. But the pink-frosted face was frightening, and after all his father was a urologist; expert advice on peeing was something he couldn't afford to turn down. He thought of iron filings floating down from his bladder; he saw the

145

stout snout of a chisel pushing its way down his urinary tract like a raft.

"God, what's in me?" he asked his father.

"Feels like it's rusted shut, doesn't it?" the good doctor said. "Now let me see it."

Fred let his hand drop to his knee, listening for the *plop* on the bathroom floor.

"Who was it?" his father asked, touching the tip of his life.

"Elsbeth Malkas!" he crooned, hating his betrayal of her but finding nothing delicious enough in his memory of her to make protecting her worthwhile.

Elsbeth Malkas! His toes stuck out so straight he thought he'd fall. Elsbeth Malkas! Bring her in here, stretch her out, discover what in hell she hides in that deceptive snatch of hers . . .

"Clap," his father said, and like most things his father said, it sounded like a command. And Fred thought, *Clap?* Oh no, please be careful. No one should clap anywhere near it now. God, don't anyone clap please . . .

Then his mother came to the bathroom door and called his father to the phone. "It's Cuthbert Bennett," she said.

"For Fred?"

"No, for you," she told the good doctor, following him down the hall, looking anxiously back at Fred, who was as white as an Elsbeth Malkas canvas. "Edmund," she followed, chirping, "be nice to Cuthbert. He's just lost his father, and I think he wants your advice."

Fred came grimacing after them down the hall, watched his father pick up the phone, slumped against the wall and waited.

"Yes, hello, Cuthbert," his father said in a kindly tone, plastering the mouthpiece with blood-pink shaving lather. "Yes, of course, what is it?" Then his whole face changed and he shot a look at Fred like a killer-dart. Far off, in a tiny sound of panic, Fred heard Couth's hysterical voice; his father stared down the hall at him, shocked, as the voice over the phone went on and on. "No no, not here. I'll see you in my office," his father said irritably, and Fred simply had to smirk, a breaking grin. "In an hour, then," his father said, holding in his rage. "All right, in *half* an hour," he said, louder. Fred slouched haughtily

146

against the wall, then dissolved in a cackling fit as his father shouted into the phone, "Well, don't pee, then!" Hanging up, he glared at Fred, now laughing uncontrollably against the wall.

"Why can't Cuthbert pee?" his mother asked, and his father wheeled on her, his wild head in a gory froth.

"*Clap!*" he shouted at her. He frightened the poor woman; she began to clap.

918 Iowa Ave.
Iowa City, Iowa

Nov. 3, 1969

Dr. Edmund Trumper
2 Beach Lane
Great Boar's Head, New Hampshire

Dear Dr. Trumper:

As I understand your feelings, if Fred had *not* brought me back pregnant from Europe and married me, you would have continued to support him through graduate school. You have never made it clear, however, that if I *hadn't* been pregnant, you might have continued your support of Fred. Well, frankly, this all strikes me as both insulting and unfair. If Fred didn't have a wife and child to support, he would not really need your money. He could pay for himself through graduate school with part-time jobs and scholarships. And if I hadn't been pregnant, *I* could have gotten a job to support the remainder of his studies. In other words, the situation we are now in requires your support more than both situations you claim you would have supported us in. What exactly is it you don't approve of? That I was pregnant? That Fred didn't wait to do things in the order *you* did them in? Or is it just me in particular whom you simply don't like? It's like some moral punishment you are handing out to Fred, and don't you think that someone over twenty-five shouldn't be treated this way? I mean, you had this money set aside for Fred's education, and I can understand you not being willing

147

to support his wife and child too, but isn't it sort of childish to refuse to pay for his education as well?

Yours,

Biggie

918 Iowa Ave.
Iowa City, Iowa

Nov. 3, 1969

Dr. Edmund Trumper
2 Beach Lane
Great Boar's Head, New Hampshire

Dear Dr. Trumper:
Fred's letters to you have, I think, been what you'd call "hints." I am not going to hint around. *My* mother and father give us what they can so that Fred can finish his goddamn Ph.D., and I think that you should give us at least what you were planning to give Fred for his education before I came pregnantly along and upset your plans for him. I also think that your wife would agree with me, but you bully her.

Biggie

918 Iowa Ave.
Iowa City, Iowa

Nov. 3, 1969

Dr. Edmund Trumper
2 Beach Lane
Great Boar's Head, New Hampshire

Dear Dr. Trumper,
You are a prick. Please forgive my language, but that's what you are. A prick for making your own son suffer and casting aspersions on his manner of

148

marrying me and having Colm and all. Just because he wasn't a doctor when he did it. Even so, your Fred has done quite well for Colm and me. It's just that this last year, with all the pressures on him to finish his thesis and look for a job, he is getting very depressed. And you haven't helped him any—with all you've got, too. My own parents haven't half your luxury, but they contribute something. Did you even know, for example, that your Fred has sold football pennants and borrowed no small sums from his friend Couth, who obviously cares more for us than you do? You prick with your principles, you. A fine fucking father you are, is all I can say.

Your daughter-in-law,
(Like it or not!)

Biggie

That muddy November afternoon, I sat in my window watching Fitch, the grim raker, standing soldierly on his immaculately dying lawn. Fitch was on guard, his rake at the ready; he scanned the mess of leaves on all his neighbors' lawns, waiting for one to stray his way. In the rain gutters of his house, leaves lurked above him, waiting for him to turn his head; then they would swoop down. But I sat there with intolerant thoughts toward the harmless old fool. May your entire yard cave in, Fitch.

In my lap were the carbons of Biggie's three letters, and she sulked over my shoulder. "Which is the best one?" she asked. "I couldn't decide."

"Oh, my God, Big . . ."

"Well, it's high time somebody told him how it is," she said. "And I didn't notice that you had anything to say."

"Biggie . . . oh, Christ," I went on. "A prick, Biggie? Oh, my God . . ."

"Well, he *is* a prick, Bogus. You know very well . . ."

"Of course he is," I said to her. "But what is the effect of telling him?"

"What's been the effect of *not* telling him, Bogus?"

" 'You prick with your principles, you,' " I read in horror. "That's *two* pricks, Big. That's twice you've said it . . ."

149

"Well, do you like the other letters better?" she asked. "What do you think of the reasonable one, or the short one?"

"God. Biggie. which one did you send?"

"I told you, Bogus," she said. "I couldn't make up my mind—"

"Oh. thank God!" I groaned.

"So I sent all three of them." Biggie said. "Let the prick take his pick."

And I felt the wind blow down Fitch, sweep him light as a leaf down the block and cram him under a parked car!

918 Iowa Ave.
Iowa City, Iowa

Nov. 4, 1969

Mr. Cuthbert Bennett
Caretaker/ The Pillsbury Estate
Mad Indian Point
Georgetown, Maine

My Dear Couth:

In the afterglow of your nice phone call, Biggie and I are sitting up tonight, spending imaginary fortunes and considering the alternative: a hara-kiri duet. See the two of us, squatting across from each other on the newly waxed linoleum floor. Biggie is carving out my stomach with the bread knife; I prefer the steak slicer for disemboweling her. We're quite absorbed in our work. We're being careful to smother our screams, not wanting to wake up Colm.

Colm, we agree, will go to Biggie's good parents in East Gunnery, Vermont. He'll grow up to be a skier and a wood-chopper, ruddy and craggy and so strongly mired in his New England nose-tones that he'll never care to trouble himself with another language—like Old Low Norse. The mumbled tongue of his ancestors. close and far.

It's not that I don't agree with everything Biggie told my father. It's only that I wish she hadn't blown

150

her tact. Because I fear my father has to be treated like a Pope before he'll bestow blessings, and if you call the Pope a prick, will he still pray for you?

In the meantime, Biggie and I sit tracing her letter eastward. I see Biggie's blunt truth tilting a mail van in Chicago, her heavy message felling a postal employee in Cleveland. An ember of its heated feeling cools in the sea breeze on the coastal route between Boston and Great Boar's Head, where our mail is invariably delivered in the early afternoon. My mother will be home to open it, but Biggie swears it was addressed to my father alone, *not* to Dr. & Mrs., in which case, recalling my mother's awe of the good doctor, she will not open it. She'll lay it on the counter below the liquor cabinet.

My father will come home at four, having just removed a bladder spigot or told some octogenarian that such an operation is advisable; having just fussily shaved himself in his tidy office-bathroom; having removed from his hands all traces of the surgical powder that helps the gloves slide on and off. He will allow my mother to peck his clean-shaven cheek; he'll fix himself a neat Scotch—after holding up the glass to light, to make sure it's been properly washed. Then he'll see the letter. He'll pinch it all around, to see if there's a check enclosed, and my mother will say, "Oh, no, dear. It's from Iowa City. It's not a patient; it's from Fred, don't you think?"

My father will take off his suit jacket, loosen his tie, meander through the den to the sunporch window and remark on whether the tide is high or low, as if, mystically, it will influence where he sits. It never seems to.

He'll sit down in his same red-leather throne, crush the same hassock under his heels, sniff his scotch, sip it, and *then* he'll read Biggie's letters.

If it went out in the noon mail yesterday, it's at least past Chicago today, if not already through Cleveland, and through Boston by tomorrow, and in Great Boar's Head tomorrow or the day after.

At which time, Couth, if you'd be so kind, please enter your darkroom and print two absolutely *solid* photographs, one all-white and one all-black; one is hope and the other is doom. Mail them both to me. I will return to you the one that doesn't suit my occasion.

> Wishing you, Couth, infinite varieties
> of Hope and Freedom
> From the Fear of Doom.

> Love,
> Bogus

Imagining good Couth by the rainy sea, his wild hair sailing in a nor'easter blowing Bar Harbor to Boothbay. Couth with one of his fuddy sea prayers for my letter held aloft, the empty Pillsbury mansion behind him, a ramble of rooms for his lonely play.

I remember the end of that one funny summer when we moved into the boathouse with its crammed little bunk beds.

"Top or bottom, Big?"

"Get up there . . ."

While Couth lolled in the Big House after the Pillsburys had gone home for the fall.

Some younger son phoned to say he might be coming. "My mother gone. Couth?"

"That's true. Bobby."

"Aunt Ruth won't be there, will she?"

"Right again. sir."

"Well. Couth. I suppose you've moved into the Big House now. I wouldn't want to put you out, so we'll take the boathouse."

"Who's we, Bobby?"

"A friend and myself, Couth. But I'd appreciate your telling Father I was alone for the weekend."

"Sorry. Bobby, there are people in the boathouse. Friends of mine But another couple of bedrooms in the Big House could easily be . . ."

"One bedroom will do it, Couth. With a double . . ."

In the poolroom, while Biggie helped Colm build a fire, Couth and I racked up the balls.

152

"It won't be so private this fall," Couth said sadly, "now that some of the Pillsbury kids have reached fucking age. They'll be bringing their lays up for the weekends. But after November it'll get too cold for them."

The great mansion still was heated strictly with coal, wood stoves and fireplaces. Couth loved the winters best, with the whole run of the house to himself, fussing with wood and coal all day, banking the fires at night, trying to keep the chemicals from freezing in his darkroom. With Colm after supper, Couth worked down there on a series of Colm pulverizing a clamworm on the dock. Colm grinding it with a sneaker, halving it with a piece of shell; Colm requesting a replacement worm.

In the darkroom, Colm refused to talk; he just watched his image emerging from Couth's chemical baths. He was not at all amazed at his underwater development; he took miracles for granted; he was more impressed by being given a second chance to view the mangled clamworm.

Couth also printed from a double negative: one of Colm on the dock, the other of just the dock from the same angle. The structure was slightly out of focus around the edges, since the two docks did not quite mesh, and Colm appeared to be both on the dock and under it, the grain of the wood spread over his hands and face, his body laid out in planks. Yet he sits up (how? in space?). I was stunned by the image, though I shared Biggie's dislike for it, the boy with the wood imposed over him was strangely dead. We mentioned to Couth the incredible paranoia one felt about one's own children. Couth showed the image to Colm, who disregarded it since it was not a clear reproduction of the worm.

The girl whom Bobby Pillsbury brought "home" for the weekend thought it was "almost like a painting."

"Nell is a painter," Bobby told us all.

Seventeen-year-old Nell said, "Well, I work at it."

"Some more carrots, Nell?" Couth asked.

"It's such a lonely photograph," she told Couth; she was still staring at the picture of Colm with his face under the dock. "This place, you know—in the winter, I mean—it must pretty well sort of collaborate with your vision."

Couth chewed slowly, aware that the girl was gone on him. "My vision?" he said.

"Yeah, well," said Nell, "you know what I mean. Your world-view, sort of."

"I'm not lonely," Couth said.

"Yes, you are, Couth," Biggie said. Colm—the real Colm, his face ungrained with wood—spilled his milk. Biggie held him in her lap and let him touch her boob. Beside her, Bobby Pillsbury sat in love with Biggie.

"It's a very untypical photograph for Couth," I told Nell. "Seldom is the image so literal, and almost never does he use such an obvious double exposure."

"Can I see more of your work?" Nell asked.

"Well," Couth said, "if I can find it."

"Why not have Bogus just tell her about it," Biggie said.

"Up yours, Big," I said, and she laughed.

"I've been working on some short stories," Bobby Pillsbury announced.

I took Colm from Biggie and stood him on the table, aimed at Couth.

"Go get Couth, Colm," I said. "Go on . . ." And Colm began to walk with a brute glee across the salad, avoiding the rice.

"Bogus . . ." Biggie protested, but Couth stood up at his end of the table, his arms held out for Colm, now bearing down on him through the mussel shells and corncobs.

"Come to Couth," Couth said. "Come on, come on. Want to see some more pictures? Come on, come on . . ."

Colm went sprawling over a basket of rolls and Couth swept him up and bore him dizzily off to the darkroom, the girl named Nell followed devotedly.

Bobby Pillsbury watched Biggie push her chair back from the table. "Can I help you with the dishes?" he asked her. I gave Biggie a gleeful pinch under the table; Bobby thought her blush was meant for him. He began to clear the table in clumsy swoops, and I retired to the darkroom to watch Couth dazzle Bobby's girl. As I left her with this bumbling would-be lover, Biggie caught my eye with a comic look of mock lust for Bobby.

But later, in our boathouse racks, as Couth slept with Colm in the master bedroom of the Big House, and Bobby

154

Pillsbury and his young girl Nell were or were not reconciled, Biggie was cross with me.

"He was a perfectly nice boy, Bogus," she said. "You shouldn't have left him alone with me."

"Big, you're not telling me you grabbed a quickie in the kitchen?"

"Oh, shut up." She shifted in the bottom bunk bed.

"Did he really try, Big?" I asked her.

"Look," she said coolly, "you know nothing happened. It's just that you made it awkward for the kid."

"I'm sorry, Big, really. I was just fooling . . ."

"And I'll admit I was flattered," she said, and then paused a long time. "I mean, it was sort of nice," she said. "A young kid like that really wanting me."

"You're surprised?"

"Aren't you?" she asked me. "You don't seem that interested."

"Oh, Biggie . . ."

"Well, you don't," she said. "You might pay more attention to who's interested in me, Bogus, and not abuse it."

"Biggie, it was just a dumb evening. Look at Couth with that girl Nell—"

"That brainless twat . . ."

"Biggie! A young girl . . ."

"Couth is the only friend you've got that I like."

"Well, good," I said. "I like Couth too."

"Bogus, I could live like this. Could you?"

"Like Couth?"

"Yes."

"No, Big."

"Why?"

I thought about it.

"Because he doesn't own anything?" Biggie asked, but that was stupid; that didn't matter at all to me, either. "Because he doesn't seem to need any other people around him?" She was edging around it. "Because he lives on the ocean all year round?" Which has nothing to do with anything we're talking about, I thought. "Because he can put a lot into his photographs and not need to put much into his life?" She was a prodder, Biggie was. I forgot the question.

"So you could live here with Couth, Big?" I asked her, and she was quiet for a long time.

"I said I could live like this," she said. "Not with Couth. With you. But like Couth lives."

"I'm not handy with anything," I said. "I couldn't be a caretaker for anything. I couldn't even replace a fuse in a complicated house like this, probably . . ."

"That's not what I mean," she said. "I mean, if you could be content like Couth. You know, *peaceful?*"

I knew.

In the morning, from Biggie's lower bunk we watched Couth and Colm out of the boathouse porthole. On the low-tide mudflats, Couth was taking Colm exploring, carrying his camera and a burlap potato sack to gather the odd sea-leavings off the mud.

In the breakfast nook of the Big House, Biggie served blueberry pancakes to a silent Bobby Pillsbury, a nervous Nell, Couth and Colm, a bubble of display. The contents of the potato sack were for us all to enjoy: a razor-clam shell, a skate's tail, the transparent, paper-thin skeleton of a sculpin, a dead gull, the severed head of a bright-billed tern and the jutting lower jawbone of what might be a seal, a sheep, or a man.

After breakfast, Couth arranged the carnage on our plates and photographed it, suggesting some weird, cannibalistic meal. Though Nell's interest in Couth's photography seemed to end with this, I watched Biggie watching Couth patiently arranging his table settings. Colm appeared to find Couth's work the logical extension of child's play.

"Do you ever do nudes?" asked Nell.

"Models are expensive," Couth said.

"Well, you should ask your friends," Nell told him, smiling.

"Biggie?" Couth asked, but he looked at me. I was balancing Colm on his head on the pool table.

"Search me," I told him. "Ask *her*."

"Biggie?" Couth called. She was in the kitchen with the breakfast pans. Bobby Pillsbury and Nell handled the long pool cues at the end of the living room. "Will you model for me, Biggie?" I could hear him asking her in the kitchen.

156

Bobby Pillsbury flexed his pool cue like a fly-fisherman's rod. Nell bent hers like a bow, and I was suddenly aware of how red in the face poor, upside-down Colm was. I righted him dizzily on the pool table, and heard Couth add cautiously, "I mean, you know, naked . . ."

"Yeah, just a minute, Couth," said Biggie. "Let me finish these dishes first."

But Couth envied children more than wives. He used to tell me that he thought more of offspring than of mates. Though Biggie touched him, I think Colm got to him more. He used to ask me what I did with Colm; he was amazed that I had to think hard for an answer. All I could tell him was that children changed your life.

"Well, sure, I'd think they would," he said.

"But I mean, they make you paranoid."

"You were always paranoid."

"But with children, it's different," I said, not knowing how to explain what was so different. I once wrote Merrill about it. I said that children gave you a sudden sense of your own mortality, which was clearly something that Merrill Overturf had no sense of; he never answered me. But I simply meant that you noticed how your priorities had changed. For example, I used to like motorcycles; I couldn't ride one after Colm was born. I don't think it was just responsibility; it's just that children give you a sense of time. It was as if I'd never realized how time moved before.

Also, I had this feeling about Colm that seemed unnatural. That is, I desired to bring him up in some sort of simulated natural habitat—some kind of pasture or corral—rather than the gruesome real natural habitat itself, which seemed too unsafe. Bring him up in a sort of dome! Create his friends, invent a satisfying job, induce limited problems, simulate hardships (to a degree), fake a few careful threats, have him win in the end—nothing too unreasonable.

"You mean, sort of graze him, like a cow?" Couth said. "Well, but he'd become a little bovine, wouldn't he?"

"Cattle are *safe,* Couth, and they're *content.*"

"Cattle are cattle, Bogus."

Biggie agreed with Couth. When Colm was allowed to

157

tricycle around our block, I fretted. Biggie said it was necessary to give the child self-confidence. I knew that; still, I lurked in the bushes around the block, following him unseen. I had a notion of the father as guardian angel. When Colm would see me peeling back a branch and peering out at him from the hedge, I'd tell him that it was actually the hedge that interested me. I was looking for something; I'd try to interest him in such safe scrutiny too. Better than riding your tricycle into danger! Come live a placid life in the untroubled hedge.

I even found a place I thought was suitable for a controlled environment: the Iowa City zoo. No life and death struggles or failures there.

"We always come here," Colm would complain.

"Don't you like the animals?"

"Yes . . ." But in winter there were only four or five animals. "Mommy takes me *there*," Colm would say, pointing across the river to downtown Iowa City and the university buildings.

"There's just people there," I'd tell him. "No raccoons." Just people; if we went there, we might see one of them crying—or worse.

So coming home from People's Market, I'd take Colm through the zoo. In November, when the monkeys had gone south or indoors, and Biggie and I had been waiting a week to hear from my offended father, Colm and I brought the breakfast bread home through the zoo, and left most of it there.

Feeding the vile raccoons, an entire snarling clan of them in their stony cell, Colm was always concerned that the smaller ones got no bread. "That one," he'd say, pointing to a cowardly one, and I'd try to reach the little bastard with a wad of bread. Every time, some fat and surly one would get there first, bite the coward in the ass, steal the bread and wait for more. Is this good for a child to see?

Or the molting American bison, looking like the last buffalo? His legs as thin as some awkward wading bird's, his mottled coat falling off in hunks, like old furniture in need of reupholstering; a giant, tottering sofa with the stuffing hanging out.

Or the cold, wizened bear, in a brick pit with a swinging innertube he never played with, surrounded by his own awful reeking flaps.

"What's the tire for?" Colm asked.

"For him to play with."

"How?"

"Oh, swing on it, bat it around . . ."

But the tire, unbatted and unswung, hung over the ever-sleeping bear like a taunt. The animal himself probably lived in dread of what it was for. I had growing doubts about the fitness of this zoo habitat for Colm; perhaps the downtown streets would be better for the child, after all.

And then, that November, there was the disaster in the duck pond, where usually I felt most at ease with Colm. The soot-white domestic ducks scrounged the breaded pond; we awaited the striking visitations at this time of year from the bold, bright, wild ducks flying south. Iowa lay in a Midwest flyway, and the pond at the Iowa City zoo was perhaps the only place a duck could rest between Canada and the Gulf without being shot at. We used to watch them land there, a cautious flying wedge with a scout sent down first to test the landing; then he would quack the safe news up to the rest. Such color was a new thing in the zoo; the dull inhabitants were stirred up by the arrival of these real-world travelers: red-eyes, mallards, canvasbacks, blue- and green-winged teal, and the splendid wood ducks.

That November I held Colm's hand and watched the lowering V in the sky, imagining this tired and crippled gaggle coming in to rest, blasted over the Great Lakes, shot down in the Dakotas, ambushed in Iowa! The scout landed like a skater on glass, gave a brazen quack at the old-maid ducks ashore, thanked God for the wonder of no artillery, then called his flock down.

In they came, breaking their flight patterns, splashing down in a great reckless dash, astonished at all the floating bread. But one duck hung back in the sky. His flying was ragged, his descent unsure. The others seemed to clear the pond for him, and he dropped down so suddenly that Colm grabbed my leg and clung to it as if he were afraid the duck was going to bomb us. It appeared that the bird's landing gear was fouled, his wing controls damaged, his vision blurred. He came in at too steep an angle, attempt-

159

ed to correct his position with a weak veer, lost all resemblance to a duck's grace and struck the pond like a stone.

Colm flinched against me as a choral quack of condolences came from the ducks ashore. In the pond, the downed duck's little ass protruded, a spatter of feathers floating around him. Two of his former flock paddled out to prod him, then left him to float there like a feathered bobber. His mates quickly turned their worried attention to the bread, anxious that at any moment a thrashing dog would swim out to retrieve their comrade. Were they shooting with silencers now? The irony of death descending on the Iowa City zoo.

All I said to Colm was, "Silly duck."

"Is he dead?" Colm asked.

"No, no," I said. "He's just fishing, feeding on the bottom." Should I add: They can hold their breath a long time?

Colm was unconvinced. "He's dead."

"No," I said. "He was just showing off. You know, you show off sometimes."

Colm was reluctant to leave. Clutching the maimed breadloaf, he looked over his shoulder at the crash-landing duck—former stunt pilot, bizarre bottom-feeding bird. Why this suicide? I wondered. Or had he been wounded, bravely carrying gunshot for many troubled landings, at last losing control here? Or was it just some midair seizure of natural causes? Or drunk, having last fed in a fermenting soybean bog?

"I wish, Bogus," Biggie said, "that when you know you'll be going to the zoo, you'd buy *two* loaves of bread so there'd be one left for us."

"We had a wonderful walk," I said. "The bear was asleep, the raccoons were fighting, the buffalo was trying to grow a new coat. And the ducks," I said, nudging the ominously silent Colm, "we saw this silly duck land in the pond . . ."

"A dead duck, Mommy," Colm said solemnly. "He crashed up."

"Colm," I said, bending down to him. "You don't know he was dead." But he knew, all right.

"Some ducks just die," he said, being irritably patient with me. "They just get old and die, is all. Animals and

160

birds and people," he said. "They just get old and die."
And he looked at me with worldly sympathy, obviously
feeling sad to be stunning his father with such a hard
truth.

Then the phone rang and visions of my own terrible
father blotted all else from my brain: Daddy with a five-
minute speech prepared, an analysis of the emotional imbalance in Biggie's letters, puffing his pipe at his end of the
phone. I believe there was supreme rationality in his tobacco. Suppertime in Iowa, after-dinner coffee in New
Hampshire; a phone call timed on his terms, like him. But
also like Ralph Packer, inviting himself for supper.

"Well, answer it," Biggie said.

"*You* answer it," I said. "You wrote the letters."

"I'm not picking that thing up, Bogus, not after what I
called him, the prick."

As we faced the ringing, unanswered phone, Colm slid a
kitchen chair over and climbed up to reach it.

"I'll get it," he said, but both Biggie and I lunged for
him before he picked it up.

"Let it ring," Biggie said, looking frightened for the first
time. "Why not just let it ring, Bogus?"

We did just that. We rode out the ringing.

Biggie said, "Oh, can't you just see him? Breathing into
the phone!"

"I'll bet he's just livid," I said. "The prick."

But later, after Colm had fallen out of bed and
bawled—and needed trundling to Biggie's broad chest, and
some reassurance about a peculiar nightmare involving a
zoo—I said, "I'll bet that was just Ralph Packer, Big. My
father wouldn't call us. He'd write us—he'd write a fucking opus."

"No," Biggie said. "It was your father. And he'll never
call again." She sounded glad.

That night Biggie rolled back against me and said, "Let
it ring."

But I just dreamed. I dreamed that Iowa was playing
out of town and took me with them. They used me for the
opening kickoff. From yards deep in my own end zone, I
ran all the way upfield for a miraculous touchdown. Of
course I was horribly jarred along the route, even chopped,

161

quartered, halved, ground, gouged and swiped; but somehow I emerged, severely crippled but upright, churning into the enemy's virgin end zone.

Then there's the aftermath: I am carried off the field by the Iowa cheerleaders and toted along the sidelines, past the seething, jeering enemy fans. Little sweatered nymphs bear me along; my near-limp and bloodied arm brushes one of their cold, pink legs; somehow I sense both the smoothness and the prickle. I look giddily up at their young, tear-streaked faces; one brushes my cheek with her hair, perhaps trying to remove the grass stain on my nose or dislodge the cleat embedded in my chin. I am light to carry. These strong young girls bear me under the stadium, through a bowel-like tunnel. Their high voices echo, their shrill concern for me pierces me more than my pain. To some linen-covered table, then, where they spread me out, remove my encrusted armor, marvel and wail over my wounds. Above us the stadium throws down its muted din. The girls sponge me off. I go into shock; I shiver; the girls lie across me, fearing that I'll chill.

I am so cold that I have another dream; I'm in a duck blind in the New Hampshire salt marshes with my father. I am wondering how old I am; I don't have a gun, and when I stand on tiptoe, I can just reach my father's throat.

He says, "Be quiet." And, "Jesus, see if I ever bring you with me again."

I am thinking: *See if I come!*

Which I must have dreamed aloud, because Biggie said, "Who asked you?"

"What, Big?"

"Let it ring," she said, asleep again.

But I lay awake contemplating the horror of having to look for a real job. The notion of earning a living . . . The phrase itself was like those other obscene propositions offered on a men's-room wall.

17 : Reflections on the Failure of the Water Method

The procedure for making an appointment with Dr. Jean Claude Vigneron is unpleasant. The nurse who answers his phone does not care to hear a description of what ails you; she only wants to know if this is a convenient time for your appointment. Well, no. Well, she's sorry. So you tell her you'll find the time.

The waiting room at Vigneron's office is comfy. A former Norman Rockwell cover for *The Saturday Evening Post* is framed on the wall; also, a Bob Dylan poster. Also, you can read *McCall's, The Village Voice, The New York Times, Reader's Digest* or *Ramparts*—but no one reads. They watch Vigneron's nurse, whose thigh, rump and swivel chair protrude into the waiting room from her typing alcove. They also listen when the nurse asks for a description of what ails you. A certain pattern is evident.

"What are you seeing the doctor for?"

Incoherent whispers.

"What?"

Louder incoherent whispers.

"How long has your urine been this way?"

What way? everyone pretending to read is dying to ask.

Urology is so awesomely foul and debilitating a specialty that I took Tulpen with me for support. The office presented its usual puzzle. A child the color of urine sat cramped beside her mother; perhaps she had not peed for weeks. A stunning young girl, dressed entirely in leather, sat aloof with *The Village Voice*. No doubt, she was infected. And an old man quaked by the door, his tubes and valves and spigots so ancient and malfunctioning that he probably pissed through his navel into a plastic bag.

"What are you seeing the doctor for?"

"The water method has failed." Intense curiosity is provoked in the waiting room.

"The water method?"

"Failed. Utterly."

"I see, Mr. . . . ?"

"Trumper."

"Do you have pain, Mr. Trumper?" I sense that the mother with the swollen child is anxious; the girl in leather grips her paper tight.

"Some . . ." A mysterious answer; the waiting room is on edge.

"Would you tell me, please, just what . . ."

"It's stuck."

"Stuck?"

"Stuck shut."

"I see. Shut . . ." She looks through my record, a long history of being stuck shut. "And you've had this trouble before?"

"The world over. Austria to Iowa!" The waiting room is impressed by this worldly disease.

"I see. It's what you saw Dr. Vigneron about before?"

"Yes." Incurable, the waiting room decides. Poor fellow.

"And have you been taking anything?"

"Water." The nurse looks up; the water method is clearly unknown to her.

"I see," she says. "If you'll have a seat, Dr. Vigneron will see you in a moment."

Crossing the waiting room to Tulpen, I saw the mother smile kindly at me, the child stare, the stunning young girl cross her legs, thinking, If it's stuck shut, stay away from me. But the poor old man with his faulty tubes did not respond; hard of hearing, perhaps, or totally deaf, or peeing through his ear.

"I should think," Tulpen whispered, "that you've had enough of this."

"Enough of what?" I said too loudly. The mother tensed; the girl flapped her paper; the old man shifted uncomfortably in his chair, his terrible insides sloshing.

164

"This," Tulpen hissed, tapping her fist in her lap. "This," she said, with a careful gesture taking in this collection of the urinary-wounded. There's always a rare fraternity in doctors' offices, but in the office of a specialist the intimacy is worse. There are clubs for veterans, for people with high I.Q.'s, for lesbians, for alumni, for mothers who gave birth to triplets, persons in favor of saving the elm, Rotarians, Republicans and Neo-Maoists, but here was a forced association: people who have problems peeing. Call us Vigneronists! We could meet once a week, have contests and exhibitions—a kind of track and field meet of urinary events.

Then Dr. Jean Claude Vigneron came into the waiting room from the secret innards of his office, wafting over us the swarthy smell of Gauloises. We Vigneronists sat in great awe: Which of us would be called?

"Mrs. Cullen?" Vigneron said. The mother stood up nervously and cautioned her child to be good while she was gone.

Vigneron smiled at Tulpen. The untrustworthy French! "You waiting to see me?" he asked her. An outsider among these assembled Vigneronists, Tulpen stared back at him, unanswering.

"No, she's with me," I told Vigneron. He and Tulpen smiled.

When the doctor went off with Mrs. Cullen, Tulpen whispered, "I didn't think he'd look like that."

"Look like what?" I asked. "What should urologists look like? Bladders?"

"He doesn't look like a bladder," Tulpen answered, impressed.

The child sat there timidly listening to us. If her mother was the patient, I thought, why did the child look so swollen and yellow? I determined that her appearance was the result of not being allowed to pee. About Colm's age, I thought. She was worried about being alone, and restless too; she peeked at the nurse and watched the old man. She was getting upset, so I tried some reassuring conversation. "Do you go to school?"

But it was the stunning young girl in leather who looked up. Tulpen simply stared at me and the child ignored the question.

165

"No, I don't," said the surprised leather girl, with a look right through me.

"No, no," I said to her. "Not you." Now the child stared at me. "I mean *you*," I said to her, pointing. "Do you go to school?" The child was embarrassed and felt threatened; obviously she had been told never to talk to strangers. The young girl in leather regarded the child-molester icily.

"Your mother will be right back," Tulpen told the little girl.

"She's got blood in her pee," the child informed us. The nurse swiveled into view, with a quick look at me which said that my brain must be stuck shut too.

"Oh, your mother will be all right," I told the child. She nodded, bored.

The stunning young girl in leather looked at me as if clearly to inform me that she did not have blood in her pee, so don't ask. Tulpen stifled a giggle and pinched my thigh; I examined the roof of my mouth with my tongue.

Then the old man who had been so silent made a strange sound, like an oddly suppressed belch or a pinched fart or a massive, creaking shift of his whole spine, and when he tried to stand up, we saw a stain the color of burned butter spreading on the loose stomach of his shirt and making his pants cling tight to his skinny thighs. He lurched sideways, and I caught him just before he fell. He weighed nothing at all and was easy to hold upright, but there was an awful reek to him and he clutched at his belly; there was something under his shirt. He looked grateful, but terribly embarrassed, and all he could say was, "Please, the bathroom ..." flopping his bony wrist in the direction of Vigneron's inner office. Against the stain which his shirt soaked up like a blotter, I could see the outline of a curious little bag and a hose.

"The damn thing is always spilling," he told me as I steered him as fast as I could to the nurse, who was just swiveling out of her chair.

"Oh, Mr. Kroddy," she said scoldingly, plucking him out of my arms as if he were a hollow doll. She muscled him down the long hallway, waving me irritably back to the waiting room and continuing to reprimand him. "You simply have to empty it more often, Mr. Kroddy. There's just no need to have these little accidents . . ."

But he kept crooning over and over, "The damn thing, the goddamn thing! There's just never any place to go, people get so upset, in men's rooms you should see all the looks . . ."

"Can you unbutton your shirt by yourself, Mr. Kroddy?"

"The goddamn fucking thing!"

"This isn't at all necessary, Mr. Kroddy . . ."

In the waiting room, the child looked frightened again and the tight-assed, snotty girl in leather stared straight at her paper, smug, superior and harboring what awful secret between her legs. No one would know. I hated her.

I whispered to Tulpen, "The poor old guy was all *hoses*. He had to go into this little sack." That damned girl in leather looked coolly up at me, then down at her paper while we all listened to what sounded like the nurse flushing old Mr. Kroddy away.

I looked straight up at that aloof leather lady and asked her, "Do you have the clap?"

She didn't look up; she froze. But Tulpen gouged me hard with her elbow and the child looked up gratefully. "What?" she asked.

Then the young woman looked hard at me. But she couldn't hold her fierce expression; for the first time something human broke over her face—her lower lip curling under, her teeth trying to hold her lip still, her eyes suddenly aswim—and I just felt cruel and awful.

"You shit, Trumper," Tulpen whispered, and I went over to the girl, who now held her face down on her knees, rocking in her chair and crying softly.

"I'm sorry," I told her. "I don't know why, really, I said that . . . I mean, you seemed sort of insensitive . . ."

"Don't listen to him," Tulpen told the girl. "He's just crazy."

"I just can't believe I've got the clap," the girl said, sobbing. "I don't go doing it all around, you know, and I'm not dirty . . ."

Then Vigneron came back, returning the mother to her swollen child. He had a folder in his hand. "Miss De-

167

Carlo?" he asked, smiling. She stood up quickly, wiping her tears.

"I have the clap," she told him, and he stared at her. "Or maybe I *don't* have it," she added hysterically as Vigneron peered into her folder.

"Please, in my office," he said to her, guiding her quickly past us. Then he looked at me, as if somehow I'd given this girl her disease while she was in the waiting room. "You're next," he said, but I stopped him before he could move.

"I'll have the operation," I said, shocking both him and Tulpen. "I don't need to see you. I just want an appointment for the operation."

"But I haven't examined you."

"No need to," I said. "It's the same old thing. The water didn't help. I don't want to see you again except for the operation."

"Well," he said, and I was delighted to see that I'd ruined his perfect record—he wasn't ten for ten with *me*—"Ten days or two weeks," he said. "You'll probably want some antibiotic in the meantime, won't you?"

"I'll stick with the water."

"My nurse will call you when we've set a time at the hospital, but it will be at least ten days or two weeks, and if you're at all uncomfortable . . ."

"I won't be."

"You're sure?" Vigneron said; he tried to smile.

"Still ten out of ten?" I asked him, and he looked at Tulpen and blushed. *Vigneron blushed!*

Matter-of-factly I gave Vigneron's nurse the phone number for Ralph Packer Films, Inc., and the number at Tulpen's. Recovering, Vigneron handed me a packet of some capsules, but I shook my head.

"Please, no nonsense," He said. "It's better to operate when you're free from any infection. Take one of these a day, and I'll have to see you the day before we operate, just to check." Now he was being strictly businesslike. I took the capsules from him, nodding, smiling, waving over my shoulder, and walked Tulpen out of there. I think I must have swaggered.

And I didn't think, until I was out on the street, about whatever happened to old Mr. Kroddy. Was he having a hose replaced? I shivered, drew Tulpen up against my hip and jostled her along the sidewalk, warm and bouncy, her breath close enough to smell, sweet with candy mints, and her hair whipping my face.

"Don't worry," I said. "I'm going to have a fine new prick, just for you."

She slipped her hand in my pocket, rummaging through change and my Swiss Army knife. "Don't *you* worry, Trumper," she said. "I like the old prick you are."

So we abandoned work for the day and went back to her apartment, though we knew that Ralph expected us at the studio. It was always a touchy time for Ralph when he was dropping one project and picking up another; we noticed late salary checks and signs above the phone: FLEASE ENTER IN THE FUCKING BOOK (↓) YOUR LONG-DISTANCE CALLS!

Tulpen might have guessed that there was more involved in skipping work than my want of her. I didn't care for the subject of Ralph's new film, the subject being me. A tedious outline of interviews with Tulpen and me, and a little gem later in which Ralph planned to include Biggie.

"I must tell you, Ralph, that my enthusiasm for this project is not what it might be."

"Thump-Thump, do I have integrity or do I not?"

"It is your point of view which remains to be seen, Ralph."

For weeks we'd been handling some dull distribution for other film makers, and giving special showings of *Ralph Packer: Retrospective!* for film societies, student groups, museums and the Village matinées. It was better to be on a project again, even this project, and the only really nasty argument Ralph and I'd had so far was the title.

"It's just a working title, Thump-Thump. I often change the title when we're finished."

Somehow I doubted his flexibility about this one. He was calling the film *Fucking Up.* It was a common utterance of his, which made me suspect that he liked it far too well.

"Don't worry, Trumper," Tulpen told me, and in that long afternoon at her apartment I didn't. I changed the record stack; I made Austrian *Tee mit Rum,* swizzled with a cinammon stick and heated on a hot plate by the bed; I ignored the phone, which woke us once at dark. Vacuum-sealed from the city, we didn't know whether it was supper, a midnight snack or an early breakfast we were hungry for; in that kind of timeless dark which only city apartments can give you, the phone clamored on and on.

"Let it ring," Tulpen said, scissoring me fast around my waist. It occurred to me that this line should be a part of *Fucking Up,* but I let it ring.

18 : One Long Mother of a Day

It begins, actually, the night before, with an argument, wherein Biggie accuses Merrill Overturf of childish, escapist pranksterism and further claims that I have been able to heroize Merrill only because he has been missing from my life for so long—implying, harshly, that the real Merrill, in the flesh, would even put me off, at least at this moment in my life.

I find these accusations painful and counterattack by accusing Overturf of courage.

"Courage!" Biggie hoots.

She goes on to imply that I am no reliable authority on courage, having no courage myself—having cowardice to spare, in fact. The example given for my cowardice is that I am afraid to call my father and have it out with him about my disinheritance.

Which witlessly prompts me to bluster that I will phone the old prick, anytime—even now, though by the dark Iowa night around us, I vaguely suspect that it's a poor hour for a phone call.

"You will?" says Biggie. Her sudden respect is frightening. She gives me no time to change my mind; she's thumbing through papers, looking for the one on which we once wrote down the Great Boar's Head number.

"What will I say, though?" I ask.

She is starting to dial.

"How about, 'I called to ask you if your mail was being delivered.' "

Biggie frowns and dials on.

"How about, 'How are you? Is the tide in or out?' "

Grimacing over her fast fingerwork, Biggie says, "At

171

least we'll *know*, for God's sake ..." and hands me the ringing phone.

"Yes, at least we'll know, all right," I say into the mouthpiece and it echoes back as if it were being spoken to me by some operator of uncanny perception. The phone rings and rings, and I give Biggie what must be a relieved look: A-ha! He's not at home! But Biggie points at my wrist watch. Back East, it's after midnight! I feel my jaw slacken.

Biggie says sternly, "It'll serve the prick right."

Far from groggy, my father curtly answers the phone. Of course doctors are used to being called up in the middle of the night. "Dr. Trumper here," he says. "Edmund Trumper. What is it?"

Biggie is balancing on one leg as if she's got to pee. I can hear my watch tick, and then Daddy says, "Hello? This is Dr. Trumper. Is anything wrong?"

In the background, I hear my mother murmur, "The hospital, Edmund?"

"Hello!" my father shouts into the phone.

And my mother hisses, "You don't suppose it's Mr. Bingham? Oh, Edmund, you know his heart ..."

Still teetering on one foot, Biggie glares at me, appalled by the cowardice she sees in my face; she grunts fiercely at me.

"Mr. Bingham?" says my father. "Can't you get your breath again?"

Biggie stamps her foot, utters a small-animal cry.

My father advises, "Don't try to breathe too deeply, Mr. Bingham. Listen, you just hold on. I'm coming right over ..."

Scurrying in the background, my mother calls, "I'll get the hospital to send the oxygen, Edmund—"

"Mr. Bingham!" my father yells into the phone as Biggie kicks the stove, emitting a snarl from her curved mouth. "Bring your knees up to your chest, Mr. Bingham! Don't try to talk!"

I hang up.

Convulsed with something almost like laughter, Biggie lunges past me, into the hall, into the bedroom and slams the door. Her sucking sounds, her crazy lip noises sound

172

like choking, something like poor Mr. Bingham with his real and faltering heart.

Unnoticed by the night watchman, I spent the night in the Iowa Library Ph.D. thesis alcoves, in one of a long fourth-floor row of cubbies which are usually crammed with sweaty scholars, each with his Coke bottle. A dollop of Coke in each bottle, honey-thick, with several cigarette butts floating. You can hear them hiss when they're plunked in, several cubbies down from your own.

Once, his thesis near the finishing point, Harry Petz, a graduate student from Brooklyn, who was reading documents in Serbo-Croatian, heaved himself backward in his chair on casters and shot out of his cubby in reverse; peddling his feet faster and faster down the aisle, he whizzed past all of us, the entire length of the cubby row. He smashed against the fourth-floor thermopane at the end of the aisle, cracking both the glass and his head, but not careening four floors to the library parking lot below, where Harry Petz must have had visions of himself splattering on the hood of someone's car.

But I would never do such a thing, Biggie.

There is a touching scene in *Akthelt and Gunnel* when Akthelt is dressing and arming himself to go out and fight the ever-warring Greths. He is donning his shin pads and shoulder pads and kidney guards and tin cup, ritualistically shielding and spiking his vital parts, while poor Gunnel is wailing at him not to leave her; ritualistically, she is taking off her clothes, unbraiding her hair, unbuckling her anklets, unsheathing her wrists, unthonging her corset, while Akthelt goes on collaring his throat with chains, fastening his coccyx-spikes, etc. Akthelt is trying to explain to Gunnel the object of war (*det henskit af krig*), but she doesn't want to listen. Then Old Thak, Akthelt's father, bursts in on them. Old Thak has been arming and dressing himself for the war too, and his chest zipper, or something, is stuck and he needs help with it. Of course he is embarrassed to see his son's lovely young wife all distraught and half nude, but he remembers his own youth and realizes what Akthelt and Gunnel have been arguing about. So Old Thak attempts an ambiguous gesture; he wants to try to please them both. He gives sweet Gunnel a lusty goose

173

with his thorny old hand, at the same time saying wisely to Akthelt, *"Det henskit af krig er tu overleve"* ("The object of war is to survive it").

Which struck me as the object of graduate school—and possibly my marriage. Such comparisons struck me hard in those days.

Walking through the library parking lot in which Harry Petz tried to land, I spy young Lydia Kindle lurking for me near a sea-green and arklike Edsel. She wears a pear-colored suit, snug, short-skirted and rather grown-up.

"Hi! That's my Edsel there!" she says. And I think, This is much too much.

But there's a kind of safety at the midthigh of her skirt and I know her knees, so they don't frighten me. It's a relief to feel her leg rise and fall under my head, her foot busy at the brake and accelerator.

"Where are we going?" I ask in a doomed tone and turn a little in her lap, which there's so little of.

"I know," she says, and I look up her suit-front, past her slight breasts to her chin; I see her teeth gently holding her lower lip. At the throat of her suit, her blouse is a deep rust-yellow; it gives that tint to her jaw, like a buttercup. And I remember Biggie and me in a field below the monastery at Katzeldorf, with a bottle of the monks' wine in the buttercups. I held a handful of the flowers to her nipple; it turned her vivid orange and made her blush. Then she held a cluster under my own sunny part. I believe it turned me strictly yellow.

"Actually, this isn't my Edsel," says Lydia Kindle. "It's my brother's, but he's in the service."

New perils everywhere I turn. Lydia Kindle's strapping brother, a punchy Green Beret, coming after me with deft chops to the clavicle, his terrible vengeance brought down on me for defiling his sister and his Edsel.

"Where are we going?" I ask again, feeling her hard thighs bounce under my head on what must be a rough road. I see dust swirl by the windows; I see a flat sky not bent by a single tree, not laced with any powerlines.

"You'll see," she says, and her hand strays off the wheel to brush my cheek—with the faintest, most innocent perfume at her wrist.

174

Then into a low ditch and out again; I can tell that we've even left the dirt road because there's no dust at the windows and the car dips deeper on a softer surface; occasional snapping sounds, which in Iowa can only be corn stubble or hog bones. We're headed in a different direction too, because the sun warms my kneecaps from a new slant. Then there are some tire-slipping noises, like a squeegee on wet grass. I fear we'll be stuck miles from anywhere, that overnight we and the Edsel will settle forever in some soybean bog. "With only the ducks to cry over us," I say, and Lydia peers down at me, looking slightly alarmed.

"A fellow took me here once," she says. "Sometimes there's a hunter or two, but no one else. Anyway, you can always see the hunters' cars."

Some fellow? I think, wondering if she's already been defiled. But she guesses my thinking and says hurriedly, "I didn't like him. I made him bring me back. But I remember how we got here." And her tongue darts out a moment, to wet each corner of her mouth.

Then shade, and an incline; the ground is firmer and bumpier; I hear rustling under the Edsel and smell pine pitch—in Iowa, of all places! A branch lashes the car, which makes me jump and bump my nose on the steering wheel.

When Lydia stops, we're in a dense grove of new pine, old deadfall, flat-leafed fern and spongy, half-frozen hunks of moss. Mushrooms are about. "See?" she says, opening her door and sliding her legs out. Finding it wet and cold out there, she sits, her back to me, dallying her feet above the ground.

We're on a knoll, in a scruffy thatch of tree and shrub. Behind us are cut corn and soybean fields; in front and well below, what must be part of the Coralville Reservoir lies frozen at its fringes, open and choppy in the middle. If I were a hunter, I'd take my stand on this hill, deep in the ferns, and wait for the lazier ducks to fly this shortcut between one feeding ground and another. They'd come over low to the ground here, especially the fat, sluggish ones, their bellies bright with a glance of the sun off the lake.

But leaning against the Edsel's armrest, I extend my foot to the small of Lydia Kindle's back, and for just a moment feel like propelling her out her open door. But I just touch her spine, and she looks over her shoulder at me before she swings her legs inside and shuts the door.

There's a blanket in the car-boot, and an older-looking girl in her dorm has bought beer, she tells me. There's a nice cheese, too, and a warm, circle loaf of pumpernickel and apples.

Climbing over the front seat, she lays this picnic spread in back, and we hunch the blanket over our shoulders, tentlike and cozy. Under the blanket, a bit of cheese sticks to a tiny blue vein on Lydia's wrist. She snares it with her fast tongue, watching me watch her; her legs are crossed under her in such a way that her knees face me.

"Your elbow's in the bread," Lydia whispers, and I giggle witlessly.

She squirms her legs and shakes the blanket around us for crumbs; I watch the bread roll to the floor; I see her skirt lift to her hipbone as she pulls me further up in her lap. She has baby-pink and baby-blue flowers on her slip, flowers too reminiscent of one of Colm's early crib blankets. She says, "I think I love you." But I hear a measure to each word, so deliberate that I know she's practiced saying this. As if she too feels it didn't sound quite right, she amends it: "I think I know I love you." Pressing her fine, thin leg against my side, she shifts to one hip and gently tugs my head to her thigh. My heart hits her knee.

There are the same damn flowers on her panties, too. A baby in her bunting; such frilly, flowered things for Junior Misses.

She squirms again and gives a weak pull on my ears, aware that I've seen her flowers. "You don't have to be in love with me," she says, and again I hear the practiced measure. Somewhere, I know, in Lydia Kindle's dormitory room, there's a piece of notebook paper with this conversation written out like a script, scribbled on, revised, perhaps footnoted. I wish I knew what responses she has written for me.

"Mr. Trumper?" she says, and as I kiss her under her hem, I feel a tiny muscle slack. She tugs my head up to her bird's breast, her suit jacket open, her blouse a thin shiver over her cool skin.

176

"Vroognaven abthur, Gunnel mik," I recite. Old Low Norse is safest in such circumstances.

With the slightest shudder, she sits up against me, but even an ark like an Edsel is awkward, and there's much wriggling before she's free of her suit jacket. My hunting-coat snags on the rear-window handle; sitting back against her, bobsled style, I manage to unlace my cloddy boots while her hands braille-read my shirt buttons. Turning back to her, I find she's unbuttoned herself, but she is hunching on her knees, arms folded over her bra; she shivers as if she was undressing for some unsure dip in a winter river.

Almost relieved, she stalls against me, happy to be hugged still semiclothed, her skirt unzipped but only half down one hip. Her damp hands skitter across my ribs and pinch the unfortunate fold that curls slightly over my belt.

Lydia Kindle says, "I never have, you know . . . I have never . . ."

I drop my chin to her sharp, bony shoulder and brush her ear with my mustache. "What does your father do?" I ask, and feel her sigh, both let down and relieved.

"He's in burlap," she says, her fingers finding my kidneys. And I think, He's in burlap! All the time? Wrapped in it, dressed in it, sleeping in it . . .

"He can't be very comfortable," I say, but her hard collarbone is numbing my jaw.

Lydia says, "You know—feed bags, grain sacks . . ."

Imagining Lydia Kindle's huge father, hefting a hundred-pound burlap duffel of onions and swinging it against my spine, I wince.

Lydia straightens up on her knees, pulling away from me, her hands at her hips, working down her skirt; she has the smallest bulge of a tummy under her flowered slip. Seeing her hands so busy, I slip her bra straps off her shoulders. "I'm so small," she apologizes in a tiny voice as I drop my pants down to my ankles. Hoisting my feet over the front seat, my clumsy heels strike the horn; with all the windows closed, it sounds as if it's from another car, and Lydia suddenly crouches against me, allowing me to unhook her bra. The label reads: A YOUNG PRETTY-PIECE UNDERTHING. How true.

I feel her hard breasts pushed against me and I shrug

177

off my shirt, aware that the fly of my boxer shorts is gaping, and how she's staring down at me; she's rigid, but her hips help me get off her slip. There's a mole, and the brief V of flowers, baby-pink and baby-blue.

She says, "You've got such tiny nipples." Her fingers wonder over them.

I cup her small, round breasts—just oranges to the touch—with her nipples as hard as the knuckle that is digging into my leg. Slowly I lay her down, getting one glimpse of her body, taut and ribby, and one look at her up-poking breasts, a tint of powder in her narrow cleavage. Then she pulls my head down to the powder spot, but I feel my stomach tighten at the scent. It reminds me of Colm's baby shampoo; the label says: NO TEARS!

She says, "Please . . ."

Please what? I think, and hope she won't make this my decision. I have such trouble with decisions.

Kiss a soft, straight line down to her navel; see the marks her panties' waist band has grooved on the small swell of her belly. It bothers me that I can't remember when or how her panties came off. Was it her decision or mine? It strikes me as an important bit of forgetting. My rough chin rests on that fluffed fringe. When I move, when she first feels my kiss, she scissors my head hard and gives my hair two quick painful tugs. But then her thighs relax; I feel her hands slide off my head and cup my ears, so that I can hear the sea in stereo—or the Coralville Reservoir rising, making our odd hill an island; to maroon us under the dusk-flying ducks, over the dust-choked odor drawn up like groundfog from the soybean fields.

One of my ears is released; the sea rings one-sided, monaural. I catch a flash of Lydia's free hand swooping along the floor and fumbling in her pear-colored suit jacket. What is in the sleeve? She says, "There's a rubber. A girl in my dorm . . . had one."

But I can't fit my hand up her jacket cuff, and she's obliged to shake her suit, saying, "There's a secret pocket in the lining of the wrist . . ." What for?

Her breasts are parted: I see her lip held in her teeth; I see her ribcage quickly lift, hold itself up and slide the tinfoil-wrapped rubber down her belly to my forehead; then her ribs fall, and the queer, small swell to her belly quivers; her hips shake. Out the corner of my eye I see her arm swinging free, her wrist slack; wadded in her palm, like a sponge ball, is what must be the heart of the pumpernickel, torn from the center of the fresh loaf. Her thighs tense and slap my face hard, then fall flush to the seat, and the hand that holds the bread-heart lets the dark wad fall.

I hear the tinfoil tear and crinkle; I wonder if she hears it too. I lay my head on her breasts and hear the flutter-step of her heart. Her elbow is propped on the seat, her forearm dangled over the floor. Her wrist is so sharply bent that it looks broken; her long fingers point down, unmoving, and the cloudy sun through the window is just strong enough to glint off her high school ring; it is too big for her finger and has slipped askew.

I shut my eyes in her powdered cleavage, noting a sort of candy musk. But why does my mind run to slaughter-houses, and to all the young girls raped in wars?

Her thighs close gently on my shielded part, and she asks, "Aren't you going to do the *other?*"

And my frail part shrinks in its thin, pinching skin; it recedes when Lydia Kindle flexes her thighs.

Again she says, "Please . . ." And in a very small voice, "What's wrong?"

Slowly I raise myself off her, kneeling between her legs; I feel her fingers stronger on my shoulders; there's a blue, thread-thin vein that's pulsing in her cleavage, a diagonal between her far-parted breasts. As if she's conscious of her heartbeat showing, she drops one arm across herself, and with the other hand hides her crotch. A YOUNG PRETTY PIECE! saved, for a while. And for whom?

I feel the rubber roll up. While Lydia Kindle, swinging her legs off the seat, says, "I never even asked you to be in love with me or anything. I mean, I've never done this before, or that *other,* and it just didn't even matter what you really thought of me—I mean, to me. Don't you even know that? Oh, my God . . . Shit, and I thought *I* was pretty naïve . . ."

As if she's got the cramps, she bends over, her face on one knee, a lash of hair in the corner of her mouth, and in that familiar angle between her elbow and her knee, the breast nearest me is simply too small and perfect to swing; it points like a thing painted on her, too perfect to be real.

"It's complicated," I try to tell her. "No one should ever leave things up to me."

I fumble with the latch and open my door for the cold, reviving pain of the air. Standing cold and naked in the wet, crunchy moss, I hear Lydia rummaging through the car. Turning, I duck my boots; she's on all fours in the back seat, shoveling my things out the door. Wordless, I gather each article as it falls and make a ball of my stuff and clutch it to my chest. Brainless, Lydia Kindle tosses her own clothes from the back seat to the front seat, and from the front seat to the back seat, and then from the back seat to the front seat . . .

I say, "Let me drive you home, please."

"*Please?*" she shrieks, and over the knoll, like stones thrown over my head, a low rush of ducks wings by, black in the dusk; startled, they veer off, honking to see this naked fool with his clothes held over his head.

Now watch Lydia, dashing nude around the inside of the Edsel. She is locking all the doors. Still nude, she slips behind the steering wheel, her fine nipples brushing the cold ring of the horn. The Edsel convulses, belches and blurts a thick gray wad of exhaust out its rusted pipe. For a second, though I make no effort to move, I believe Lydia is going to run over me, but she surges in reverse. Jacking the wheel, she spins herself back into the tire ruts that mark our coming here. Wrenching the hard-to-turn Edsel, her breasts at last move like live things. I fear for her nipples on the horn ring.

It's not until I watch her Edsel rocketing over the soybean bog that I realize my predicament. *He died of exposure on the duck-flown shores of the Coralville Reservoir!*

So I began to slog through the soybeans, keeping my jogging eyes on the spattered Edsel, churning through the far field of corn stubble. I could barely make out the pale line of the road by which we must have come. Running nude and slippery through this swampland, I gambled that if I cut along the shore line of the reservoir, I might intersect the road ahead of her and be able to flag her down.

By then, she might be in more of a mood to be flagged down. Flag her down with what? I wondered. With my strangely-clad part?

My clothes bundle high and dry in my armpit, I dug through the painful saw grass and spongy muck along the thin-iced edge of the reservoir. A black burst of coots took flight in front of me; once or twice I sank to my knees, feeling terrible oozy and decaying things in the bog slime. But always I kept my clothes bundle high and dry.

Then I was into some uncut corn, bent broken stalks, the running painful on the crinkling cornhusks underfoot, as dry and sharp and brittle as thin pottery. There was a slight pond between me and the flat line of the road; it was not so firmly frozen as it looked, and I crashed waist-deep striking a downed fence underwater, the fenceposts just visible at either side of the pond, with the barbwire slanting under. But I was too numb to feel any of the cuts.

By now I could foresee our lucky collision. Lydia's sea-green Edsel had a dust tail like a kite trying to leave the ground. Reaching the ditch of the road just ahead of her, I was too exhausted to wave; I simply stood there, my bundle of clothes casually under one arm, and watched her roar by, her breasts as straight in front of her as headlights. She didn't even turn her head, and her brake lights never flickered. Stupefied, I jogged a little in her dusty wake—so thick a dust that I stumbled off the road's crown and had to grope my choked way along.

I was still trotting as her Edsel increased the distance between us, when I saw, so close I almost ran into it, a shabby-red pickup truck parked along the side of the road. I sagged against the truck's door handle, seeing that I wasn't more than six feet from a hunter busy cleaning a duck on the pickup's hood. He had the floppy neck of the bird draped over the arm of the side-view mirror, while blood and clotted parts spilled to the road, and down feathers stuck to his gutting knife and thick thumb.

When he saw me, he almost cut his wrist off, with a sudden wrench that squeegeed the duck over the hood and skidded it wetly down the fender away from him, and he cried out, "Holy shit, Harry . . ."

I panted. "No," I gasped, convinced that I wasn't a

Harry yet, not seeing the man in the driver's seat of the truck; his elbow wasn't more than a few inches from my ear.

"Holy shit, Eddy ..." the driver answered, so close to me that I jumped.

I took a minute more of panting to compose myself, then asked casually, "Are you going to Iowa City?"

They gaped at me for a long time, but I was too proud and too weary to unwrap my bundle and dress myself.

Then Harry said, "God, are *you* going to Iowa City?"

"They won't let you into Iowa City like that," said Eddy, still holding the gory duck.

Dressing in the road beside their truck, I noticed that my condom was still attached. But if I'd removed it, it would have been too much like admitting to these hunters that I really did wear such a thing. I dressed right over it, simply ignoring it.

Then we all got in the truck, amid much changing of seats and bickering about who'd drive. Eddy finally took the wheel and said, "Jesus. We saw your little friend go by."

"If she *was* your friend ..." Harry said to me. But wedged in between them, I didn't answer. I could feel my feet warming and bleeding in my boots beside the bloody ducks.

Cautious Harry kept the guns between the door and his knee, putting them far from my reach, understandably not trusting a run-around nudist and madman.

"Jesus," said Eddy, as if still trying to convince himself. "She was just batting like hell down that old road ..."

"She almost swiped you," said Harry.

"Well, Christ, I was staring so hard," Eddy told him, leaning across my lap, "I almost forgot to get out of her way." He paused, then added, "Holy shit, she had such a nice little pair on her, setting right up there, behind the wheel. It was almost like she was *driving* with them ..."

"Well, God, I was up here in the cab," Harry said. "I could see her whole *thing*. Shit! I was looking right down in her lap!" He paused, then added, "... such a nice little bush ..."

Envious Eddy said defensively, "Well, I saw her pair, anyway. I got a good look."

I almost entered the conversation then; I wanted to say, "I got a pretty good look myself." But I looked down at the floor at a duck's slack neck and upturned, downy belly; the feathers near the neat slit, the careful gash, were soaked with the blood.

Then, loud beside me Eddy said, "Sweet Jesus, here she is again!" All of us stared at the sea-green Edsel parked at the side of the road ahead.

"Slow down, " Harry said, but I thought, Please don't slow down too much.

Slowly we cruised past her, three gawking faces turning to look her over. Harry and I turned around and watched the Edsel shrink behind us while Eddy used the mirror, swearing softly, "Shit shit shit, oh shit . . ."

"Oh, shit," echoed Harry.

But I was relieved to see Lydia Kindle dressing behind the wheel, applying the finishing touches, buttoning up under our gapes; it showed me she was somewhat sane again.

And how sane she looked! There was such a cold, unrecognizing look in her face—unsurprised to see me in the truck, or not even noticing; or poised enough, in an awful adult way, to pretend, with frightening composure, not to notice any of us.

The violation was complete; Lydia Kindle was defiled more perfectly than any pervert could have planned it.

I shifted my throbbing feet, Eddy farted and Harry answered him. Inches from my boot, the viscous eye of the duck was drying up, the shine dulled.

"Jesus," I said.

"Yeah, shit," said Eddy.

"Yeah, Jesus," Harry said.

Grief shared; we were a threesome of disappointment.

On Interstate 80, the sea-green Edsel hurtled past us. Eddy honked his horn and Harry cried, "Go, you little honey!"

And I thought: Lydia Kindle will probably transfer to another section of freshman German language lab.

Eddy took the Clinton Street exit, bringing us in by City Park. As we crossed the river, Harry began to pluck a duck, savagely seizing great clumps of down in his fist and stuffing the feathers out the side-vent window. But half the feathers blew back inside, and his sloppy speed tore the duck's oily skin. Harry didn't seem to mind; fiercely intent, he ravaged on. A feather stuck to Eddy's lip; he spat and rolled down his window, creating a cross gale. Suddenly the cab was awhirl with feathers. Harry hooted and threw a handful of them at Eddy, who swerved onto the shoulder of the road and swiped at mad Harry's throttled bird, reaching across my lap and clucking like a loon.

Along the riverbank, several cold strollers watched with alarm the giddy flight of this enormous leaking pillow careening into town.

When we had passed the park, all the streetlights came on and Eddy slowed down, gazing at the row of lamps lit all the way up Clinton Street as if he'd witnessed a miracle. "Did you see?" he asked, like a child.

Embedded in his duck Harry hadn't seen anything, but I told Eddy, "Yes, they all came on at once."

Turning to look at me, Eddy choked, opening his mouth, gagging and shouting, "You've got feathers in your mustache!" Reaching across and grabbing Harry's knee, he shrieked, "Christ, would you look at his mustache!"

The duck a near-pulp in his lap, Harry stared at me with hostility before seeming to remember who I was and how I'd got there. Not giving him time to respond with what I feared might be a pawful of feathers crammed down my throat, I turned back to Eddy, and in a small voice, very faint, asked, "Would you mind letting me out here? This is fine."

Eddy slammed on the brakes with a great grinching noise and a jolt that lurched busy Harry headfirst into the dash. "Christ!" he shouted, holding the duck like a bandage against his forehead.

"Thank you very much," I said to Eddy, and waited for Harry to slide out of the seat. Sliding after him, I caught a brief vision of my feathered mustache in the rear-view mirror.

Standing on the running board, Harry offered me the duck. "Go on, take it," he begged. "We got a shitload."

"Christ, yes," Eddy said. "And better luck next time."

"Yeah, fella," Harry said.

"Thank you very much," I said, and not knowing exactly where to hold the sorry duck, I gingerly took it by its rubbery neck. Harry had plucked it quite cleanly, though it seemed to be internally crushed. Only the wing tips and head were still feathered: a lovely wood duck with a multicolored face. There weren't more than three or four pellet wounds in it; the ugliest wound was the naked slit where it had been dressed out. His great feet felt like armchair leather. And there was a dried, see-through bead of blood, like a small dull marble, on the tip of his beak.

On the curb, along the riverbank sidewalk, I waved to those generous hunters. And heard, just before the slamming of the door, Harry saying, "Jesus, Eddy, did you smell the cunt on him?"

"Shit, yes," said Eddy.

Then the door slammed, and I was stung with sand spray from the pickup's whining tires.

All down Clinton Street, the dust of their leaving rises and billows under the hoods of the streetlights, while across the river, on the bank that looks like an Army barracks—stacked with the war-built Quonset huts, now called Married Student Housing—two neighborly wives snap their sheets off a shared clothesline.

Slowly, I get my bearings and decide which way home lies. But when I take my first step I totter off the sidewalk and howl. It's my feet; they've thawed. Now I can feel each gash from the underwater barbwire, each shard of corn stubble in my soles. Trying to stand, I feel a pellet-like object under the arch of my right foot; I suspect that it's one of my severed toes, rolling loose in my blood-warm boot. I scream again, provoking mute stares from the two women across the river.

More people scuttle from the Quonset huts, like bomb survivors; student fathers with books in hand or children riding on their wife-sized hips. Someone from this tribe yells over to me, "What the hell's the matta, fella?"

But I can think of nothing that would pinpoint it. Let them guess: A man who's been ravaged by the ravaged duck he holds?

"What are you screaming for?" cries one Mrs. Sheet,

185

veering about on the riverbank like a ship tipped by her sail.

I search their gathering for the most likely Samaritan. Scanning beyond them, I spot a friend weaving between the Quonset huts on his racing bicycle: Ralph Packer, frequent, illicit visitor to these depressed areas of Married Student Housing. Smooth-pedaling Ralph on his racer, stealthily gliding among the harried wives.

"Ralph!" I hoot, and see his front wheel wobble, watch him flatten himself over the handlebars and dig for cover, darting out of sight behind a hut. I shriek, "Ralph *Paaack*-er!" The racer is propelled like a shot; Ralph runs a slalom course between the clothesline posts. But this time, he looks across the river, trying to identify his would-be assailant; no doubt, he is forever imagining student husbands with dueling pistols. But he sees me! Why, it's just Bogus Trumper, out walking his duck.

Ralph weaves among the onlookers, haughtily pedaling down to the shore. "Hello!" he calls. "What are you doing?"

"The most awful screaming," says the woman under sail.

"Thump-Thump?" Ralph calls.

But all I can say is "Ralph!" I detect a witless sort of ecstasy in my voice.

Ralph balances, back-pedals, then lunges forward, raising his front wheel off the bank and slithering ahead. "Up, Fang!" he commands. If there's a man who can leave rubber smoldering with a bicycle, it's philandering Ralph Packer.

The bridge rails cut him up and paste him together, a collage of feet and spokes crossing the river to me. Oh, help is here. I put my weight on one knee and gently wobble to my feet, but I don't dare take a step. I hold my duck up.

Staring at the plucked bird and at my feathered mustache, Ralph says, "Jesus, was it a fair fight? From here, it looks like a draw."

"Ralph, help," I say. "It's my feet."

"Your *feet?*" he says, and rests the racer against the curb. As he tries to steady me someone over the river starts hollering, "What's the matta with him?"

186

"It's his *feet!*" Ralph shouts, and the crowd stands under the clotheslines, troubled and murmuring.

"Easy, Ralph," I tell him, tottering to his bike.

"This is a very light bicycle," he tells me. "Be careful you don't bend the crossbar."

I don't see exactly how I can avoid bending it, should it decide to bend, but I perch as weightlessly as possible under the sloped-back handlebars and wedged between Ralph's knees.

"What do you mean, your feet?" he says, wobbling us down Clinton Street. Some of the married students wave.

"I stepped on lots of stuff," I say vaguely.

Ralph warns me not to dangle my duck so far over the handlebars. "That bird could snag in my spokes. Thump-Thump . . ."

"Don't take me home," I say, thinking that I should clean myself up a bit.

"Benny's?" says Ralph. "I'll buy you a beer."

"I can't wash my feet at Benny's, Ralph."

"Well, that's true."

Unsteadily, we arrive downtown. It is still light but growing darker; Saturday night begins early here because it's over so soon.

Shifting my weight on the crossbar, I feel my forgotten condom crinkle. Attempting to adjust myself, I neatly insert my toe between the chain guard and the rear wheel; the pain makes the sky pitch. Lying toppled on the pavement in front of Grafton's Barber Shop, Ralph makes a loud vowel sound. Several sheeted men raise their shaved skulls above the backs of their barber chairs, watching me writhe on the sidewalk as if they were owls—and me, a club-footed mouse.

Ralph released unspeakable pressure by removing my boots, then whistles at the multitude of flaklike wounds, boil-sized swellings and punctures caked with mud. He takes charge. Back on the bicycle, he holds my boots, laced together, in his teeth, while I balance myself and the duck on the crossbar, fearful of my bare feet in the terrifying spokes.

"I can't go home like this, Ralph," I plead.

"What if that duck has friends?" he asks, my laces slipping through his teeth, causing him to lunge with his

187

mouth as if he meant to eat the boots. "What if that duck's friends are looking for you?" he grunts, turning up Iowa Avenue.

"Please, Ralph."

But he says, "I have never imagined feet like yours before. I'm taking you home, baby." Our timing is perfect. My rotten car is smoking by the curb; Biggie is just back from shopping, and the car is trying to breathe again, throbbing and overheated from its mile-long journey at twenty miles an hour.

"Slip me into the basement, Ralph," I whisper. "There's an old sink in there. At least I can wash my face . . ." I am remembering the scent which the hunters found so gloriously a part of me. And the feathers in my mustache? There's no need for Biggie to think that I plucked this duck with my mouth.

We totter over the side lawn past my retired neighbor, Mr. Fitch, still raking so that the snow will have clean, dead grass to fall on. I wave the duck at him unthinkingly, and the old codger says brightly, "Ho! I used to do some hunting myself, but I don't get around like I used to . . ." He stands like some brittle ice carving, propped on his rake, not at all puzzled by the absence of a gun. In his day they probably used spears.

Ralph scoops me off by the cellar-door, and though it's quite clear to Mr. Fitch that I'm in no condition to walk on my own, he doesn't seem troubled; in his day, no doubt, casualties were to be expected on a rugged duck hunt.

I am carried into the cellar like a bag of coal, wearing my boots like a yoke on my shoulders, and finding the cool slime of the cellar floor most soothing to my feet. Ralph's ursine head looms through the opening. "All right, Thump-Thump?" he asks, and I nod. As he closes the flaps quietly, he slips in some last words. "Thump-Thump, I trust some day you'll tell me about this . . ."

"Sure, Ralph."

Then I hear Biggie's voice from the kitchen window. She says, "Ralph?" and I creep deeper into the cellar.

"Hi, Big!" says Ralph cheerfully.

"What are you doing?" There is cold suspicion in her voice. That's my good Biggie, never fraternizing with the

188

likes of lecherous Ralph Packer. Though it's a foolish moment for it, I feel proud of her.

"Um," says Ralph.

"What are you doing in our cellar?" Biggie asks.

"Well, I wasn't exactly *in* your cellar, Biggie."

I grope blindly toward where I think the cellar sink is, knowing there's little time before I'm discovered, making up whole novels in my mind.

"Playing a game, Ralph?" says Biggie, more playfully than I like. I can't help thinking, Don't let up on him, Big. Be merciless.

Ralph laughs unconvincingly just as I step directly on the trap that's always laid for Risky Mouse, the fierce wombat trap, the crusher of small spines. I think it sprung directly on one of those boil-like wounds the barbwire made, because the whole cellar seemed to light up and I could see everything around me for a moment, just as if the light switch by the stairs had gone on. I couldn't stop the scream, because I didn't realize what I'd stepped on until it was at a crescendo. Its forceful volume must have shattered poor Fitch into thousands of tiny ice cubes beside his rake.

"What was that?" Biggie shouted.

Ralph, the coward, surrendered instantly. "Thump-Thump. He's in the basement . . ." He added gratuitously, "It's his feet," as through the cellar window I saw him sprint across the lawn to his getaway bike.

Mr. Finch, in a voice miles away, said, "Good hunting!"

To Fitch, Biggie said, *"What?"*

"Good hunting!" Fitch repeated, while I wore the mousetrap like a shoe to the sink, opened the rusty faucet and frantically sloshed my face in the dark.

"Bogus?" Biggie called; she thumped on the kitchen floor above me.

"Hi! It's just me!" I yelled up to her.

Then the real light came on, and I could see Biggie's lower half at the top of the stairs; I could also see well enough to remove the mousetrap.

"Bogus? What's going on?"

"Stepped in the damn mousetrap," I muttered.

Biggie sat down at the top of the stairs, allowing me to

look up her skirt. She said, "But what were you doing down here, anyway?"

I had already surmised that it was going to get complicated. The answer prepared, I said, "I didn't want to frighten you with my feet. Thought I'd clean myself up a bit . . ."

She leaned forward, confused, and stared at me. From the bottom step, I tilted the sole of one foot up at her; a dramatic gesture; she squeaked. Then I held up the duck.

"See the duck, Big?" I said proudly. "I've been hunting, but it's hell on the feet."

Well, that threw her off—that, and the artful way I propelled myself up the stairs on my knees. In the hall, still kneeling, I handed her the duck, which she promptly dropped.

"Bringing home the dinner," I said winningly.

"It looks like someone's already eaten it."

"Well, we've got to wash it, Big. Clean it up a bit, then roast it in wine."

"Give it brandy," Biggie said. "Perhaps we can revive it."

Then Colm toddled down the hall and sat next to this oddly feathered surprise. *May he remember me as the father with fancy presents of all kinds.*

Colm protested when Biggie slung him over her hip and helped me down the hall to the bathroom.

"Easy, oh easy, my feet," I murmured.

Biggie examined me all over, searching for some specific explanation. In my ear? Under my mustache?

"You went hunting?" she began again.

"Yes . . . You know, I've never been interested in hunting before . . ."

"That's what I thought," she said, nodding. "But you went hunting and you shot a duck?"

"No, I don't have a gun, Big."

"That's what I thought," she said, pleased enough so far. "So someone else shot this duck and gave it to you?"

"Right!" I said. "But it was hell on the feet, Big. I was retrieving them in the marshes. Didn't want to get my boots wet, but I didn't know there'd be so much stuff on the bottom."

"What are boots for?" said Biggie as she started to

draw a bath for me. I sat on the toilet, and remembered that I had to go. "Your pants didn't get wet, either," she remarked.

"Well, I took them off too. There were just those guys there, and I couldn't see getting all messed up."

Testing the water, Biggie pondered this. Colm crept to the bathroom door and peered down the length of the hall at the peculiar bird.

Then I had my fly open, and my feet painfully spread to straddle the hopper. I fumbled myself out and commenced to pee, while Biggie stared grimly at my pecker and watched me fill up the condom. Until the pressure and lack of noise was suddenly, awfully apparent to me, and I gazed down to see my growing balloon.

"And just who went on this little hunting party, Bogus?" Biggie yelled. "You and Ralph Packer and a pair he picked up?"

"Scissors!" I screamed. "For God's sake, Big. Please. this could make an awful mess . . ."

"You shit!" she screamed, and Colm fled down the hall to his friend the peaceful duck.

I feared Biggie would start stomping on my bleeding feet—as soon as she was logical again—so I struggled out of the bathroom, first on my heels, then more comfortably banging along on my knees, cradling the bulbous rubber in one hand. Colm clutched the duck, determined not to let his charging father take it away.

As I was only a few feet from the kitchen door, mid-hall, someone knocked on the front door at the hall's end and called, "Special Delivery! Special Handling!"

"Come in!" Biggie screamed from the bathroom.

The mailman entered, waving a letter. It happened so suddenly that he startled Colm, who shrieked back down the hall, dragging the duck after him. I waddled three more painful knee steps to the kitchen door, still clutching my balloon, and rolled out of sight into the kitchen.

"Special Delivery! Special Handling!" the mailman announced again flatly—not having been forewarned of the possibility that he might ever be in need of a more appropriate remark.

I peeked out of the kitchen. Obviously the mailman was pretending to be totally blind. Biggie, now at the end of the hall, appeared to have forgotten that she'd told anyone to enter, and was glowering at the mailman; in her mind, he was in some way connected with my hunting trip.

Bless his poor brains, the mailman shouted once more, "Special Delivery! Special Handling!" then dropped the letter in the hall and ran.

Skidding the duck along in front of him, Colm edged toward the letter. Another surprise! And Biggie, thinking that I too might have escaped, hollered, "Bogus!"

"Here, Big," I said, ducking back into the kitchen. "Oh, please just tell me where the scissors are."

"On a hook under the sink," she said mechanically, then added, "I hope you cut the whole thing off."

But I didn't. As I snipped in terror over the sink, I saw Colm crawl past the door, shoveling the duck and the letter down the hall.

"There's a letter, Big," I said weakly.

"Special Delivery, Special Handling," Biggie mumbled, the dullness heavy in her voice.

I flooded the nasty thing down the drain. In the hall Colm squawked as Biggie took his duck, or the letter. I looked at the bruised toes on one foot and thought, At least it wasn't your neck, Risky Mouse. Now Colm was garbling affectionately, talking to what must have been the duck. I heard Biggie ripping the letter. Without the slightest change in her flat voice, she said, "It's from your father, the prick . . ."

Oh, where have you gone, Harry Petz? After your splendid attempt, do they keep you in a nailed-down chair? Would you mind, Harry, if I borrowed your track-tested racing seat? Would you think me plagiaristic if I took a turn on your well-oiled casters and had a go at that fourth-floor window and that parking lot below?

19 : Axelrulf Among the Greths

There is a moment in *Akthelt and Gunnel* when the subtle depths of a mother's priorities are probed. Akthelt wishes to take his young son Axelrulf along with him on his newest campaign against the warring Greths. The lad is only six at the time, and Gunnel is distraught that her husband could conceive of such heartlessness. *"Da blott pattebarn!"* she exclaims. "The mere baby!"

Patiently Akthelt asks her what, precisely, she is afraid of. That Axelrulf will be slain by the Greths? If so, she should remember that the Greths always lose. Or is it that the talk and habits of the soldiers are too coarse for the boy? Because she should at least respect her husband's taste; the boy will be well protected from such excesses. *"Dar ok ikke tu frygte!"* ("There is nothing to fear!"), Akthelt insists.

Shyly, Gunnel confesses what she fears. "Among the Greths," she tells him, not looking him in the eye, "you will take a woman."

This is true; Akthelt always takes a woman when he is off warring. But he still doesn't see what the matter is. *"Nettopp ub utuktig kvinna!"* he shouts. *"Nettopp tu utukt . . . sla nek ub moder zu slim."* ("Just a fucking woman. Just to fuck . . . she won't be a mother to him").

The distinction is lost on Gunnel. She fears that young Axelrulf will associate the role of the Greth fucking-woman with his own mother's role—that Gunnel herself will be debased in her son's eyes, by association. With fucking.

"Utukt vinnas!" ("Fuck women!"), Akthelt tells his old father Thak.

193

"Utukt kvinnas urt moders!" ("Fuck women *and* mothers!"), bellows old Thak.

But that's not the point. The point is that Akthelt left Axelrulf at home with his mother; he did it Gunnel's way, after all.

Hence, though not necessarily sympathetic to the Mother & Fucking Theory of the Greth Women, Bogus Trumper at least had some background reading to prepare him for Biggie's feelings about Colm—specifically, Biggie's feelings about Colm and that Greth whore, Tulpen.

Since it was difficult for Trumper to leave New York, and since visits to Biggie and Colm made everyone uncomfortable, especially Bogus, Biggie did allow Colm to make a rare trip to New York—on one condition: "That girl you live with—Bull Pen, is that her name?—in that apartment you're going to keep Colm in—well, I mean it, Bogus, I don't think you should be too familiar with her around him. After all, he remembers when you used to sleep with *me* . . ."

"Jesus, Big," Trumper told the phone, "he remembers when *I* used to sleep with you too, so what about Couth, Big? What about *him?*"

"I don't have to send Colm to New York, you know," Biggie said. "Please just understand what I mean. He lives with me, you know."

Trumper knew that.

The arrangements had been exhausting. The fretful synchronizing of watches; the repetition of the flight number; the willingness of the airline to allow an unescorted five-year-old on board (Biggie had to lie and say he was six) provided his pickup at the destination was certain, provided it was not an over-crowded flight, provided he was a calm child, not easily given to panic at twenty thousand feet. And did he get motion sickness?

Trumper stood nervously with Tulpen on the greasy observation deck at La Guardia. It was early spring weather—nice weather, really, and probably a nice day up where Colm was, twenty thousand feet above Manhattan. The air at La Guardia, however, was like a giant bottled fart.

"The poor kid is probably terrified," Trumper said. "All alone in an airplane, going around and around New York. He's never even been in a city before. Christ, he's never even been in an airplane before."

But Trumper was wrong. When Biggie and Colm left Iowa, they had flown away, and Colm had loved every minute of it.

However, airplanes did not agree with Trumper. "Look at them circling up there," he said to Tulpen. "Must be fifty of the fuckers stacked up and waiting for a free spot to land."

Though such stackups are imaginable, and even probable, there were none on this day; Trumper was watching a squadron of Navy jets.

Colm's plane landed ten minutes early. Fortunately Tulpen saw it come in while Trumper was still raving about the Navy jets; she also caught the number of the arrival gate over the loudspeaker.

Trumper was already mourning Colm as if the plane had crashed. "I should never have let him fly," he cried. "I should have borrowed a car and picked him up right at his back door!"

Leading the still-ranting Trumper off the observation deck, Tulpen got him to the gate in time. "I'll never forgive myself," he was babbling. "It was just pure selfishness. I didn't want to have to drive all that distance. And I didn't want to have to see Biggie, either."

Tulpen glanced through the gate at the passengers. There was only one child, and he held a stewardess by the hand. The top of his head came to her waist, and he was coolly sorting out the crowd; it looked as if the stewardess was holding his hand because she simply wanted to, or needed to; he simply tolerated her. He was a handsome boy, with lovely skin like his mother's but dark, blunt features like his father's. He wore a pair of lederhosen knickers, a rough pair of hiking boots and a fine tyrolean wool jacket over a new white shirt. The stewardess held a rucksack in her hand.

"Trumper?" Tulpen said, pointing out the boy. But Trumper was looking the wrong way. Then the boy spotted Bogus, dropped the stewardess's hand, asked for his rucksack and pointed out his father, who now was doing a mad pirouette, looking everywhere but the right place. Tulpen had to forcefully aim him in Colm's direction.

"Colm!" Bogus cried. After he had swooped down on the boy and picked him up, he realized that Colm had grown up a little and no longer liked being picked up, at least not in public. Of all things, Colm wanted to shake hands.

Trumper dropped him and shook hands. "Wow!" Trumper said, grinning like a fool.

"I got to ride with the pilot," Colm said.

"Wow," said Bogus, in a kind of hush. He was looking at Colm's Austrian costume, thinking of Biggie getting Colm all fancied up for the trip, dressing the poor kid like a showpiece for an Austrian travel agency. Bogus had forgotten that he had bought the whole outfit for Colm, including the rucksack.

"Mr. Trumper?" the stewardess asked him, being dutifully careful. "Is this your father?" she asked Colm. Bogus held his breath, wondering if Colm would admit it.

"Yup," said Colm.

"Yup, yup, yup," said Trumper all the way out of the terminal. Tulpen carried Colm's rucksack and watched the two of them, struck by Colm's inheritance of Bogus's peculiar way of ambling.

Bogus asked Colm what was in the pilot's cockpit.

"There was a lot of electricity," Colm told him.

In the taxi, Bogus bubbled about the number of cars. Had Colm ever seen so many? Had he ever smelled air this bad? Tulpen held the child's rucksack in her lap and bit her lip. She was about to cry; Bogus hadn't even introduced her to Colm.

That awkwardness took place at Tulpen's apartment. Colm was fascinated by the fish and turtles. What were their names? Who had found them? Then Bogus remembered Tulpen, and remembered, too, that she'd been just as nervous about Colm coming as he had. She wanted to know, What did five-year-olds eat, what did they like to do, how big were they, when did they go to sleep? Suddenly Bogus realized how important he was to her, and it chilled him. Almost as fiercely as he wanted Colm to like him she wanted Colm to like her.

"I'm sorry, I'm sorry," he whispered to her in the

196

kitchen. She was preparing a snack for the turtles so that Colm could feed them.

"It's all right, it's all right," she said. "He's a beautiful child, Trumper. Isn't he beautiful?"

"Yes," Bogus whispered, and went back to watch Colm with the turtles.

"These live in fresh water, right?" said Colm.

Trumper didn't know.

"Right," said Tulpen. "Do you ever see any turtles in the ocean?"

"Yes, I have one," Colm said. "Couth caught him, a *big* one." He spread his arms—too wide, Trumper thought, for any turtle Couth could have caught around George-town, but a fair exaggeration for Colm. "We have to change his water every day. Sea water; that's salt water. He'd die in here," he said, peering into one of Tulpen's elaborate tanks. "And these turtles," he said, his voice bright with discovery, "they'd die in my tank at home, right?"

"Right," Tulpen said.

Colm turned his attention to the fish. "I had some min-nows, but they all died. I don't have any fish." He watched their bright colors intently.

"Well," Tulpen told him, "you pick out your favorite one there, and when you go home you can take it with you. I've got a little bowl a fish can travel in."

"Really?"

"Sure," Tulpen said. "They eat special food, and I'll give you some of that too, and when you get it home, you'll have to get a tank for it, with a little hose thing which puts air in the water—" She was showing him the fixture, on one of her aquariums, when he cut her off.

"Couth can make one," Colm said. "He made one like that for my turtle."

"Well, good," Tulpen said. She watched Trumper slip off to the bathroom. "Then you'll have a fish to go with your turtle."

"Right," said Colm, nodding eagerly and smiling at her. "But not in the same water, right? The fish has to have fresh water, not salt water, right?" He was a very exact little boy.

"Right," Tulpen told him. She listened to Bogus, in the bathroom, flushing himself away.

They went to the Bronx Zoo: Colm and Bogus, Tulpen, Ralph Packer and Kent, along with about two thousand dollars' worth of movie equipment. Packer shot Bogus and Colm riding the subway out to the Bronx during that long ugly stretch when it is above ground.

Colm watched the laundry flapping from the grimy apartments in the grimy buildings alongside the tracks. "Boy, don't those clothes get dirty?" he asked.

"Yup," Bogus said. He wanted to throw Ralph Packer, Kent and the two-thousand-dollar movie equipment off the subway, preferably at high speed. But Tulpen was being very nice, and Colm obviously liked her. She was trying hard, of course, but there was more than enough that was natural about her to make Colm feel at home with her.

Colm had never liked Ralph, though. Even when he'd been a baby and Ralph had come to their place in Iowa, Colm didn't like him. When the camera ran on and on, Colm would stare into the lens until Ralph stopped, put down the camera and stared back. Then Colm would pretend he was bored and look away.

"Colm?" Bogus whispered. "Do you think Ralph would live in fresh water or sea water?" Colm giggled, then whispered to Tulpen and told her what Bogus had said. She smiled and told Colm something, which he passed back to Bogus. The camera was running again.

"Oil," Colm whispered.

"What?" said Bogus.

"Oil!" Colm said. Ralph would live in oil.

"Right!" said Trumper, flashing a grateful look at Tulpen.

"Right!" Colm shouted. Aware that the camera was running again and aimed at him, he proceeded to stare Ralph Packer down.

"The kid keeps looking at the camera," Kent told Ralph.

With exaggerated patience, Ralph leaned across the aisle and smiled at Colm. "Hey, Colm?" he said gently. "Don't look at the camera, okay?"

Colm looked at his father, seeking guidance on whether or not he had to obey Ralph.

198

"Oil," Bogus whispered.

"Oil," repeated Tulpen, like a chant. Then she started laughing, and Colm broke up too.

"Oil," Colm chanted.

Kent appeared typically baffled by the experience, but Ralph Packer, who was at least a keen observer of detail, put his camera down.

And after the zoo—the pregnant animals, the molting coats, the controlled little kingdom, from wart hog to cheetah—and after God knows how many feet of film, not of the animals but of the main character, Tulpen, Bogus and Colm ditched Ralph and Kent and the two thousand dollars' worth of movie equipment.

Ralph never really put the camera away. It hung in that heavy shoulder bag like a pistol in a holster, but you knew it was a pistol of large caliber, and you never forgot that it was loaded.

Tulpen and Bogus took Colm to a puppet show for kids in the Village. Tulpen knew all about such things: when museums put on films for kids, when there were dances and plays and operas and symphonies and puppet shows. She knew about them because she herself was more interested in seeing them than things for adults; most of *those* were awful.

Tulpen hit it right every time. After the puppet show they went to a place to eat called The Yellow Cowboy, which was full of old film posters from Western movies. Colm loved it and ate like a horse. Afterward, he fell asleep in the taxi. Bogus had insisted they take a cab, not wanting Colm to see any subway happenings at night. In the back seat, Trumper and Tulpen almost fought over whose lap Colm was going to lie in. Tulpen gave in and let Trumper hold him, but she kept her hand on Colm's foot.

"I just can't get over him," she whispered to Trumper. "I mean, you *made* him. He's part *you*." Trumper looked embarrassed, but Tulpen went on anyway. "I didn't think I loved you this much," she told Bogus. She was crying a little.

"I love you too," he said hoarsely, but he wouldn't look at her.

"Let's have a baby, Trumper," she said. "Can we?"

"I have a baby," Trumper said sourly. Then he made a face, as if he couldn't stomach the self-pity he'd heard in his own voice.

She couldn't stomach it either. She squeezed Colm's sleeping foot. "You selfish bastard," she told Bogus.

"I know what you mean, but I do love you, I think," he said. "It's just such a fucking risk."

"Suit yourself, Jack," Tulpen said, and let go of Colm's foot.

Tulpen took Biggie's request that she and Trumper not be too familiar with each other more seriously than Trumper did. She arranged for Colm to sleep in her bed, facing the turtles and fish. Bogus was to sleep with him, if he could remember not to reach out and goose the child in the middle of the night. She slept on the couch.

Trumper listened to Colm's sweet breathing. How fragile children's faces are in sleep!

Colm woke up from a dream in the half-light before dawn, wailing and shaking, whining for a drink, demanding that the fish be quiet, claiming that a mad turtle had attacked him, then falling asleep again before Tulpen could bring him the water. She couldn't believe that a boy could be so worldly in the daytime and in such terror at night. Trumper told her that it was perfectly natural; some kids have rough nights. Colm had always been a wild sleeper, hardly ever passing two nights in a row without an outcry, mysterious and never explained.

"Understandable," he muttered to Tulpen. "Considering who the kid's lived with."

"I thought you said Biggie was good with him," Tulpen said, worried. "And Couth too, you said. You mean Couth?"

"I meant *me*," Trumper said. "Fuck Couth," he mumbled. "He's a wonderful person . . ."

Tulpen was also struck by how totally children wake up in the morning. Looking out the window, Colm was a babble of talk, thinking what he wanted to do, prowling Tulpen's kitchen.

"What's in the yogurt?"

"Fruit."

200

"Oh, I thought it was lumps," Colm said, eating on.

"Lumps?"

"Like in cereal," said Colm. A-ha! Bogus thought, so Biggie is lousy with cereal. Or perhaps the overtalented Couth is responsible for the lumps?

But now Colm was talking about museums, wondering if there were any in Maine. Yes—for ships, Tulpen thought. Here in New York there were ones for paintings and sculpture and natural history . . .

They took him to one for machines. That's what he wanted. There was a giant contraption at the main entrance, a jumble of gears, levers, steam whistles and hammering rods as high as a three-story ceiling, as wide as a barn.

"What does it do?" Colm asked, standing transfixed by its terrible energy. The thing sounded as if it was constructing a building for itself.

"I don't know," said Trumper.

"I don't think it actually *does* anything," Tulpen said.

"It just sort of works, right?" said Colm.

"Yup," said Trumper.

There were hundreds of machines. Some were delicate, some were violent, some you could start and stop yourself, some were terribly noisy bashers and others appeared to be resting—like the great, potential animals in zoos who are always asleep.

In the big tunnel leading out of the building, Colm stopped and felt the wall with his hand, absorbing the vibration of all those machines. "Boy," he said. "You can feel them."

Trumper hated machines.

Another museum was showing W.C. Fields in *The Bank Dick*, so they took Colm to it. Both he and Trumper howled throughout the film, but Tulpen fell asleep. "I guess she doesn't like the movie," Bogus whispered to Colm.

"I think she's just tired," Colm whispered. After a pause, he added, "Why does she sleep on the couch?"

Deftly changing the subject, Trumper said, "Maybe she doesn't think the movie's so funny."

"But it is."

"Right," said Trumper.

"You know what?" Colm whispered thoughtfully. "Girls don't like funny things so much."

"They don't?"

"Nope. Mommy doesn't, and ... what's her name?" he asked, poking Tulpen.

"Tulpen," Trumper whispered.

"Tulpen," said Colm. "She doesn't like funny things either."

"Well ..."

"But you do, and I do," Colm said.

"Right," Trumper whispered. He could listen to the kid for days, he thought.

"Couth thinks things are funny, too," Colm went on, but Trumper lost him there. He watched W.C. Fields drive the terrified bank robber out to the end of the dock overhanging the lake. Fields said to the robber, "From here on, you'll have to take the *boat*." Colm was doubled up, laughing so hard that he woke Tulpen, but Trumper couldn't even manage a convincing smile.

During Colm's last night in New York, Bogus Trumper had a nightmare about airplanes and this time it was Trumper who woke up Colm and Tulpen with his howls.

Colm was wide-awake, popping questions and looking for turtles who might have attacked his father. But Tulpen told him that it was okay; his father had just had a bad dream. "I have those sometimes, too," Colm confessed, and he looked very sympathetically at Bogus.

Because of the dream, Bogus decided to borrow Kent's car and drive Colm back to Maine.

"That's silly," Biggie said on the phone.

"I'm a good driver," Trumper said.

"I know you are, but it will take so long. He can fly to Portland in an hour."

"Unless he crashes in the Atlantic," Bogus said. Biggie groaned. "All right," she said. "I'll drive to Portland and meet him, so you won't have to drive all the way to Georgetown."

A-ha! thought Trumper. What is there in Georgetown that I shouldn't see? "Why can't I come to Georgetown?" he asked.

202

"God," said Biggie. "You certainly can, if you want to. I didn't think you'd want to. I just thought, since I was going to drive to Portland, anyway, to meet the plane . . ."

"Well, have it your way."

"No, have it *yours*," said Biggie. "Have you had a nice time?"

He did it Biggie's way. He borrowed Kent's awful car and drove to the Portland Airport. Tulpen packed them a lunch and bought a lovely little fishbowl for the fish Colm selected, a big purple fantail. Colm couldn't see that Tulpen was crying over his shoulder when she hugged him goodbye, and she snarled at Trumper on the sidewalk when he tried to hug her.

Before they were even out of New York State, Colm found a joint-roller in Kent's filthy glove compartment and four old marijuana cigarettes. In a panic about being busted—in front of his boy!—Bogus asked Colm to empty the contents of the glove compartment into a litter-bag, and the first moment they were alone on the road, Trumper threw the whole mess out the window.

Somewhere in Massachusetts Bogus realized that he'd thrown out all the registration papers for the car, and probably Kent's driver's license as well; all of the pot apparatus would be found with Kent's name and address. He decided to tell Kent that the glove compartment had been robbed.

Trumper relaxed driving through New Hampshire. He took the longer shore road along the Maine coast to stretch out his last moments with Colm. He had some thoughts about Biggie, and about Couth, and about what Biggie might have told Colm about his father, or even about his father's girl. But they were not dark thoughts; they were sometimes sad thoughts, but they were kind. Biggie was not poisonous.

"Do you like Maine?" he asked Colm.

"Oh, sure."

"Even in the winter?" asked Trumper. "What can you do near the ocean in the wintertime?"

"Walk on the beach in the snow," said Colm. "And

watch the storms. But we're going to put the boat back in the water when I get home . . ."

"Oh?" said Trumper. "You and Mommy?" He was asking for it, he was leading purposefully.

"No," said Colm. "Me and Couth. It's Couth's boat."

"You like Couth, don't you?"

"I sure do."

"Did you have a nice time in New York?" Trumper begged.

"I sure did."

"I like Couth and Mommy, too," said Bogus.

"So do I," Colm said. "And I like you," he said, "and . . . what's the girl's name?"

"Tulpen."

"Yup, Tulpen. I like her," said Colm, "and you, and Mommy, and Couth."

Well, that wraps it up, Trumper thought. He didn't know what he felt.

"Do you know Daniel Arbuthnot?" Colm asked.

"No, I don't."

"Well, I don't like *him* so much."

"Who is he?"

"He's a kid in my school," Colm said. "He's just a stupid kid."

At the Portland Airport, Biggie asked Trumper if he wanted to come to Georgetown; it was only another hour's drive and he could stay the night; Couth would like to see him. But Trumper felt that Biggie would really rather he didn't come, and he would rather not either.

"Tell Couth I'm sorry, but I have to get back to New York," he said. "Ralph's all hot to trot with a new film."

Biggie looked at the ground. "Who's the main character?" she asked, and when Bogus stared at her—a How Did You Know? stare—she said, "Ralph's been up. He flew up one weekend and talked to me and Couth." She shrugged. "I don't mind, Bogus," she said. "But I can't understand why you would have anything to do with a film about . . . about *what?*" she said angrily. "That's what I'd like to know."

"You know Ralph, Big. I don't think *he* knows what the movie's about."

"Do you know he tried to sleep with me?" she asked. "Again and again," she said, working herself into a rage. "Jesus, even when he came for the weekend, he even tried then, with Couth around and all."

Trumper just shuffled. "That girl," said Biggie, and Trumper looked up. "Tulpen?" Biggie asked.

"Right," said Colm. "Tulpen . . ."

They moved around to the other side of the car. Colm was absorbed in unwrapping the fishbowl, which was covered with tinfoil and tied with a ribbon.

"What about her?" Trumper asked.

"Well, Ralph says she's nice," Biggie said. "I mean, really nice."

"Yes, she really is."

"Well, he wants to sleep with her too," Biggie said. "You should know . . ."

Trumper wanted to tell Biggie that Ralph had already slept with Tulpen, and that he might still be sore that he couldn't any more, but that there really wasn't anything else to it, but he didn't say anything; he just looked as if he was going to try.

"Bogus," Biggie said. "Please don't say you're sorry. Just this once, don't say something like that. You always say it."

"But I *am* sorry, Big."

"Don't be," she told him. "I'm very happy, and so is Colm."

He believed her, but why did it make him so angry?

"Are you?" she asked.

"What?"

"Are you happy?"

He guessed he was, sort of, but he evaded an answer. "We had a nice time, Colm and I," he told her. "We went to the zoo and a puppet show . . ."

"And a museum!" said Colm. By now he had the fishbowl unwrapped and was holding it up to show Biggie. But the fish was floating on top of the water.

"Oh, it's lovely," Biggie said.

"It's dead," said Colm, but he didn't seem very surprised.

"We'll get you another one," Trumper said. "You can

come down again," he added, not looking at Biggie. "Would you like that?"

"Sure."

"Or your father can come see us," Biggie said.

"Sure, and I could bring a fish with me," Bogus said.

"There was a yellow one and a red one, too," Colm told Biggie. "And all kinds of turtles. Maybe a turtle wouldn't have died so easy."

A small plane took off nearby, and Colm watched it. "I wish I could have taken the plane back," he complained. "It doesn't take so long on the plane, and maybe the fish wouldn't have died."

Fish-killer Trumper felt like saying, Maybe the great Couth can revive it. But he didn't really feel like saying that at all; in fact, he felt like a shit for even thinking it.

20: His Move

He left his wife and kid in Iowa,
and he bought a one-way ticket.

—Ralph Packer, from the narration of *Fucking Up*

He stands on the dark sidewalk, shielded from the streetlight by a shrub, and pays his respects to Biggie's lighted window, and to Mr. Fitch, night watchman for his own and neighboring lawns. Fitch waves to him, and Bogus starts his tender-footed limp toward town, slow steps along the grassy strip between the sidewalk and the street; in the shadows between the lamp-posts he blunders into someone's pile of leaves.

"Got to get up early to get those ducks!" shouts Mr. Fitch, who is capable of believing anything.

"Right!" calls Bogus, and bleeds downtown to Benny's, where he finds Ralph Packer in a wallow of beer. Ralph, however, is sobered by Trumper's pained and spectacular appearance.

Packer is sensible enough to intervene when Bogus starts an assault on a harmless fat student in a white Ghandi robe who wears the sign of the Tao and electrocuted hair. Bogus is telling him, "If you say you love everyone, I'm going to disembowel you with a glass ashtray . . ." He picks one up and adds, *"This* glass ashtray."

Packer beerily ushers Bogus out onto Clinton Street and hobbles him along the curb to his racing bicycle. With the unfeeling stamina of the indestructibly drunk, Ralph pedals the two of them down to the river, across the bridge, and up the long, lung-killing hill to the university hospital. There Trumper is treated for festering foot wounds, chiefly punctures and lacerations, and is released.

All day Sunday Trumper kept prone, reclining on Ralph's couch, his throbbing feet stacked on a pile of pillows. Feverish visions in Ralph's nasty two-room apartment: smelling Ralph's mongrel, whom Trumper called Retch, and the odor of hair oil which seeped upward through the floorboards from a Jefferson Street barbershop below Ralph's rooms.

Once the phone rang, on a table behind his head. After some groping Bogus managed to answer it, and a strange angry lady informed him that he could go fuck himself. He didn't recognize the voice, but whether it was his fever or a clear-headed conviction, he didn't for a moment believe that the call was intended for Ralph.

By nightfall, Bogus had shaped several emotional impulses into what could vaguely be called a plan. Overturf, indulging his sense of drama, would have called it a scheme.

Trumper struggled to remember the brief letter from his father which had been torn up and hurled in tiny pieces to Risky Mouse:

Son:

I have had to think very seriously about everything, and I should at first say that I am most disapproving of the various ways you have conducted yourself, both in your personal life and in your career goals.

It is strongly against my better judgment that I have concluded to make you a loan. Understand: this is not a gift. The enclosed check for $5,000 should be ample to put you on your feet again. I will not be so inhuman as to set a specific interest rate on this figure, or to set a specific due date for its return. Suffice it to say that I hope you will consider yourself responsible to me for this money, and that you will accept this responsibility with a gravity quite lacking in your past behavior.

Dad

Bogus was capable of remembering that he had not torn up the check and hurled it into the basement too.

The next morning Trumper took slow, swollen steps to the bank. A day's transaction included the following: a deposit of five thousand dollars, which prompted the personal congratulations of Bank President Shumway; a twenty-minute wait in President Shumway's now-cordial office while the bank processed a new numbered checkbook for him (the old one was home with Biggie); a withdrawal of three hundred dollars in cash; and the theft of fourteen courtesy matchbooks from the little basket on the counter by the teller's window ("I intend to rob you," he whispered to the startled teller, then grabbed the matches).

Trumper limped to the post office and wrote out checks to the following:

> Humble Oil & Refining Co.
> Sinclair Refining Co.
> Iowa-Illinois Gas & Electric
> Krotz Plumbing
> Northwestern Bell Telephone Co.
> Milo Kubik (Peoples Market)
> Sears, Roebuck & Co.
> Office of Financial Aid, State University of Iowa
> Lone Tree Co-operative Credit Union
> Shive & Hupp
> Addison & Halsey
> Cuthbert Bennett
> The Jefferson International Travel Agency

Lacking was a check for the several thousand dollars owed National Defense Loans—government money for education, which he assumed must emanate from the U.S. Department of Health, Education and Welfare. Instead, he sent H.E.W. a note in which he declared himself "unwilling and unable to pay this debt, on the grounds of receiving an incomplete education." Then he went to Benny's, drank fourteen draughts and played a lot of violent pinball until Benny called Packer to come take him away.

At Ralph's, Bogus phoned a cable he wanted sent:

> Herr Merrill Overturf
> Schwindgasse 15/2
> Vienna 4, Austria

>> Merrill
>>   I am coming
>>   Boggle.

"Who's Merrill?" said Ralph Packer. "Who's Boggle?"

Trumper hadn't heard a word from Overturf since the last time he'd been in Europe, with Biggie, more than four years before. If Ralph had known this, or known anything, for that matter, he might have tried to stop Trumper. Conversely, it later occurred to Bogus that Ralph might have some thoughts about Biggie being left alone.

The next morning, Trumper had a phone call at Ralph's apartment from Lufthansa Airlines. They had botched his reservation to Vienna and had him booked on a flight from Chicago, to New York, to Frankfurt. For some unexplained reason, this would cost him less, even if he took a businessman's flight from Frankfurt to Vienna. Especially if I hitch-hike from Frankfurt, Trumper thought.

"Frankfurt?" said Ralph Packer. "Jesus, what's in Frankfurt?"

He told Ralph his "plan," sort of.

At four in the afternoon, Ralph phones Biggie and informs her that Bogus is "besotted at Benny's and about to get into a losing fight." Biggie hangs up.

Ralph calls back. He suggests Biggie bring Colm and the car right away, and that together they can safely stow Bogus in the trunk.

After Biggie hangs up again, Ralph encourages the three silent customers in Benny's to make a lot of background rumpus for the next attempt. That call rings unanswered for almost five minutes while Bogus, near to giving up hope, crouches behind a shrub on Mr. Fitch's well-kept lawn. Finally he sees Biggie and Colm leave.

Ralph stalls Biggie at Benny's door with grim tales of

blood, beer, teeth, ambulances and policemen before Biggie suspects the hoax and walks boldly past Ralph into the bar. There is a drunk girl, all alone, playing pinball; there are two men in a booth by the door talking cheerfully. Biggie asks Benny if there's been a fight here.

"Yes, about two months ago . . ." Benny begins.

When Biggie darts outside, she finds that Ralph Packer has moved her car somewhere, and is strolling down the sidewalk with Colm. Packer won't reveal where he's parked the car until she threatens to call the police.

When she gets home, Bogus has been and gone.

He took his tape recorder and all the tapes; his passport; not his typewriter but all his thesis work on the translation of *Akthelt and Gunnel*. God knows why.

He cleaned out the refrigerator, putting all the food in the basement for Risky Mouse. He destroyed the trap.

By Colm's pillow he left a toy duck, with real feathers, made by Amish farmers. It cost $15.95, the most Trumper had ever spent for a toy.

By Biggie's pillow he left the new checkbook, with a remaining balance of $1,612.47, and a large, French-uplift mauve bra. It was the right size too. In one of the big cups, he crumpled a handwritten note: Big, there was truly none finer.

This is all Biggie discovers of his trip home. She can't know, of course, about his other accomplishment. If Mr. Fitch ever cared to be nosy, he could describe for Biggie the sight of Bogus groping through the garbage cans outside his house and rescuing the abandoned duck, by now in an advanced state of decomposition. Fitch registered no surprise when Trumper wrapped up the duck in a plastic bag. Nor would Fitch ever describe Trumper's search for a sturdy box into which the bag containing the duck was crammed, along with a note reading, "Dear Sir: Please count your change."

The package was mailed to Bogus's father.

Watching Biggie's stormy return from behind Fitch's shrub, Bogus hung around just long enough to make sure that she didn't jump out any windows. At his see-through curtain with Mrs. Fitch, watching Bogus behind the shrub, Fitch had enough good sense to recognize secrecy when he

211

saw it and didn't come out on his porch to make any inappropriate remarks. Once Bogus turned and saw the old couple observing him. He waved; they waved back. *Good old Fitch: he must have fussed for years with the Bureau of Statistics, but now he lets things ride. Excepting his lawn, the man knows how to retire.*

Later Bogus went to the library, to mull over his little-used alcove, not really expecting to find anything he'd want to take with him. Predictably, he didn't. His cubby-neighbor, M.E. Zanther, discovered him "doodling on an otherwise blank page," he later reported. Zanther remembered this well, because when Trumper left the library, Zanther slunk into Trumper's alcove to read the doodles. Actually, Bogus was hiding around the end of the row of cubbies. What Zanther saw was the crude beginnings of a poem about Harry Petz, a badly drawn obscene drawing, and, broadly printed with a Magic Marker across the surface of the desk blotter, HI, ZANTHER! ARE YOU RUNNING OUT OF THINGS TO READ?

"One thing I've noticed," said Dr. Wolfram Holster, Trumper's thesis chairman, "is that witless behavior can be a very calculated thing." But that was much later; at the time, he was thoroughly bamboozled.

Trumper called Dr. Holster and begged for a ride to the nearest Iowa airport with the quickest connection to Chicago. This would have been Cedar Rapids, about three-quarters of an hour from Iowa City, and Dr. Wolfram Holster was not in the habit of cultivating familiar relationships with his students. "Is this an emergency?" he asked.

"There's been a death in the family," Trumper told him.

They were almost at the airport, Trumper not speaking a word, when Holster asked, "Your father?"

"What?"

"Your *father*," Holster repeated. "The death in the family . . ."

"My own," said Trumper. "*I'm* the death in the family . . ."

Holster drove on, maintaining a polite pause. "Where are you going?" he asked after a while.

"I prefer to fall to pieces abroad," Trumper answered. Holster remembered that line; it was from Trumper's translation of *Akthelt and Gunnel*. On the battlefield at Plock, word comes to Akthelt that his wife, Gunnel, and his son, Axelrulf, have been foully molested and dismembered back home at the castle. Thak, Akthelt's father, suggests that they postpone their planned invasion of Finlandia. "I prefer to fall to pieces abroad," Akthelt tells his father.

So Dr. Holster suspected some melodramatics on the part of Trumper.

Actually, what Holster didn't suspect was more interesting. The whole passage—the battlefield at Plock, the business about Gunnel and Axelrulf being foully molested and dismembered, and Akthelt's comment—was bunk. Trumper had lost track of the plot, needed more work to show Holster, and had invented all of it. Later, he had thought of a way to revive Axelrulf and Gunnel; it was a case of mistaken identity.

So actually Trumper's line was original, after all.

"I prefer to fall to pieces abroad."

Holster's reaction must have shaken Trumper up a bit.

"Have a good time," Dr. Wolfram Holster told him.

The Lufthansa flight for Frankfurt was less than half full at the takeoff from Chicago. It picked up a few more passengers in New York, but it was still pretty empty. Even with all the seats available, a Lufthansa stewardess sat down beside Trumper. Perhaps I look like I'm going to throw up, he thought, and promptly felt sick.

The stewardess's English wasn't very good, but Bogus didn't feel up to speaking German yet. He'd be speaking it soon enough.

"Dis your furzt flighct?" the stewardess asked him in a sensuous guttural. Most people don't know what a lovely language German is, Trumper reflected.

"I haven't flown in a long time," he told the stewardess, wishing that his stomach wouldn't bank and circle with the plane.

Over the Atlantic they leveled off, climbed, then leveled off again. When the lighted sign saying PLEASE FASTEN

213

SEAT BELTS went off, the nice stewardess unfastened hers. "Vell, here ve go," she said.

But before she could get up, Trumper tried to lunge past her into the aisle, forgetting that his own seat belt was still attached. He was jerked back against her, knocking her back in her seat. He vomited in her lap.

"Oh, I'm sorry," he gurgled, thinking how he'd lived for the last few days on beer.

The stewardess stood, holding her skirt up, making a tray of it, and smiled, or tried to. He said again, "Oh, I'm sorry."

She told him sweetly, "Pleeze, don't vorry about it."

But Bogus Trumper didn't hear her. He saw the blackness out his window and hoped it was only the sea. He said again, "Really, I *am* sorry . . ."

The stewardess was trying to get away from him to empty her skirt. But he caught her hand not looking at her and staring out the window fixedly, and said again, "I really am sorry, really! Fuck it, anyway, damn it! But I *am!* So very fucking sorry . . ."

The stewardess knelt awkwardly in the aisle beside him, balancing her skirtful of slop. "Pleeze, you . . . hey, you!" she crooned. But he began to cry. "Pleeze don't even tink about it," she pleaded. She touched his face. "Look, pleeze," she coaxed. "You von't believe me, but dis happens all der time."

21 : Home Movies

Kent ran the projector. It was a pretty beat-up print of the original which Tulpen had crudely spliced together so they could see how the concept was working.

Trumper ran the recorder. His tapes were as crudely cut as the film; they weren't always in sync, and he kept having to ask Kent to slow down the projector or speed it up or stop it altogether, and he was constantly fussing with the speed of the tape too. Altogether, it was about as amateurish an operation as Trumper had been privileged to see since he'd started working with Ralph. Most of the camera shots were hand-held, as jumpy as a TV newsreel, and most of the film was silent; the separately taped sound track would be laid over later. Ralph had practically given up on using sync-sound. Even the film itself was substandard—high speed, grainy stuff—and Ralph, normally a wizard with light, had overexposed and underexposed half of the footage. Ralph was also a very patient genius in the darkroom, yet some of the footage looked as if the film had been handled with pliers and blotched with chemicals invented for the removal of rust rather than the development of film.

An excellent film craftsman, Ralph had done all this on purpose; in fact, some of the light holes in the film had been handmade with a jackknife. Since there wasn't a speck of dust in his darkroom, Ralph must have swept half of New York with the reels to achieve the mess he had. Perhaps when the film was distributed, if it ever was, Ralph would stipulate the use of a crushed plastic lens on the projector.

When Packer wanted to run through the whole crude beginning again, Trumper felt he'd had it.

"It's looking good," Ralph said. "It's looking *better*."

"You want to know what it sounds like?" Trumper said, slamming the buttons on the recorder. "It sounds like it was taped in a tin-can factory. And you know what it looks like? It looks like your tripod got stolen and that you were so poor you had to pawn your light meter to be able to buy the cheapest film stock in Hong Kong."

Tulpen coughed.

"It looks," said Trumper, "like your darkroom was in a windowless building being sand-blasted."

Even Kent didn't say anything. He probably didn't like it either, but he had great faith in Ralph. If Ralph had asked him to load a camera with Saran Wrap, Kent would have tried it.

"It looks like home movies," Trumper said.

"It *is* a home movie, Thump-Thump," Ralph told him. "Can we run through the first reel just once more, please?"

"If this tape will even hold together," Trumper said. "I ought to copy it. It's got more splices than actual tape. It's about as stable as a pubic hair," he said.

"Once more, Thump-Thump?" Ralph asked.

"If I have to stop it just once," Trumper said, "the whole thing will fall apart."

"Then we'll run it straight through, okay, Kent?" Ralph said.

"The film might break too," Kent suggested.

"Let's just try it, shall we?" Ralph said patiently. "Just once more."

"I'll pray for you, Ralph," said Bogus. Tulpen coughed again. Nothing was meant by it; she simply had a cold. "Ready, Kent?" Trumper asked.

Kent advanced the film to the opening frame and Trumper located the sound he wanted. "Ready, Thump-Thump," Kent said.

The name was reserved for Ralph's use alone; Trumper didn't like being called Thump-Thump by fucking Kent. "What did you say, Kent?" he asked.

"Huh?" said Kent.

Ralph stood up, and Tulpen put her right hand in

Trumper's lap, leaned across him and with her left hand flicked the tape to PLAY. "Go, Kent," she said.

The film opens with a medium shot of Trumper in a delicatessen in the Village. It is a big, crowded lunch-counter, and you can pick out sandwich makings as you move along, ending up with a whopper at the cash register. Trumper moves slowly, scrutinizing the pastrami, pickles and spiced ham, nodding or shaking his head to the men behind the counter. There is no sync-sound.

The voice-over is Packer's, narrating from the tape. "He's very cautious now—like someone who's been stung has an eye open for bees, you know?"

Trumper looks suspiciously at his sandwich. "It's natural, I guess, but he just won't get involved in anything."

Ralph's voice-over rattles on about Trumper's lack of involvement until we cut to another angle: Trumper standing by the condiment counter, applying mustard and relish. A pretty girl is looking self-consciously at the camera, then at Trumper to see if he might be someone famous. She also wants the mustard. Trumper slides it along the counter to her without looking at her, then carries his sandwich out of frame. The girl stares after him, as Tulpen's voice-over says, "I think he's very careful with women. A good thing, too, by the way . . ."

Cut: Trumper and Tulpen are entering her apartment, both of them lugging groceries. There is no sync-sound. Ralph, voice-over, says, "Well, naturally *you'd* think so. You live with him."

Tulpen and Bogus are putting groceries away in the kitchen; she is chattering in an apparently normal monologue; he is sullen, throwing an occasional irritated look at her, then at the camera. "I mean, he's just nice with me," Tulpen's voice-over says. "I think he's aware of the dangers, that's all . . ."

Walking straight into the camera's lens, Trumper makes an obscene gesture.

Cut: a series of stills, family photographs of Trumper, Biggie and Colm. Ralph's voice-over: "Well, he ought to be aware of the dangers, of course. He was married before . . ."

Tulpen: "He misses the child."

217

Ralph: "And the wife?"

Cut: Earphones on, Bogus is working on the tapes in Ralph's studio. There is no sync-sound. The sound track is a montage of fragments we've already heard from the various voices-over: "It's natural, I guess ..." "I think that's a good thing . . ." "You live with him . . ." "And the wife?"

Trumper appears to be switching these fragments on and off by his fingerwork at the tape recorder. Then Tulpen comes into frame, says something and points to something out of frame just beyond the two of them.

Another angle: with the bits from the voices-over still the only sound, Trumper and Tulpen are looking at a tangled mess of tape which has spun off a reel and is spilling into a great wormy pile on the floor. Trumper shuts something off: *clunk*. With this noise, the frame freezes to a still. There continues to be no sync-sound. Ralph's voice-over says, "Stop it, right there! Now the title—hold it right there . . ." Then the titles for *Fucking Up* appear over the frozen image. "Music," says Ralph's voice-over, and in turn they appear over the frozen image: Bogus Trumper, in stop-action, is stooping to attempt to untangle a mess of spilled tape. Tulpen is looking on.

22 : Slouching After Overturf

He was very lucky to hitch a ride from the Frankfurt Airport to Stuttgart with a German computer salesman who was proud of his company's Mercedes. Trumper wasn't sure whether it was the drone of the autobahn or the salesman's own peculiar drone that put him to sleep.

In Stuttgart he spent the night at the Hotel Fehls Zunder. Apparently, from the rows of photographs in the hotel lobby, Fehls Zunder had been a diver on the German Olympic Team of 1936; there was a photo of him in midair at the Berlin Games. The last photo showed him on the deck of a German U-boat, leaning on the port rail beside the *Fregattenkapitän;* FEHLS ZUNDER, FROGMAN, LOST AT SEA, read the caption.

There was also an unexplained photograph of dark, empty ocean, the shoreline—France? England?—in the distance. A white X had been painted on the crest of a heavy swell. The caption, ripe with irony, said: HIS LAST DIVE.

Trumper wondered where Fehls Zunder had learned to swim and dive in Stuttgart. From his fifth-floor window, Bogus contemplated a double-gainer which would have placed him precisely in the middle of a glistening puddle in the tram tracks below the hotel.

Bogus's longest dreams are about heroes. Accordingly, he dreams of Merrill Overturf sterilizing his hypodermic needle and syringe in a little saucepan, and boiling a test tube of Benedict's solution and pee to check his urine sugar. Merrill is being almost dainty in some impossibly large American kitchen; it's the kitchen at Great Boar's Head, where Bogus has never seen Merrill. Dr. Edmund

219

Trumper is reading the newspaper and Bogus's mother is making coffee as Merrill squeezes a medicine dropper of pee into a test tube, plinking exactly eight drops into the Benedict's solution.

"What's for breakfast?" Trumper's father asks.

Merrill is watching the timer on the stove. When the little bell rings, Dr. Edmund Trumper's soft-boiled egg is done, simultaneously with Merrill's urine.

Merrill cools his pee in a fancy spice rack while Trumper's father fingers the steaming eggshell. Merrill shakes his test tube; Dr. Edmund strikes the egg a glancing blow with his butter knife. Merrill announces that his urine sugar is high. "At least two percent," he says, waving the opaque reddish mixture. "Clear blue would be negative . . ."

Something hisses. Actually, it's a large Mercedes bus below Trumper's Stuttgart window, but Bogus concludes that it's Merrill loading his syringe.

Then the three of them are sitting around the breakfast table. As Bogus's mother pours coffee, Merrill lifts his shirt and pinches up a small roll of his belly. Trumper smells alcohol and coffee as Merrill rubs his bit of fat with a cotton wad, then flicks the needle in like a dart and smoothly pushes the plunger.

Another hiss, louder than before, and Bogus rolls over and bumps into the wall of the Hotel Fehls Zunder; for a moment, the kitchen at Great Boar's Head tilts and slips off the bed. Hearing the crash, and another hiss, Trumper wakes up on the floor, with a fleeing vision of Merrill pumping himself full of air.

Now Merrill floats near the ceiling of Trumper's strange room at the Hotel Fehls Zunder, and somewhere, dimmed by the hiss of the bus doors opening and closing outside, Bogus hears his father say, "This is not a usual symptom of insulin reaction . . ."

"My urine sugar is too high!" shrieks Merrill, skidding like a helium balloon across the ceiling to the transom above the door, where Bogus sees the girlish face of a total stranger peering through one of the transom's tiny windowpanes. Actually, the glass is in splinters on the floor of Trumper's room, and the embarrassed hotel maid, on her hall stepladder, tells Trumper that she's sorry for the disturbance; she was just wiping the glass when a pane fell out.

Bogus smiles; he doesn't catch the German right away, so that the maid is forced to carry on. "It just fell right out when I was wiping it," she explains, then tells him she will come back with a broom.

Trumper dresses himself in the bedsheet; draped in it, he moves suspiciously to his window, trying to locate the real hiss. Whether the Mercedes bus looks so new and shiny and inviting, or whether he actually notes how much money he has, he splurges and takes such a bus to Munich—riding high and drowsily on the sightseeing deck through Bavaria; dreaming vaguely a sort of stepped-up cycle to Overturf's careless treatment of his diabetes. Merrill shooting the insulin, watching his urine sugar plummet; Merrill suffering an insulin reaction on a Vienna *Strassenbahn*, jangling the dog tags around his neck until the conductor, who's about to throw this weaving drunk off the tram, reads the bilingual messages printed on the tags:

> *Ich bin nicht betrunken!*
> I am not drunk!
>
> *Ich have zuckerkrankheit!*
> I have diabetes!
>
> *Was Sie sehen ist ein Insulinreaktion!*
> What you're seeing is an insulin reaction!
>
> *Füttern Sie mir Zucker, schnell!*
> Feed me sugar, quick!

Merrill gobbles sugar, Lifesavers, mints, orange juice and chocolate, raising his fallen sugar count so that he's out of insulin reaction and headed in the opposite direction, toward acidosis and coma. Which requires that he take more insulin. Which starts the cycle over again. Even in dreams, Trumper exaggerates.

Coming into Munich, Bogus tries to be objective; he unearths his tape recorder and on the bus records this statement: "Merrill Overturf and other irregular people are unsuited to conditions demanding careful routines. Di-

221

abetes, for example . . ." (Thinking, Marriage, for example . . .)

But before he can shut the recorder off, the man next to him asks in German what Trumper is doing, fearful, perhaps, of an interview. Feeling the tape is already botched, and sure that the man understands only German, Trumper keeps the tape running and replies in English, "Just what is it, sir, that you have to hide?"

"I speak English rather quite some well," the man replies, and they ride in deathly silence into Munich.

To make peace, at the bus terminal Bogus lightly asks the offended passenger who Fehls Zunder was. But the man expresses some distaste for the question; not answering, he hurries off, leaving Bogus to endure the stares of several nearby eaves-droppers, for whom the name Fehls Zunder seems to have rung an unpleasant bell.

Feeling foreign, Trumper wonders, with considerable surprise, What am I doing here? He bumps awkwardly along a strange Munich street, suddenly unable to translate the German shop signs and voices garbling around him, imagining all the terrors that could be taking place in America at this moment. A run-amok tornado lashing the Midwest lofts weighty Biggie forever out of Iowa. Colm is buried by a blizzard in Vermont. Cuthbert Bennett, drinking in his darkroom, accidentally swallows a highball glass of Microdol-X, retires to the seventeenth bathroom and flushes himself out to sea. While Trumper, isolated from these dreadful events, drains a heavy beer in the Munich Bahnhof, having decided to take the train from here to Vienna. He is aware that he's been waiting for the point in his trip when he'll be suddenly exhilarated, struck with the adventure of returning.

It's not until he arrives, still unfeeling, in Vienna that he considers the possibility that adventure is a time and not a place.

He wandered down the Mariahilferstrasse until the awkwardness and weight of his tape recorder and the other items in his duffel wearied him into waiting for a *Strassenbahn*.

He got off the tram at Esterhazy Park, near which, he remembered, there was a large secondhand shop; here he

222

bought a secondhand typewriter with odd German symbols and umlaut keys. For his purchase, the shopkeeper agreed to give him a generous exchange of schillings for his German marks and U.S. dollars.

Trumper also bought an ankle-length overcoat; the epaulettes had been torn off the shoulders and there was a neat, small bullet hole in the back, but otherwise it was in stunning shape. He proceeded to outfit himself as a sort of postwar spy, in a baggy, broad-shouldered suit, several yellow-white shirts and a six-foot purple scarf. The scarf could be arranged in various ways and made a tie unnecessary. Then he bought a suitcase with more straps and buckles and thongs than it had room. But it fitted with the rest of his attire. He looked like a traveling spy who had been a passenger on the Orient Express between Istanbul and Vienna since 1950. Finally, he purchased a hat like the one Orson Welles wore in *The Third Man*. He even mentioned the film to the shopkeeper, who said he must have missed that one.

Bogus sold the duffel for about two dollars, then lugged his recorder, extra shirts and the new typewriter in the spy's suitcase through Esterhazy Park, where he ducked into a large bush to pee. His rustling in the hedges alarmed a passing couple. Her look was anxious: A girl is being raped, or worse! His reaction was a sneer: A couple with no better place to do it. Trumper emerged from the hedge alone and with great dignity, lugging the suitcase in which a severed body could be stuffed. Or was he a parachutist who had just made a quick change out of uniform, his dismantled bomb safely hidden in the suitcase, now making his casual way to the Austrian Parliament?

The couple hurried away from his ominous costume, but Bogus Trumper felt just right. He felt the way he ought to look for an Overturf hunt through Vienna.

He took another *Strassenbahn* to the Inner City, riding around to the Opera Ring and leaving the tram at Kärntner Strasse, the city's biggest nighttime alley, smack downtown. If I were Merrill Overturf, *if I were still in Vienna*, where would I be on a Saturday night in December?

Trumper stalks quickly through the little streets off the Neuer Markt, looking for the Hawelka, the old Bolshevik *Kaffeehaus* still popular with assorted intellectuals, students and opera cashiers. The coffeehouse gives him the same cold shoulder he remembers—the same lean hairy men, the same big-boned sensual girls.

Nodding to an apparent prophet at the table by the door, Bogus thinks, Years ago there was one like you, dressed all in black, but his beard was red. And Overturf knew him, I think . . .

Trumper asks the fellow, "Merrill Overturf?"

The man's beard seems to freeze; his eyes dart as if his mind is remembering all the codes it ever learned.

"Do you know Merrill Overturf?" Bogus asks the girl who's sitting nearest the frozen beard. But she shrugs, as if to say that if she did, it hardly matters now.

Another girl, a table away, says, *"Ja,* he's in films, I think."

Merrill in films?

"Films?" says Bogus. *"Here,* you mean? In films here?"

"Do you see a camera running?" asks the fellow with the beard, and a waiter passing between them cringes at the word *Kamera.*

"No, here—in Vienna, I mean," Trumper says.

"I don't know," says the girl. "Just films is all I heard."

"He used to drive an old Zorn-Witwer," Trumper says to no one in particular, searching for identifying marks.

"Ja? A Zorn-Witwer!" a man with thick glasses says. "A fifty-three? A fifty-four?"

"Ja? A fifty-four!" Bogus cries, turning to the man. "It had an old gearshift that slid in and out of the dash; it had holes in the floorboards—you could see the road moving. It had lumpy upholstery . . ."

He stops, seeing several Hawelka customers observing his excitement. "Well, where is he?" Trumper asks the man who knows Zorn-Witwers.

"I knew the *car,* was all I said," the man answers.

"But *you've* actually seen him . . ." Bogus turns back to the girl.

"Ja, but not in a while," she says, and the boy she's with gives Bogus an irritated stare.

"How long since you've seen him?" Bogus asks her.

"Look," the girl says, annoyed. "I don't know any more about him. I just remember him, is all . . ." Her tone silences those around her.

224

Trumper stares at her, disappointed; perhaps he begins to sway, or else his eyes roll, because a high-bosomed, thick-maned girl with neon-green eyeshadow catches his arm, pulling him down to her table.

She asks, "You have problems?" He tries to pull away, but she coaxes him more gently. "No, seriously, what is the problem?" When he doesn't respond, she tries him in English, even though he's spoken German all along. "You have troubles, do you?" She trills the word "troubles" in such a way that Bogus sees it floating, like a written word: Tttrrrubbles.

"You need help?" the girl asks, returning to German.

There's a waiter near them now, darting nervously. Trumper remembers that the waiters at the Hawelka always seemed fearful of tttrrrubbles.

"You sick?" the waiter asks. He takes Trumper's arm, causing him to strain against the girl's grip and drop his laden suitcase. It makes an unlikely *clank*, and the waiter backs off, awaiting the explosion. People nearby eye the suitcase as if it's stolen or lethal, or both.

"Please, just talk to me," says the neon-green girl. "You can tell me everything," she claims. "It's all right." But Bogus gathers up his suitcase, looking away from this fierce female. . . . who would make a fine Den Mother for some Erotic Club.

Everyone stares while Trumper checks to see if his fly is closed. He distinctly remembers removing a condom . . .

Then he's out of there, not quite escaping the prophecy of the strange bearded fellow in black near the door. "It's around the corner," says the prophet with such conviction that Bogus shudders.

He turns out on the Graben, cutting toward Stephansplatz. It wasn't around *that* corner, he reassures himself, thinking that the prophet must have been speaking figuratively, which is the safe and sneaky way all prophets speak.

He means to look next for Merrill in the Twelve Apostles' Keller, but he loses his way and ends up in the Hohner Markt, all of whose wooden vegetable and fruit stands are tarpaulined for the night; he imagines the venders asleep under the canvas. The place looks like an outdoor morgue. The Twelve Apostles' Keller always was a bitch to find.

He asks a man for directions, but it's clearly the wrong person to ask; the man just gawks at him.

"*Kribf?*" he says, or something like that. Trumper doesn't understand. Then the man makes certain odd motions, as if reaching into his pockets for smuggled watches, fake meerschaum pipes, dirty pictures or a gun.

Bogus runs back to Stephansplatz and up the Graben. Finally, he stops under a streetlight to read his watch; it's past midnight, he's sure, but he can't remember how many time zones he's crossed since Iowa, or even if he's thought about this before and already corrected his watch. It says it's 2:15.

A well-dressed woman of uncertain age comes toward him on the sidewalk, and he asks her if she has the time.

"Sure," she says, and stops beside him. She is wearing a rich-looking fur coat, with her hands in a matching muff; and fur boots, with heels, which she shifts. She stares at Trumper, puzzled, then extends her elbow to him. "It's this way," she says, a little annoyed that he hasn't taken her arm.

"The time?" he says.

"Time?"

"I asked, 'Do you have the time?' "

She stares, shakes her head, then smiles. "Oh, the *time*—what time is it?" she says. "The *hour*, you mean?"

Then he realizes that she's a whore. He's on the Graben, and the first-district prostitutes cover the little streets off the Graben and the Kärntner Strasse at night.

"Uh," he says, "I'm sorry. I don't have the money. I just wondered, did you know what time it is?"

"I don't have a watch," the prostitute tells him, looking both ways along the street; she doesn't want to discourage a potential customer by being seen with Trumper. But no one's around except another prostitute.

"Is there a pension near here?" Bogus asks. "Not too expensive."

"Come on," she says, and walks off ahead of him to the corner of Spiegelgasse. "Down there," she points to a blue neon light. "The Pension Taschy." Then she walks away, heading down the Graben toward the other prostitute.

"Thank you," Bogus calls after her, and she waves her

226

muff over her shoulder, exposing for a second one un-gloved, elegant, long-fingered hand with winking rings.

In the lobby of the Pension Taschy are two other pros-titutes who have stepped in out of the cold and stand stamping their boots, slapping their pink calves together. In the light of the lobby, eyeing Trumper's long-traveled mustache and suitcase, they don't bother to smile.

From the window of his room at the Taschy, Trumper can see one side of the mosiac roof of Saint Stephen's Cathedral, and also watch the whores clicking down his street to catch a late bite at the American Hamburger Spa a block up the Graben from Spiegelgasse.

At this apparently late hour the prostitutes are bringing few customers to the Taschy, where they're provided with a few dozen rooms on the second floor. But Trumper can hear them guiding men through the halls below him and see them escorting men down the Spiegelgasse sidewalk to the lobby.

One by one, the men depart alone, and Trumper hears the flushing of the second-floor bidets. It's this late-hour plumbing that makes him bold enough to ask Frau Taschy if he can take a bath. Reluctantly she draws him one, then waits outside the bathroom while he splashes about—*lis-tening, to make sure I don't draw another drop.*

Bogus was ashamed of the color of the bath water and hastily pulled the plug, but Frau Taschy heard the first thick gurgle and from the hall cried that she'd attend to the cleaning up. Embarrassed, he left her his ring to scrub, but couldn't help noticing the slight catch in her breath when she viewed it.

Frau Taschy had been pleasant enough when he'd regis-tered, but as he stepped clean and chilled into his room, he noticed she'd done more than turn down his bed. His suitcase had been opened and the contents were neatly ar-ranged on the broad window seat, as if the Frau had taken a careful inventory in preparation for an outstand-ing debt.

Though the room was unheated, he felt drawn to sit down for a moment at his new typewriter and try out all those funny umlauts. He wrote:

227

My room at the Taschy is three floors up, one block down Spiegelgasse from the Graben. The first-district whores use the place. They are first-class. I stay with nothing but the best.

Then Frau Taschy interrupted him, reminding him of the lateness of the hour and that his typing was noisy, but before he could ask her what late hour it was, she crept off. He heard her pause on the stair landing, and when she descended he resumed his typing:

Frau Taschy, an old hand at estimating a lodger's fate, can decipher pending doom from rings left in bathtubs.

Then he typed three lines of German diphthongs and attempted to write the typing-test sentence about the quick brown fox and the lazy dog, using only umlaut vowels. Or was it a lazy frög?

Listening for Frau Taschy, he heard another bidet flush and remembered the whores. He wrote:

In Vienna, prostitution isn't simply legal; it's both aided and controlled by law. Every whore is issued a sort of license to practice, renewable only with regular medical checkups. If you're not a registered prostitute, you can't legally be one.

Merrill Overturf used to say, "Don't ever buy until you see their safety stickers."

Just as officially, uncertain hotels and pensions in each district are licensed to handle the trade. Prices are supposedly fixed for both hotels and whores, and the first district has the youngest, prettiest and most expensive of them. As you move away from the Inner City, the whores in the outer districts grow older, uglier and more economical. Overturf was fond of remarking that he lived on a fifteenth-district budget.

Then Bogus got bored with writing and went to his window and watched the sidewalk. Below was the whore with

228

the fur coat and matching muff. He tapped the double-pane window and she looked up. He turned his face back and forth in the window for her to see, trying to catch just enough light from his night table to show her who he was, thinking that from below he must resemble some embarrassed exhibitionist not quite daring to hold still.

But she recognized him and smiled up at him. Or she smiled out of habit, recognizing him only as someone simply male, summoning her inside. She pointed up to him and wagged her finger; again he saw the bright, bejeweled hand. When she started for the door, Trumper tapped fiercely on the glass: No, no! I'm not calling you inside. I was just saying hello . . . But she looked as if she took his wild tapping for excitement, and she actually skipped, tossing her face up to him. From a distance he couldn't see a trace of her make-up; she might have been a flirting cheerleader agreeing to a ride home after the game.

He thumped out into the hall, still wearing his towel; it rose over his navel when he straddled the stairwell and caught the draft of the closing lobby door below. He recognized the woman's hand on the banister, sliding up to the first landing. When he called down to her, her head jutted out of the stairwell and she looked right up his skirt, giggling like a fresh girl.

He shouted, *"Nein!"* But she moved up another landing, and he shouted, *"Halt!"* Again her face darted into the stairwell space and he pinched his towel together with his knees. "I'm sorry," he told her. "I didn't mean for you to come up." Her mouth turned down at one corner, causing sudden crow's feet to delta from her eyes; now she looked in her thirties, perhaps forties. But she kept coming.

Trumper stood like a statue, and she stopped a step below him, breathing in short, perfumed gasps, the outdoors cold still radiating off her clothes, her face nicely flushed. "I know," she said. "You only wanted to ask me the *time?*"

"No," he said. "I recognized you. I just tapped on the window to say hello."

"Hello," she said. Now she exaggerated her breathing, leaning on the banister, growing older in front of him, *just to make me feel especially bad.*

"I'm sorry," Bogus told her. "I don't have anything to give you."

She stared at his towel and touched the corners of her mouth. She really was quite lovely. In the first district, they often are. Not so whorish; more elegance than burlesque. Her coat was nice; her hair was simple and looked clean; her bones had taste.

"Really, I would like to," Bogus said.

Again she stared cruelly at his towel, and said—too sweetly, playing a mock mother to him—"Put some clothes on. Do you want to catch a cold?"

Then she left. He followed her nice hand along the banister all three flights down, then padded back to his typewriter; he was about to command his keys to be lyrical, to make some unembarrassed statement of self-pity, when he was interrupted by one more flushing bidet below, and by Frau Taschy scratching outside his door. "No more typing, please," she said. "People are trying to sleep."

People are trying to screw, she meant. His typing disturbed their rhythm or their consciences. But he didn't touch his funny foreign keys; they could prepare their lyrics overnight. Looking down on Spiegelgasse he observed the whore he'd twice misled arm in arm with another prostitute, headed for a coffee break. He thought about how the years must be for them, pacing young and glittering along the Kärntner Strasse and the Graben, then moving out, district by district, year by year, past the Prater amusement park and along the dirty Danube, getting mauled by factory workers and technical high school students for half the fare they had once charged. But it was at least as fair as the real world, perhaps fairer, because the district you ended up in wasn't always a predictable downfall, and in real life you couldn't always choose a glittering beginning.

Out the window, Bogus watched the ringed woman with her muff—once more the cared-for hand animated her talk with another whore; her hand snaked out in the cold, brushed something off the other woman's cheek. A speck of soot? A tear turned to ice? Some smudge made by her last mate's mouth?

With envy, Trumper regarded this careless, real affection.

Trumper went to bed, lying rigid until he had warmed a

pot. He heard a bidet flush and decided he could never all asleep to that lonely music. He danced nude across the oom, retrieved his tape recorder from the window seat nd scurried back to bed. Fumbling through a box of apes, he found his 110-220 converter, plugged in the earhone jack, and clutched the earphones to his chest to varm them. "Come in, Biggie," he whispered.

REWIND.

PLAY . . .

23 : Taking It Personally

(Fade In: A medium shot of the Pillsburys' boathouse, exterior, and the ramp leading down to the ocean. Cuthbert Bennett is scraping down an old rowboat like the ones whaling men used, and Colm is helping him. They're talking animatedly to each other) presumably Couth is explaining the algae, kelp, barnacle and crustacean world stuck to the boat's bottom, but there is no sync sound. The voices are Ralph Packer's and Couth's)

RALPH: Let me put it another way: I mean, you're living with his wife and child. Has that put a strain on your friendship with him?

COUTH: I think it must be very hard for him—but because of what he feels for her, that's all. It's hard for him to be around her and the boy now. It's got nothing to do with me; I'm sure he's still fond of me.

CUT.
(In the Packer studio, Bogus speaks [sync sound] into camera)

BOGUS: I couldn't be happier about who she's living with. Couth is an absolutely wonderful person . . .

CUT.
(The boathouse again, with Couth and Colm, voices over)

COUTH: I know I'm very fond of him . . .

RALPH: Why didn't the marriage work?

COUTH: Well, look, you should ask her that, really.

RALPH: I just meant, you must have an opinion ...

COUTH: Ask her. Or him ...

CUT BACK.
(In the studio, Bogus speaks [sync sound] into camera)

BOGUS: Shit—ask her!

CUT.
(On the deck in Maine, Biggie is reading a storybook to Colm. There is no sync sound; the voices over are Biggie's and Ralph's)

BIGGIE: Did you ask him?

RALPH: He said to ask you.

BIGGIE: Well, I'm sure I don't know. I know that even if I knew why it couldn't change anything, so what does it matter?

RALPH: Who left whom?

BIGGIE: What does it matter?

RALPH: Shit, Biggie ...

BIGGIE: He left me.

CUT BACK.
(Bogus in the studio)

BOGUS: Well, she asked me to leave. No, actually, she *told* me to ...

CUT.
(Biggie is sitting with Colm and Couth around an outdoor

table under a large umbrella set up on the Pillsbury's dock. It is a deliberately formal, stilted scene, and the three of them look distrustfully at the camera. There is sync sound; Ralph [offstage] is interviewing them)

BIGGIE: I had no idea he was going to stay away, for so *long*, I mean ...

COUTH: She had no idea where he was, even.

BIGGIE: *(looking hard at camera, speaking to Ralph angrily)* You knew more than anyone, you bastard. You knew where he was going—you even helped him! Don't think I don't remember ...

CUT.
(Ralph Packer in the editing room of his studio, running film strips through a machine. Other strips clipped to rods overhead hang down all around him. There is no sync sound)

RALPH *(voice over)*: That's true ... I knew where he was going, all right, and I helped him to leave. But he *wanted to* leave!

(He pushed the heavy splice lever of the machine down emphatically)

CUT.
(The first in a series of still photographs. Bogus and Biggie in an Alpine Village, leaning against a strange old car and smiling at the photographer. Biggie looks sexy in her stretch ski clothes)

RALPH: (v.o.) He went back to Europe, that's where he went. Maybe he was nostalgic ...

(Another still: Biggie and Bogus clowning in a big rumpled bed, the covers pulled up to their chins)

RALPH: (v.o.) He never made it clear why he went to Europe, but he mentions this friend he had ... a Merrill Overturf.

(Another still: a strange-looking fellow wearing a weird hat is sitting in an old Zorn-Witwer, '54, grinning at the camera out his rolled-down window)

BIGGIE: (v.o.) That's him, all right. That's Merrill Overturf.

CUT BACK.
(The table and umbrella on the dock. With sync sound, Biggie speaks into camera)

BIGGIE: Merrill Overturf was absolutely crazy, completely mad.

CUT BACK.
(Bogus in the studio [sync sound])

BOGUS: No! He wasn't; he wasn't crazy at all. She never really knew him like I did. He was about the most sane person I've ever known ...

CUT BACK.
(In the editing room, Ralph raises the splice lever and looks through more film strips)

RALPH: (v.o.) It's very hard to get anything very concrete out of him. He takes it all so *personally*. He can really be uncooperative sometimes ...

(He chomps the splice lever down again)

CUT. *(Sync sound)*
(A dazzling series of stage lights are set up outside the closed bathroom door in Tulpen's apartment. Inside the bathroom a toilet flushes. Kent moves into frame, waiting in ambush at the bathroom door with a big microphone in his hand. Bogus opens the door, zips up his fly, looks up

235

surprised into camera. He is angry; he bats Kent aside and glares at camera)

BOGUS: *(Yelling, his face distorted)* Would you fuck off, Ralph!

24 : How Far Can You Get
with an Arrow in Your Tit?

It warmed his heart to find Overturf still listed in the phone book at the same address, with the same number. But when he tried to call from the lobby of the Taschy, there was a strange whirring cry over the phone, some sort of signal. He asked Frau Taschy, who informed him that the noise meant that the number was no longer in service. Then he realized that the phone book was more than five years old, and that his own name was listed in it—at the same address, with the same number.

Trumper walked to Schwindgasse 15, apartment 2. A brass nameplate on the door said: A. PLOT.

Rather like Merrill, Bogus thought. Beating on the door, he heard scuffles, perhaps a growl. He pushed and the door opened, but only so far as the ball-and-chain device would let it. It was fortunate that it didn't open further, because the large German shepherd inside the apartment was only able to get the tip of his snarling muzzle in the crack of the door. Trumper jumped back unbitten, and a woman—blond, her hair in curlers, her eyes angry or frightened or both—asked him what in hell he meant by trying to sneak into her apartment.

"Merrill Overturf?" he said to her, standing well back on the landing in case she let her German shepherd out.

"You're not Merrill Overturf," she told him.

"No, of course, I'm not," he said, but she closed the door. "Wait!" he cried after her. "I just wanted to know where he was . . ." But he heard her voice speaking low, presumably on the phone, and left quickly.

Out on the Schwindgasse, he looked up at what had once been Overturf's famous window box. Merrill had grown pot in it. But now the window box contained only some purplish dead plants poking out through a dusting of snow.

A child wheeled her tricycle up to the lobby door and got off to open it. Bogus helped her.

"Does Merrill Overturf live in this building?" he asked her. She either caught his accent or had been told never to speak to strangers, because she looked at him as if she had no intention of answering.

"Where do you think Herr Overturf went?" he asked her gently, helping her get her trike inside. But the little girl just stared at him. "Herr Overturf?" he said to her slowly. "Do you remember? He had a funny car, he wore funny hats . . ." The little girl didn't appear to know anything. Upstairs the big dog barked. "What happened to Herr Overturf?" Bogus tried once more.

The little girl was edging her tricycle away from him. "Dead?" she asked him; it was a guess, he felt sure. Then she ran away, streaking towards the stairs, leaving him with a chill equaled only by the one he felt when he heard a door open above, heard the woman with the haircurlers yelling at the child, heard the clatter of what had to be the big dog's toenails coming downstairs.

Trumper fled. The little girl didn't know anything anyway; that was clear. With some astonishment, he realized that the father of the child must be named A. Plot.

With a bag of sidewalk-roasted chestnuts, Bogus slouches in the general direction of the Michaelerplatz, where there's a grotesque statue he remembers. A Zeus-like giant of a man, or a god, is struggling with sea monsters, snakes, birds of prey, lions and young nymphets; they are dragging him down to the main spigot of a fountain that splashes his chest; his mouth gapes in strain—or perhaps he is thirsty. The whole work is so overwrought that it's hard to tell whether Zeus is in control, or whether the creatures draped around him are wrestling him down or trying to lift him up.

238

Bogus recalls weaving through the Michaelerplatz one night, drunk with Biggie. They had just swiped some huge white radishes as long as carrots off a horsecart. Passing by this monstrous eternal struggle in the fountain, Bogus boosted Biggie up and she placed a radish in the gaping god's mouth. For energy, she said.

Thinking he'll feed the wrestler a chestnut, Trumper is surprised to find the fountain shut off. Or the spigot has frozen; it spouts a thick, blunt phallus, a rigid, wax-gobbed candle, and the Zeus figure's chest is layered with ice. Somehow, though the pose is the same, the struggle appears to be over. He's dead, thinks Bogus, and there's no point in feeding chestnuts to the dead. He regrets the demise of the god, finally conquered by the snakes and sea monsters, lions and nymphets. Trumper knows: It was the nymphets who finally got to him.

Surely Biggie would be miserable to hear the news. Surely she *is* miserable.

Biggie, it may be hard for you to believe this, but ... when you go duck hunting, you wear a condom. It's an old sportsman's trick against the cold. You see, all the duck hunters slip on a condom before they go retrieving fallen birds from icy waters—when they don't have dogs, which we didn't. It works on the same principle as a wetsuit ...

Or—wandering now through the Habsburg's courtyard, the Plaza of Heroes—*the reason I was wearing that unmentionable rubber, which I neglected to remove, was because of my new part-time job as a demonstration model for the Student Health Service's class for freshmen in Sex Education. I was too embarrassed to tell you about it. They hadn't told me there would be a session on contraception. Of course the class was surprised.*

But Bogus feels the cold eyes of the stony cupids on him; passing under these Baroque cherubs and the pigeons perched on the formidable palace buildings, he knows that Biggie is no sucker. *She is already too familiar with the improbability of me.*

He watched the *Strassenbahnen* tilting along the Burg Ring, their sharp bells gonging at the intersections. Inside, the streetcar passengers steam and smear the windows, and the men look like overcoats hung on a clothes rack

239

with people in them. They jostle and sway with every lurch of the tram; their hands on the overhead rails are above the windows, and Bogus can see only that their arms are raised, like children in school, like soldiers at a rally.

Wanting to kill the afternoon, Trumper reads his way around a tattered kiosk. The afternoon, he feels, would die most painlessly at some Sunday matinée for kids, and miraculously he finds one, up Stadiongasse and behind the Parliament building.

There are many short subjects and an American Western. Trumper travels to Ireland, sees the happy peasants. In Java the travel guide tells the audience about the national pastime: boxing with your feet. But Bogus and the children are restless; they want the Western. And here it comes at last! Jimmy Stewart, speaking German, almost in time with the dubbed-in German voice. The Indians did not want the railroad. That was the plot.

Jimmy Stewart pumped a carbine from his hip, and it might have been a pre-ravaged Shelly Winters with an arrow sunk in her ample bosom. Whoever she was, she rolled off the caboose, down a gully, into a creek where she was trampled by wild horses—just passing by—and lecherously mauled by an Indian who was too chicken to attack the train. She was forced to endure all these things until she could locate the derringer stuffed in her bleeding cleavage, with which she blew a large hole through the Indian's throat. Not until then did she stand upright and sodden, all the creek- and blood-soaked parts of her garments clinging to her, and yell, *"Hilfe!"*—all this while wrenching away at the arrow stuck in her heaving tit.

Stopping for a greasy sausage and a glass of new wine, Trumper sat in the Augustiner Keller listening to an ancient string quartet and reflecting that Hollywood stunt women would be very interesting to meet, but that he hoped not all of them had hair in their cleavage.

As he walked back to the Taschy, the street lamps came on, but spastically, fading on and off, without a trace of the clockwork precision of Iowa City; as if Viennese electricity was a recent, unsure improvement over gas.

Outside a *Kaffeehaus* on Plankengasse, a man spoke to

him. *"Grajak ok bretzet,"* he seemed to say, and Trumper paused, trying to place this queer language. *"Bretzet, jak?"* the man said, and Trumper thought, Czech? Hungarian? Serbo-Croatian? *"Gra! Nucemo paz!"* man shouted. He was angry about something and waved his fist at Trumper.

Bogus asked, *"Ut boethra rast, kelk?"* Old Low Norse never hurt a soul.

"Gra?" the man said suspiciously. *"Grajak, ok,"* he added with more confidence. Then he shouted eagerly, *"Nucemo paz tzet!"*

Bogus was sorry he didn't understand, and began to say in Old Low Norse: *"Ijs kik . . ."*

"Kik?" the man interrupted, smiling at Bogus. *"Gra, gra, gra! Kik!"* he cried, trying to shake Trumper's hand.

"Gra, gra, gra!" replied Bogus, and shook hands with the man who weaved and mumbled, *"Gra, gra,"* nodding with greater conviction before he turned away and stumbled off the curb, veering across the street stooped over; like a blind man groping for the opposite sidewalk, he aimed his feet and protected his crotch with his hands.

Bogus thought that it had been like a conversation with Mr. Fitch. Then he glumly noted a crumpled scrap of newspaper on the sidewalk; it was unreadable, printed in what looked like the Cyrillic alphabet, the letters looking more like music than parts of words. He looked around for the little man, but there wasn't a trace of him. The article, torn from some paper in the queer language, looked important—phrases underlined with a ballpoint pen, comments scribbled emphatically in the margins in the same script—so he pocketed the strange scrap.

Trumper felt his mind floating. Back at the Taschy, he tried to focus on something familiar enough to bring it back home. He attempted to write a review of the Western movie, but his typewriter's umlaut keys distracted him, and he found that he'd forgotten the film's title. *How Far Can You Get with an Arrow in Your Tit?* Just then, as if by association, the bidets downstairs began their nightly flushing.

Bogus caught his own reflection in the ornate French window reaching nearly to the ceiling; he and his typewriter occupied only the bottom-corner pane. In an effort to rescue his small and sinking soul, he tore the review out of his typewriter and, avoiding umlauts, tried to write to his wife.

Pension Taschy
Spiegelgasse 29
Vienna 1, Austria

Dear Biggie:

Thinking of you, Colm, and you too, Biggie—the night your navel distended in East Gunnery, Vermont. You were in your eighth month, Big, when your bellybutton turned inside out.

We rode three hours from Great Boar's Head in Couth's old airy Volkswagen, with the sunroof missing. In Portsmouth it was cloudy; and in Manchester, Peterborough and Keene, it was cloudy too. And in each place, Couth said, "I hope it doesn't rain."

Three times I traded seats with you, Big. You were not comfortable. Three times you said, "Oh God, I'm so *big!*"

"Like a full moon," Couth told you. "You're lovely."

But you bitched away, Biggie—still smarting, of course, over my father's crude manner of referring to our lewd and irresponsible mating.

"Think of it this way," Couth told you. "Think how happy the baby will be having parents so close to its own age."

"And think of the *genes*, Big," I told you. "What a masterful bunch of genes!"

But you said, "I'm tired of thinking about this baby."

"Well, you two will be together this way," Couth said. "Think of all the decisions you don't have to make now."

"There wouldn't have been *any* decisions," you told poor Couth, who was only trying to cheer you up. "Bogus would never be marrying me if I wasn't going to have this baby."

But all I said was, "Well, here we are in Vermont," looking up through the hole in the roof at the rusty girders of the bridge over the Connecticut.

You wouldn't let it drop, though, Biggie, even though we'd had this conversation several times before, and I wasn't about to be drawn into it again.

You said to me, "Bogus, you wouldn't have married me, ever. I know it."

And Couth, bless him, said, "Then *I'd* have married you, Biggie—at full moon, half moon or no moon at all. I'd have married you, and I still would, if Bogus wasn't going to. And think what that would have been like, now I ask you . . ." Then, hunched over the wheel, he turned his fabulous smile to you—showing you how he could manipulate with his tongue his front-four false teeth.

Which at least put a small smile on your face, Biggie. You were a little less pale when we got to East Gunnery.

But in the Pension Taschy, Bogus was distracted when he thought of East Gunnery. Reading over what he'd written, he decided he didn't like it. The tone seemed wrong to him, so he tried again, beginning after the line, ". . . when your bellybutton turned inside out."

We hid Couth and his Volkswagen in the lower field and walked up the long dirt driveway to your father's farm. Here comes the child bride, with a bundle in her belly! And I suspect I accused you of cowardice for not writing some word of this to your parents.

"I wrote them about you, Bogus," you told me. "Which is more than you ever warned your parents."

"Only not about your condition, Big," I remarked. "You said nothing about that."

"No, not about that," you said, tugging your tight raincoat away from yourself, trying to create the illusion that your coat was swollen only because you had your hands in your pockets.

I looked back at Couth, who waved a little fearfully, looming out of his sunroof like some hairy, human periscope.

"Couth can come up to the house too," you said. "He doesn't have to hide in the field." But I told you that Couth was shy and felt better hiding in the field. I didn't mention that I thought we might appear more forgivable if we walked in alone, or that it would be nice to know that Couth and his car were safe in the pasture, in case I had to leave.

The most anxious time, I think, was when, passing by your father's jeep, you said, "Oh, my father's home too. God, Father, Mother, *everybody!*"

Then I reminded you that it was Sunday.

"Then Aunt Blackstone is here too," you said. "Aunt Blackstone is quite deaf."

They were eating dinner, and you kept your hands in your raincoat pockets, twirling your coke-bottle shape around the dining-room table, saying, "This is Bogus. You know, I *told* you! I *wrote* you!" Until your mother began to glide her eyes down your front, Biggie, and your deaf Aunt Blackstone said, "Hasn't Sue put on the old weight, though?" to your mother. Who stared rather stonily. And you said, "I'm pregnant." Adding, "But it's all right!"

"Yes! It's all right!" I cried out witlessly, watching your father's unmoving fork, dripping pot roast and an onion, poised an inch from his open mouth.

"It's all right," you said again, smiling at everyone.

"Of course it is," said Aunt Blackstone, who hadn't really heard.

"Yes, yes," I mumbled, nodding.

And your deaf Aunt Blackstone, nodding back to me, said, "Certainly *yes!* all that fat German food in her, putting the old weight on. Besides, the child hasn't skied all summer!" And looking at your dumbstruck mother, Aunt Blackstone said in her shrill, clear voice, *"Gracious,* Hilda, is that any way to greet your daughter? I can remember *you* always put the old weight on and off, any time you pleased ..."

While at the Taschy, two bidets flushed simultaneously, and Bogus Trumper lost the memory part of his mind. And perhaps other, closely related parts of his mind, as well.

25 : Getting Ready for Ralph

In the fishy dark, the turtle murk of Tulpen's apartment, Trumper sat up in bed hopping mad and as rigid as a cigar-store Indian. Lately he'd developed a habit of furious fuming. He would concentrate fiercely on not moving at all, on simulating a brooding statue. It was a sort of isometric which eventually exhausted him. He was having trouble sleeping again.

"Oh, come on, Trumper," Tulpen whispered to him. She touched his wooden thigh.

Trumper concentrated on the fish. There was a new one who especially irked him, a beige sort of blowfish whose gross practice was to smear its translucent lips against the aquarium wall and belch little trapped bubbles against the glass. Unable to escape, the gas would bounce back into the fish, which would then swell up. As it grew larger, its eyes got smaller, until suddenly the air pressure inside it would propel it away from the glass, rather like a balloon someone has blown up and then released. In reverse, the beige blowfish would career about the tank like a rotary motor broken loose. The other fish were terrified of it. Trumper wanted to prick it with a pin at the pinnacle of its swollen state. The fish always seemed to be facing Trumper when it began to bloat itself. It was a stupid way of antagonizing the enemy; the fish should have known better.

Actually, Trumper disliked *all* the fish, and his present irritation was enough to set him to imagining how he would dispose of them. Go out and buy a terrifying fish-eating fish, an omnivore which would scour the tank of every other swimming, crawling, gliding thing—and then eat all the shells, rocks, algae, and even the air hose. Then it would gnaw its way through the glass, let the water out and die for lack of oxygen. Even better: flopping about on the dry aquarium floor, it would have the good sense to eat itself. What an admirable omnivore! Immediately he wanted one.

The phone rang again. Trumper didn't move, and the sidewise glance darted in Tulpen's direction convinced her that she'd better not answer it, either. A few minutes before, he had answered the phone, and that call had been partially responsible for his destructive impulses toward helpless fish and for his cigar-store-Indian imitation.

It had been Ralph Packer who had called. Though Bogus and Tulpen had just gone to bed, Ralph wanted to come over right away with Kent and several thousand dollars' worth of movie equipment. He wanted some footage of Tulpen and Bogus going to bed.

"Jesus, Ralph," Trumper said.

"No, no!" Ralph said. "Just going to bed, Thump-Thump. You know, domestic stuff—bathroom routine, teeth brushing, taking off clothes, little familiar affections, shit like that . . ."

"Good night, Ralph."

"Thump-Thump, it won't take half an hour!"

Trumper hung up and turned to Tulpen. "I don't understand," he shouted, "how you ever could have slept with him."

That set a lot of things off.

"He was interesting," Tulpen said. "I was interested in what he did."

"In bed?"

"Shove it, Trumper."

"No, really!" he yelled at her. "I want to know! Did you like sleeping with him?"

"I like sleeping with you much better," she said. "I did not sustain an interest in Ralph in that way."

Her voice had some ice in it, but Trumper didn't seem to care. "You realized it had been a mistake," he prodded.

"No," she said. "I just wasn't interested in doing it any more. It wasn't any mistake. I didn't know anybody else, then . . ."

"And then you met me?"

246

"I stopped sleeping with Ralph before I met you."

"Why did you stop?" he asked.

She rolled over in bed, so that her back was to him. "My twat fell out," she said to the wall of aquariums.

Trumper didn't say anything; he began his trance then.

"Look," Tulpen said a few minutes later. "What is it? I just didn't feel much for Ralph that way. But I liked him, and I still like him, Trumper. Just not in that way . . ."

"Do you ever think about sleeping with him again?"

"No."

"Well, *he* thinks about sleeping with you again."

"How do you know?"

"Interested?" he asked. She swore to herself and turned away from him. He felt himself turning to stone.

"Trumper?" she asked him later; he'd been still a long while. "Why don't you like Ralph, Trumper? Is it the film?"

But it wasn't that, really. After all, he could have simply refused; he could have said that it touched him too deeply. But it didn't, and he had to admit that he had an interest in it. It was not a therapeutic interest, either; he knew he was basically a ham, and he liked seeing himself in a movie.

"It's not that I don't like Ralph, exactly," he answered. She rolled over, touched his wooden thigh, and said something he didn't hear. Then . . . he thought of killing the fish, and when the phone rang again, he would have killed the first person who touched it.

He had a cramp in his back from sitting up straight for so long, and Tulpen left him alone for a while before she tried again. "Trumper? You know, you don't make love to me enough. Not nearly enough."

He thought about that. Then he thought about his pending operation, about Dr. Vigneron and the water method. "It's my prick," he said at last. "I'm going to get it fixed up, so I'll be good as new."

But he liked making love to Tulpen very much, and he was worried by what she said. He thought about making love to her right now, but he had to get up to pee.

In the bathroom he studied himself in the mirror and watched the fear come into his expression when he had to pinch himself open before he could go. It was getting worse. Vigneron had been right again; you sometimes *did* have to wait a few weeks for minor surgery.

It seemed essential to him that he make love to Tulpen right away, but then—perhaps because he recognized something in his expression in the mirror—he thought of Merrill Overturf and pissed so hard that tears came to his eyes.

He was in the bathroom a long time, until Tulpen, groggy, called to him from the bed. "What are you doing in there?" she called.

"Oh, nothing, Big," he said, then tried to swallow it back.

When he came back to bed, she was sitting up, the covers tight around her, crying. She'd heard him say it, all right.

"Tulpen," he said, putting his arm around her.

"No, 'Biggie,' " she whispered.

"Tulpen," he said, and tried to kiss her.

She shoved him away; she was out to get him now. "I'll tell you one thing," she said. "Old Ralph Packer never called me anyone else's name."

Trumper moved away and sat at the foot of the bed.

"And you want to know what?" she yelled. "I think it's bullshit that you don't make love to me enough because of your old prick!"

Then the beige blowfish came up to the glass again, stared at Trumper and went through its gross routine once more.

What Tulpen said was true and he knew it. What pained him worse was that this conversation wasn't new. He'd had it all before—a number of times—with Biggie. So he sat at the foot of the bed, wished for catatonia and achieved it. When the phone rang a third time, he didn't care whether it was Ralph or not. If he could have moved, he would have answered it.

Tulpen probably felt just as lonely, because she answered it. "Sure," Bogus heard her say tiredly. "Sure, come on over and make your fucking movie."

But Trumper still sat there like a stone worrying about the next transition. To be in Ralph's movie required that he get out of the movie he was in now, didn't it?

Then Tulpen put her head in his lap, her face turned up

248

to him. It was a gesture—she had many of them—as if to say, Okay, a bridge in our complex landscape is now at least defined, though not yet crossed. Maybe it can be.

They stayed in that position for a long time, as if that were as good a way as any to get ready for Ralph.

"Trumper?" Tulpen whispered finally. "When you *do* make love to me, I really like it."

"So do I," he said.

26 : *"Gra! Gra!"*

Just how long his mind was lost he didn't know, or how
fully he'd recovered it by the time he was aware of some
more writing in the typewriter before him. He read it, wondering who had written it, poring over it like a letter he'd
received, or even like someone else's letter to someone else.
Then he saw the dark, crouching figure in the bottom corner of his French windows and startled himself by suddenly sitting upright and moaning, while simultaneously in
the mirroring window, a terrifying gnomelike replica of
himself reared up and bleared like a microscopic specimen.

It was when he recognized the moan as his own that he
also heard the growing commotion downstairs in the
Taschy lobby, or perhaps as close as the second floor. Not
remembering where he was, he opened his door and
screamed some hysterical gibberish at the faces peering
from the open doorways up and down the hall. Matching
him terror for terror, three faces screamed back at him,
and Trumper tried to identify the other noise, which was
rising like fire from the second floor.

Which tape is this? When was I in an asylum?

Cautiously he crept toward the stairwell; all along the
hall no one ventured out a doorway—for fear, perhaps,
that he'd scream at them again.

Up the stairwell, Frau Taschy's voice reached him. "Is
he dead?" she asked, and Trumper heard himself whisper,
"No, I am not." But they were talking about someone
else.

He moved down to the half-landing and saw a crush of
people milling in the hall below. One of the whores was
250

saying, "I'm sure he's dead. No one ever passed out on me like that—never."

"You shouldn't have moved him," someone said.

"I had to get him off me, didn't I?" the whore said, and Frau Taschy looked scornfully down the hall at a man emerging from a room, zipping his fly, carrying his shoes under one arm. The whore emerging behind him said, "What is it? What's wrong?"

"Someone died on Jolanta," someone said, and they all laughed.

"You were too much for him," said another of the ladies, and Jolanta, who was wearing only her girdle and stockings, said, "Maybe he just had too much to drink."

Along the hall, dark and head-down men burst from rooms, carrying their clothes, as darting in their movements as startled birds.

"He's too young to be dead," Frau Taschy said, which seemed to make the scurrying men sidle past her even more fearfully. It was as if they'd never thought of it before: *fucking can be dangerous. It can even kill the young!*

Such a notion hardly came as a surprise to Trumper, who moved confidently down from the half-landing into the sex-smelling hall, as if his mind had now adjusted and accepted the creature in the window as his own reflection, or as if he were asleep. In fact, he wasn't sure that he wasn't.

The whore said, "He went cold all over. I mean *cold.*"

But in the doorway of the stricken screwer's room, Frau Taschy said, "He moved! I swear he did!"

The gathering in the hall was almost equally divided between those who moved away from the doorway and those who moved closer in order to see.

"He moved again!" Frau Taschy reported.

"Touch him!" said the whore who'd been involved. "Just feel how cold he is."

"I'm not going to touch him, you can bet your life," the Frau said. "But you just *look* and tell me he's not moving."

Trumper moved closer; over a warm, perfumed shoulder he saw through the doorway a shocking flash of nude

251

white rump aquiver on the rumpled bed; then the doorway filled and cut off his vision.

"Polizei!" someone yelled, and a man carrying all his clothes in a hasty wad bolted nude from a room down the hall, looked at the crowd and then hobbled back into his room. *"Polizei!"* someone repeated as three policemen came down the hall abreast, in step—the two flanking the broader one, solidly in the middle, flicking open any closed door along the way. The one in the middle stared straight ahead and brayed, "Don't anyone try to leave."

"Look, he's sitting up," Frau Taschy remarked to the doorway.

"Where's the trouble?" the middle policeman asked.

Jolanta said, "He blacked out. He went cold, right on top of me." But when she approached the middle policeman, one of the flankers cut her off.

"Move back," he said. "Everyone move back."

"What's happened here?" the middle policeman asked. The long gloves above his wrists were creased where his wrists cocked on his hips.

"Jesus, if you'll just let me," said the whore who'd been shoved off, "I can tell you all about it."

The same policeman who'd cut her off said, "Well, do it, then."

Then Frau Taschy cried, "He's getting up! He's not dead! He never was!" But by the ensuing crash and groan, Bogus knew that the revival had been momentary.

"Oh, dear," the Frau muttered.

Then the voice came up from the floor of the room, a voice just beginning to thaw out, slow and faint through all those chattering teeth. *"Ich bin nicht betrunken"* ("I am not drunk") the voice said. *"Ich habe Zuckerkrankheit"* ("I have diabetes").

The middle policeman parted the mob at the doorway and swaggered roughly into the room, stepping on the outstretched hand of the pale creature curled on the threshold; the other hand weakly twitched at a tinny batch of tangled dog tags hung around the creature's neck.

"Was Sie sehen ist ein Insulinreaktion" ("What you're seeing is an insulin reaction"), the creature droned. It was like a recorded voice, an answering service.

252

"Füttern Sie mir Zucker, schnell!" ("Feed me sugar, quick!"), the voice cried.

"Oh, sure," the policeman said. "Oh, sugar. You bet." And he stopped to lift Merrill Overturf, as limp as an empty bathrobe, off the floor.

"Sugar, he says," the policeman quipped. "He wants sugar!"

"He's a diabetic," Trumper told a whore near him, and he reached out to touch Merrill's crumpled hand. "Hello, old Merrill," Bogus said, before one of the flanking policemen, apparently misinterpreting the gesture toward the draped Overturf, dropped an elbow in Trumper's solar plexus and sent him spinning into a soft, musky lady who fiercely bit this surprise attacker in the neck. Out of breath, Bogus flayed out, trying to make words with his hands, but the two policemen pinned him against the banister and bent his head back, upside down in the stairwell. Upside down, Bogus saw Merrill carried down the stairs to the lobby. Competing with the creaking of the opening lobby door, Merrill's voice sang out, brittle and frail, *"Ich bin nicht betrunken!"* Then the lobby door shut on his high, thin wail.

Trumper fought for breath to explain. But he had only managed to grunt, "He's not drunk. Let me go with him," before one of the policemen squeezed his lips tight together, kneading them like bread dough.

Bogus shut his eyes and heard a whore say, "He's a diabetic." While one of the policemen grumbled in Trumper's ear, "So you want to go with him, do you? What do you want to get your hands on him for?" When Trumper tried to shake his head and explain through his mushed mouth that he'd only reached out to touch Merrill because he was a friend, the whore said again, "He's a diabetic. He told me. Let him go."

"A diabetic?" said one policeman. Bogus felt his pulse throb behind his eyes. "A diabetic, eh?" the policemen repeated. Then they snapped Bogus upright and took their hands off his mouth. "Are you a diabetic?" one of the policemen asked him; they both stood warily, not touching him but ready to.

"No," Bogus said, feeling his stinging mouth, then said "No" again, sure that they hadn't heard him because his mouth was full of burrs. "No, I am not a diabetic," he said more distinctly.

So they grabbed him again. "I didn't think he was one," one policeman said to the other. As they bustled him through the lobby and outside into the first shock of cold, Bogus heard the faint, tired explanation of the whore behind them, calling, "No, no . . . Jesus. *He's* not the diabetic. Oh, Christ, I just meant he told me that the *other* one was . . ." Then the lobby door shut her off and left Bogus in motion on the sidewalk, flanked by the two policemen hustling him away.

"Where are we going?" Bogus asked them. "My passport's in my room. For Christ's sake, I don't have to be treated like this! I wasn't attacking that fellow—he's my fucking friend! And he's got diabetes. Take me where he is . . ." But they just stuffed him into a green *Polizei* Volkswagen, cracking his shins on the seat-belt fixture and bending him over double to fit him the way they wanted him in the backseat. They handcuffed him to a neat little metal loop fastened on the floor in back, so that he was forced to ride with his head between his knees. "You must be crazy," he told them. "You don't care what I say." He turned his head; through the peepsight between his calf and his bent knee he could spot the policeman riding with him in the back. "You're an anus," Trumper told him. "And so's the other one." He swung his head so that he bumped the back of the driver's seat and drew out a short oath from the driver.

The back-seat policeman said, "You take it easy, okay?"

"You gaping anal pore!" Trumper told him, but the policeman only leaned forward, almost politely inquisitive, as if he hadn't quite heard. "Your mind has syphilis," Trumper said, and the policeman shrugged.

The front-seat policeman asked, "Doesn't he speak any German? I know he was speaking some German; I heard him, I think. Tell him to speak German."

Bogus felt a chill jerk his spine upward and make his hands rattle the handcuffs. I could have sworn I was speaking German!

In German Trumper shouted, "You asshole!" Too late to move his head, he saw the black hard-rubber truncheon flick in the policeman's hand.

254

Then he heard the radio. A voice said: "A drunk ..."
And he heard his own voice murmur, *"Ich bin nicht be-trunken ..."* Then he regretted saying anything, seeing the truncheon lash out and hearing the *thwock!* against his ribs, not really feeling it until his next breath.

"A drunk," the radio reported. He tried not to breathe again.

"Breathe, please ..." said the radio-announcing voice. He breathed, and went cold all over.

"He went cold all over," said a recorded whore.

"You mother," Trumper mumbled. "You recorded whore ..." And the truncheon fell across his ribs, his wrists, his kidneys and his mind.

It took him a long time to swim out to the exact place in the Danube where he could see the underwater tank. Treading water and keeping a landsight on the light at the Gelhafts Keller's dock, he saw the tank's barrel swing up to where he thought he could almost touch it, or where it was perfectly aimed to blast him. Then the tank's top hatch opened, or seemed to, or at least fluttered in the water. Who is down the tank's hatch? Wouldn't somebody be interested to know they were there? But then he thought, I am in a Volkswagen, and if there's a hole in the roof, I am safe with Couth.

Then the bidets flushed and rinsed his mind.

Just how long his mind was lost he didn't know, or how fully he'd recovered it by the time he was aware of some more writing in the typewriter before him. He read it, wondering who had written it, poring over it like a letter he'd received, or even like someone else's letter to someone else. Then he saw the dark, crouching figure in the bottom corner of his French windows, and startled himself by suddenly sitting upright and moaning, while simultaneously in the mirroring window, a terrifying gnomelike replica of himself reared up and bleared like a microscopic specimen.

When he opened the door to the hall, he was met by a sea of faces—whores with their customers, Frau Taschy and a cop.

"What's the matter?" several of them said.

"What?"

"What's the trouble here?" the cop asked.

"What were you screaming about?" Frau Taschy asked.

"Drunk," a whore whispered.

Like a recording, Trumper said, *"Ich bin nicht betrunken."*

"You were screaming, though," Frau Taschy said. The cop stepped closer, peering behind Bogus into the room.

But the cop said only, "Been writing, eh?" Trumper looked for the cop's truncheon. "What are you looking at?" the cop asked him. He had no truncheon.

Bogus stepped softly back into his room and closed his door. He stuck his finger in his eye; it hurt. He felt his neck where the whore had bitten him; he felt no pain. His wrists and ribs where he'd been whacked by the truncheon weren't tender.

Listening to the murmur in the hall outside, he packed. *They are willing the door off its hinges.* But they weren't; they were only standing there when he came out. He felt that if he didn't take charge, they would take charge of him. So he said with great dignity, "I'm leaving. It's impossible to work here with all your noise." To Frau Taschy he held out what he figured to be more than enough money, but she made up some wild tale about his having been there for a couple of months. He felt confused; with the cop right there, he thought he'd better pay her what she asked for. His passport was peeking out of the pocket of his spy suit, and when the cop asked to see it, he nodded to the pocket, making the cop reach in gingerly for it.

Then Bogus made one last check, just to be sure. "Merrill Overturf?" he said. "He's a diabetic?" But no one seemed to respond; in fact, some of the crowd looked away from him, pretending not to hear, as if their embarrassment for him was so great that they feared that at any second he would take off his clothes.

Outside, the cop followed him for a block or two—waiting, no doubt, to see if he would leap in front of a car or dive through a store window. But Bogus set a brisk pace, walking as if he had in mind some place to go, and the cop fell back and disappeared. Trumper was alone, then, circling the Graben on safe little side streets; it took him a while to locate the Kaffeehaus Leopold Hawelka, and he hesitated before going in, as if he knew everyone who would be there, even as if his search for Merrill had never really progressed beyond his first inquiries here.

Inside, he saw the nervous waiter and smiled at him. He saw the young girl who'd known Merrill in some way at some other time. He saw the heavy girl with the neon-green eyeshadow, the Head Den Mother, who was briefing a table of disciples. What he wasn't quite prepared for was the great-bearded prophet who sat almost hidden behind the door—like the toughies who check ID's in America, or the wise-ass ticket-takers at dirty movies. When the prophet spoke, he bellowed, and Bogus wheeled around suddenly to see who was shouting.

"Merrill Overturf!" the prophet boomed. "Well, did you find him?" Whether it was the volume of the voice or the fact that it rendered Trumper motionless, frozen in an awkward pivot stance, almost all the Hawelka customers seemed to think the question was directed to them; they froze too, suspended over their coffees, mired in their rummed teas, beers and brandies; fastened, unchewing, to whatever they'd been gnawing.

"Well, *did* you?" the prophet asked impatiently. "Merrill Overturf, you said, wasn't it? Weren't you looking for him? Did you find him?"

All the Hawelka waited for an answer. Bogus balked; he felt as if he were a reel of film being rewound before he was finished.

"Well?" said the neon-green girl softly. "Did you find him?"

"I don't know," Trumper said.

"You don't know?" the prophet boomed.

With a sickening sympathy in her voice, the neon-green girl begged him. "Here, come and sit, you. You've got to get this off your mind, I think. I can tell . . ."

But he whirled himself and his bulky suitcase toward the door, hitting the waiter in the groin with it and causing that natty, agile man to fold—maintaining, for just a moment, a neat balancing feat with the sliding coffees and beers on his tray.

The prophet made a grab for Bogus at the door, but Bogus slipped by him, hearing the prophet announce, "He must be on something . . ." Just before the door closed, he heard the prophet call, "Ride it out. You'll come down . . ."

Outside the Hawelka, someone in the shadows touched his hand with something like affection.

"Merrill?" Bogus asked in a whimper.

"Gra! Gra!" the man said, turning like a quarterback and thrusting a parcel, *Whunk!*, in Trumper's stomach. When he straightened up, the man was gone.

Stepping to the curb, he held the parcel up to the light; it was a firm, white-papered package, tied up with white butcher's string. He undid it. It looked like chocolate in that neon light, smooth and dark, queerly sticky to the touch; it gave off a minted smell. A mentholated slab of fudge? Queer gift. Then he bent closely over it, sniffed it deeply and touched it with his tongue. It was pure hashish, a perfectly cut rectangle slightly larger than a brick.

A clamor rose in his head as he tried to imagine what it was worth.

In the fogged-up window of the Hawelka, he saw a hand rub a peepsight out to the street. A voice inside announced, "He's still there."

So then he quickly wasn't. He didn't intend to go back out on the broad Graben; it was just the direction he happened to jog in that brought him out onto this glittery whoreful street. He crammed the hashish brick into his suitcase.

He didn't intend to speak to anyone, either; it was just that when he saw the lady in the fur coat with the matching muff, he saw she'd changed her clothes. No more fur coat, no more muff; she wore a spring suit, as if it were warm.

He asked her if she had the time.

27 : How Is Anything Related to Anything Else?

Ralph was attempting to explain the structure of his film by comparing it to a contemporary novel, Helmbart's *Vital Telegrams*.

"The structure is everything," he said. Then he quoted a blurb from the book jacket which said that Helmbart had achieved some kind of breakthrough. "The transitions—all the associations, in fact—are syntactical, rhetorical, *structural;* it is almost a story of sentence structure rather than of characters; Helmbart complicates variations on forms of sentences rather than plot," it read.

Kent nodded a lot, but Ralph was more anxious that Trumper and Tulpen understand him. The comparison to Helmbart's work was supposed to cast some needed light on Tulpen's editing and Trumper's sound tracking. "Do you see?" Ralph asked Tulpen.

"Did you like that book, Ralph?" Tulpen asked.

"Not the point, not the point, not the fucking point!" said Ralph. "I'm interested in it only as an example. Of course I didn't like it."

"I thought it was awful," Tulpen said.

"It was almost unreadable," said Trumper, marching off to the bathroom with the book under his arm. In fact, he hadn't even looked at it yet.

He sat in the bathroom surrounded by messages, due to the fact that the phone was in the bathroom. Ralph had moved it there when he became suspicious of the number of long-distance calls, which none of them would admit to making. He was sure that people were dropping in off

Christopher Street to make long-distance calls. They sneaked in, according to his theory, when he and Bogus and Tulpen and Kent were busy in the other rooms of the studio. But someone dropping in like that wouldn't dream of looking for the phone in the bathroom.

"Suppose they drop in to use the bathroom?" Trumper had asked.

But the phone was installed there, anyway. The walls, the flush-box lid, the mirror and the shelves were dotted with reminders, phone numbers, urgent requests and Kent's garbled translations of messages.

Taking the phone off the hook, Trumper opened *Vital Telegrams*. Ralph had remarked that the success of the structure made it possible to open the book at random and understand everything immediately, no matter where you began. Trumper opened it in the middle and read Chapter 77 from beginning to end.

Chapter 77

From the moment he saw her, he knew. Still, he persisted.

We felt at once that the ball-joint system was all wrong for the blivethefter. Why, then, did we force it?

The very second the goat was slain, we saw we were in for it. Pretending otherwise was absurb. Yet Mary Beth lied.

There was no sense whatsoever to the socket wrench being put to such a use. But it just might have worked.

There was nothing in the least amusing about the vile disembowelment of Charles. Strange we weren't shocked when Holly laughed.

With his feet as they were, Eddy could not have had much hope. To have seen him, though, you would have thought he still had toes.

"Don't come near me!" Estella wailed, holding out her arms.

We knew that the thought of chickpeas with bagels defied the concept of spreading. Still, they were both brown.

There was, of course, no logic to the dwarf's fear of Harold's rather large cat. But if you've ever spent some time down on your knees, you're surely aware of how differently things appear from down there.

That was Chapter 77. Curious about the vile disembowelment of Charles, Trumper read it again. He liked the bit about chickpeas and bagels. He read the chapter a third time and was irked that he didn't know what was wrong with Eddy's feet. And who was Estella?

Ralph knocked on the bathroom door; he wanted to use the phone.

"I understand the dwarf's fear of Harold's rather large cat," Trumper told him through the closed door. Ralph went away, swearing.

What Trumper had some difficulty understanding was what relation Helmbart's work had to Ralph's film. Then he thought of one: perhaps neither of them meant anything. Somehow that made him feel better about the film. Relaxed, he approached the toilet. But he was too relaxed; he'd forgotten to pinch himself open. A hose with an obstructed nozzle is difficult to aim. He pissed in his shoe, jumped back and elbowed the phone into the sink. Wincing, he awkwardly peed his way back to the toilet. In his condition, although it hurt to go, it hurt worse to stop.

So much for relaxing, he thought. He was reminded of one of the many lessons to be learned from *Akthelt and Gunnel*, the forbidding story of Sprog.

Sprog was Akthelt's bodyguard, armor bearer, valet, knife sharpener, head huntsman, chief scout, favorite sparring partner and trusted whore fetcher. When they were visiting captured towns, Sprog tasted everything that Akthelt was served before Akthelt would eat it.

Old Thak had given Sprog to Akthelt for Akthelt's twenty-first birthday. Akthelt was more pleased by Sprog than by any of his horses, dogs or other servants. For Sprog's birthday, Akthelt gave him a highly favored captured Greth woman named Fluvia. Akthelt had been quite taken by Fluvia himself, so you can see how much he thought of Sprog.

Sprog was not a Greth. There were no captured Greth men; only Greth women were captured. Greth men were forced to dig a large pit, then were stoned senseless, flung into it and burned.

One day Old Thak had been returning from a war along the coast of Schwud when his scouts rode up to him and reported that the beach ahead was blocked by a long row-

261

boat, in front of which stood a man holding a huge driftwood log like a light mallet. Old Thak rode ahead with his scouts to see this phenomenon. The man was only about five feet tall, with curly blond hair, but his chest seemed to be about five feet around too. He was neckless, wristless and ankleless; he was simply a great chest with almost jointless limbs and a face as featureless as an anvil topped by blond curly hair. A driftwood log two feet thick rested lightly on his shoulder.

"Ride over him," Old Thak told one of his scouts, and the man charged this strange stumpy apparition who had blocked the beach with a rowboat. The giant dwarf swung the driftwood log like a fungo bat against the horse's chest, killing the animal instantly, then tore the scout out of the tangled stirrups and folded him up, breaking his back easily. Then he picked up his driftwood racket and stood in front of his rowboat again, staring down the beach to where Old Thak was watching with the other scout.

Trumper remembered thinking that the other scout must have been shitting his pants at that moment.

But Old Thak was not so wasteful as to sacrifice another scout. He recognized great bodyguard potential when he saw it, so he sent the scout hightailing it back to the legion. Thak wanted the thing alive.

About twenty men with nets and long gaffs eventually captured the super troll who blocked the shore of Schwud. It was a lieutenant of these men who first called the creature Sprog. *Da Sprog*—a rough translation would be the Devil's Toad—a kind of super toad who impersonated the Devil, or through whom the Devil hopped around on the earth, was a fixture of their religion.

But all that was nonsense. Sprog was as easy to train as a falcon, and he became as loyal to Old Thak as Thak's best dog, Rotz. So it was a demonstration of fatherly affection when Old Thak parted with Sprog and made a gift of him to his son Akthelt.

Trumper interrupted his memory of the tale to wonder if it had been at this point in life when Sprog had begun to relax and think that he had it made. Probably not, he reflected, because Sprog suffered some kind of inadequacy complex during his first few years with Akthelt. Old Thak had been less demanding, and Sprog had found the master-dog role comfortable. But Akthelt was Sprog's own age and tended to be more familiar with servants; in fact, Akthelt liked to drink with Sprog, and Sprog no longer knew what his place was. He was very loyal to Akthelt, of course, and would have done anything for him, but he was also treated just enough like Akthelt's friend to be confused. Equality is a rare and minor theme in *Akthelt and Gunnel,* though it emerges in its typically disruptive fashion here.

One night, Akthelt and Sprog got very drunk together in the tiny village of Thith, and then staggered home to the castle through an orchard, having contests to see who could uproot the biggest trees. Sprog won, of course, and perhaps that irritated Akthelt. Whatever the reason they were crossing the moat arm in arm when Akthelt asked Sprog if he would be hurt if Akthelt slept with Sprog's new wife, Fluvia. After all, they were friends . . .

Perhaps the confusion was suddenly lifted from Sprog's life by this proposal. He must have realized that Akthelt could have simply taken Fluvia whenever he wanted to, and maybe he thought that by asking permission Akthelt was bestowing equality on Sprog.

Which apparently Sprog was not prepared for, because he not only gleefully told Akthelt to take his pleasure with Fluvia, but went barreling off to the royal quarters to take *his* pleasure with Akthelt's Gunnel. Akthelt had said nothing whatever about that. Obviously, Sprog had read the situation wrong.

Trumper could imagine poor Sprog rocketing down the labyrinthine corridors to the royal quarters like a five-foot bowling ball. *That* was when Sprog relaxed.

Ralph came and beat on the bathroom door again, and Trumper wondered what was on his mind. He looked at the book in his hands somehow expecting it to be *Akthelt and Gunnel,* and was disappointed when he saw it was only Helmbart's *Vital Telegrams.* When he opened the door, Ralph followed the phone cord to the sink. He didn't seem surprised to find the phone there; he dialed it in the sink, listened to the busy signal in the sink and hung up in the sink.

Jesus, I should keep a diary, Trumper thought.

That night he tried. After he had made love to Tulpen, questions were raised. Analogies leaped to his mind. He thought of Akthelt stumbling in on the dark Fluvia, who was expecting her thick Sprog. Fluvia had been frightened at first because she thought it *was* Sprog. Fluvia and Sprog had an agreement never to make love when Sprog was drunk, because Fluvia was afraid he might break her spine. There was also an untranslatable word that had to do with how Sprog smelled when he drank a lot.

But Fluvia quickly guessed who was making love to her, perhaps because her spine wasn't breaking, or by his royal odor. "Oh, my Lord Akthelt," she whispered.

Again Trumper thought of poor, deceived Sprog barreling down to the royal quarters, lusting after Gunnel. Then he thought of babies and contraceptive devices and making love to Biggie as compared to making love to Tulpen. His diary was blank.

He remembered how Biggie always forgot to take her pill. Bogus would hang the little plastic dispenser from the light cord in the bathroom so that she would think of contraception every time she pulled the light on and off, but she hadn't liked the idea of the pills hanging out in public. Whenever Ralph was in the house, she got especially angry about it. "Take your pill today, Biggie?" Ralph would ask her, coming out of the bathroom.

Tulpen, on the other hand, had an intrauterine device. Biggie, of course, had *had* an ill-fated I.U.D. in Europe, but she left it there. Trumper had to admit that there was an added something about the I.U.D. You could feel it in there, like an extra part, a spare hand or tiny finger. Every so often it poked. He liked it. It moved around, too. With Tulpen, he never knew where he was going to come in contact with the string that felt like a finger. In fact, on this particular night he hadn't come in contact with it at all. It worried him, and remembering that Biggie lost or dissolved hers, he had asked Tulpen about it.

"Your device," he whispered.

"Which device?"

"The one with the string."

"Oh, how *was* my string tonight?"

"I never felt it."

"Subtle, huh?"

264

"No, really, are you sure it's okay?" He worried about it often.

Tulpen was quiet under him for a while; then she said, "Everything's fine, Trumper."

"But I couldn't feel the string," he insisted. "I nearly always feel it there." Which wasn't very true.

"Everything's fine," she repeated, curling up against him.

He waited for her to fall asleep before getting up to try his hand at beginning a diary. But he didn't even know what day it was; he couldn't have guessed the date within a week. And his head seemed so cluttered with *things*. There were a million images from the film on his mind, both real and imagined. Then Helmbart's puzzling passage about Eddy's feet returned to haunt him. And there was *Akthelt and Gunnel* to consider; he couldn't seem to get beyond the image of Sprog barreling through the castle, his hopes erect.

He did manage a sentence. It didn't seem to be a diary sort of sentence; in fact, it was a real cliff-hanger of an opening line. But he wrote it in spite of himself:

"Her gynecologist recommended him to me."

What a way to begin a diary! The question struck him: How is anything related to anything else? But he had to begin somewhere.

Take for example . . . Sprog.

He watched Tulpen curl into a tighter ball on the bed; she tugged his pillow to her, scissored it between her legs and then slept quietly again.

One thing at a time. What happened to Sprog?

28 : What Happened to the Hashish?

In East Gunnery, Biggie, your mother puts us in separate rooms, even though that forced your mother to sleep with Aunt Blackstone and put your father on the hall sofa. And we forgot about poor Couth waiting for word in the lower field. He spent the night in his airy Volkswagen and woke up in the morning as stiff as a spring-back chair.

But there wasn't that much unpleasantness around the dinner table after the announcement—excepting, of course, the difficulty in making deaf Aunt Blackstone understand the conditions. *"Pregnant,"* you said. "Aunt Blackstone, I'm pregnant."

"Rent?" said Aunt Blackstone. "Rent what? Who's renting? What's to rent?"

So the incriminating news needed shouting, and when Aunt Blackstone finally got it, she couldn't see what all the fuss was about. "Oh, *pregnant,"* she said. "How nice. Isn't that something?" She fixed her gaze on you, Biggie, marveling at your metabolic wonder, glad to know the young were still fertile; at least there was one thing about the young that hadn't changed.

We were all quite understanding of your mother, tolerating her taking it for granted that we sleep in separate rooms; only your father was bold enough to imply that we must have slept together at least once before, so what was being saved? But he let it drop, seeing, with the rest of us, that your mother needed to be sustained by some formality. Perhaps she felt that though her daughter had been violated and stained beyond childhood, there was no reason why her daughter's room couldn't remain pure. Why tarnish the teddy bears on the headboard of the bed, or all the

266

little trolls on skis, lined up so innocently along the dresser-top? Something needed to be left intact. We could all see that, Biggie.

And in the morning, we met in the bathroom. I knocked Aunt Blackstone's teeth into the sink; they chattered noisily around and around the bowl, a mouth on the roam. This made you laugh while you clipped your toenails over the tub—my first taste of domesticity.

Outside the bathroom door, your mother was nervous. "There's another bathroom upstairs," she called twice, as if she feared you could get pregnant again, have twins or worse.

And you whispered to me, Biggie, as I sloshed water into my armpits, "Do you remember, Bogus, when you tried to wash in the bidet in Kaprun?" And my member shrunk from that icy memory.

In the morning, Trumper spoke into his dream, and into the soft hair nesting on his pillow. "Do you remember . . .?" he began, but he failed to recognize the perfume and drew back from the figure on the bed beside him.

"Remem . . ." the whore said sleepily. She didn't understand English.

After she'd gone, all he could remember of the whore was her rings, and how she'd used them. It was a game she fancied: reflecting little facets of light, caught in the many-faced stones, all over her body and his. "Kiss this one here," she'd say, indicating a flickering spot of light. When she moved her hands, the little mirrored edges of light moved with them, racing bright squares and triangles over her deep-cut navel and down her taut thigh.

She had long, lovely hands and the sharpest, quickest wrists he'd ever seen. She played a fencing game with her rings too. "You try to stop me," she said, squatting opposite him on the teetering Taschy bed while she feinted, parried and thrust her flickering wrists at him, scratching him here and there with a ring's sharp edge, but never hard enough to break the skin.

When he was on top of her, she raced her rings over his back. Once he caught a glimpse of her eyes; she was watching her rings' prism patterns chase across the ceiling as she moved under him with slight and careless shrugs.

In the Josefsplatz he stopped walking around the fountain and wondered how he'd gotten there. He tried to remember how much he'd paid the whore, or even when he had. He couldn't remember the transaction at all and checked his empty wallet for some clue.

In his suitcase, the fine smell of mentholated chocolate laced with catnip made him swoon, and he remembered the hashish brick. He imagined paying for his lunch with a sliver of it—picking up a table knife, slicing off a wafer-thin strip and asking the waiter if that would do.

In the American Express office he found himself asking for Merrill Overturf at the information counter, behind which a man tilted his puzzled head, consulted a map in front of him, then a larger map behind him.

"Overturv?" the man asked. "Where is it? Do you know the nearest town to it?"

After this was straightened out, Trumper was directed to the mail desk. There a girl firmly shook her head; American Express had no permanent mailbox in Merrill's name.

Bogus wanted to leave a note anyway. "Well, we can hold it at the desk for him," the girl told him. "But just for a week or so. Then it's a dead letter."

A dead letter? Apparently even one's words could die.

On a bulletin board in the front lobby there were little notices about all sorts of matters:

ANNA, FOR GOD'S SAKE COME HOME!

SPECIAL TELETAPE REPLAY NFL GAME OF THE WEEK/ REG. SHOWING EV. SUN. @ P.M. 2 & 4/ ATOMIC ENERGY COMM., KÄRNTNER RING 23, WIEN I/U.S. PASSPORT REQUIRED.

KARL, I'M BACK AT THE OLD PLACE.

PETCHA, CALL KLAGENFURT 09-03-79 BEFORE WEDS., ELSE RIDE WITH GERIG TO GRA, MEET HOFSTEINER AFTER II THURS. EVE/ ERNST

To these, Trumper added:

MERRILL, LEAVE SOME WORD FOR ME/ BOGGLE

He was standing on the Kärntner Ring sidewalk, feeling the warm, springlike weather and wondering why December felt like this, when the man with apple cheeks and a bow tie first spoke to him. The man's mouth was so plump and round that his natty mustache was almost circular. Trumper wasn't a bit surprised to hear him speak English; he looked like a gas-station attendant Trumper had known in Iowa.

"Say, are you American too?" the man asked Bogus. He reached to shake Trumper's hand. "My name's Arnold Mulcahy," he said, shaking hands with a firm grip, a rapid pump. Bogus was trying to think of something polite to say when Arnold Mulcahy jerked him right off his feet with a perfectly executed falling arm-drag. For a cherub, he moved very fast; he was behind Bogus before Bogus could get off his hands and knees and had already torn the suitcase right out of Bogus's grasp. Then he slapped a double chicken-wing on Trumper and flattened him right down to the sidewalk.

Trumper was a little dizzy as a result of encountering the sidewalk with his forehead, but he wondered if perhaps Arnold Mulcahy was an old wrestling coach he'd known. He was trying to place the name when he saw the car pull up to the curb and two men get out quickly. Someone stuck his head into Trumper's suitcase and took a deep sniff. "It's in here, all right," he said.

The car doors were all open. I'm having this dream again, Trumper thought, but his shoulders really did feel as if they were popping out of their sockets and the two men helping Arnold Mulcahy throw Bogus into the back of their car felt very real.

In the back seat, they frisked him so fast and thoroughly that they could have told him the number of teeth on his pocket comb. Arnold Mulcahy sat up front reading Trumper's passport. Then he unwrapped the hashish brick, sniffed it, touched its sticky resin and licked it with his toady tongue. "It's pure stuff, Arnie," said one of the men in the back seat with Bogus. His English was pure Alabama.

"Yup," said Arnold Mulcahy, who wrapped the hashish back up, returned it to Trumper's suitcase, and then leaned over the front seat and smiled at Bogus. Arnold

269

Mulcahy was about forty, twinkling and plump; among other things, Trumper was thinking that Mulcahy had just executed the best falling arm-drag and double chicken-wing that he had ever had the misfortune to experience in his entire wrestling career. He was also thinking that all the men in the car were about forty, and probably American. They were not all twinkling and plump, however.

"Don't you worry, my good boy," Arnold Mulcahy told Bogus, still smiling at him. His voice was a poor nasal imitation of W.C. Fields. "Everyone knows you're quite innocent. That is to say, almost innocent. What we mean is, we haven't noticed you trying to give the dope back." He winked at the men sitting on either side of Bogus. They released his arms, then, and let him rub his sore shoulders.

"Just one question, son," Mulcahy said. He held up a little scrap of paper; it was the note Bogus had left for Merrill on the bulletin board at American Express. "Who's Merrill?" Mulcahy asked, and when Trumper just stared at him, he went on. "Would this Merrill be a prospective buyer, son?" he asked, but Trumper was afraid to talk. He thought that whoever they were they knew more than he did, and he wanted to wait and see where the car was going. "My good boy," Mulcahy said, "we know you didn't mean to get the dope, but we can only guess what you were going to do with it." Trumper didn't say a word. The car rounded the Schwartzenburgplatz, circling behind the spot where they'd picked him up. Trumper realized he'd seen too many movies; there was an astonishing similarity between the cops and the crooks, and he didn't know for sure which these men were.

Arnold Mulcahy sighed. "You know," he said, "I personally think we may have saved you from an act of crime. Your only crime so far is one of omission, but if this Merrill character is someone you were planning to sell the stuff to—now that's another sort of crime." He winked at Bogus and waited to see if Bogus was going to respond. Bogus held his breath.

"Come on," said Arnold Mulcahy. "Who's Merrill?"

"Who are *you?*" said Bogus.

"I'm Arnold Mulcahy," said Arnold Mulcahy, who held out his hand and winked. He wanted to shake hands again, but Bogus still remembered the falling arm-drag and double chicken-wing, and he hesitated before accepting Arnold Mulcahy's firm grasp.

"Got just one more question for you, Mr. Fred Trumper," Arnold Mulcahy said. He stopped shaking Trumper's hand and suddenly looked as serious as a plump, twinkling man could look. "Why did you leave your wife?" he asked.

29 : What Happened to Sprog?

He was de-balled with a battle-ax. Then he was exiled to the coast of his native Schwud. To remind him of his castration, his lewd wife, Fluvia, was exiled with him. All this was the customary punishment for sexually assaulting a member of the royal family.

When I asked her why her gynecologist recommended that she have her intrauterine device removed, she does this infuriating thing with her hot-shit tit—flipping the big bosom of hers as if to tell me that her contraceptive device, or lack of one, is entirely her business.

"*When* did he take it out?" I ask, and she shrugs, as if she can't be bothered to remember. But I can remember that it's been several times now that I haven't felt its little string touching me in there.

"Why didn't you tell me, for God's sake? I could have been using a rubber."

She mumbles casually that her gynecologist would not have recommended a rubber, either.

"What!" I scream. "Why did he recommend that you have the thing pulled out in the first place?"

"For what I wanted," she hedges, "it was the first thing that was recommended."

I still don't get it; I suspect the poor girl doesn't understand reproduction. Then I realize I do not understand the girl.

"Tulpen?" I ask her slowly. "What is it you wanted for which removing your I.U.D. was recommended?" And of course she doesn't need to answer; making me phrase the question has been enough. She smiles at me and blushes.

"A *baby?*" I say. "You want a baby?" She nods, still smiling. "You might have told me," I say, "or even asked me."

"I've already tried that," she says smugly, about to flip her tit again, I can tell.

"Well, I ought to have something to say about this, dammit."

"It will be my baby, Trumper."

"Mine too!" I scream.

"Not necessarily, Trumper," she says, flitting across the room like one of her aloof fish.

"Who else have you slept with?" I ask her, dumb.

"No one," she says. "It's just that you don't have to have any more to do with the baby than you want to." When I look skeptical, she adds, "You won't have any more to do with it than I let you, either, you shit."

Then she waltzes into the bathroom with a newspaper and four magazines, waiting for me ... to do what?! Fall asleep? Leave her alone? Pray for triplets?

"Tulpen," I tell the bathroom door. "You might already be pregnant."

"Move on if you want to," she says.

"Jesus Christ, Tulpen!"

"There's no need to feel trapped, Trumper. That's not what babies are for."

She's in there for an hour and I'm forced to pee in the kitchen sink. Thinking. It's just two days until I'm operated on—maybe they should sterilize the whole works while they're at it.

But when she came out of the bathroom, she looked less tough and more vulnerable, and almost instantly he found himself wanting very much to be what she wanted him to be. He was thrown off guard by her question, though. She asked it shyly and sweetly. "If you do have much to do with the baby," she said, "if you want it, that is, would you like a boy or a girl?"

Damn him, he hated himself for remembering the crude joke Ralph had once told him. There's this girl, see, and she's just been knocked up, and she says to her boyfriend, "You wanna girl or boy, George?" George thinks for a minute and then says, "A stillborn."

"Trumper?" Tulpen asked again. "A boy or a girl? Do you care which?"

"A girl," he said. She was excited, playful, drying her hair in a big towel, flouncing around the bed now.

"Why a girl?" she asked. She wanted to keep the ball rolling; she liked this talk.

"I don't know," he mumbled. He could lie, but elaborating on the lie was hard. She held his hands, sat down on the bed in front of him and let the towel fall off her hair.

"Come on," she said. "Because you've already had a boy? Is that it? Or do you really like girls better?"

"I don't know," he said irritably.

She dropped his hands. "You don't care, you mean," she said. "You don't really care, do you?"

That left him with no place to go. "I don't want any baby, Tulpen," he said.

She frisked through her hair with the towel, which made it hard to see her face. "Well, I do want one, Trumper," she said. She let the towel drop and looked straight at him, as hard as anyone, except Biggie, had ever looked at him. "So I'm going to have one, Trumper, whether you're interested or not. And it won't cost any more than it ever has," she said bitterly. "All you have to do is make love to me."

Right then, he wanted very much to make love to her; in fact, he knew he'd *better* make love to her, quick. But what mush his mind was! His brain was well trained at evasion. He was thinking of Sprog . . .

That old horse-basher, the uprooter of trees, thumping through the royal quarters, bowling over the guard of the royal bedchamber. Then into the lavish bed. No doubt a veiled and perfumed Gunnel lay there waiting for her Lord Akthelt. Enter the five-foot toad. Did he hop on her?

Whatever he did, he didn't do it fast enough. The text reports that Gunnel was "nearly humbled by him." Nearly.

Apparently Akthelt heard Gunnel screaming all the way down in the servants' quarters as he lay deep in the lush grip of Fluvia. It never occurred to him that his lady was being attacked by Sprog; he just recognized his lady's scream. He pulled out of Fluvia, flapped on his codpiece and hot-hoofed it up to the royal quarters. There he and seven castle guards netted the thrashing Sprog and pried

274

him loose from the fainting Lady Gunnel with the aid of several fireplace tools.

According to custom, castrations always took place at night, and the very next evening poor Sprog's balls were lopped off with a battle-ax. Akthelt did not attend the event; neither did Old Thak.

Akthelt mourned for his friend. It was several days before he even asked Gunnel if Sprog had actually . . . well, got her, if she knew what he meant. She did; Sprog had not. Somehow that made Akthelt feel even worse, which made Gunnel rather angry. In fact, Akthelt and Old Thak had to persuade her from publicly demanding that Fluvia be thrown to the wild boars.

The wild boars were in the moat, for some reason Trumper had never been able to translate; it didn't make any sense. Moats were supposed to be full of water, but perhaps this one had a leak they couldn't fix, so they had wild boars charging around in there instead. It was just another example of what a ragged old ode *Akthelt and Gunnel* was. Old Low Norse was not known for its tight little epics.

For example, the matter of the legend of Sprog isn't even brought up until pages and pages after Sprog and Fluvia are exiled to the coast of Schwud. The legend says that one day a weary, ravaged traveler passes through the kingdom of Thak and begs for a night's rest at the castle. Akthelt asks the stranger what adventures he's had—Akthelt loves a good story—and the stranger tells this ghastly tale.

He was riding on the fine white sand of the beaches of Schwud with his handsome young brother when the two of them came upon a dusky lewd wench whom they took to be some wild fisherwoman, abandoned by her tribe and hungry for a man. Therefore the stranger's young brother fell upon her there on the beach, as she clearly indicated she wanted him to, and proceeded to satisfy himself. But this only partially slaked the thirst of the wench, so the stranger himself was about to mount the wild woman when he saw his brother swiftly seized by a round, blond, beastlike man "whose chest could inhale the sea." As the stranger watched with horror, his brother was bent, broken, snapped, crunched, folded and otherwise mangled by

275

this terrible blond god "with a center of gravity like a ball."

The beach ball was Sprog, of course, and the woman on the sand who had laughed, moaned and implored the stranger to take her quick was Fluvia.

One way to look at it was that it was nice to know they were still together after all this time, still a team. But the stranger didn't look at it that way; he ran. He ran to where he and his brother had tethered their horses.

Both animals were dead, their chests staved in. They looked as if they'd been hit by a huge battering ram, and beside them lay a log which no man could have lifted. So the stranger had to keep running, because Sprog ran after him. Luckily the stranger had once been a messenger by profession, so he could run very fast and for a long time. He ran with great long easy strides, but whenever he looked back, there would be Sprog, who was so short that he ran like a woodchuck, thumping along on his little stunted legs. But he kept up.

The stranger ran a few miles, looked back, and there was Sprog. He had no style but he had a set of lungs like a whale.

The stranger ran all through the night, stumbling over rocks, falling, getting up, straggling along unable to see. But whenever he stopped, he could hear, not far behind and coming closer, the sound of Sprog thumping along like a five-foot elephant and breathing like a winded bear.

In the morning, the stranger crossed the border of Schwud and reeled into the town of Lesk in the kingdom of Thak. He stood gasping in the town square, his head bowed and his back to what he was sure would be thumping up behind him at any minute. He stood there for hours before the kind people of Lesk took him in and gave him breakfast and told the stranger that this was why none of the young men of Lesk ever went swimming off the shore of Schwud any more.

"*Da Sprog,*" said a young widow, making the sign of the toad on her breast.

"*Da kvinna des Sprog*" ("The *woman* of Sprog,") said a young man with only one arm who had escaped. He rolled his eyes.

That was what had happened to Sprog.

276

And Bogus Trumper? What had happened to him? He had fallen asleep sitting up, his chin resting on the shelf by the turtle aquarium, his brain at last lulled by the gurgle of the air hose.

Tulpen had curled up beside him on the bed for an hour, waiting for him to wake up and make love to her. He didn't wake up, though, and she had stopped waiting. She'd waited quite long enough for him, she thought, so she lay back in the bed and watched him sleep. She smoked a cigarette, though she never smoked. Then she went into the bathroom and threw up. Then she ate yogurt. She was pretty upset.

When she returned to bed, Trumper was still there, sleeping next to the turtles. Before she went to sleep herself, she got the idea that if only she could find two of those big air-horns that diesel trucks have, she could blow one in each of his ears and scramble his brains so completely that it might wipe his memory clean. She thought that would help.

She probably wasn't far wrong. It would be hard for most people to sleep with their chins on a shelf, but Bogus was dreaming about Merrill Overturf.

30: What Happened to Merrill Overturf?

Once Trumper had read a magazine article on espionage. He remembered that the U.S. Treasury Department controls the Federal Narcotics Bureau and the Secret Service, and that the C.I.A. coordinates all government intelligence activities. This seemed plausible; at least, he wasn't worried any more.

He was in a rear office of the American Consulate in Vienna, so he supposed he wasn't going to be murdered and dumped in the Danube—not yet, anyway. If he still had any doubts about where he was, they vanished when the vice-consul intruded on them nervously.

"I'm the vice-consul," he apologized to Arnold Mulcahy, who was apparently more important than a vice-consul. "I wish to inform you about your man out there, please . . ." Arnold Mulcahy went to see what the trouble was.

According to the vice-consul, one of Mulcahy's thugs, a big man with a livid burn scar, was frightening away people who were coming to take the U.S. immigration exam. In two minutes Mulcahy returned; the man with the burn scar had come to *take* the immigration exam, he told the vice-consul with some asperity. "Let him in," he advised. "Any man that mean-looking is good for something." Then he settled down to work on Bogus Trumper.

They had the goods on Trumper, and the bads too. Did he know he was a "missing person" back in America? Did he know that his wife was wondering where he'd gone?

"I haven't been gone so long," Trumper said.

Mulcahy suggested that his wife thought he'd been gone
278

long enough. Trumper told him who Merrill Overturf was. He said that he'd had no plans to do anything with the hashish, though he probably would have sold it if someone had come along wanting to buy. He told him that a whore had taken all his money and that he was a little uncertain about things in general.

Mulcahy nodded; he knew all this already.

Then Bogus asked him to help him find Merrill Overturf, and it was then that Mulcahy made his deal. He would find Merrill Overturf, but first Bogus would have to do something for Arnold Mulcahy, for the U.S. government and for the innocent people of the world.

"I guess I don't mind," Bogus said. He really wanted to find Merrill.

"You *shouldn't* mind," said Mulcahy. "Also, you need plane fare home."

"I don't know if I'm going home."

"Well, *I* know," Mulcahy said.

"Merrill Overturf is in Vienna. I think," Trumper said. "I'm not going anywhere until I find him."

Mulcahy called in the vice-consul. "Locate this Overturf character," he ordered. "Then we can get on with it."

"It" was then explained to Bogus Trumper. It was pretty simple. Trumper would be given a few thousand dollars in U.S. hundred-dollar bills. Trumper was to hang around the Kaffeehaus Leopold Hawelka, wait for the man who said *"Gra' Gra!"* all the time and who'd given Trumper the parcel of hashish, and to give the man the money when he showed up. Then Trumper was to be taken to Schwecat Airport and be put on a plane to New York. He would take the hashish brick with him; his luggage would be searched at Kennedy Airport customs; the hashish brick would be discovered; he would be seized on the spot and driven away in a limousine. The limousine would take him anywhere he wanted to go in New York City, and then he would be free.

It all seemed pretty straightforward. The reasons for all this escaped Trumper, but it was obvious that no one was going to do any explaining.

Then he was introduced to a Herr Doktor Inspektor Wolfgang Denzel, who was apparently an agent at the Austrian end. Inspektor Denzel wanted as much of a description of the man who had said *"Gra! Gra!"* as Trumper could give. Trumper had seen Herr Doktor Inspektor Denzel before; he was the natty, agile waiter whose tray of coffee and beers Trumper had spilled.

The only part of the deal that Bogus didn't like was getting on a New York plane as soon as he had handed over the money. "Don't forget about Merrill Overturf," he reminded Mulcahy.

"My good boy," said Arnold Mulcahy. "I'll go with you in the cab to the airport, and this Overturf character will be sitting right there with us."

If Mulcahy wasn't quite the sort of man you'd actually trust, he was at least the sort whose efficiency you could have confidence in.

Bogus went to the Hawelka and sat around with his few thousand dollars for three nights running, but the *"Gra! Gra!"* man never showed up.

"He'll show," said Arnold Mulcahy. His overpowering confidence was chilling.

On the fifth night, the man came into the Hawelka. He didn't pay any attention to Bogus, though; he sat far away and never looked at him once. When he paid the waiter—who of course was actually Herr Doktor Inspektor Denzel—and then put on his coat and headed for the door, Bogus thought he should make his move. Walking right up to the man as if he'd suddenly recognized an old friend, he called, *"Gra! Gra!"* and grabbed the man's hand and pumped it. But the man looked petrified; he was trying so hard to get away from Bogus that he didn't even utter one little *"Gra!"*

Bogus went right after him out the door and down the sidewalk, where the man tried to break into a jog to get free. *"Gra!"* Bogus screamed at him again, and spinning the man around to face him, he took the envelope with all the money in it and crammed it into his trembling hand. But the man threw the envelope away and ran off as fast as he could.

Herr Doktor Inspektor Denzel came out of the Hawelka and picked the envelope up off the street. "You should have let him come to *you*," he told Trumper. "I think you scared him off." Herr Doktor Inspektor Denzel was a genius at understatement.

In the cab to Schwecat Airport, Arnold Mulcahy said, "Suffering shit! Boy, did you ever blow it!"

Merrill Overturf was not in the cab.

"It's not *my* fault," Bogus told Mulcahy. "You never told me how I was supposed to give the money to him."

"Well, I didn't think you'd try to cram it down his throat."

"Where's Merrill Overturf?" Trumper asked. "You said he'd be here."

"He's not in Vienna any more," Mulcahy said.

"Where is he?" Trumper asked, but Mulcahy wouldn't tell him.

"I'll let you know in New York," he said.

They were late getting to New York; there'd been a delay on their Lufthansa flight. The runway in Frankfurt, their first stop, was stacked up, so they missed their first connection to New York, a TWA flight, and ended up on a big Pan Am 747. Their luggage, however, had gone through earlier on the TWA flight. No one could explain how this happened, and Mulcahy was nervous about it. "Where'd you put the stuff?" he asked Trumper.

"In my suitcase," Trumper said, "with everything else."

"When they find it in New York," Mulcahy said, "it would be good if you pretended to run away—you know. Not too far, of course; let them catch you. They won't hurt you or anything," he added.

Then Kennedy was stacked up, so they circled New York for an hour. It was late afternoon when they landed, and it took them an hour to locate their bags. Mulcahy left Bogus before he went through the customs declaration gate.

"Anything to declare?" the man said, winking at Bogus. He was a big, warm-faced Negro with hands like a black bear's feet, and he started pawing through Bogus's suitcase.

There was a pretty girl in line behind him and Trumper turned around and smiled at her. *Won't she be surprised when they arrest me?*

The customs man had taken out the typewriter, the recorder, all the tapes, and half of Trumper's clothes, but he hadn't found the hashish yet.

Bogus looked around nervously, the way he thought a

281

potential smuggler would look around. By now the customs man had the suitcase completely emptied on the counter and was pawing back over all the stuff. He looked up at Bogus, worried, and whispered to him, "Where *is* it?"

Then Bogus started pawing through all the stuff with him; they went through it twice more, with the line behind them growing and grumbling, but they couldn't find the hashish.

"All right," the customs man said to him. "What did you do with it?"

"Nothing," Bogus said. "I packed it, I know I did, honest."

"Don't let him get away!" the customs man yelled suddenly, apparently figuring he'd better go ahead with the plan. Bogus did what Mulcahy had told him to and started to make a run for it. He ran out through the gate with the customs man yelling at him and pointing and setting off a horn that had a jarring shriek to it.

Trumper got all the way through the exit ramp and up to where the taxis were waiting before he realized that he'd probably escaped, so he ran back. As he neared the customs gate, a policeman caught up with him, "Christ, at last!" Trumper said to the cop, who looked puzzled and handed Bogus the envelope containing the few thousand dollars. Trumper hadn't given it back to Mulcahy, who hadn't asked for it; it must have fallen out of his pocket when he'd run through the terminal.

"Thank you," Bogus said. Then he ran back down the exit ramp, where he was finally captured by the Negro customs man who hadn't found the hashish.

"Now I've got you!" the man yelled, holding Bogus gently around the waist.

In a funny, formica-covered room, Arnold Mulcahy and five other men were hopping mad.

"Suffering shit!" Mulcahy yelled. "Someone must have picked it off in Frankfurt."

"The suitcase was in New York for six hours before you got here," one of the men told him. "Someone could have picked it off here."

"Trumper?" Mulcahy said. "Did you really pack the thing, boy?"

"Yes, sir."

They whisked him into another room, where a man who looked like a male nurse searched him all over and then left him alone. A long time later, he was brought some scrambled eggs, toast and coffee, and after another long wait Mulcahy reappeared.

"There's a limousine here for you," he told Bogus. "It will take you anywhere you want to go."

"I'm sorry, sir," Trumper said. Mulcahy just shook his head. "Suffering shit . . ." he said.

On the way to the car, Trumper said, "I hate to ask you this, but what about Merrill Overturf?"

Mulcahy was pretending not to hear. At the limousine he opened the door for Trumper and then shoved him inside quickly. "Take him anywhere he wants to go," he told the driver.

Bogus rolled his window down quickly and caught Mulcahy's sleeve as he was trying to turn away from the car.

"Hey, what about Merrill Overturf?" he said.

Mulcahy sighed. He opened the briefcase he was carrying and took out a photostated copy of an official-looking document with the raised seal of the American Consulate stamped on it. "I'm sorry," Mulcahy said, handing the photostat to Trumper. "Merrill Overturf is dead." Then he smacked the roof of the car, shouted to the driver, "Take him anywhere he wants to go!" and the car pulled away.

"Where to?" the driver asked Trumper, who sat in the back seat like an armrest or some other stationary part of the car itself. He was trying to read the document, which in officialese seemed to be called an Uncontested Obituary, and concerned one Overturf, Merrill, born Boston, Mass., Sept. 8, 1941. Father, Randolph W.; mother, Ellen Keefe.

Merrill had died nearly two full years before Bogus had returned to Vienna to find him. According to the document, he had bet an American girl named Polly Crenner—whom he had picked up at American Express—that he could find a tank on the bottom of the Danube. He had taken her to the Gelhafts Keller out on the Danube and Polly had stood on the dock and watched Merrill swim out in the Danube holding a flashlight over his head. When he located the tank, he was going to call to her; she

283

had insisted that she wouldn't go in the water until he'd found it.

Miss Crenner had waited on the dock for about five minutes after she could no longer see the flashlight bobbing around; she thought that Merrill was kidding around. Then she'd run into the Gelhafts Keller and tried to get some help, but since she didn't speak any German, it took some time for her to make herself understood.

Overturf might have been drunk, Polly Crenner said later. Evidently she hadn't known he was a diabetic, and neither, apparently, did the consulate, for it wasn't mentioned. In any case, the cause of death was listed as drowning. The identification of Merrill's body had not been completely confirmed. That is, a body had been found three days later that was snagged on an oil barge bound for Budapest, but since it had gone through the propellers a few times, no one could be sure.

The story of the tank was never confirmed. Polly Crenner said that Merrill had started hollering about a minute before she lost sight of the flashlight that he'd found the tank, but she hadn't believed him.

"I would have believed you, Merrill," Bogus Trumper said aloud.

"Sir?" the driver said.

"What?"

"Where to, sir?" the driver said.

They were cruising past Shea Stadium. It was a warm, balmy night and the traffic was fierce. "This stretch is slow," the driver informed him unnecessarily. "It's the Mets and the Pirates."

Trumper sat baffled over that for a long time. It was December when he'd left and he couldn't have been gone more than a week or so. *They're playing baseball already?* He leaned forward and looked at himself in the rear-view mirror of the limousine. He had a lovely, flowing mustache and a full beard. His back-seat window was still rolled down and the steamy New York summer air rolled over him. "Jesus," he whispered. He felt frightened.

"Where to, sir?" the driver repeated. He was obviously getting a little nervous about his passenger.

But Trumper was wondering if Biggie was still in Iowa—if it was *summer* already. Jesus Christ! He couldn't

284

believe he'd been gone so long. He looked for a newspaper or something with a date.

What he found was the envelope with a few thousand dollars in it. Arnold Mulcahy was a more generous man than he at first appeared.

"Where to?" the driver said.

"Maine," said Trumper. He had to see Couth; he had to clear his head.

"Maine?" the driver said. Then he got tough. "Look, buddy," he said, "I ain't taking you to Maine. This car don't go out of Manhattan."

Trumper opened the envelope and handed the driver a hundred-dollar bill. "Maine," Trumper said.

"Yes, sir," said the driver.

Trumper leaned back, smelled the wretched air and felt the heat. He didn't quite know it yet—or he couldn't make himself believe it—but he'd been away for almost six months.

31 : A Pentothal Movie

(159: *Medium shot of Trumper putting down a small overnight suitcase in front of the reception desk at a hospital. He looks around anxiously; Tulpen, smiling next to him, takes his arm. Trumper asks the nurse behind the desk something and she gives him some forms to fill in. Tulpen is warmly attentive to him while he struggles with the papers*)

DR. VIGNERON (*voice over*): It's a very simple operation, really, though it does seem to frighten the patient a good deal. It is minor surgery, five stitches at the most . . .

(160: *Close-up of a medical drawing of the penis. A hand, presumably Vigneron's, draws with a black crayon on the penis*)

VIGNERON (*v.o.*): The incision is made at the opening, here, to simply widen the passage. Then the sutures hold it open, here, so that it won't grow back the way it was. It will try to do that, anyway, by the way . . .

(161: *Long shot of a nurse leading Trumper and Tulpen down an aisle of the hospital. Trumper peers nervously into every room, bumping his suitcase against his knees as he walks*)

VIGNERON (*v.o.*): There's just one night in the hospital to prepare you for surgery in the morning. Then rest the

286

next day and perhaps stay that night too, if you're still
... uncomfortable.

(162: *Medium shot of Trumper getting awkwardly into a
hospital gown; Tulpen helps him tie the string in back.
Trumper stares at the patient with whom he shares his
room, an old man with tubes running in and out of him
who lies motionless on the bed next to Trumper's. A nurse
comes and deftly pulls the curtains around the bed, shutting off this view*)

VIGNERON *(v.o.):* ... to put it another way, it is forty-eight
hours of pain. Now, that is not so very much pain, is it?

(163: *Sync sound. Medium shot of Ralph Packer interviewing Dr. Vigneron in Vigneron's office*)

PACKER: There is some psychological pain, I imagine ...
you know, a sort of penis fear?

VIGNERON: Well, I suppose some patients would feel ...
You mean like a castration complex?

(164: *A male nurse is shaving Trumper, who lies rigidly
on his hospital bed watching the man's razor zip through
his pubic hair*)

PACKER *(v.o.):* Yeah, castration ... Or, you know, afraid
the whole thing will get cut off. By mistake, of course!
(*He laughs*)

(165: *Same as 163, in Vigneron's office*)

VIGNERON *(Laughing):* Well, I assure you, I have never
made a slip-up in that area!

PACKER *(Laughing hysterically):* Well, of course not ...
No, but I mean if you're the sort of patient who's at all
paranoid about your prick ...

(166: *Sync sound. Medium shot of Trumper lifting the
sheets, peering under at himself, letting Tulpen peek too*)

287

TRUMPER: You see? Like a baby!

TULPEN (*Staring hard*): It's like you're going to *have* a baby ...

(*They look at each other, then look away*)

(167: *Sync sound. Same as 163 & 165. In Vigneron's office, both Packer and Dr. Vigneron are laughing loudly and uncontrollably*)

(168: *Medium shot. Trumper, sitting up in bed, waves goodbye to Ralph and Tulpen, who waves back from the foot of his bed*) .

VIGNERON (*v.o., as if leaving instructions with a nurse*): No solid foods tonight, and nothing to drink after ten o'clock. Give him the first injections at eight tomorrow morning; he should be in the operating room by eight-thirty ...

(*Tulpen and Ralph walk out of frame together, escorted by a nurse. Trumper glowers after them darkly*)
DISSOLVE

After which, you can bet your ass, I did not dissolve. I lay feeling my smooth-shaven parts—the lamb's neck fleeced for the slaughter!

I also listened to the gurgling man beside me, a man who was fed like a carburetor; whose tubes, whose intake and output, whose simple functioning, seemed to rely on a mechanical sense of timing.

I was not worried about my operation, really; I had anticipated it to death. What did worry me was the degree to which I had become predictable even to myself, as if the range of my reactions had been analyzed, discussed and criticized to the point where I was as readable as a graph. I wished I could shock them all, the fuckers.

It was nearly midnight when I convinced the nurse that I simply had to call Tulpen. The phone rang and rang. When Ralph Packer answered, I hung up.

(169: *Sync sound. Close-up from dissolve. At her bathroom mirror Tulpen brushes her teeth; her shoulders are bare; presumably, so is the rest of her*)

PACKER (*Offstage*): Do you think the operation will change him? I don't mean just physically . . .

TULPEN (*She spits, looks in the mirror, then talks over her shoulder*): Change him how, then?

RALPH (*o.s.*): I mean psychologically . . .

TULPEN (*Rinses, gargles, spits*): He doesn't believe in psychology.

RALPH: (*o.s.*): Do you?

TULPEN: Not for him, I don't . . .

(170: *Sync sound. Medium shot of Tulpen in the bathtub, soaping her breasts and underarms*)

TULPEN (*With occasional looks at camera*): It's a very simplistic whitewash to attempt to cover very deep and complicated people and things with very easy generalizations, superficialities—you know. But I think it's just as simplistic to assume that everyone is complex and deep. I mean, I think Trumper really does operate on the surface . . . Maybe he *is* a surface, just a surface . . .

(*She trails off, looks warily at camera, then at her soapy breasts, and self-consciously slides down in the water*)

TULPEN (*Looking at camera, as if Ralph were the camera*): Come on, let's call it a night.

(*The phone rings offstage and Tulpen starts to get out of the tub*)

RALPH (*o.s.*): Shit! The phone . . . I'll get it!

TULPEN (*looking offstage after him*): No, let me—it might be Trumper.

RALPH (*o.s., answering the phone; Tulpen, listening, freezes*): Yeah, hello? Hello? Hello, goddam you ...

(*The camera is jerky; it tries to back up awkwardly as Tulpen steps out of the tub. Clumsily embarrassed, she wraps herself in a towel as Ralph steps into frame with her. He wears a light meter around his neck and points it at her, then down at the tub*)

RALPH (*Irritably, he takes her arm and tries to steer her back to the tub*): No, come on. We'll have to shoot this all over again ... the goddam phone!

TULPEN (*Pulling away from him*): Was it Trumper? Who was on the phone?

RALPH: I don't know. They hung up. Now, come on, this won't take a minute ...

(*But she wraps herself tighter in the towel and moves away from the tub*)

TULPEN (*angry*): It's late. I want to get up early. I want to be there when he comes out of the anesthesia. We can do this tomorrow.

(*She looks up, exasperated, at the camera. Suddenly, Ralph looks angrily at the camera himself, as if he just realized it was still running*)

RALPH (*Shouting at camera*): Cut! Cut! Cut! Sweet Jesus, Kent! Stop wasting film, you royal fuck-up!
BLACK OUT

Early in the morning they came and emptied the pots, hoses and receptacles of all kinds belonging to the man beside me. But they did nothing for me; they wouldn't even feed me.

At eight o'clock a nurse took my temperature and gave

me a numbing shot in both legs, high up on the thigh. When they came to wheel me down to the operating room, I couldn't walk very well. Two nurses supported me while they made me take a leak, but I still had *feeling* down there, and I was worried that the shots hadn't worked the way they were supposed to. I remarked on this to the nurse, but she didn't seem to understand me; in fact, my voice sounded strange even to me and I couldn't understand what I said either. I prayed I would be lucid in time to stop them from cutting.

In the operating room there was a stunning, full-bosomed woman in a green uniform like the kind all the surgery nurses wear, and she kept pinching my thighs and smiling at me. She was the one who stuck the needle leading to the dextrose jug into my vein; then she bent my arm in a special way, taped the needle to it, and then taped my arm to the table. The dextrose running down the yellowy hose was gurgling into me; I could follow it right down to my arm.

I had a thought about Merrill Overturf: If they had ever operated on him, they wouldn't be able to use dextrose, would they, since it's mostly sugar? What would they use?

With my free right hand, I reached over and pinched my penis. I could still feel everything, and this frightened me a lot. What was the sense of putting my thighs to sleep?

Then I heard Vigneron's voice, but I couldn't see him; instead, I saw a short, genial, spectacled old geezer who I guessed was the anesthetist. He came over and poked at the dextrose needle, then slid a jug of Pentothal alongside the dextrose jug and ran the hose from it right alongside the dextrose hose. Rather than stick the Pentothal needle in me, he stuck it into the dextrose hose, which I thought was very clever.

The hose to the Pentothal had a clamp on it, and I saw that the drug wasn't running into me yet. I watched it closely, you can bet your ass, and when the anesthetist asked me how I felt, I boomed in a great loud voice that I still had plenty of feeling in my prick and that I hoped they were all aware of it.

But they all just smiled as if they hadn't heard me—that

291

anesthetist, the green nurse and Vigneron himself, now standing over me.

"Count to twelve," the anesthetist told me. He started the Pentothal running then, by unclamping the hose, and I watched the stuff trickle down until it mingled with the dextrose in the main rubber vein.

"One two three four five six seven," I said very fast. Only it took forever. The Pentothal changed the color of the dextrose running down toward my arm. I watched it run right up to the hub of the needle, and when it entered my arm, I cried, "Eight!"

Then a second passed, which took two hours, and I woke up in the postoperative room—the recovery room, whose ceiling looked so much like the ceiling in the operating room that I thought I was still in the same place. Hovering over me was the same stunning green nurse, smiling.

"Nine," I said to her, "ten, eleven, twelve . . ."

"We'd like you to try to urinate now," she said to me.

"I just went," I said. But she rolled me over on my side and slid a green pan under me.

"Please just try," she coaxed. She was awfully nice.

So I started to go, even though I was sure I had nothing to pee. When the pain came, it was like an awareness of someone else's pain in another room—or even more distant, in another hospital. It was quite a lot of pain; I felt sorry for the person enduring it; I was all through peeing before I realized that it was *my* pain, realized that the operation was over.

"Okay, okay, okay, now," the nurse said, smoothing back my hair and wiping the sudden, surprised tears off my face.

Of course, what they had spared me was the double pain of anticipating peeing that first time. But I couldn't see it that way. It was a betrayal; they had tricked me.

Then I went away again into dizzy sleep, and when I came back I was in my hospital room, Tulpen sitting there beside the bed, holding my hand. When I opened my eyes, she was smiling at me.

But I pretended that I was still drugged senseless. I stared right through her. There's more than one who can play the tricks and surprises, you can bet your ass . . .

32 :   Another Dante, a Different Hell

The driver had worked for the limousine service for about three years. Before that, he'd driven a cab. He liked the limousine service better; nobody tried to stick him up or maul him, it was more leisurely, and the cars were elegant. He'd had the Mercedes for the past year and he loved to drive it. Occasionally, he'd gotten out of the city—once as far as New Haven—and he loved the feel of the car on the open road. That was what he thought the "open road" was: driving to New Haven. It was as far as he'd ever been out of New York City. He had a family and three kids, and every summer he talked with his wife about taking his vacation out West, driving the whole family out there. But he didn't own a car himself; he was waiting until he could afford a Mercedes, or until the limousine service let an old one go cheap.

So when he contracted to drive Bogus to Maine, the driver undertook the journey as if someone had told him to drive to San Francisco. *Maine!* He thought of men who hunted whales, ate lobster for breakfast and wore rubber boots all year long.

He talked for two hours before he realized that his passenger was either asleep or in a trance; then he shut up. His name was Dante Calicchio, and he realized that this was the first time since he'd stopped driving a cab that he was spooked by a passenger. He thought that Bogus was crazy, and he put the hundred-dollar bill in his jockey shorts, right in the pouch where he could find it. Maybe he'll give me another one, he thought. Or try to take this one back.

Dante Calicchio was short and heavy, with a salad of

293

black hair and a nose which had been broken so many times that it appeared to flap. He'd been a boxer; he liked to say of his style that he always led with his nose. He'd been a wrestler too, and had cauliflower ears from that. A lovely set, all folded and swollen and lumpy, like two unmatched wads of dough slapped on the sides of his face. He chewed gum loudly, a habit he'd developed years ago when he gave up cigarettes.

Dante Calicchio was an honest man who was curious about the way other people lived and what other places were like to live in, so he was not unhappy to be driving this nut to Maine. It was just that when they got north of Boston, and it was dark, and the traffic thinned out and almost disappeared, he got a little scared about driving off into this wilderness with a man who hadn't opened his mouth since they'd passed Shea Stadium.

The toll-booth attendant at the New Hampshire Turnpike looked at Dante's chauffeur uniform, stared into the plush back seat at Bogus in a trance, and then, since there were no other cars in sight, asked Dante where he was going.

"Maine," Dante whispered as if it was a holy word. "*Where* in Maine?" the attendant asked. Maine, in general, was only twenty minutes away from his daily life.

"I don't know where," Dante said, as the attendant handed him his change and waved him on. "Hey, sir?" he said, turning to Bogus. "Hey, where in Maine?"

Georgetown is an island, but in Trumper's mind it was even more of an island than it really is. It's the sort of island that might as well be a peninsula, because it's connected to the mainland by a bridge; there are none of the inconveniences of a real island. But Trumper was thinking of the lovely isolation Couth contributed to the place. But then Couth could probably give you a sense of isolation in Kennedy Airport.

Bogus wondered how he might best approach Biggie, realizing only now how much he missed her. She'd never stay in Iowa during the summer. At this moment she was probably in East Gunnery, helping her father and letting her mother help her with Colm. It was even conceivable that her abandonment had inspired an I-told-you-so sort

294

of negative invitation from his own parents, but surely Biggie would have declined those helping hands.

In any case, she certainly would have written to Couth to ask if he knew where his friend Bogus was, and Couth would know where *she* was, and what her feelings were about her runaway husband. Perhaps Couth had even seen them and could tell him how Colm had changed.

"Hey, sir?" someone was asking him. It was the man in the front seat in the doorman's uniform. "Hey, where in Maine?" he asked.

Trumper looked out the window; they were coming through the deserted rotary by Portsmouth Harbor, crossing the bridge to Maine. "Georgetown," he said to the driver. "It's an island. You'd better stop and get a map."

And Dante Calicchio thought, *An island!* Sweet Jesus, how am I supposed to *drive* to an island, you frigging crazy bastard . . .

But Dante got a map and saw there was a bridge from the mainland at Bath, across a tidal inlet of the Kennebec River, to Georgetown Island. As he crossed the bridge sometime after midnight, Bogus rolled down the back windows and asked him if he could smell the sea.

What Dante smelled was too fresh to be the sea. The sea Dante knew smelled like the docks off New York and Newark. The salt marshes here smelled tangy clean, so he rolled down his window too. But he didn't like the driving any more. The road across the island had loose, sandy shoulders, was narrow and winding and didn't have a median stripe. Also, there weren't any houses, just dark black pine trees and stretches of high salt grass.

Also, the night was alive with sounds. Not horns and mechanisms, or tires squealing or unidentified human voices or sirens, but things—frogs and crickets and sea birds and foghorns out at sea.

The lonely road and the terrible sounds scared the shit out of Dante Calicchio, who kept sizing up Bogus in the rear-view mirror, thinking, If this nut tries anything, I can break his back in two places before his friends jump me . . .

Trumper was calculating how long he'd stay with Couth, and whether he'd phone Biggie or just go see her when the time seemed ripe.

When the road suddenly turned to dirt, Dante slammed

on the brakes, locked the two front doors, and then the two back ones, never taking his eyes off Bogus for an instant.

"What the hell are you doing?" Trumper asked, but Dante Calicchio sat in the front seat with one eye on Trumper in the mirror and the other roaming the map.

"We must be lost, huh?" Dante said.

"No," Trumper said. "We've got about five miles to go."

"Where's the road?" said Dante.

"You're *on* it," Trumper said. "Drive on."

Dante checked the map, saw that this indeed was a road and drove on with trepidation; that is, he inched the car forward as the island narrowed down around him. A few unlighted houses appeared, solemn as moored ships, and he saw the horizon open on both sides of him; the sea was out there, the air felt colder, he could taste the salt.

Then a sign told him he was on a private road.

"Drive on," Trumper told him. Dante wished his tire chains were beside him on the seat, but he drove on.

A few hundred yards further on a sign said PILLSBURY, and the road dipped so close to the water that Dante thought the surf would break over them. Then he saw the magnificent old house with its barn-red wooden shingles, a high gabled house with a connecting garage, a boathouse and a tidy cove of the sea to itself.

Pillsbury—Dante thought he probably had one of them in the back seat. The only Pillsbury he knew was the competition for Betty Crocker. He peeked in the rear-view mirror, wondering if he was chauffeuring the crazy young heir to a cake-mix fortune.

"What month is it?" Trumper asked. He wanted to know if Couth was still alone in the place, or whether the Pillsburys would be here for the summer. They never came until the Fourth of July.

"It's the first of June, sir," said Dante Calicchio. He stopped the car where the driveway ended, and sat listening to the shrieking night—to what he imagined were whistling fish and great birds of prey, bears roaming the deep pines and an insect world of jungle ferocity.

When Trumper hustled up the flagstone walk, his eye on the one lit room in the house, the master bedroom upstairs, Dante hustled after him uninvited. He had grown up in a tough neighborhood and felt perfectly comfortable going out for a late-night six-pack when no one else would venture abroad in less than gang numbers, but the stillness of the island really threw him and he had no intention of facing the teeming animal potential singing and scuffling in those bushes and trees all by himself.

"What's your name?" Trumper asked.

"Dante."

"Dante?" Trumper said. A shot of light flickered down a hall of the house; a shaft stretched downstairs; a porch light went on.

"Couth!" Trumper yelled. "Heigh-ho!"

If there's just two of them, Dante thought, I can handle the mothers. He felt the hundred-dollar bill in his crotch for reassurance.

I could recognize old Couth through the porch door, coming to let us in: that floppy bathrobe he wears which is cut from a patchwork quilt; the way he squinted through the screen at us. It must have given him a shock to see that hairy brute chauffeur in a doorman's uniform swatting at the mosquitoes as if they were carnivorous birds, but it must have been even more of a shock to see *me.*

I could tell as soon as you let us in, Couth, that you'd been dallying with a lady when we interrupted you. You wore her many perfumes like a bathrobe under the bathrobe you wore; and from the way you stepped back from the chill of the open door, I could tell you were coming from some place warm.

But what's it matter among friends, Couth? I hugged you, picked you right up off your feet, you scrawny bugger! You sure smelled good, Couth.

Trumper lugged Couth into the kitchen, waltzing him around until they collided with a shiny new vinyl kiddie raft moored by the sink. Bogus didn't remember the Pillsburys having any small children. He sat Couth down on the butcher's block, kissed him on the forehead and left him gawking while he boomed affectionately, "Couth, I can't tell you how glad I am to see you ... Here you are saving my life again ... you're the one fixed star in the heavens, Couth! Look—my beard's nearly as big as yours, Couth . . . How *are* you? I've been awful, Couth, you probably know . . ."

And Couth just kept staring at him, and then looking at Dante Calicchio, a squat monster in uniform trying to keep politely out of the way in a corner of the kitchen and holding his driver's cap in his big-knuckled hands. While Trumper skipped around the kitchen, opening the refrigerator door, peering into the dining room, poking into the laundry alcove—where, to his mischievous delight, he saw a wooden clothesrack with some lady's silky bras and panties hung up to dry.

Plucking up the nearest bra, he waved it with a leer at Couth.

"Who is she, you sly bugger?" he cackled, and once more he couldn't resist tickling his fingers playfully in the chin of Couth's long beard.

But all Couth said was, "Where have you *been*, Bogus? Where in hell have you been?"

Trumper was quick to catch the accusing tone and knew that Couth had heard from Biggie. "You've seen her, huh?" he asked. "How is she, Couth?" But Couth looked away from him, as if he were going to cry, and Trumper quickly added, quickly scared, "Couth, I've behaved rather badly, I know . . ."

He was twisting the bra in his hands and Couth took it away from him. Then, when he saw the bra in Couth's hands, Trumper suddenly thought, *That's a mauve bra*, and he remembered buying a bra so purple—a bra so big. He stopped talking; he watched Couth slip down from the butcher's block like some slow-moving meat which had been de-boned there; Couth went into the laundry alcove and put Biggie's bra back on the clothesrack.

"You were gone a long time, Bogus," Couth said.

"But I'm back now, Couth," Bogus said, which sounded pretty stupid. "Couth? I'm sorry, but I *am* back, Couth . . ."

Some bare feet were slap-slapping down the stairs and a voice said, "Please keep the noise down or you'll wake up Colm."

The feet came toward the kitchen. Crammed in the corner by the spice rack, Dante Calicchio was attempting the

298

impossible by trying to make himself small and inconspicuous.

"Bogus, I'm sorry," Couth said gently, and touched his
arm.

Then Biggie walked in, gave Dante a look as if he were
a storm trooper who had arrived by U-boat and turned a
remarkably unflinching and unsurprised stare on Bogus.

"It's Bogus," Couth whispered to her, as if she might
not have recognized him with a beard. "It's Bogus," he repeated a little louder. "Home from the war . . ."

"I wouldn't say *home*," Biggie said. "I wouldn't say that
at all."

And I listened hard for the humor in your tone, Big; I
was really straining to hear it. But I missed it, Big. It was
absent. And the only thing I could think to say—because
of tho way both you and Couth seemed so nervous about
the hulking wop in uniform crouched under the spices—
the only thing I could do, Big, was introduce you both to
my driver. There was nothing else I could begin with.

"Uh," Trumper said, as if backing away from a punch.
"This is Dante. He's my driver."

Neither Biggie nor Couth could look at Dante; they
kept right on staring alternately at Bogus and at the floor.
And Bogus could only notice Biggie's robe, a new one—in
orange, her favorite color; in velour, her favorite material.
Her hair had grown out some, and she wore earrings,
which she'd never done before; she looked sort of tousled
and blowzy, a look he remembered her carrying well. You
just wanted to rumple yourself up with her when she
looked like that.

Then Dante Calicchio, under the strain of being introduced, tried to shoulder himself out of the corner where
he'd crammed himself and hit the spice rack with his
shoulder, propelling it with him into the center of the
kitchen where he made a hopeless grab at it; Biggie and
Couth and Bogus all rushed toward him and made things
worse. Little spice jars shattered all over the kitchen, and
Dante's last lurch for the empty rack splintered it against
the unyielding refrigerator.

"Oh, God, I'm sorry," Dante said.

Biggie prodded a little spice jar with her foot and looked straight at Bogus. "A lot of people are sorry," she said.

Upstairs, Trumper heard Colm call out.

"Excuse me," Biggie said, and walked out of the kitchen.

Trumper followed her up the stairs. "Colm," he said. "That's Colm, isn't it?" He was right behind her when she stopped, turned and gave him a look he'd never had from her before—as if she were a strange woman he'd just goosed in some vile, surprising way.

"I'll be back in a minute," she said coolly, and he let her go on upstairs alone. He lingered on his way back to the kitchen, hearing her soft voice reassuring Colm about the crash of the spice rack; from the kitchen, he could hear Couth's equally reassuring tone to Dante Calicchio. Not all the spice jars had been broken, Couth was saying, and he could build a new rack in no time.

Dante Calicchio made some remark in Italian; to Trumper, it sounded like a prayer.

Then there was the business with the pool table. Couth got to feeling badly for Dante, who felt so miserably awkward hanging around in the house, afraid of the fierce outdoors, wondering if he should call his wife, and whether he should tell the limousine service about the delay or just drive back to New York quick.

"Sir?" he asked Trumper, who was waiting for Biggie to come downstairs. "Should I go?"

But Trumper didn't know what was what. "I don't know, Dante," he said. "Should you?"

Then Biggie came back down and gave a kind of brave smile to Couth and a hard nod to Trumper, who followed her outside and out onto the night-black dock.

Then Couth asked Dante if he shot pool. This brought Dante out of trauma for a while; he shot a lot of pool, in fact. He took eight straight games from Couth and then, after secretly devising a handicap system, won three of the next four. But they weren't playing for money. The way everyone in that house acted, Dante couldn't even think about money. Actually, though, whenever he bent over to address the cue ball, he felt the hundred-dollar bill in his underwear.

"That Mr. Pillsbury," he said to Couth, still thinking that Bogus was named Pillsbury. "What's he do for all his money?"

"He opens his mail once a month," Couth said, thinking that Dante meant *the* Mr. Pillsbury. Dante whistled, swore softly and sank the fiveball in the sidepocket, the cue ball gliding back to where he wanted it. Couth, who was wondering how Bogus could afford a chauffeur, said, "That Mr. Trumper, Dante—what's *he* do for all his money?"

"Twelveball down in the right corner," Dante said. He never heard anything when he was planning a shot.

Couth was confused; he thought that perhaps Dante was being evasive. Looking out the picture window, he saw Biggie on the end of the dock, facing the ocean; by her moving hands he knew that she was talking. Ten feet away, leaning against the dock's mooring post, Bogus sat as still and silent as a barnacle—growing there, taking root.

Dante sent the cue ball whistling down the length of the table and socked the twelveball into the corner pocket, but Couth never turned from the window. Dante watched the cue ball nudge the ten away from the eight, then roll up cozily behind the fourteen, leaving him a perfect shot for the opposite corner. He was about to call it when Couth said something to the window.

"Tell him no," Couth said. It was almost a whisper.

Dante watched Couth standing there. Jesus, he thought, he opens his fucking mail once a month and they're all crazy here, the two of them nutty for that big broad. I'm not shutting my eyes tonight, baby, and I'm not letting the fuck go of this pool cue, either . . . But all Dante said was, "It's your shot."

"What?"

"It's your shot," Dante said. "I missed."

Lying was the handicap system which Dante Calicchio had devised for himself.

I threw a snail off the dock. It went *ploink!* in the water, and I thought of how long it would take that snail to get back to dry land.

And you went on and on, Biggie.

Among all the other things, you said, "Of course I can't

stop caring for you. I care about you, Bogus. But Couth really cares about me."

I threw three snails rapid-fire: *Ploink! Ploink! Ploink!*

You went on, Big. You said, "You were gone such a long time! But after a while it wasn't the time you were gone that got to me, Bogus; it was the time when you were *with* me, as I remembered it, that I didn't like . . ."

I found a cluster of barnacles with the heel of my hand and ground my palm down on them, grating it against them as if it were a cheese.

I said, "I'll give you time, Big. All the time you want. If you want to stay here a while . . ."

"I'm here for good," you said, Big.

I *ploinked!* another snail. Then a fish slapped, a tern cried, an owl spoke, and, carried on that resonant air, across the bay a dog barked.

"You say," I said, "that Couth cares for you, and for Colm too. But what do you feel for Couth, Big?"

"It's hard to say," you said, and you turned away and faced the bay. I thought you meant it was hard because you didn't have much feeling for him, but then you said, "I care for him a lot."

"Sex?" I said.

"A lot," you said. "It's okay there, too."

Ploink! Ploink!

"Don't make me tell you how much I love him, Bogus," you said. "I don't feel like hurting you. It's been a long time, and I don't feel so angry now."

"Merrill's dead, Big," I said—I don't know why. And you came over and hugged me from behind, squeezing me so hard that I couldn't turn around and squeeze you back. In fact, when I wriggled free enough to reach you, you pushed me off.

"I wanted to hold you for Merrill, Bogus," you said. "Don't you try to hold me, please."

So I let you hold me your way. If you wanted to think you were hugging Merrill, I wasn't going to stop you.

I said, "What about Colm, Big?"

"Couth loves him," you said. "And he loves Couth."

"*Everybody* loves Couth," I said, and *ploink! ploink! ploink!*

"Couth is very fond of you, Bogus," you said. "And you

can see Colm whenever you want to. Of course you're welcome to come here . . ."

"Thank you, Big."

Then you *ploinked* a snail of your own off the dock. "Bogus?" you asked. "What are you going to do?"

And I thought, *Ploink!* Then I spoke a handful: *Ploink! Ploink! Ploink! ploink-ploink-ploink!* I watched you turn away from me and looked up at the two figures silhouetted at the picture window in the pool room; they stood side by side, pool cues on their shoulders like rifles during a parade. But they weren't marching; they were looking down at the dock, and neither of them moved until you started up the path to the house. Then the taller, thinner figure left the window dissolving into the house to meet you; the shorter figure flexed his cue stick like a fencing foil, and then he too turned away.

Ploink! was what I thought as I heard the screen door slam.

From deep inland, beyond the salt-marsh where Couth and I once swamped a boat in the salt-stunted pines, a loon said what was on his mind.

Dante took three straight games from Biggie before he began to miss shots on purpose just so he could see her arch her body over the table with all her bends and boulder-shapes hard under her soft, slinky robe. She held her lower lip in her teeth when she stroked the ball.

Down on the dock, her two lovers, he guessed, sat close together, their legs hanging off the end, striking a bargain with a handful of snails.

Jesus, Dante thought. Who's who here, is what I'd like to know.

You have always been kind, Couth, and that suits the way you look. As fair as I am dark, you're white with freckles, whereas I am linseed oil rubbed into coarse-grained wood. Your height conceals the fact that your hips are broader than your shoulders, but you don't look broad; those long, skinny legs and your pianist's fingers and your noble, unbroken nose make you look slender. You're the only strawberry blond I've ever liked. I know that you grew your beard to hide your freckles, but I never told anyone.

We're as different in the body as a seal and a giraffe. You must be a whole head taller than me, Couth, and I can't help remembering what Biggie used to think of people bigger than herself. Come to think of it, though, she must outweigh you.

I mean, your chest could fit in her cleavage, Couth.

Biggie used to like the idea that she couldn't get her arms all the way around my chest and keep her hands locked if I chose to fill my lungs. Well, she could collapse your lungs. And when she wraps her legs around your waist, beware of your back! In fact, it's a wonder she hasn't killed you. Yet clearly you've survived.

But all I said was, "You look well, Couth."

"Thank you, Bogus."

I said, "Well, you know, she wants to stay with you."

"I know."

I threw a snail as far as I could, and you threw one too. Yours went nowhere near as far as mine, though—not with that funny, twitchy way you have of throwing. You've got a lousy arm, Couth, and for all the time you've spent on boats, you row like a bird with a broken wing. And fancy you teaching Colm how to swim.

But all I said was, "You'll have to watch Colm around the water this summer. He's approaching a dangerous age."

"Don't worry about Colm, Bogus," you said. "He'll be fine, and I hope you'll come see him, whenever you want to. And us, too—come see us, you know."

"I know. Biggie told me."

Ploink!

But you threw your snail so badly that it didn't even reach the water; it went *fip!* in the mudflats.

"I'd appreciate lots of photographs, Couth," I said. "When you make some of ... of Colm, you know, just make a print for me."

"I have some I can give you now," you said.

Ploink!

"Shit, I'm sorry, Bogus," you said. "Who could have known it would work out this way?"

"Me. I could have known, Couth ..."

304

"She'd already left you when she came here, Bogus. She'd already made up her mind, you know . . ."

Ploink!

Fip!

"What about the Pillsburys?" I asked. "What are they going to think of you living here with this woman and a child?"

"That's why we got married," you said, and I thought that I must have become a snail—that I must have thrown myself in and swallowed too much water to be hearing you right, Couth.

"You mean you *want* to get married, Couth?" I said.

"No, I mean we *did* . . . sort of."

I brooded over this for about four *ploinks*. How was it possible? It didn't seem that it could be, so I asked, "How could that be, Couth? I thought *I* was married to her."

"Well, you *were*, of course, and this . . . thing hasn't legally gone through yet," you said, "but since you . . . deserted her, it was possible to get a kind of thing proceeding. I don't understand it myself, but one of the Pillsburys' lawyers has some things already drawn up . . ."

I thought, Well, you haven't just been sitting on your hands, have you, Couth?

"We had no way of knowing when or if you'd be back, Bogus," you said. Then you went on and on about how it was almost legally necessary to go through with this, because of the tax structure and the way dependents were regarded by law. *Thank you*, I thought, when you got to the part about there being no alimony this way.

"How much do I owe you?" I said.

"I don't care about that, Bogus," you said, but I already had the envelope out and was pressing nine hundred dollars out into your fine, thin hand.

"Jesus, Bogus. Where did you get this?"

"I've struck it rich, Couth," I told you, and tried to put the envelope back in my pocket as if it were a casual gesture—as if there were other envelopes stashed all over my body, and I wasn't exactly sure which pocket this one belonged in. Then, because I thought you were going to refuse it, I started to babble, beginning no place special.

"If I can't live with them, Couth, then I'm very glad it's you. You'll take better care of them than I have, I'm sure, and I won't ever worry about them with you. It's also a wonderful part of the country to grow up in, and you can teach Colm photography."

"Biggie is going to help this summer," you said. "You know, when the Pillsburys are here—shopping and doing some cooking and taking care of the house. It will give me more time to take pictures and work in the darkroom . . ." you trailed off. "I've got a part-time job at Bowdoin in the fall. It's only forty-five minutes away. You know, just one section of students—a sort of workshop in photography. They gave me a show this spring and the students even bought a few prints."

The weight of this small talk was crushing us.

"That's great, Couth."

"Bogus, what in hell are you going to do now?" you asked me after a long silence.

"Oh, I have to get back to New York," I lied. "But I'll be up again . . . when I get settled, you know."

"It's almost morning," you said. We watched an early orange sun rise out of the sea, its faint glow striking the shore. "Colm gets up early. He can show you his animals. I built a kind of zoo in the boathouse of things I caught for him."

But I didn't want to be around to see what he looked like and if he even liked me any more. Let the grave mound grow a little grass, I always say; then it's safe to look.

But all I said was, "I've got to talk to my driver now, Couth."

When I tried to get up, you caught me by the belt and said, "Your driver doesn't even know who you are, Bogus. What's going on with you?"

"I'm okay, Couth. I'll be all right."

You stood up with me, you frail angel bastard, and you took hold of my beard and shook my head gently, saying, "Oh shit, oh shit, if we could only both live with her, Bogus, I wouldn't mind—you know that, don't you? I even asked her that once, Bogus."

"You did?" I said. I was holding your beard tight; I half felt like kissing you, but also like snatching you bald. "What did she say to that?"
306

You said, "She said no, of course. But I wouldn't have minded it, Bogus—I think."

"I wouldn't have minded it, either, Couth," I said. Which was probably not true.

Like a buoy out on the water, all of the sun was showing itself now, bobbing on the surface of the sea, and suddenly there was too much light to see you by, Couth, so I said, "Get me those photographs, will you? I have to go now . . ."

We went up to the house together, taking the flagstone steps up the boathouse path two at a time. I felt you slip the money I'd given you into my back pocket. And I remembered your bare ass one moonlight on these flagstones, where you lay singing on your belly, Couth, too drunk to stand. That girl with you—one of the two we picked up at the trailer park in West Bath—was putting on her bathing suit, fed up with trying to get you up to the house and the master bedroom. I was cozy with my half of those girls up in the boathouse loft.

I watched you strike out on the lawn, Couth, and I remember thinking to myself as I lay there smugly, not too drunk to screw, Poor Couth is never going to get a girl.

Well, Couth, I've been wrong before.

When they came into the kitchen, Biggie had just made a sandwich for Dante Calicchio. It was a large sandwich which Dante was gnawing off a serving platter shaped like a trough, and Biggie had poured him a beer which he was drinking out of a stein the size of a flower vase.

Dante was wondering who was going to go off with whom next. If this is the part where I take the big blond broad down to the dock, I won't mind, he thought.

"Will you have something to eat, Bogus?" Biggie asked.

But Couth said, "He wants to go before Colm gets up."

Who? thought Dante Calicchio. Who in hell could be sleeping through a night like this?

"Well," Bogus said, "I'd like to see him, actually, but I don't want him to see me . . . if that's not too much to ask."

"He feeds his animals in the boathouse, the first thing when he gets up," Couth said.

"And he eats his breakfast on the dock," Biggie said.

Bogus thought, A routine. Colm has a routine. How kids love a good routine. Did *I* ever establish a routine with Colm?

But all he said was, "I could watch him from the pool room, couldn't I?"

"I've got some binoculars," Couth said.

"Jesus, Cuthbert," Biggie said. Couth looked embarrassed; she did, too. Bogus thought, *Cuthbert?* When was it anyone called you Cuthbert, Couth?

In a corner of the kitchen, wary of the spice-rack debris, Dante Calicchio wolfed his sandwich, quaffed his beer and wondered if the limousine service was worried, and if his wife had called the police. Or would it be the other way around?

"We'll be going pretty soon," Bogus said to Dante. "Why don't you take a walk, get some air . . ."

Dante's mouth was stuffed so he couldn't talk, but what he was thinking was, Oh, sweet shit, you mean I got to take you back with me? But he didn't say a word, and he pretended not to see Bogus slip a big wad of money— maybe as much as a thousand dollars—into the breadbox.

Dante sat below the high-water mark on the cool wet steps leading from the dock to the boat ramp and marveled at the miniature life he saw swarming in the tide pools on the mudflats, and in the teeming crevices of the bared rocks. It was the only mud he had ever seen that he wanted to stick his bare feet in, and he sat with his trousers rolled up to his knees and his blue-white city toes asquirm in the cleanest muck he'd ever felt. On the dock above him, his dusty black city shoes and thin black city socks looked so ominous and foreign that even the gulls were wary of them. The braver terns swooped low, then shrieked off in alarm at this strange deposit left by the tide.

Out at the mouth of the bay, a lobsterman was pulling in his traps, and Dante wondered what it would be like to work with his arms and his back again, and whether he'd get seasick.

He got up and walked gingerly out on the flats, feeling a shell prick his foot now and then, wary of the squiggling life all around him. An old lobster pot lay washed up against the far mooring post of the dock; Dante made his cautious way toward it, wondering what beasts would be inside. But it was staved in and its only contents was the bait, a fish head, picked clean. Then a clamworm scuttled across his foot and he yelped and ran painfully up the shoreline. When he looked up to see if anyone had observed his cowardice, he saw a dark handsome little boy watching him. The boy was in his pajamas and he was eating a banana. "It was just a clamworm," Colm said.

"Do they bite?" Dante asked.

"They pinch," said Colm, hopping off the low side of the dock and climbing barefoot over the sharp rocks as if his feet were soled with rope. "I'll catch one for you," he said. He handed Dante his banana and walked through the shells which, Dante was sure, had ribboned his own feet. Feeling sheepish, he resisted the temptation to examine himself for cuts and watched the boy prowl the mudflats, prodding with his fingers at terrible live-looking things Dante wouldn't have poked with a pole.

"They're kind of hard to catch sometimes," said Colm, squatting down and digging up a great glob of mud. His tiny hand shot into the hole and came up with a long greenish-reddish worm which wrapped itself around his hand. Colm had it pinched just behind the head and Dante could see the thing's black pincers groping blindly in the air.

Wise-ass kid, Dante Calicchio thought. You come near me with that thing and I'll drop your banana in the mud. But Dante held his ground and let Colm walk right up to him.

"See the pinchers?" Colm asked.

"Yeah." said Dante. He thought of giving Colm back his banana, but he feared the boy might think he was making an exchange. Also, Colm was covered with mud. "Now you're too dirty to eat your breakfast," Dante said.

"No," said Colm. "I can wash, you know." He led Dante to a tide pool trapped higher up in the rocks and they washed the mud away together.

"You want to see my animals?" Colm asked. Dante wasn't sure; he was wondering what Colm had done with that worm. "What's a chauffeur?" Colm asked him. "Like a taxi?"

"Uh-huh," Dante said. As alert as a rabbit, on the look-out for the animals lurking in there, he followed Colm to the boathouse.

There was a turtle with what looked like rocks growing all over its back, and a gull Colm told Dante not to get close to—it had a busted wing and liked to peck. There was a fiercely active little animal that looked like an elongated rat, which was a ferret, Colm said. There was a zinc washtub full of herring, half of which were dead and floating on the surface; Colm scooped these up with a net, as if these deaths were commonplace.

"Cat food?" Dante asked, meaning the dead herring.

"We don't have a cat," said Colm. "They kill more than they can eat."

When they came out of the boathouse, the sun was warm enough to flush Dante's face, and a sweet, salt-smelling wind had picked up off the bay.

"You know what, kid?" said Dante. "You're pretty lucky to live here."

"I know," Colm said.

Then Dante glanced up at the house and saw Bogus Trumper at the pool-room window watching them through a big pair of binoculars. Dante knew that the boy wasn't supposed to know he was being watched, so Dante moved his bulky body between the boy and the house.

"Are you sometimes a soldier?" Colm asked, and Dante shook his head. He let Colm try on his fancy driver's cap; the kid grinned and marched a few steps up the dock. Funny, Dante thought. Kids love uniforms, and most men hate them.

Trumper watched Colm attempt a military salute. How tanned he was! And his legs seemed much longer than he remembered.

"He's going to have your length, Big," he mumbled. Biggie was exhausted; she lay sleeping on the couch in the pool room. Bogus was all alone at the binoculars, but Couth heard him. When he saw Couth looking at him, Bogus moved away from the binoculars.

"He looks fine, doesn't he?" said Couth.

"Yup, yup," said Trumper. He looked at Biggie. "I won't wake her up," he said. "You say goodbye for me." But he tiptoed up to where she lay; he seemed to be waiting for something.

Couth tried to be casual about looking out at the sea, but Trumper still didn't seem comfortable, so Couth ambled out of the pool room. Then Bogus bent over Biggie and kissed her fast and light on the forehead, but before he could straighten up, she reached a groggy hand into his hair, giving him a soft stroke and a sleepy groan.

"Couth?" she said. "Is he gone?"

He was gone, all right. He had Dante stop at an Esso station in Bath and pack the tiny icebox in the back of the limousine full of ice. In Brunswick, he bought a fifth of Jack Daniel's, and in a Woolworth's across the street, one glass.

So he was gone by the time they crossed the Massachusetts line. He sat in the plush back seat with the glass divider shut tight, and drank until the tinted windows seemed a darker green, even though the day was getting brighter. In the soundless, air-conditioned Mercedes, he slumped like a dead king riding in his cushioned coffin back to New York.

Why New York? he thought. Then he remembered that it was because Dante was going there. He took out his envelope of money and counted up to a fuzzy fifteen hundred or eighteen hundred, give or take a hundred or so. It never came out the same twice, so after he'd counted it four times he put it back in his pocket and forgot about it.

But Dante noticed, and it was the first notion he had that the nut in back might not be so rich. If you took the time to count it, you didn't have enough.

By the time they got to New Haven, Trumper was so crocked that Dante didn't even have to ask if they could stop for a minute. Dante phoned New York and got a bawling out from the limousine service and a lot of tearful shouting from his wife.

When he returned to the car, Trumper was simply too stewed to understand what Dante wanted to tell him. Dante wanted to warn Trumper that "they" were waiting for him in New York. "You mean the cops?" Dante had

311

asked the limousine service. "What do they want with him?"

"Bigger than ordinary cops," the limousine service told Dante.

"Oh, yeah? What'd he do?"

"They think he's nuts," the limousine service said.

"No shit," said Dante. "Is that a crime?"

Dante tapped on the glass divider and finally roused Bogus Trumper into some form of recognizable stare. Then Dante decided to let it go; he just waved to Trumper through the glass. Trumper smiled and he waved back.

But Dante was warming up to this nut now; he was moved by him. Even before they'd left Maine, he'd changed his mind about the guy. He'd asked Trumper if he could stop at a gift shop along the road; he wanted to get some souvenirs for his wife and kids.

Trumper had let him stop, and when Dante went inside to browse through plastic lobsters and seacoast watercolors painted on driftwood logs, Trumper looked at the photographs Couth had given him as he was leaving. There was a whole stack of pictures of Colm, big eight-by-tens: Colm on the mudflats, Colm in a boat, Colm on the beach in a snowstorm (so they had already moved in with Couth during the winter!), Colm formally posed in Biggie's lap. They were all lovely.

But the last photograph shocked Trumper. Perhaps Couth had put the photographs together too quickly and hadn't meant to include it, for it was obviously from a rather different series. It was a close-up of a nude, distorted by a wide-angle lens. The shot was focused on the woman's crotch, and she was lying in a field in such a position that the texture of the grass between her spread legs nearly matched the texture of her pubic hair; in fact, that was clearly the idea of the photograph. The wide-angle rounded the world above her, and her face was small and faraway and not in focus. But her twat was in focus, all right.

Mother Earth? Trumper thought. He didn't like the photograph, but he realized that if Couth had not included it by mistake—if Couth had meant to give it to him—that the gesture was generous and well-meaning, like Couth.

312

And also like Couth, in surprisingly bad taste. The nude was Biggie.

Trumper looked up and saw Dante coming. He opened the door of the back seat because he wanted to show Trumper what he'd bought for his children: three inflatable beach balls and three sweatshirts with MAINE! across the chest; under the letters a large lobster cocked his claws.

"That's nice," Trumper said. "Very nice."

Then Dante saw the pictures of Colm, and before Trumper could stop him, Dante picked the stack up and started leafing through them. "I want to tell you, sir," he said, "that's a fine-looking boy you got."

Trumper looked away, and Dante, embarrassed, said, "I knew he was yours. He looks just like you."

Then Dante came to the crotch shot of Biggie, and though he tried to look away, he couldn't. Finally he forced himself to slip the photograph to the bottom of the stack and handed them all back to Trumper.

Trumper was trying to smile. "Very nice," Dante Calicchio said, his mouth a hard line, fighting a leer.

Then it was New York all around me, I could tell. And Jack Daniel's Old Time No. 7 Brand Quality Tennessee Sour Mash Whiskey, 90 proof, wallowing there in my brain, its good burnt taste so thick on my tongue that I could have chewed it.

I could see them out there, wanting to get at me. They rapped the window and fucked around with the door latch, and they shouted at my big brutish good-hearted driver, "Calicchio! Open up, Calicchio!"

Then they had my door open and I caught the first one smack on his forehead with that lovely squarish bottle Jack Daniel puts his whiskey in. Some others helped the man off the floor, and then they came at me again.

I was all right when they kept their distance, but when they moved in close, I'd lose the focus. I could make out Dante, though; that good man was begging them to go easy on me. He had a persuasive way of doing it; he would put his thick-fingered hands on their throats until they gargled a queer tune and danced gently away from me. "Here, here," he kept saying. "Just don't anybody hurt him, he hasn't done anything. I just want to give him something, a little present. Now you let me do that, please." Then he'd add something in a slightly lower key, like, "You want to keep your teeth, or should I transplant them up your ass, faggot?"

They were tugging me one way and Dante was tugging me another. Then there was an awesome heave in one direction for a considerable distance, during which an unidentified man yelled out that he was being killed, and another stranger began bleating like a goat, and I was all alone and free for a minute. Then my guardian angel, Dante Calicchio, was reaching into his underwear—in his crotch, of all things—and from out of his crotch, of all places, he pulled a crinkled-up thing and stuffed it down my shirt front, saying breathlessly, "Here, here, here, for God's sake ... I think you're going to need every bit of this you can hold on to ... Now take off, if you're smart at all. *Run!*"

Then we were in rapid motion once more, and faraway from me I saw Dante Calicchio playing with two toy men. They must have weighed no more than ten pounds each, because Dante tossed one of them through the windshield of a parked car and shook the other one upside down like a rag-doll puppet until I could no longer see, because all the other people swarming around seemed to be trying to get into the game Dante was playing.

Then they had me again. They drove me around in a car with the window open, and they made me keep my head hanging out; I guess they thought I needed air. But I was not so far gone that I couldn't recall the crinkled-up thing under my shirt front, and when they were riding me up in this elevator, I slipped it out and sneaked a peek at it. It was some kind of money—I couldn't read how much—and one of the men in the elevator took it away from me.

I *think* I was in an elevator; we were in a hotel, I think. But all I thought at the time was, What a funny thing to carry in your crotch!

33 : Welcome to the Order
of the Golden Prick

Throughout Tulpen's hospital visit, I alternately dozed and stared, opening my eyes suddenly as if I'd been startled, gawking unfocused over my shoulder, acting a lolling stupor to perfection, though I had to pee something fierce.

Ralph came to visit later in the afternoon, pronounced me dead and asked Tulpen what my prick looked like. But she seemed genuinely worried and snapped at him. "I haven't seen it," she said. "He's all doped up. He doesn't know where he is."

Ralph circled the bed; he'd brought the mail, and under the pretense of looking for a place to put it, he peeked behind the drawn curtain at my roommate—the sloshing old gentleman with the erector set of intake and output tubes.

"Let's ask a nurse," Ralph said.

"Ask her what?" Tulpen said.

"To let us see it," Ralph said. "Maybe we could just lift his sheet?"

I rolled my eyes and mumbled a little German to impress them.

"He's in his Nazi period," Ralph announced, and I lay there as if lobotomized, waiting for them to say intimate things to each other or exchange touches. But they never did; in fact, they didn't appear to be getting along well at all, and I wondered if they'd seen through my pretense and were playing it cool.

When they finally left, I heard Tulpen ask the floor nurse when Vigneron would be coming around, and whether they planned to release me that night. But I didn't hear the nurse's answer; my roommate chose that moment

315

to leak or ingest something loudly, and when he'd ceased his awful, liquid tremors, they had gone.

I had to get up and pee, but when I moved I caught one of my wiry stitches on the top sheet and let out such a piercing shriek that a covey of nurses burst into the room and the old gentleman gurgled in his dreams and hoses.

Two nurses walked me to the bathroom, and I held my hospital gown out in front like a jib so that it wouldn't brush against my wounded piece.

I made the foolish error of looking at myself before trying to pee. I could not see a hole; it was scabbed shut and a black tangle of stitches made me resemble the tied-off end of a blood sausage. I stalled by asking a nurse to bring me my mail.

There was a letter from my old thesis chairman, Dr. Wolfram Holster. He had enclosed an article from *The North Germanic Languages Bulletin,* written by that old comparative literature wizard from Princeton, Dr. Hagen von Troneg, which bemoaned the lack of studies in the ancestors tongues of the North Germanic chain. From Von Troneg's point of view, ". . . any in-depth understanding of the religious pessimism in works from the Norwegian, Swedish, Danish, Icelandic and Faroese is impossible unless the task is undertaken to update the few translations we already have, and we undertake further to translate previously untranslated works from the Old West Norse, Old East Norse and Old Low Norse." Dr. Wolfram Holster's comment was that the time was certainly "ripe" for *Akthelt and Gunnel.*

In a p.s., Holster added his sympathies for what he'd learned of my "situation." He elaborated: "A thesis chairman rarely has the time to involve himself in the emotional problems of the doctoral candidate; however, in the light of such a timely and needed project, I feel a chairman must, to a more personal degree, be as constructively forgiving as he must be constructively critical." His conclusion: "Do let me know, Fred, how *Akthelt and Gunnel* is coming."

Which, in the toilet cubicle of the hospital, reduced me to laughter, then to tears. I put Holster's letter in the toilet, and this gave me the courage to piss on it.

In my wandering stupor in Europe, I had written to

Holster twice. One was a long, lying letter wherein I described my research on the tragic Icelandic queen Brünnhilde and her possible relationship to the Queen of the Dark Sea in *Akthelt and Gunnel*. Of course there is no Queen of the Dark Sea in *Akthelt and Gunnel*.

My other communication with Holster was a postcard. It was a tiny detail from Breughel's great painting, "The Slaughter of the Holy Innocents." Children and babies are being ripped out of their mothers' arms; their fathers' arms, trying to grip them fast, are being hacked off. "Hi!" I'd written on the back of the postcard. "Wish you were here!"

After a while, one of the nurses came to the bathroom door to ask if I was all right. She walked me back to my bed, where I had to wait for Vigneron to come release me.

I looked at the rest of my mail. There was a large envelope from Couth full of documents about the divorce; I was supposed to sign them. A note from Couth advised me not to actually read them; they were worded in a "tasteless fashion," he warned me, so that the divorce would be taken seriously. I didn't know who had to take it this seriously, so I went against his advice and read a little. There was something about my "gross and depraved adulterous activity." Also mentioned was my "cruel and inhuman departure from all responsibility," and my "heartless abandonment, which bordered on the degenerate."

It seemed pretty cut and dried, so I signed everything. There's not much to signing things.

The rest of my mail wasn't mail at all. That is, it was wrapped up, but it was from Ralph and there wasn't any postage. A get-well gift? A joke? A vicious symbol?

It was a kind of diploma.

ORDER OF THE GOLDEN PRICK

Greetings! Be It Known By These Present
That
FRED BOGUS TRUMPER

Having Demonstrated Exceptional Bravery, Valor,

Gallantry And Phallic Phortitude, Through Having
Dauntlessly Endured The Surgical Correction Of His
Membrum Virile, And Having Successfully Survived
A Fearsome Urethrectomy With Not Less Than Five
[5] Sutures, Is Hereby Recognized As A Full Knight

In The Brotherhood Of The Order Of The
Golden Prick
And Is Entitled To All Privileges And Braggartry
Pertaining
Thereto.

It was actually signed, too, by Jean Claude Vigneron,
Attending Surgeon, and by Ralph Packer, Chief Scribe &
Prick. But where, I wondered, was the signature of
Tulpen, Chief Mistress of Interest?

Trumper was still batty and paranoid when Vigneron
came to release him.

"Well, it went very well," Vigneron said. "And you
don't have too much pain urinating?"

"I'm just fine," said Trumper.

"You should be careful not to catch the stitches on your
underwear or bedclothes," Vigneron said. "In fact, you'll
probably be most comfortable the next few days if you
stay home and don't wear any clothes."

"Just as I thought," Trumper said.

"The stitches will fall out by themselves, but I'll want to
see you in a week, just to make sure you're all right."

"Any reason to suspect I won't be all right?"

"Of course not," Vigneron said. "But it's customary, after surgery, to have a checkup."

"I may not be here," Trumper told him.

Vigneron seemed bothered by his aloofness. "Are you
all right?" he asked. "I mean, do you feel okay?"

"Just fine," Trumper said. Conscious that he was making Vigneron uneasy, he tried to make amends. "I've never
felt better," he lied. "I'm a new man. I'm not the old prick
I was."

"Well," Vigneron said, "I'm not really in a position to
vouch for that."

318

Vigneron was right, of course; Vigneron was *always* right. It was most uncomfortable to wear any clothes.

Trumper eased himself into his underwear, a greased gauze pad stuck to the end of his penis. This kept the stitches from tangling in the weave of his clothes; they tangled in the gauze pad instead. Walking was a gingerly accomplished feat. He plucked the crotch of his pants away from himself and ambled bow-legged, like a man with live coals in the pouch of his jockstrap. People stared at him.

He took his mail and the odd gift from Ralph. On the subway he stared at an austere and formal couple who looked as if they had meant to take a cab. Would you like to see my diploma? he thought.

But when he reached the Village, nobody paid any attention to him. People down there were always walking in strange ways, and he looked no more odd than half the people he saw.

As he fumbled for his key on the landing outside Tulpen's door, he heard the splashy squeegee-sounds of Tulpen in the bathtub. She was talking to someone, and he froze.

"It's a very simplistic whitewash," she was saying, "to attempt to cover very deep and complicated people and things with very easy generalizations, superficialities—you know. But I think it's just as simplistic to assume that everyone is complex and deep. I mean, I think Trumper really does operate on the surface . . . Maybe he *is* a surface, just a surface . . ." She trailed off, and Trumper heard her sliding in the bathtub and saying, "Come on, let's call it a night."

He turned away from her door, hobbled down the landing to the elevator, out and onto the moving street. *Let's call it a night,* he thought.

If he'd waited, he would have heard the scene cut and finished, heard Ralph bawling out Kent and Tulpen asking them to leave.

But I went straight to the Christopher Street studio and let myself in through Ralph's elaborate devices and se-

319

quence of locks. I knew what I was looking for; I had some things I wanted to say.

I found the cut strips of what Ralph called "fatty tissue." These were bits of overlong footage, or scenes considered weak in some way. Tulpen had them hanging in the dust closet of her editing room.

I didn't want to destroy anything valuable; I wanted to use footage I knew was second-rate. I looked through a lot of stuff. The parts with me and Colm and Tulpen on the subway were interesting. Also, there was a long shot of me, alone, coming out of a pet shop in the Village with a fishbowl sloshing under each arm—presents for Tulpen, one day when I was in the mood. The pet-shop proprietor, who comes to the doorway to wave goodbye to me, looks like a German shepherd in a Hawaiian sport shirt. He continues to wave long after I've left the frame.

I did a little rough splicing; I knew that I didn't have much time, and I wanted to do a good job of laying the sound strip over the footage.

My cock hurt so much that I took off my pants and underwear and walked around bare-ass, being careful to avoid the edges of tables and the backs of chairs. Then I took my shirt off, too, because it brushed against me, especially when I sat down. So then I was naked except for my socks. The floor was cold.

It was getting light out when I finished; I moved the projector into its place in the viewing room and dropped the screen down so that they'd know right away that something had been set up for them. Then I ran through the footage once, just to check.

It was a short reel. I marked the can with adhesive tape; THE END OF THE MOVIE, it said. Then I rethreaded the projector, advanced the film to just the right place, and adjusted the focal length; all they had to do was switch it on, and this is what they would see:

Bogus Trumper with his son, Colm, riding on a subway. The pretty girl with the nice breasts, the one who can make Colm laugh and Trumper touch her, is Tulpen. They are sharing a secret, but there's no sound. Then my voice-over says, "Tulpen, I am sorry. But I do not want a child."

CUT.

320

Bogus Trumper is leaving the pet shop, the fishbowls under his arms, and the German shepherd in a Hawaiian sport shirt waves goodbye to him. Trumper never looks back, but his voice-over says, "Goodbye, Ralph. I don't want to be in your movie any more."

It was a pretty short reel, and I remember thinking that they could probably stay awake through it.

I was looking around for my clothes when Kent let himself into the studio. A girl was with him; Kent was always bringing girls into the studio when he was sure we weren't going to be there. That way, he could show them around as if he owned the place, or was responsible for all that machinery in some grand way.

He was pretty surprised to see me, all right. He noticed I was wearing green socks. And I don't think Kent's girl ever knew that a person's pecker could look like mine. "Hello, Kent," I said. "Have you seen my clothes?"

They discussed the operation while Kent tried to reassure his girl and Trumper agonizingly put on his gauze pad and underwear. Then Bogus told Kent that under no circumstances was he to preview the little reel that lay in wait on the projector; it was meant for Ralph and Tulpen to watch together, and would Kent be so kind, please, as not to touch *anything* until they were all there to watch it together.

Kent read the adhesive tape on the reel can. "The end of the movie?" he asked.

"You bet your ass, Kent," Trumper said. Then he walked out holding his crotch out in front of himself.

He might have waited. If he had, Kent might have told him about the bathtub scene they'd shot. If he'd waited longer, he might have noticed that Ralph and Tulpen didn't come to the studio together, or even from the same direction.

But he didn't wait. Later he thought about how he had this infuriating habit of leaving too soon. Later, after Tulpen had straightened him out about her nonrelationship with Ralph, he had been forced to confess that he'd never even had a good reason for leaving at all. In fact, Tulpen pointed out, he had simply made up his mind to go some time before, and that anyone looking for excuses to leave can always find them. He didn't argue.

But now, with his raw new prick, he let a little of the morning pass, then went to Tulpen's apartment when he was sure that she'd be at the studio. There he picked up some of his things, and a few things that weren't his; he stole a cereal bowl and a bright orange fish for Colm.

It was a long bus ride to Maine. The pit-stops were endless, and in Massachusetts it was discovered that a man in the rear of the bus had died; a sort of quiet heart attack, the other passengers assumed. The man had meant to get off in Providence, Rhode Island.

Everyone seemed afraid to touch the dead man, so Bogus volunteered to lug him off the bus, though it nearly cost him his prick. Perhaps all the others were afraid of catching something, but Bogus was more appalled at the fact that the man was unknown to everyone around him. The driver looked in the man's wallet and discovered that he lived in Providence. The general reaction was that it was more bothersome to have missed your stop than to have died.

In New Hampshire Trumper felt compelled to introduce himself to someone and struck up a conversation with a grandmother who was on her way home from a visit with her daughter and son-in-law. "I guess I just can't understand the way they live," she told Bogus. She didn't elaborate, and he told her not to worry.

He showed her the fish he was bringing to Colm. He'd refilled the cereal bowl with fresh water at every pit-stop along the way. At least the fish was going to make it. Then he fell asleep and the bus driver had to wake him up.

"We're in Bath," the driver told him, but Trumper knew he was in limbo. What's worse, he thought, I've been here before.

What had made this leaving different from the first leaving was not necessarily a sign of health. That is, it was easier this time, and yet he hadn't really wanted to go. All he knew was that he had never finished anything, and he felt a need, almost as basic as survival, to find something he could finish.

Which made him remember Dr. Wolfram Holster's let-

322

ter, flushed down a hospital toilet with bloody pee, and that was when he decided to finish *Akthelt and Gunnel*.

Somehow the decision was uplifting, but he was aware that it was a queer thing to feel positive about. It was as if a man, whose family had for years assailed him about finding something to do, had sat down one night to read a book, only to be interrupted by a disturbance in the kitchen. It was just his family, laughing about something, but the man flung himself upon them, throwing chairs, punches and vile language until they all lay bruised and cringing under the kitchen table. Then the man turned to his horrified wife and said to her encouragingly, "I'm going to finish reading this book now."

One mauled member of his family might have dared to whisper, "Big deal."

Still, the decision was enough to give Trumper a sort of frail courage. He dared to call up Couth and Biggie and ask if one of them would pick him up at the bus station.

Colm answered the phone, and the pain when Trumper heard his voice seemed greater than if he'd tried to pass a peach pit through his sutured prick. But he was able to say, "I have something for you, Colm."

"Another fish?" Colm asked.

"A live one," Trumper said, and looked at it again to make sure. It was doing fine, it was probably seasick from the sloshing in the cereal bowl, and it certainly looked small and delicate, but it was still swimming around, by Christ.

"Colm?" Trumper said. "Let me speak to Couth or Mommy. Someone's got to come get me at the bus station."

"Did the lady come with you?" Colm asked. "What's her name?"

"Tulpen," Trumper said, passing another peach pit through his prick.

"Oh, yeah, *Tulpen!*" Colm said. He obviously liked her a lot.

"No, she didn't come with me," Trumper told him. "Not this time."

34: Into a Life of Art:
Prelude to a Tank on
the Bottom of the Danube

You asshole, Merrill! You were always hanging around American Express, waiting for lost little girls. I guess you found one, and she lost you, Merrill.

Arnold Mulcahy told me it happened in the fall. A restless time, eh, Merrill? That old feeling of needing to find someone to spend the winter with.

I know how it must have been; I was familiar with your American Express approach. I'll hand it to you, Merrill; you could cultivate a marvelous look. It was the former fighter-pilot look; the ex-Grand Prix Racer who'd lost his nerve, and perhaps his wife too; the former novelist with a writer's block; the ex-painter, out of oil. I never knew what it was you *really* were. The unemployed actor? But you had a great look; you had the aura of an ex-hero, a former *somebody*. Biggie said it right: women liked to think they could bring you back to life.

I remember the tour buses from Italy unloading in front of American Express, and the collection of sneering onlookers watching the clothes, imagining the money. A mixed group would leave the bus. Older ladies, unselfconsciously speaking English, expecting to be taken advantage of, wise enough not to mind looking foreign and perhaps stupid. Then a younger crowd—embarrassed even by being associated with such a crowd. They would try to set themselves apart and to look fluent in four languages. They wore a cool disdain for their fellow tourists, their
324

cameras inconspicuous, their luggage not excessive. You would always pick the prettiest one of these, Merrill. This time her name was Polly Crenner.

I can visualize it. The girl at the information counter, perhaps with a copy of *Europe on $5 a Day*, reading through a furnished list of the pensions she can afford. You would come up to the counter briskly and speak a rapid German to the information man—some pointless question, like asking if anyone's left a message for you. But the German would impress Polly Crenner; she'd at least look at you, then turn away when you glanced at her and pretend to be reading something interesting.

Then, casually, you would say in *English*—the language making her aware that you and anybody else can tell she's American—"Try the Pension Dobler. A nice spot, on Plankengasse. Or the Weisses Huf, on Engelstrasse; the woman there speaks English. You can walk to them both. Do you have much luggage?"

Reading this as a pickup, she would only indicate her luggage with a nod; then she'd wait, ready to refuse your gentlemanly offer to carry her bags for her.

But you never offered, did you, Merrill? You'd have said, "Oh, that's not much to carry," and thanked the information man in your polished German when he returned to tell you there were no messages for you. *"Auf Wiedersehen,"* you'd say, and then walk out—if she'd let you get away. Polly Crenner must not have let you go, Merrill.

What then? Your usual comic tour of Old Vienna? "What's your interest, Polly? The Roman or the Nazi period?"

And some of your invented history, Merrill? "You see that window, the third one from the corner, fourth floor up?"

"Yes."

"Well, that's where he hid when they were all looking for him."

"Who?"

"The great Weber."

"Oh . . ."

"Every night he'd cross this square. Friends left food for him in this fountain."

And Polly Crenner would feel the old suspense and ro-

325

mance settle on her like dust from the Holy Land. *The great Weber!* Who was he?

"The assassin took a room in the opposite building—just there."

"The assassin?"

"Dietrich, the miserable bastard." And you'd glare at the assassin's window, Merrill, like a raging poet. "It cost just one bullet, and all Europe felt the loss."

Polly Crenner would stare at the fountain where food for the great Weber had been stashed. But *who* was the great Weber?

The dull old city glowing like a live coal all around her, Polly Crenner would ask, "What are you doing in Vienna?" And which mystery would you have used on her, Merrill?

"For the music, Polly. I used to play, before . . ."

Or, more enigmatically, "Well, Polly, I had to get away . . ."

Or, more daringly, "When my wife died, I wanted nothing more to do with the opera. But somehow I haven't been able to break completely clean . . ."

Then what, Merrill? Perhaps your Erotic Art Tour (E.A.T., INC.)? And if the weather was nice, surely you would have taken Polly Crenner to the zoo. A heavy walk through the Schönbrunn Gardens. You used to tell me, Merrill, that the animals inspired sexual notions. A sip of wine on the terrace, watching the giraffes rub necks? Then into the tried-and-true patter: "Of course, this was all bombed . . ."

"The zoo?"

"In the war, yes . . ."

"How awful for the animals!"

"Oh, no. Most of them were eaten before the bombing."

"People ate them?"

"Hungry people, yes . . ." Here you would look worldly-sad as you reflectively extended a peanut to an elephant. "Well, it's natural, isn't it?" you'd ask Polly Crenner. "When we were hungry, we ate them. Now we feed them . . ." I imagine, Merrill, that you would have made that sound profound.

And then?

Maybe there was urgent mail you were waiting for, and

would Polly mind stopping by your apartment for a minute so that you could check? Doubtless she didn't mind.

Somewhere along here there would be talk of swimming while the nights were still warm—which would prompt that nice awkwardness of having to go to your place so you could put on your bathing suit, and having to go to her place so she could slip into hers. Oh, you were smooth, Merrill.

But you blew it! You just had to bring up that one about the tank in the Danube, didn't you? True or not, you had to mention the story.

"Die Blutige Donau," you would say. *"The Bloody Danube.* Have you read it?"

"It's a book?"

"Yes, by Goldschmied. But of course it hasn't been translated."

Then you would drive her out past the Prater.

"What do you call this car?"

"A Zorn-Witwer, fifty-four. Quite rare."

Crossing the old canal, you'd pour on the chilly mystique of Goldschmied's prolific river history. "How many men at the bottom of the Danube? How many spears and shields and horses, how much iron and steel and debris of thousands of years of war? 'Read the river!' writes Goldschmied. *'That's* your history! Read the river!' "

Who is Goldschmied? Polly would be wondering. Ah, pretty Polly, but who was the great Weber?

Then you'd say, "I know a piece of the river, a piece of that history." She would wait out your pregnant pause. "Remember the Ninth Panzer Division?" you'd say, and then go on, not waiting for her answer. "The Ninth Panzer sent two scout tanks into Floridsdorf on the night of New Year's Eve, 1939. The Nazis wanted to move a tank company into Czechoslovakia, and their armory was out along the Danube The scout tanks were looking for trouble in Floridsdorf. There'd been some die-hard resistance out there, and the scouts wanted to divert any saboteurs' intentions on the big tank drive at the river. Well, the scout tanks got the diversion they were seeking. One of them was blown to bits in front of a factory which made dry milk. The other tank panicked. It got lost in the warehouse monotony of Floridsdorf and ended way up on the

Old Danube—the old canal that's blocked off. Did you see? We just drove over it."

"Yes, yes," Polly Crenner would answer, history crushing down on her.

Then you'd stop the Zorn-Witwer at Gelhafts Keller, Merrill. You'd open Polly Crenner's door for her, and she'd bubble, "Well, what happened?"

"To what?"

"The tank."

"Oh, the *tank* . . . Well, it was lost, see."

"Yes . . ."

"And it was New Year's Eve, remember. Very cold. And this wild bunch of resistance people, they were chasing it . . ."

"How do you chase a tank?"

"With a lot of nerve," you'd say. "They kept close to the buildings and tried to disable it with grenades. Of course, the tank gunner was doing some damage; he was blowing half of the suburbs in two. But the people kept after the bastard and finally cornered the tank down on the bank of the old canal. Blocked off, right? The water pretty still and pretty shallow—therefore frozen pretty solid. They forced the thing out on the ice; it was the tank's only chance to get away . . . Well, when the tank was right in the middle, they rolled some grenades out across the ice . . . It sank, of course."

"Wow." Polly Crenner would say, both to the story and to the great beer-steined walls of Gelhafts Keller, through which you would be strolling her, Merrill, right out onto the dock.

"There," you would tell her, pointing out into the Old Danube, where tiny boats with lanterns were paddling lovers and drunks about.

"What?" she would say.

"There! The tank—that's where it broke through the ice. That's where they sank her."

"Where?" Polly Crenner would ask, and you would gently pull her pretty head close to yours and make her sight along your outstretched arm at some black point way out on the water.

And you'd whisper, "There! Right out there she went down. And she's still there . . ."

"No!"

"Yes!"

Then, Merrill, she would ask what in hell you'd brought a flashlight for.

You asshole, Merrill . . .

That was, in fact, what Trumper said when the federal men, if that's who they were, steered him out of the elevator at the tenth floor of the Warwick Hotel in New York City.

A well-dressed couple who were waiting for the elevator observed the men guiding Trumper down the hall. One of the Feds said, "Good evening."

"Good evening," the couple mumbled warily.

"You asshole, Merrill," Trumper said.

They took him to room 1028, a two-room suite on the corner which looked up the Avenue of the Americas to the park. From the tenth floor, New York certainly looked like fun.

"You asshole," Trumper said to Arnold Mulcahy.

"Give him a shower, boys," Mulcahy told his men. "Make it very cold." They did. They brought Trumper back to the room wrapped in bath towels, his teeth chattering, and sank him like a sash weight into a voluptuous chair. One of the men even hung up Trumper's espionage suit, and another found the envelope with the hundred-dollar bills in it. That was handed to Mulcahy, who then asked all the men to leave.

Mulcahy had his wife with him, and they were both dressed up. Mulcahy was in a formal dinner shirt with black tie, and his wife, a motherly, fretful sort of person, wore an evening dress which looked like an old prom gown. She examined Trumper's suit as if it were the hide of a freshly skinned beast, then asked him sweetly if he'd like anything—a drink? a snack? But Trumper's teeth were still chattering too much for him to talk. He shook his head, but Mulcahy poured him some coffee anyway.

Then Arnold counted the diminished money in the envelope, whistling softly and shaking his head. "My boy," he said, "you certainly have a hard time adjusting to a new situation."

"That's only human, Arnold," Mulcahy's wife said. He

silenced her with a businesslike look, but she didn't seem to mind being excluded from the conversation. She smiled at Bogus and told him, "I care as much for Arnold's boys as if they were *my* boys, too."

Trumper didn't say anything. He didn't think he was one of Arnold Mulcahy's "boys," but he wouldn't have put money on it.

"Well, Trumper," Arnold Mulcahy said, "I can't seem to get rid of you."

"I'm sorry, sir."

"I even gave you a head start," Mulcahy said. He recounted the money and shook his head. "I mean, I got you home again and gave you a little pocket liner—that wasn't even part of the deal, you know, boy?"

"Yes, sir."

"You went to see your wife," Mulcahy said.

"Yes, sir."

"Sorry about that," Mulcahy said. "Maybe I should have told you."

"You *knew?*" Trumper asked. "About Couth?"

"Yes, yes," Mulcahy said. "We had to find out who you were, didn't we?" He took a large manila folder off his dresser, sat down and thumbed through it. "You can't blame your wife, boy," he said.

"No, sir."

"So here you are!" said Mulcahy. "Embarrassing, really. I took some responsibility for you, you see. And you stole a chauffeur! And came back in no condition to be left alone . . ."

"I'm sorry, sir," Trumper said. He really was sorry. He sort of liked Arnold Mulcahy.

"You cost that poor chauffeur his job, boy," Mulcahy said. Trumper tried to remember Dante; dimly he recalled some strange heroics by him.

Mulcahy took about five hundred dollars out of the envelope, then handed the rest back to Trumper. "This is for the chauffeur," he said. "It's the least you can do."

"Yes, sir," Trumper said. Rudely, he counted his remaining money; there was eleven hundred dollars the first time he counted it, but the second time there was only nine.

"That will get you back to Iowa," said Mulcahy. "If that's where you're going . . ."

"I don't know . . . I don't know about Iowa."

"Well, I don't know much about the thesis business," said Mulcahy, "but I don't think there's much money in it."

"Arnold," Mrs. Mulcahy said; she was fastening an elaborate brooch. "We really will be late for the performance."

"Yes, yes," Mulcahy said. He got up and looked at his tuxedo jacket before putting it on; he didn't seem to know which way it went. "Ballet, you know," he said to Trumper. "I love a good ballet."

Mrs. Mulcahy touched Trumper's arm affectionately. "We never go out in Washington," she confided. "Only when Arnold's in New York."

"That's nice," Trumper said.

"Do you know the ballet?" Mulcahy asked him.

"No, sir."

"All those flitty people up on their toes," Mrs. Mulcahy chided.

Mulcahy grumbled as he fought himself into his tuxedo jacket; clearly, he must have been a ballet nut to put himself through this. Bogus had remembered him looking like an ambassador, but when he saw Mulcahy in evening dress, he knew that the man really didn't fit the role. Clothes didn't hang well on him; in fact, they appeared as if they'd been flung on him, wet, and when they dried, they chose to go their own peculiar and wrinkled way.

"What are you going to do now, boy?" Mulcahy asked.

"I don't know, sir."

"Well, dear," Mrs. Mulcahy told Bogus, "you should start with a new suit." She went over and plucked at it as if it might still be in danger of shedding.

"Well, we have to go," Mulcahy said, "and you've got to get out of those towels."

Bogus gathered up his clothes and moved delicately toward the bathroom; his head had something heavy and aching inside it, and his eyes felt so dried out that they felt fried; it hurt to blink.

When he came out, one of the federal men who'd brought him there was standing around with the Mulcahys. "Wilson," Mulcahy said to the man, "I want you to take Mr. Trumper wherever he wants to go—within the confines of Manhattan Island."

"Yes, sir," Wilson said. He looked like a hired killer.

"Where *will* you go, dear?" Mrs. Mulcahy asked.

"I don't know, ma'am," Trumper said. Mulcahy riffled through the manila folder again. Trumper caught a glimpse of a photo of himself and one of Biggie.

"Look, boy," Mulcahy said, "why don't you go see this Ralph Packer?" He pulled out a paper-clipped wad, with Ralph's hairy photo on top.

"He's in Iowa, sir," Trumper said. He couldn't imagine Ralph's history requiring as much authentication as Arnold Mulcahy seemed to hold in his hand.

"The hell he's in Iowa," said Arnold Mulcahy. "He's right here in New York, and doing rather well for himself, too, I might add." He handed Bogus a stack of newspaper clippings. "The missing persons people looked into your friend Packer quite extensively," Mulcahy said. "He was the only one who had an idea where you'd gone."

Bogus tried to visualize what missing persons people looked like. He saw them as invisible, materializing in the form of lampshades and subtle bathroom fixtures which asked you questions while you slept.

The clippings were reviews of Ralph's first movie, the National Student Film Festival winner, *The Group Thing*, whose sound track had been done by Bogus. The film had been shown in the art houses around New York; Ralph now had a studio in Greenwich Village and the distribution for two more of his films had already been contracted. One of the reviews of *The Group Thing* even mentioned how good the sound track was. "Bogus Trumper's infinite sound devices," it said, "are confident, ambitious techniques, extremely well crafted for such a low-budget film." Trumper was impressed.

"If you want my advice," said Mulcahy, "that's a better bet than that thesis business any day of the week."

"Yes, sir," Trumper said obediently, but he couldn't quite imagine Ralph actually getting money for what he did.

Mulcahy gave the hired killer named Wilson Packer's studio address, but the man, whose right eyebrow had just been shaved and stitched back together, seemed troubled about something.

"For heaven's sake, what's the matter with you, Wilson?" Mulcahy asked.

"That driver," Wilson mumbled.

"Dante Calicchio?" Mulcahy prompted.

"Yes, sir," Wilson said. "Well, the police want to know what they should do with him."

"I already told them to let him go," Mulcahy said.

"I know, sir," Wilson grumbled, "but I guess they'd like to have you confirm that personally, or something."

"Why, Wilson?"

"Well, sir," Wilson said, "the guy sure did a lot of damage, even though he didn't really know who we were, or anything. He was really pretty berserk."

"What happened?" Mulcahy asked.

"Well, some of our boys are in the hospital," Wilson said. "You know Cowles?"

"Yes, Wilson."

"Well, Cowles has a broken nose and a few ribs cracked. And you know Detweiller, sir?"

"What about Detweiller, Wilson?"

"Both collarbones busted, sir," Wilson said. "The guy was some kind of wrestler ..."

Suddenly Mulcahy looked interested. "A wrestler, Wilson?"

"Yeah, and a boxer too, sir," Wilson said. "You know Leary?"

"Yes, of course," Mulcahy said eagerly. "What happened to Leary?"

"Had his cheekbone cracked, sir. The wop just cold-cocked him with a hook. He was mostly a body puncher, sir, but he was getting off those hooks pretty good ..." Wilson gingerly touched his stitched eyebrow and smiled a little sheepishly. Arnold Mulcahy was smiling too. "And Cohen, sir. He threw Cohen through a windshield of a car. Cohen's got all kinds of lacerations and some water on the elbow."

"Really?" said Mulcahy. He seemed enormously pleased.

"So, sir," Wilson said, "the police thought you might want to reconsider and let them keep the guy a while. I mean, that wop's sort of dangerous, sir."

"Wilson," Mulcahy said. "Get him out, *tonight,* and bring him here after the ballet."

"After the ballet, sir? Yes, sir," Wilson said. "You just want to bawl him out a little, huh?"

"No," said Mulcahy. "I think I'll offer him a job."

"Yes, sir," Wilson said, but he seemed pained. He looked at Trumper in a surly way. "You know, kid," he told Trumper, "it beats me why anybody'd want to fight over you."

"It beats me too," said Bogus. He shook Arnold Mulcahy's hand and smiled at Mrs. Mulcahy.

"Get a new suit." she whispered to him.

"Yes, ma'am."

"Forget your wife," Mulcahy whispered to him. "That's the best thing."

"Yes, sir."

The thug called Wilson was holding Trumper's well-traveled suitcase, less in friendliness than as a gesture of insult—as if Trumper wasn't capable of carrying it. He wasn't, either.

"Goodbye!" said Mrs. Mulcahy.

"Goodbye," Trumper said.

"God, I *hope* so," said Arnold Mulcahy.

Bogus followed Wilson out of the hotel and into a battered car. Wilson set the suitcase heavily in Bogus's lap.

Trumper rode in silence to Greenwich Village, but Wilson swore and gestured at every odd-looking, queerly dressed person he saw on the crowded sidewalks. "You're going to fit right in here, you fucking freak," he told Trumper. He swerved to avoid a tall black girl walking two handsome dogs and yelled out the window at her, "Eat me!"

Bogus tried to hang on just a little longer. A vision of Ralph Packer as savior; an odd role for Ralph, but then he saw Packer on a bicycle, crossing the Iowa River.

"Well, here we are, hair-pie," Wilson said.

One hundred nine Christopher Street was lit. There was still hope in the world. Bogus noted it was a quiet street with daytime shops, a luncheonette, a spice store, a tailor. But apparently it linked more night-traveled areas; lots of people were walking through it without stopping.

"You missing anything?" Wilson asked him. Bogus felt

for the money envelope; yes, he had it, and he was holding his suitcase in his lap. But when he looked puzzled, he
saw that Wilson was holding the crinkled-up thing that
Dante Calicchio had taken out of his crotch. Bogus
remembered then that it was a hundred-dollar bill.

"I guess you lost this in the old elevator, right?" Wilson
said. Clearly he wasn't going to give it back.

Trumper knew he wasn't up to a fight; he'd never have
been up to a fight with Wilson, anyway. But he felt sort of
plucky; he was dancing light-headed on only the fringe of
the real world. He said, "I'll tell Mulcahy."

"Mulcahy doesn't want to hear from you," Wilson said.
"Just you try to find out who Mulcahy even *is*." He put
the crumpled-up bill in his pocket and kept on smiling.

Trumper didn't really have much interest, but Wilson
angered him enough to make him think. He opened his
door, slid the suitcase out on the curb and sitting half in,
half out, he said, "I'll tell Dante Calicchio." He grinned at
Wilson's puffy, freshly stitched eyebrow.

Wilson looked as if he was about to hit him. Trumper
kept grinning but he thought, I really *am* crazy. This
bohunk is going to beat me to death.

Then a kid wearing a knee-length, Day-Glo orange
bush-jacket came out on the sidewalk in front of RALPH
PACKER FILMS, INC. It was Kent, but Bogus didn't know
him yet. Kent approached the car, bent down and peered
in the window. "There's no parking here," Kent said offi-
ciously.

Wilson was looking for some diversion, and he clearly
didn't like Kent's looks. "Shove off, cunt-head," he snapped.

Kent shoved off; he went back inside the studio, perhaps
to get a gun, Bogus thought.

"You shove off too," Wilson said to Bogus.

But Trumper had gone beyond sense; he wasn't being
brave, just fatalistic; he thought he didn't care. "Dante
Calicchio," Bogus said slowly, "can make of you, Wilson,
something a dog wouldn't eat."

There was some faraway swearing in RALPH PACKER
FILMS, INC. Wilson threw the crumpled-up hundred-dollar
bill over Bogus's shoulder out onto the sidewalk, and
Bogus barely had time to roll out the open door before
the thug gunned the car ahead, the door handle catching

335

Trumper's pants' pocket and spinning him down to the curb.

Trumper picked up the hundred-dollar bill before he picked himself up; he'd skinned his knees, and he sat on his suitcase with his pants pulled up, peering at his wounds. When he heard people coming out of the film studio, he fully expected a horde of Ralph's henchmen who, as surrogates for Wilson, would kick him to pieces in the street. But there were only two people: the kid in Day-Glo orange and the instantly recognizable shuffling gait of the hairy man beside him.

"Hello, Ralph," Trumper said. He thrust the hundred-dollar bill into Ralph's paw and got up off the suitcase. "Get my bag, would you, boy?" he said. "I understand you're in need of a sound tracker."

"Thump-Thump!" Ralph cried.

"It was the other one," Kent mumbled. "The guy who was driving the car . . ."

"Get the suitcase, Kent," Ralph said. He put his arm around Bogus, looked him over, noticed blood and worse. "Jesus, Thump-Thump," Ralph said, "you don't exactly look as if you've found the Holy Grail." He unwrapped the hundred-dollar bill, which Trumper snatched back.

"No Holy Grail to be found, Ralph," Bogus said, trying very hard not to wobble.

"You've been duck hunting again, Thump-Thump," Ralph said, steering him toward the studio door. Bogus managed a faint smile at this joke. "Jesus, Thump-Thump, I think the ducks won again."

At the steep step down to the viewing room, Bogus lost his balance and had to let Ralph carry him into the place. Here I go, he said witlessly to himself. Into a life of art. It didn't seem to be the life for him, but right now, he thought, any life would do.

"Who *is* he?" Kent asked. He hadn't liked what Bogus had said about sound tracking. Kent was the sound man now; he was appallingly bad at it, but he thought he was learning.

"Who is he?" Ralph laughed. "I don't know," he said, and leaned down to where Bogus sat slumped on the projector bench. "Who are you, really, Thump-Thump?" he teased.

But Trumper was giddy with relief, almost reduced to senseless giggles. It's amazing how you can drop your guard down among friends. "I'm the Great White Hunter," he said to Ralph. "The Great White Duck Hunter." But he couldn't even sustain the joke and his head lolled on Ralph's shoulder.

Ralph tried to guide him through the studio. "This is the editing room where we . . ." Bogus fought falling asleep on his feet. In the darkroom, the smell of chemicals was too much for him: the chemicals, the old bourbon, Mulcahy's coffee and the darkroom-reminder of Couth. His elbow slipped into a tub of stop bath, he slopped some fixer on his pants and threw up in a developer tank.

Ralph helped him out of his clothes, rinsed him off over the darkroom sink and searched through Trumper's suitcase for some clean clothes. He found none, but he had some old clothes of his own at the studio, and he dressed Trumper in them. A pair of yellow corduroy bell-bottom pants; Trumper's feet stopped at the knees. A cream-colored blouse with ruffles and puffed sleeves; Trumper's hands stopped at the elbows. A pair of green cowboy boots; Trumper's toes reached to their arch. He felt like a dwarf clown of Robin Hood's Merrymen.

"Great White Duck Hunter not feeling so good?" Ralph asked.

"I'd like to sleep for about four days," Trumper admitted. "Then I want to make movies, Ralph. Lots of movies, lots of money. Buy some new clothes," he mumbled, stumbling in Ralph's yellow bell-bottoms. "And a sailboat for Colm."

"Poor Thump-Thump," Ralph said. "I know a good place for you to sleep." He rolled up the absurd bell-bottoms so that Trumper could more or less walk, then called a cab.

"So that's the great Thump-Thump," Kent said; he had heard stories. He sulked in a wing of the viewing room, holding a reel like a discus he would have liked to have thrown at Bogus. Kent saw his sound-tracking career being preempted by this clown called Thump-Thump who looked like an Elizabethan puppet in Ralph's big clothes.

"Get the suitcase, Kent," Ralph said.

"Where are you taking him?" Kent asked.

And Trumper thought, Yes, where am I going?

"Tulpen's," Ralph said.

It was German. Trumper knew the word; *Tulpen* means tulips in German. And Trumper thought, That certainly sounds like a nice place to sleep.

35: Old Thak Undone!
Biggie Puts On Weight!

Biggie and Couth were lovely to him. Without any talk about it, they made up the extra bed in Colm's room. Colm went to bed about eight, and Trumper would lie on the other bed, storytelling until Colm fell asleep.

The story he told was his own version of *Moby Dick*, which seemed appropriate for that sea-house. Colm thought whales were wonderful, so the story according to Trumper was the whale-as-hero, Moby Dick as unvanquished king.

"How big is he?" Colm asked.

"Well," Trumper said, "if you were floating in the water and his tail slapped you, you'd be worse off than an ordinary fly getting hit with a fly swatter." A long pause from Colm. In the fishbowl above his bed, he watched the fragile orange fish from New York, the bus-ride survivor.

"Go on," Colm said.

And Trumper went on and on. "Anyone with any sense would have known enough to leave Moby Dick alone," he said. "All the other whaling men just wanted to hunt the *other* whales. But not Captain Ahab."

"Right," said Colm.

"Some of the other men had been hurt or had lost their arms and legs hunting whales, but it didn't make them *hate* whales," Trumper said. "But . . ." and he paused . . .

"But not Captain Ahab!" Colm cried out.

"Right," said Trumper. The wrongness of Ahab grew clear.

"Tell me about all the things sticking into Moby Dick," Colm said.

"You mean the old harpoons?"

"Right."

"Well, there were old harpoons," Trumper said, "with ropes still hanging off them. Short harpoons and long harpoons, and some knives, and all the other kinds of things that men had tried to stick into him . . ."

"Like what?"

"Splinters?" Trumper wondered. "Sure, from all the boats he'd smashed, he picked up splinters. And barnacles, because he was so old; and seaweed all over him, and snails. He was like an old island, he'd picked up so much junk; he wasn't a clean white."

"And nothing could kill him, right?"

"Right!" said Trumper. "They should have left him alone."

"That's what *I'd* do," Colm said. "I wouldn't even try to *pat* him."

"Right," Trumper said. "Anybody who's smart would know that." And he waited for the refrain . . .

"But not Captain Ahab!" Colm said.

You should always tell stories, Trumper knew, in such a way that you make the audience feel good and wise, even a little ahead of you.

"Do the part about the crow's nest," Colm said.

"High up on the mainmast," Trumper orated dramatically, "he could see what looked like a couple of whales, way off . . ."

"Ishmael," Colm corrected him. "It was Ishmael, right?"

"Right," said Trumper. "Only it wasn't two whales, it was *one* whale . . ."

"A very big one."

"Right," said Trumper. "And when the whale spouted, Ishmael yelled . . ."

" '*Thar she blows!*' " yelled Colm, who did not appear very sleepy.

"Then Ishmael noticed there was something *funny* about this whale."

"It was white!" Colm said.

340

"Right," said Trumper. "And it had things stuck onto it everywhere . . ."

"Harpoons!"

"Barnacles and seaweed and birds!" said Trumper.

"Birds?" said Colm.

"Never mind," Trumper said. "It was the biggest damn whale Ishmael had ever seen, and it was white, so he knew who it was."

"Moby Dick!" Colm screamed.

"Ssshhh," said Trumper. They calmed down together; they could hear the ocean slapping the rocks outside, creaking the dock, flapping the boats on their moorings. "Listen," Trumper whispered. "Hear the ocean?"

"Yes," whispered Colm.

"Well, the whaling men hear it just like that, *slap slap* against the ship. At night, when they sleep."

"Right," Colm whispered.

"And the whales come sniffing around the ships at night."

"They *do?*" said Colm.

"Sure," said Trumper. "And sometimes they brush against the ship a little, or bump it."

"Do the men know what it is?"

"The smart ones do," said Trumper.

"But not Captain Ahab," Colm said.

"I guess not," Bogus said. They lay quietly listening to the ocean, waiting for a whale to bump the house. Then the dock creaked and Bogus whispered, "There's one!"

"I know," said Colm in a hoarse voice.

"Whales won't hurt you," Trumper said, "if you leave them alone."

"I know," Colm said. "You should never *tease* a whale, right?"

"Right," Trumper said, and they both listened to the sea until Colm fell asleep. Then the only alert life in the room was the thin, vermilion fish from New York, kept alive by constant care.

Trumper kissed his sleeping son goodnight. "I should have brought you a whale," he whispered.

It wasn't that Colm didn't like the fish; it was just that Trumper wished for something more durable. Colm liked the fish very much, in fact; with Biggie's help, he'd written

341

a thank-you note to Tulpen, a most roundabout way for Trumper to apologize for the theft.

"Dear Tulpen," Biggie said. Then, letter by letter, she had to tell Colm how to spell. "D-E-A ..." Biggie said. With fierce concentration, Colm carved the letters with his pencil clutched tight in his fist.

Bogus was shooting pool with Couth.

"Thank you for the little orange fish," Biggie dictated.

"Thank you *very much?*" Colm suggested.

"T-H-A ..." Biggie said. Colm carved.

Bogus blew every shot he took. Couth was relaxed and played his usual lucky game.

"I hope sometime you'll come see me in Maine," Biggie dictated.

"Right," said Colm.

But Biggie knew better. When Colm was asleep, she said to Bogus, "You left her, didn't you?"

"I think I'll be back with her, sometime," Bogus said.

"You always do think that," said Biggie.

"Why did you leave her?" Couth asked.

"I don't know."

"You never do," Biggie said.

But she was kind, and they talked easily about Colm. Couth was sympathetic to the idea of Bogus finishing his thesis, but Biggie didn't see it that way. "You hated it out there," she said, "and you weren't ever really interested."

Bogus couldn't think of an answer. His picture of himself returning to Iowa alone in no way resembled his memory of Iowa with Biggie and Colm. Biggie didn't pursue the point; perhaps she saw that too.

"Well, you ought to do something, I think," Couth said.

Everyone more or less agreed to that.

Bogus laughed. "It's important to have an image of yourself," he said. He'd gotten a little looped on Couth's apple brandy. "I think you have to start with a superficial image, like Graduate Student or Translator, something with an easy name. Then you hope you can broaden the image a little."

"I don't know what I started with," Couth said. "I just said, 'I'm living like I want to,' and that was a start.

Later, I became a Photographer, but I still think of myself more as just a Living Man ..."

"Well, but you're very different from Bogus," Biggie said. There was a silence in honor of her authority on that subject.

Bogus said, "Well, it just didn't work thinking of myself as a Film maker, or even a Sound Tracker. I never really believed it." And he thought, or a Husband, either; I never really believed that. But a Father ... Well, that was a clearer feeling.

There wasn't much else that was clear, though. Couth commented on the appropriate symbolism of the Maine fog around the house, and Bogus laughed. Biggie said that men were so queerly involved with themselves that simple things escaped them.

With the excuse of too much apple brandy, that was too deep a subject for either Couth or Bogus to pick up. They went to bed.

Bogus was still awake when Biggie and Couth made love in their room down the hall. They were quite discreet, but it was too familiar a silent tension for Bogus to mistake it. Surprised at himself, he realized that he was happy for them. It seemed the best thing in his life that they seemed so happy—that, and Colm.

Later, Biggie used the bathroom, then came quietly into Colm's room and checked his covers. She seemed about to check the covers on Bogus, too, until he whispered to her, "Goodnight, Biggie." She didn't come near him then; it was dark, but he thought she smiled. She whispered, "Goodnight, Bogus."

If she'd come near him, he'd have grabbed her, and Biggie never misread signals of that kind.

He couldn't sleep. After three nights with them, he was aware of himself as an imposition. He went down to the kitchen with *Akthelt and Gunnel;* time for a little worn Old Low Norse and a big glass of ice water. He liked the feeling of all of them asleep, and him their guardian, taking the night watch.

Affectionately he murmured some Old Low Norse and read over the part where Old Thak is killed. Betrayed in the fjord of Lopphavet! Slain by the foul Hrothrund and

343

his cowardly band of archers! Old Thak is lured into the fjord by a false message: that from the vantage of the cliffs above Lopphavet, he can observe Akthelt's fleet returning from the great naval victory at Slint. Standing on the prow of his ship, Thak glides close under the cliffs, but just as he is ready to leap ashore, Hrothrund and his archers let fly at him from their ambush in the woods. Thak's man at the rudder, Grimstad, turns the ship out of range, but Old Thak is too riddled with arrows to even fall down; as prickled as a pincushion, he clings to the jib like a failed hedgehog.

"Find the fleet, Grimstad," Thak says, but he knows it will be too late. Faithful Grimstad tries to make him comfortable on the foredeck, but there is no flat surface on the old king's body; there's no way he can even lie down. "Let me lie in the sea," he says to Grimstad. "I am so full of wood that I shall float."

So Grimstad ties a line to Thak and lowers him overboard; he fastens the line to the gunwale of the ship and tows Old Thak out of the cold fjord of Lopphavet. Trailing behind his ship, Thak bobs in the sea like a buoy full of darts.

Grimstad sails out to meet Akthelt's fleet, returning all happy and gory from its great naval victory at Slint. Akthelt sails alongside his father's ship; "Hail, Grimstad!" he calls. But Grimstad can't bear to tell Akthelt about Old Thak. Akthelt's ship comes closer, and he spots the line tied to the gunwale; his eyes follow it to the curious sea anchor dragging behind, the feather ends of some arrows still above water. Thak is dead.

"Lo! Grimstad!" Akthelt calls, pointing to the line running from the gunwale. "What lies astern?"

"That is your father," Grimstad says. "Foul Hrothrund and his bastard archers betrayed us, my lord!" And while the great Akthelt beats his breast and the deck of his ship, he realizes what Hrothrund's plot must have been: to kill Thak and seize his ship; to sail out to meet the fleet flying Old Thak's flag; and to ambush Akthelt too, as the ships came together. Then, commanding the fleet, Hrothrund would return to claim the kingdom of Thak, would take Akthelt's castle and violate Akthelt's tender wife Gunnel.

All this boils through Akthelt's mind while he tugs on

the line with violent heaves, bringing the body of Thak aboard. He thinks of the long, sharp instruments Hrothrund had in mind for him, and of the thick, blunt instrument he has in mind for Gunnel!

Akthelt smears his body with the blood of his father, orders himself lashed to the mainmast and commands his men to whip him with the shafts of the fatal arrows until his own blood runs with his father's.

"Are you all right, my lord?" Grimstad asks.

"Soon we'll be back at the castle," Akthelt says oddly. But he has a curious thought; he wonders if Gunnel would have liked Hrothrund.

Early in the morning, Colm found Bogus sleeping on the kitchen table.

"If you come down to the dock," Colm said, "then I can come down to the dock too." So they went, Trumper having difficulty aiming his feet.

It was high tide; far out in the eddy the gulls were circling a large mass of seaweed and flotsam—from the look of it, what was left of a castaway rowboat. Trumper was thinking of Old Thak, but when he looked at his son he knew what Colm was thinking.

"Is Moby Dick still alive?" Colm asked.

Trumper thought, Well, why not? I can't provide the kid with God or a reliable father, and if there's something worth believing in, it ought to be as big as a whale.

"I guess he'd be pretty old," Colm said. "Very old, right?"

"He's alive," Trumper said. They looked out to sea together.

Trumper wished he could really produce Moby Dick for Colm. If he'd had a choice of any miracle he could perform, he would have chosen just that: to make the bay roll and swell, inspire a cacophony of gulls to circle overhead, raise the Great White Whale from the depths and make him leap like a giant trout, let them both be showered by the spray of his splashing fall as they stood in awe on the dock, have Moby Dick roll ponderously in the water—show them his scars, his old harpoons and things (but spare Colm the sight of the rotted Ahab lashed to the whale's great side); then watch the whale turn and steam out to sea, leaving them with the memory.

"He really is alive?" Colm asked.

"Yes, and everyone leaves him alone."

"I know," said Colm.

"But no one hardly ever sees him," Trumper said.

"I know."

But a wild part of Trumper's brain was chanting, *Show yourself, old Dick! Up out of that water, Moby!* Such a miracle, he knew, would have been as much a gift to himself as to Colm.

It was time to leave. At the car he even tried joking with Biggie and Couth, saying how nice it was to see them, but that he knew he was inhibiting them. He spoke German playfully to Biggie and had a mock boxing match with Couth. Then, to part on a note of lighthearted humor, he kissed Biggie goodbye and patted her ass. "You're putting on a little weight, Big," he chided.

She hesitated and looked at Couth. Couth nodded, and Biggie said, "That's because I'm pregnant."

"Pregnant!" Colm repeated gaily. "Yah! She's going to have a baby, so I'll have a brother or a sister ..."

"Or maybe both," Couth said, and everyone smiled.

Bogus couldn't think of a thing to do with his hands, so he held out one to Couth. "Congratulations, old boy," he said, like a voice underwater.

Couth scuffed the ground and said he'd better see if the car would start. Trumper gave Colm another hug, and Biggie, her face turned away, but smiling, said, "Be careful." To Couth? To Bogus? To both of them?

"I love seeing you, always," Trumper said to everyone, and fled.

36: Akthelt Beset with Doubt!
Trumper Grinds to a Halt!

In Iowa his old stitches fell out. A great new hole was in his penis. He wondered if Vigneron had meant to make the opening so big. Compared with what he'd been used to, he now had a bathtub drain.

He went to see a doctor, just any old doctor; there was no provision for specialists in his Student Health Policy. He feared the diagnosis; some former veterinarian amazed at his prick?

"You say this was done in New York?"

But the doctor was a young South American; all the foreigners in the medical school appeared to be given the lowliest cases. The young doctor was very impressed.

"That's a beautiful meatoplasty," he told Bogus. "Really, I've never seen such a neat job."

"But it's so *big*," Bogus said.

"Not at all. It's perfectly normal."

That shook him; it made him aware of how abnormal he must have been.

That doctor's visit constituted his sole entertainment in Iowa. He lived in his library alcove with *Akthelt and Gunnel* and slept in a spare room in Dr. Holster's basement. By his own choice he left and entered the basement through the cellar door; Holster would gladly have let him use the front door. Sunday dinners he ate with Holster and his married daughter and her family. The rest of his meals consisted of pizza, beer, sausage patties and coffee.

A girl in the adjoining library alcove was also doing a

347

translation. It was from Flemish: "a religious novel, set in Bruges." Occasionally they'd look at each other's dictionaries, and once she asked him to dinner at her place. "I'm a good cook, believe it or not," she said.

"I believe it," he said. "But I've stopped eating."

He had no idea what the girl looked like, but in their library and dictionary way they remained friends. There was no other way for him to have friends. He didn't even drink his beers at Benny's because Benny was always trying to drum up conversation about some half-mythical "old gang." Instead, he drank a few beers every night at a shiny bar frequented by the residue of the fraternity-sorority set. One night, one of the frat boys asked Bogus when he planned to take a bath.

"If you want to beat me up," Trumper said to him, "go ahead."

A week later, the same guy came up to him. "I want to beat you up now," he said. Trumper didn't remember him, and he executed a competent side leg-dive, picked up the guy's legs and ran him like a wheelbarrow into the jukebox. The frat boy's friends threw Trumper out of the bar. "Christ," Bogus said, bewildered. "He was a nut! He said he wanted to beat me up!" But there were two dozen other bars in Iowa City, and he didn't drink much anyway.

He worked on the translation with a dull, enduring sort of energy. He went all the way through it to the ending before he remembered that there were a lot of verses in the middle section that were made up, and others that were not even translated. Then he recalled that even some of his early footnotes were lies, and parts of the glossary of terms too.

In the back of his mind was a harsh echo he referred to frankly as Tulpen. She had always been one for facts. So he simply started over again and went through the whole translation straight. He looked up every word he didn't know, and conferred with Holster and the girl who knew Flemish about the ones he couldn't find. He wrote an honest footnote for every liberty, and a flat, direct introduction explaining why he had not tried to put the epic in verse but had elected to use simply prose. "The original verse is awful," he wrote. "And my verse is worse."

348

Holster was enormously impressed with him. Their only argument was over Holster's insistence that Trumper make some introductory remarks "placing" *Akthelt and Gunnel* in perspective in the broader picture of North Germanic literature.

"Who cares?" Trumper asked.

"*I* care!" Holster yelled.

So he did it, and he didn't lie, either. He mentioned all the other, related works he knew of, then admitted to knowing nothing about the writings in Faroese. "I don't have the slightest idea as to whether this work has any relation to Faroese literature in this period," he wrote.

Holster said, "Why don't you just say, 'I prefer to reserve judgment on the relationship of *Akthelt and Gunnel* to the Faroese hero-epics, as I have not researched Faroese literature extensively.' "

"Because I haven't researched it at all," Trumper said.

Ordinarily Holster might have insisted on his point, or claimed that Trumper *should* research Faroese writings, but Trumper's demonic work habits had so impressed Holster that the old thesis chairman let it go. In fact, he was rather a nice man. One Sunday dinner, he asked, "Fred, I would suppose that this work is a kind of therapy for you?"

"What work isn't?" Trumper said.

Holster tried to draw him out. He didn't mind Trumper living in his basement like a rarely seen mole, and occasionally he would call down into the basement and ask Bogus upstairs for a drink. "If *you're* having one," Trumper would say.

The only thing Bogus wrote that wasn't part of his thesis was an occasional letter to Couth and Biggie, and even more occasional letters to Tulpen. Couth wrote back and sent him pictures of Colm; Biggie sent him a package once a month with things like socks and underwear and Colm's finger paintings in it.

He didn't hear from Tulpen. What he wrote her was almost purely descriptive of how he was living: Trumper as monk. But at the end of every letter he would add hesitantly, "I want to see you, really."

Finally he did hear from her. She sent a postcard of the Bronx Zoo which said: "Words, words, words, words ..."

as many times as it took to nearly fill the postcard. At the bottom she left just enough room to add, "If you wanted to see me, you'd do it."

But he threw himself into the end of *Akthelt and Gunnel* instead. Only once—when he heard the girl who knew Flemish crying in her library alcove and didn't go ask her if he could help—did he stop long enough to consider that *Akthelt and Gunnel* might not be good for him.

Akthelt and Gunnel ends rather badly. It's all because of the foul temper Akthelt gets into while he's tied to the mainmast, smeared with his father's gore and being flagellated with the shafts of the father-murdering arrows. Moreover, when his fleet arrives back in the kingdom of Thak, Akthelt discovers that Hrothrund has come to Akthelt's castle, attempted to abduct the Lady Gunnel, failed (or changed his mind), and fled.

Akthelt searches the whole kingdom for the father-murdering, would-be rapist without success. Then he comes home to the castle, wondering why Hrothrund failed to abduct the Lady Gunnel (or changed his mind about it). Did he even try? And if so, how far did he get?

"I didn't even see him!" Gunnel protests. She'd been in the garden when Hrothrund had come to abduct her. Maybe he simply couldn't find her; it was a big castle, after all. Also, most of the people who had seen Hrothrund weren't yet aware of Thak's murder; therefore his appearance wasn't any big deal until the fleet returned and told the evil tale. *Then* people went around saying, "Why, that foul Hrothrund was just here!"

Akthelt is confused. Was Hrothrund the only one involved in the plot? Someone reminds him that it was just last Saint Odda's Fest when Gunnel was seen to dance with Hrothrund.

"But I always dance with lots of people on Saint Odda's!" Gunnel protests.

Akthelt behaves queerly. He demands a full search of the castle's laundry room and unearths one unclaimed pair of leather clogs, one unclaimed stained petticoat, and one unclaimed and boastfully large codpiece. Holding this grubby bundle at arm's length, he confronts Gunnel and attempts to make elaborate sense out of the evidence.

350

"*What* evidence?" she cries.

Hrothrund is not to be found anywhere in the kingdom of Thak. Reports trickle in from the coast that Hrothrund is at sea, is hiding in the northern fjords, is looting small and defenseless towns along the coast. A worthless pirate! Also, the reports imply, Hrothrund is less interested in looting for gold and food than he is in *sport*. (In Old Low Norse, *sport* means rape.)

Akthelt delves dangerously deeper into himself. "What is that mark there?" he asks Gunnel, fingering an old bruise on the back of her downy thigh.

"Why, from my horse, I think," Gunnel says sweetly— at which Akthelt bashes her in the face.

She cannot go on being wronged this way, so she begs her husband to allow her to try to capture foul Hrothrund by her wiles and prove her innocence before all. But Akthelt fears the trick will be on him, so he denies her request. But she persists. (All this stupid intrigue is the most trying point in the text, actually.)

Finally, after a lot of dithering for twenty-two stanzas, Gunnel loads a rich boat with wares, her maidservants and herself, intending to sail north up the coast, hoping to lure an attack from Hrothrund. But when Akthelt discovers her design, he believes the lure is really set for him; in a rage, he casts her rich ship, her maidservants and Gunnel herself adrift. With no man to sail them and no weapons to guard them, the defenseless ship full of hysterical, useless females sails north up the fjord toward Hrothrund, and despite the pleading from many in the kingdom of Thak, Akthelt refuses to follow.

The expected happens, of course; Hrothrund falls upon them. What a self-fulfilling prophecy to haunt Akthelt for all his remaining days! His wife was faithful, but by suspecting her, he casts her into infidelity. What else could Gunnel do when her maidservants are beset by a boatload of hairy archers, and she herself is faced with the ruthless swine Hrothrund?

Actually, what Gunnel does is pretty fucking shrewd. "Well met, Hrothrund!" she hails him. "For months, tales of your brave insolence have reached us. Make me your queen and our lord Akthelt will be undone!"

Hrothrund fell for it, too, but it cost her. For days and

351

nights in his foul ship's cabin hung with animal skins, Gunnel gave up her body to his savage, slimy ways, until at last he fully trusted her. He would take her, unarmed, without his knife or broad-ax by his bedside, and rut like a contented beast, leaving her gasping. He was fool enough to think it was pleasure that made her gasp.

Then she had him. One day she told him about a safe cove he could sail into for the night; there, friends in favor of Akthelt's overthrow would meet them. So Hrothrund sailed right into the cove where the lookouts of Akthelt's fleet were always stationed. She led Hrothrund right into it. Then, in the long night, Gunnel gave herself to him so untiringly that she finally had him spread out, spent and groggy, beside her. Though barely able to move herself, she had cherished this moment for so long that her will was not to be denied. Groaning her way from his stinking bed, she took up his broad-ax and cut off his smug, ugly head.

Then, perfumed with the aroma of her sex, Gunnel sweetly asked the cabin guard to fetch her a bucket of fresh eels. "For his lord," she said, letting her robe bare her shoulder, and the dolt fetched her the eels quick.

In the morning, Akthelt's fleet fell upon Hrothrund's boats and massacred everyone above deck, including Gunnel's faithful maidservants long since defiled and humbled by the filthy archers. Then did the bold, righteous and avenging Akthelt stride to Hrothrund's cabin door and cleave it with his two-edged sword, expecting to find his false lady in the arms of the cowardly father-murderer.

But Gunnel sat waiting for him in her best gown, and on the night table in front of her was the severed head of Hrothrund, stuffed with live eels. (In the kingdom of Thak, a legend claimed that this recipe would never let a man's brain rest.)

Akthelt dropped on his knees before her, whimpering his apologies and begging forgiveness for the burden he had forced her to bear. "I bear another burden," Gunnel said coldly. "Hrothrund's spawn is in my belly. You shall have to bear that for me too."

By this time Akthelt was ready to accept almost anything from her, so he agreed abjectly.

"Now," she said. "Take your true wife home."

Akthelt did so, and bore his burden well enough until the child of Hrothrund was born. But he could not fathom her affection for the child; to him, the spirit of the father-murderer, wife-raper lived within the babe, so he slew it and threw it to the wild boars in the moat. It would have been a girl.

"I could forgive you much," Gunnel told him, "but I will never forgive you this."

"You'll learn to," he said, but he wasn't so sure. He slept badly—and alone—while Gunnel roamed the castle every night like a streetwalker whose price was too high for any passer-by.

Then, one night, she came to his bed and made violent love to him, saying she at last felt reconciled to him. But in the morning, she asked the chamber girl for a bucket of fresh eels.

After that, the kingdom of Thak went the way of most kingdoms whose leadership is up for grabs. Gunnel was completely off her rocker, of course. She herself announced Akthelt's death at the morning session of the Council of Elders. She brought Akthelt's head, crammed with eels, to the meeting, placed it on a meat board and set it before the Elders, plunk in the middle of the great table. For years she had been in the habit of serving exotic dishes at these weekly meetings, so many of the Elders were caught off guard.

"Akthelt is dead," she announced, putting the dish down.

One of the Elders was so old that his eyesight was gone. He groped his hand toward the head on the table, which was his customary manner of identifying Gunnel's exotic dishes. "Live eel!" he exclaimed. The Elders were not sure what to do.

The obvious successor to the throne was young Axelrulf, Akthelt and Gunnel's only son, who was now in charge of the occupation of Flan. The Council of Elders sent a messenger to him, informing him of his father's murder at his mother's hand and pointing out that the kingdom of Thak was in danger of division without strong leadership. But Axelrulf was having an awfully good time among the Flans. They were a handsome, hedonistic and civilized people, the living was easy, and Axelrulf had never had political ambitions. At least, that was part of his reasoning. "Tell Mother I'm very sorry," he told the messenger.

In the meantime, some of the Elders were conspiring to appoint one of their own to the throne, and to murder Axelrulf should he come back to claim his birthright. That was the larger part of Axelrulf's reasoning for not being interested in the position. He was no fool.

What happened then was what *always* happens. When no strong leader emerged, the kingdom of Thak erupted in chaotic and ineffectual rebellion. At the castle, Gunnel became obsessed with a rash of lovers, and there were more buckets of fresh eels. Finally, of course, she took a lover who was not so spent and love-drugged as he looked, and he cut *her* head off. He didn't bother with the eels, though.

Finally, when the kingdom of Thak was hardly even a kingdom any more, but a disorganized land with hundreds of tiny, feuding fiefs, what happened then was what *always* happens too.

Young Axelrulf rode up from Flan. In fact, he liked the Flans so much that he brought an army of them into the kingdom of Thak and took over the whole mess very easily. He made peace in the kingdom by killing all the feuders who wanted war. So Thak became Flan, sort of, and Axelrulf married a nice Flan girl named Gronigen.

In the last stanza of *Akthelt and Gunnel,* the anonymous author slyly implies that the story of Axelrulf and Gronigen is probably not much different from the story of Akthelt and Gunnel. So why not stop it here?

Bogus Trumper was more than willing to agree. When he had finished all four hundred and twenty-one stanzas, it seemed a pretty empty accomplishment. In part this was because he had been so honest a translator that there was nothing of his own in the whole work. So he added something.

Remember the part where Gunnel cuts off Hrothrund's head? And then Akthelt's head? Well, Trumper added an implication that she cut off more than heads. It fit, after all. It suited the story, it certainly suited Gunnel, and most of all, it suited Bogus. He really believed that Gunnel *would* have cut off more than their heads, but that for

354

reasons of etiquette guiding the literature of the time, the author had been obliged to discreetly edit certain details. Anyway, it made Trumper feel better and gave him a small stake of his own in the translation.

Dr. Holster was very pleased with *Akthelt and Gunnel*. "Such a *rich* work!" he exclaimed. "Such a basic pessimism!" The old man moved his arms like a symphony conductor. "Such a crude story! Such a violent, barbaric people! Even sex is a blood sport!"

The notion was no surprise to Trumper. He was a little uneasy, however, that Holster had especially liked the implication he had added, and when the old man suggested a footnote to emphasize the boldness of such an act, Bogus declined by saying he didn't care to draw attention to it.

"And the part with the eels!" cried Holster. "Think of it! She cut off their pricks! How perfect—but I just couldn't imagine it!"

"I could," said Fred Bogus Trumper, B.A., M.A., Ph.D.

So finally he had finished something. He packed and reread his mail. With nothing to occupy him, he felt as if his pulse had slowed down, as if his blood was reptile-thick.

There hadn't been any more mail from Tulpen. His mother had written about his father's ulcer. Bogus felt a little guilty and tried to think of a gift. After some thought, he went to a fancy-food store and sent his father a prime boned Amish ham. Too late, he wondered if ham was good for an ulcer, and quickly sent a letter apologizing for the gift.

He heard again from Couth. Biggie had delivered an eight-pound baby girl, named Anna Bennett. Another Anna. Trying to imagine the baby, Trumper remembered that the ham he'd sent his father also weighed eight pounds. But he felt so happy for Couth and Biggie that he sent them a ham too.

And he heard from Ralph. Typically, a mysterious letter. It mentioned nothing about Trumper abandoning a film career or leaving Ralph Packer Films Inc. in the lurch, but said simply that he thought Trumper should at least come see Tulpen. Surprisingly, Ralph spent most of the letter describing the girl he was living with now, someone called Matje, "like the herring, you know?" The girl was "not voluptuous, but a brimming person," and Ralph added that "even Tulpen likes her."

Trumper had no picture of what in hell was going on. He understood why Ralph had really written the letter, though; Ralph wanted Bogus's permission to release the film. *Fucking Up* was done, Trumper knew.

Bogus left the letter unanswered for a few weeks. Then one night after his thesis was finished and he was feeling especially aimless, he went to see a movie. It was a film about a homosexual airline pilot who is afraid of rain. By some slip-up, he sleeps with a sympathetic stewardess, who cures him of both his nasty homosexuality and his fear of the weather. Evidently he was afraid of rain *because* he was a homosexual. It was a sloppy and offensive movie in every way, Trumper thought, and afterward he sent a telegram to Ralph. "You have my permission," the telegram said, and it was signed, "Thump-Thump."

Two days later Trumper said his goodbyes to Dr. Holster. *"Gaf throgs!"* Holster hailed him cheerfully. *"Gaf throgs!"*

This was an inside joke from *Akthelt and Gunnel*. When people in the kingdom of Thak wanted to congratulate one another for a job well done, a war well fought or sex well made, they said *"Gaf throgs!"* ("Give thanks!"). They even had a Thanksgiving Day devoted to such feelings; they called it Throgsgafen Day.

It was a perfect September football weekend when Trumper lugged his suitcase and his thesis bound copy of *Akthelt and Gunnel* to the Iowa City bus station. He had his Ph.D. and his memories of selling pennants and buttons and bells. He guessed he was going to look for a job. After all, what was a Ph.D. for? But it was a bad time of year to look for a teaching post; the academic year had just begun. He was too late for this year, and it was too early to find an opening for next year.

He felt like Maine, seeing the new baby and being with Colm. He knew he'd be welcome there for a while, but he couldn't live there. He felt like New York, too, and seeing Tulpen, but he didn't know how to introduce himself. He had an image of how he'd *like* to return—as someone triumphant, like a cured cancer patient. But he couldn't decide what disease he'd had when he left, so he hardly knew if he was cured.

He spent a long time looking at a Greyhound map of the United States before buying a ticket to Boston. He supposed there was much to recommend Boston, in the dim light of teaching jobs; furthermore, he had never seen the birthplace of Merrill Overturf.

Also, on the Greyhound map of the United States, Boston was roughly halfway between Maine and New York. And on a map of *me*, he thought, that's about where I am.

37 : Audience Craze, Critical Acclaim and Rave Reviews for *Fucking Up*

Variety announced that "Ralph Packer's newest film is clearly the best thing to come out of the so-called underground this year. Of course this distinction could conceivably be awarded to any film with some content and style, but Packer's film is even subtle. He has at last expanded his documentary approach to a finely focused situation; he is dealing with characters at last, instead of groups, and technically, his work is as fine as ever. Admittedly, not many viewers will find much to interest them in Packer's rather self-centered and inert main character, but . . ."

The New York Times said, "If an era of commercially successful, low-budget films is truly upon us, we may at last give birth in this country to the vital documentary style which the Canadians have been producing with such excellence in recent years. And if small, independent film makers can ever achieve widespread and major theater-distribution, then the sleight-of-hand style—which Ralph Packer has at last found a home for, in his 'F——ing Up'—is going to be much imitated. I am not sure that it is a truly enriching or satisfying style, but Packer has sharpened his craft well. It is Packer's *subject* which eludes me. He doesn't develop a subject; he simply keeps bringing it up . . ."

Newsweek called the film "An elaborately polished, honed, slicked-over, bantering movie which disguises itself as a quest: to explore the psyche of its main character—

through a choppy montage of pseudo-interviews with the character's former wife, present girlfriend, dubious friends, and with irritating interruptions from the main character himself, who plays a cute game of pretending he wants nothing to do with the movie. If that were true, he would indeed be wise. Not only does the film never get to the bottom of what makes the main character tick, but the film stops ticking long before its end."

Time, honoring a long tradition of disagreeing with *Newsweek*, trumpeted: "Ralph Packer's 'F——ing Up' is a beautifully compressed film—quiet and understated in every way. Bogus Trumper, credited with the film's innovative sound track, gives a fine acting performance in the role of an aloof, tight-lipped failure with one busted marriage in his past, one cool and shaky relationship in the present—an absolute paranoiac victimized by his own self-analysis. He is the unwilling subject of Packer's uncannily delicate scrutiny, which takes the form of a trim, point-blank documentary which pieces together and overlaps interviews and random comments with some exquisitely straight and deceptively simple shots of Trumper doing perfectly ordinary things. It is a film about making a film about someone involved in making a film, but Trumper emerges as a kind of hero when he rejects all his friends *and* the movie—Packer's subtle way of putting down a psyche-picking belief in the discovery of any true motives . . ."

Trumper read all these in his father's den at Great Boar's Head.

"Is that the *Time* review?" his mother asked him. "I like the *Time* review."

His mother had collected and saved all the reviews, and apparently the reason she liked the one from *Time* was that it mentioned Trumper by name. She hadn't seen the movie and didn't seem to realize that it was about her son's cruel, sad life. Neither did the reviewers.

His father said, "I don't suppose it will ever be shown up here."

"All the films we want to see never get up here," his mother said.

The film hadn't gotten out of New York yet, though it was scheduled to be shown in Boston, San Francisco and a few other, big-city art cinemas. It might reach a few large campuses too, but it wasn't likely to turn up in Portsmouth, New Hampshire—thank God. He himself hadn't seen the film yet.

He'd been through a month of teacher interviews in and around Boston and had come home for a weekend now and then, to console his father's ulcer and to appear grateful—which he truly was—for the new Volkswagen his father had given him. A kind of graduation present, he supposed.

It looked more and more likely that he'd have to wait until spring to find a job; he had discovered that his new Ph.D. had about the same appeal and importance at an interview as having freshly shined shoes. About the only openings at this time of year were in the public high schools, and somehow a Ph.D. in comparative literature, with a thesis in Old Low Norse, did not seem suitable training for a class in world culture, from Caesar to Eisenhower, and English composition. Also, he didn't even know how to look at a sixteen-year-old.

His father fixed himself another milk and honey, and made Bogus another bourbon with an expression on his face that revealed how much he'd like to trade stomachs with his son.

Bogus read some more of his mother's collection of reviews.

The New Yorker said that it was "rare and refreshing to see an American film with enough self-confidence to trust in a light touch. What Packer manages with his crew of nonactors should make some of our superstars feel insecure—or at least angry with their screenwriters. Lead actor Bogus Trumper (whose sound tracking is just a *bit* too clever) is remarkably effective in portraying the self-protective, shallow cool of a man who has failed to communicate with women beyond a self-satisfying level . . ."

"The women are beautiful!" proclaimed *The Village Voice.* "What's missing in Packer's film is any clue whatsoever as to why two such frankly open and stunningly complete women would have anything to do with such a weak, enigmatic, unfulfilled man . . ."

Playboy termed the film "hip and complex, with the

360

sexual vitality of the characters just barely concealed, like the impression of a voluptuous body under silk . . ."

Though it enjoyed "the vivid pace of the film," *Esquire* found the ending "a cheap emotional device. The pregnancy scene is simply an old and overused gimmick for soliciting audience response."

What pregnancy scene? wondered Bogus.

The Saturday Review, on the other hand, found the ending "pure Packer at his understated best. The light casualness of the pregnancy brings all the airy intellectual speculations up against the hard fact that she loved him . . ."

Why? Trumper thought. Who loved him? Loved whom? Was Ralph wringing sentiment from Biggie's recent child by Couth? But how had he tied that in?

Life fumbled to articulate it. "The surfacy, vignette approach almost demands a nonending sort of ending; a progression which fails to develop in depth, but instead elects to swivel a story—simply showing more facets on the surface—would be pretentious in choosing a dramatic ending centered on an inevitable event. 'F***ing Up' leads to no such inevitable event. Rather, in that last blunt image of pregnancy—brief and matter-of-fact—Packer achieves a definitive *non*-statement . . ."

A *what?* Bogus thought. He realized that he had to go see the fucking movie.

Part of the reason why he wanted to see it had nothing to do with the reviews. He wanted to see Tulpen again, but he couldn't quite bear the thought of her seeing *him.* Trumper as voyeur, and interested party, would go see *Fucking Up.*

He had a job interview at the Litchfield Community College of the Liberal Arts in Torrington, Connecticut, which was more or less on the way to New York. After his interview, he could sneak into the city and see the film.

It turned out that the job opening was for two sections of a survey of British literature and two sections of expository writing for freshmen. The chairman of the English department was impressed with Trumper's credentials, especially the Old Low Norse. "Gosh," the chairman said, "we don't even have a foreign-language requirement here."

His mind a simmering stew, Trumper got to the Village in time for the nine o'clock showing of *Fucking Up.* The sight of his name among the sound and acting credits impressed him, though he fought it. The finished version was a lot more fluid than he remembered it; he found himself looking at it expectantly, as at a photograph album full of old friends in funny clothes and ten pounds lighter. But it was all very predictable; he remembered everything, right up until the end, when he saw the scene he'd only overheard: Tulpen in the bathtub, telling Ralph and Kent that it was time for them to leave.

Then he saw the scenes he'd patched together of his own leaving. Ralph had reversed the order of their appearance. There was Trumper leaving the pet shop, saying, "Goodbye, Ralph. I don't want to be in your movie any more." There were Trumper and Tulpen and Colm on the subway to the Bronx Zoo, with Trumper's voice-over saying, "Tulpen, I am sorry. But I do not want a child."

Then came two new scenes.

Tulpen in exercise tights is performing the preparatory exercises for natural childbirth: deep-breathing, odd squat-thrusts, and the like. Ralph's voice-over says, "He left her."

Then a shot of Tulpen working in the editing room. The camera sees her from behind; she is sitting down, and only when she turns her head do we recognize her, in profile. Slowly, she acknowledges the camera's presence; she looks over her shoulder into the lens, then turns away. She couldn't care less about the camera. Offstage, Ralph asks, "Are you happy?"

Tulpen seems self-conscious. She gets up from her workbench with an odd gesture; from behind, her elbow lifts like the wing of a bird. But Trumper knows: she is lifting her lovely breast with the back of her hand.

When she turns in full-length profile to the camera, we see that she is pregnant.

"You're pregnant . . ." Ralph's voice nags.

Tulpen gives the camera a no-shit sort of look. Her hands are busy, tucking the shapeless folds of her maternity dress around her great abdomen.

"Whose baby is it?" Ralph says relentlessly.

There is no hesitation, only a casual shrug of her breasts, but she won't face the camera. "His," Tulpen says.
362

The image freezes to a still, over which the credits appear.

When the lights came on, there was a crush of Greenwich Village film addicts all around him. He sat as if anesthetized, until he realized that no one could get past his splayed knees; then he rose and walked up the aisle with the crowd.

In the lobby's miasma of sickly light and candy smells, kids were lighting cigarettes and milling around; trapped in the slow-moving crowd, Trumper overheard snatches of talk.

"What a perfect shit," a girl said.

"I don't know, I don't know," someone complained. "Packer gets more and more hung up on himself, you know?"

"Well, I liked it, but . . ." said a thoughtful voice.

"The acting was really okay, you know . . ."

"They weren't exactly actors . . ."

"Well, okay, the people, then . . ."

"Yeah, great."

"Good camera work too."

"Yeah, but he didn't *do* anything with it . . ."

"You know what I say when I see a film like this?" a voice asked. "I say, 'So what?' That's what I say, man."

"Give me the keys, motherfuck . . ."

"Another piece of shit is another piece of shit is . . ."

"But it's *relative* . . ."

"It's all the same."

"Excuse me . . ." Bogus thought of biting the slender neck of a tall girl in front of him, thought of turning and kneeing a covey of callow philosophers behind him who were calling the film "great nihilism."

Just before the door, he knew he'd been recognized. A girl with a drug-complexion and dirty-saucer eyes stared at him, then plucked her companion's sleeve. They were a part of a group, and in a minute all of them turned to regard Trumper, wedged in a clutch of people by the door. It was a double door, but half of it was stuck closed. As someone snapped it open, a cheer went up, and for a second, Trumper actually imagined the applause was for *him.* Then a young man in a Union Army uniform, who had an elegant Smith Brothers' beard and yellow teeth, blocked his way.

"Excuse me," Trumper said.

"Hey, it's *you*," the young man said, and turning to his friends, he called, "Hey, I told you—it's that *guy* . . ."

Instantly a dozen people were gawking at him in celebrity fashion.

"I thought he was taller," a girl said.

Some of the young ones—just kids, silly and laughing—followed him all the way to his car.

Another girl teased him. "Oh come home and meet my mother!" she sang.

He got into his car and drove away.

"A new Volkswagen!" a boy said with mock awe. "Far out . . ."

Trumper drove around and got lost; he'd never driven in New York before. Finally, he paid a taxi to lead him to Tulpen's apartment. He still had his key to the place. It was after midnight, but he was thinking of *other* kinds of time. Like months, and how long he'd been gone; like how pregnant Tulpen had been when the film was finished; like how much time had passed before the film was released. Though he knew better, he had an image of Tulpen as he expected her to look *now:* only a little more swollen than in the film.

He tried to let himself in, but she had fastened the safety chain. He heard her sit up startled in bed, and he whispered, "It's me."

It was a long time before she would let him in. She was in a short bathrobe, cinched tight at her waist; her belly was as flat as before; she'd even lost some weight. In the kitchen, he collided with a box of paper diapers and crunched a baby's plastic pacifier under his foot. A perverted demon in his head kept telling bad jokes to his brain.

He tried to smile. "Boy or girl?" he asked.

"Boy," she said. Looking down, she pretended to rub the sleep in her eyes, but she was wide-awake.

"Why didn't you tell me?"

"You made yourself pretty clear. Anyway, it's *my* baby."

"Mine too," he said. "You even said so, in the film . . ."

"In Ralph's film," she said. "He wrote the script."

"But it *is* mine, isn't it?" he asked her. "I mean, *really* . . ."

"Biologically?" she said crisply. "Of course it is."

"Can I see him?" Trumper asked. She was very tense, but she faked a shrug and led him past her bed to a little nook made out of stacked bookcases and more fish.

The boy slept in a huge basket, with lots of toys around him. He looked the way Colm had looked at the age of a few weeks, and a lot like Biggie's new baby, who was probably only a month or so older.

Bogus stared at the baby because it was easier than looking at Tulpen; though there's not much to see in a child that age, Trumper appeared to be reading it.

Tulpen banged around in the background. From the linen cabinet, she took some sheets and some blankets and a pillow; it was clear she was making up the couch for Bogus to sleep on.

"Do you want me to go?" he asked.

"Why did you come?" she asked. "You just saw the movie, right?"

"I've been wanting to come before," he said. When she just went on making up the couch, he said stupidly: "I got my Ph.D." She stared at him, then went back to tucking in the blanket. "I've been looking for a job," he said.

"Have you found one?" She flounced the pillow.

"No."

She beckoned him away from the sleeping baby. In the kitchen, she opened a beer for him, pouring off some for herself. "For the breasts," she said, toasting him with her glass. "It makes the milk run."

"I know."

"Oh, right, you would," she said. She played with her bathrobe belt, then asked, "What do you want, Trumper?"

But he was too slow to answer.

"You just feeling guilty?" she asked. "Because I don't need that. You owe me nothing more than your straight, honest feelings, Trumper . . . If you *have* any," she added.

"How do you live?" he asked her. "You can't work," he began, then stopped, knowing that money wasn't the issue. His straight, honest feelings were a long way down in a bog he'd been skirting for so long that now it seemed impossible to dive in and grope.

"I *can* work," she said mechanically, "and I do. I mean,

365

I will. When he gets a little older, I'll take him to Matje's while I work half-days. Matje wants to have a baby herself soon . . ."

"That's Ralph's new girl?" he asked.

"His wife," Tulpen said. "Ralph married her."

Trumper realized then that he knew absolutely nothing about anybody. "Ralph's *married?*" he said.

"He sent you an invitation," Tulpen said. "But you'd already left Iowa."

He was beginning to be aware of just how much he *had* left. But Tulpen was tired of his long interior monologues, and he guessed she didn't need any more of his silences, either. From the living room he watched her go to bed; she took her bathrobe off under the covers and threw it on the floor. "Since you remember babies, it won't surprise you that there's a two o'clock feeding," she said. "Goodnight."

He went into the bathroom and peed with the door open. He'd always left the bathroom door open; it was another of his foul habits which he only remembered in the midst of practicing them. When he came out, Tulpen said, "How's the new prick?"

What's this—*humor?* he wondered. He had no genuine instincts to rely on. "Perfectly normal," he said.

"Goodnight," she said, and as he tiptoed to his made-up couch he had an impulse to hurl his shoes against the wall and wake up the baby just to hear his piercing cries fill this empty place.

He lay listening to his own breathing, and Tulpen's, and the baby's. Only the baby was asleep.

"I love you, Tulpen," he said.

A turtle in the aquarium nearest him seemed to respond; it dove deeper.

"I came here because I want you," he said.

Not even a fish moved.

"I need you," he said. "I know that you don't need me, but *I* need you."

"Well, it's not quite like that," she said, so softly that he could hardly hear her.

He sat up on the couch. "Will you marry me, Tulpen?"

"No," she said. There was no hesitation.

"Please?" he said softly.

This time she waited, but then she said, "No, I won't."

He put on his shoes and got up. There was no other way to leave except by walking past the open alcove of aquariums around her bed, and when he reached the spot, she was sitting up, staring at him and looking furious.

"Jesus!" she said. "Are you walking out again?"

"What do you want me to do?"

"Jesus, you don't know?" she said. "I'll tell you, Trumper, if I have to. I won't marry you *yet*, but if you want to stay around a while, I could wait and *see!* If you want to stay, you should *stay,* Trumper!"

"Okay," he said. He wondered if he should take off his clothes.

"Jesus, take off your clothes," she told him. He did, and then crawled into bed beside her.

She lay turned away from him. "Jesus," she mumbled.

He lay without touching her until she rolled over suddenly, seized one of his hands and pulled it roughly to her breast. "I don't want to make love to you," she said, "but you can hold me . . . if you want to."

"I want to," he mumbled. "I love you, Tulpen."

"I guess so," she said.

"Do you love me?"

"Yes, Jesus, I guess so," she said angrily.

Slowly some instincts returned to him; he touched her gently all over. He felt where they'd shaved her; it was still stubbly. When the baby woke up for his two o'clock nipple, Trumper was out of bed ahead of her, brought the baby back to the bed and put him to her breast.

"No, the other one," she said. "Which one's harder?"

"That one."

"I get all confused . . ." she trailed off and cried softly while she nursed the child. Trumper had his memory in order; he held a diaper to her unused breast, knowing it would leak while the other was being sucked.

"Sometimes they really squirt," she told him.

"I know," he said. "They will, when you make love . . ."

"I don't want to make love," she reminded him.

"I *know*. I was just remarking on it . . ."

"You're going to have to be patient," she said. "I'm still going to say some things just because I want to hurt you."

"Sure, okay."

"You're just going to have to hang around until I don't want to hurt you any more."

"Sure, I *want* to hang around," he said.

"I don't think I'm going to want to hurt you much more," she said.

"I don't blame you," he said, which made her angry again.

"Well, it's none of your business," she said.

"Of course it isn't," he agreed.

Tenderly she said to him, "You just better not talk very much, Trumper, okay?"

"Okay."

When the baby went back to his basket, Tulpen came back to bed and snuggled up close to Trumper. "Don't you care what I've named him?" she asked.

"Oh, the baby!" he said. "Of course. What did you name him?"

"Merrill," she said, and she bore down hard with the heel of her hand on his spine. The back of his throat ached. "I must love you," she whispered. "I called him Merrill because I think you're very fond of that name."

"I am, yes," he whispered.

"I was thinking of you, see?"

He could feel her body getting angry with him again. "Yes, I know," he said.

"You hurt me like hell, Trumper, do you know that?" she said.

"Yes." He touched her stubble lightly.

"Okay," she said. "Just don't ever forget it."

He promised he never would, and then she held on to him and he dreamed his two most frequent nightmares. Variations on a water theme, he called them.

One was always Colm, in some imagined disaster which always involved deep water, the sea or cold mudflats. As always, it was too terrible to allow him to consciously remember the details.

The other was always about Merrill Overturf. He was in water too; he was opening the top hatch of a tank; it always took him too long.

At six A.M., baby Merrill's wailing woke him. Tulpen's breasts were drenching his chest and the bed had a sour-sweet smell of milk.

She covered herself with a diaper and he said, "Look at them leak. You must be aroused."

"It's because of the baby crying," she insisted, and he got out of bed to fetch the child for her. Trumper had a typical morning erection, which he did not hide.

"Have you seen my new prick?" he said, clowning. "It's still a virgin, you know."

"The baby's crying," she said, but she was smiling. "Get the baby."

"Merrill!" he said. How nice it felt to say that name out loud! "Merrill, Merrill, Merrill," he said, waltzing the baby to the bed. They had a nice debate about which breast to use; Trumper did a lot of excessive feeling around for the harder one.

Tulpen was still nursing when the phone rang. It was very early in the morning for a call, but she seemed unsurprised; watching Trumper closely, she nodded for him to answer it. He sensed he was being tested somehow, so he picked up the phone, but didn't speak.

"Good morning, young suckling mother!" said Ralph Packer. "How is the baby? How are your boobs?" Trumper swallowed while Tulpen smiled serenely. "Matje and me are on our way over," Ralph went on. "Do you need anything?"

"Yogurt," Tulpen whispered to Bogus.

"Yogurt," Trumper told the phone thickly.

"Thump-Thump!" Ralph cried.

"Hello, Ralph," Bogus said. "I saw your movie . . ."

"Terrible, isn't it?" Ralph said. "How *are* you, Thump-Thump?"

"I'm fine," Trumper said. Tulpen removed the diaper from her free tit and aimed her nipple at Trumper. "I got my Ph.D.," Trumper mumbled to the phone.

"How's the baby?" Ralph asked.

"Merrill's fine," Bogus said. Tulpen's free breast was squirting his leg. "I'm sorry I missed your marriage, Ralph. Congratulations."

"Congratulations to *you*," Ralph said smartly.

"See you soon," said Trumper and hung up.

"You okay, Trumper?" Tulpen asked. There seemed to be one cool eye regarding him, and one warm.

"Just fine," he said, covering her leaking breast with his hand. "*You* okay?" he asked.

"I'm better."

He touched her stubble and looked at his hand lying there, the way one might look at an old friend with a new beard. They were both naked, except that he still wore his right sock. Baby Merrill nursed fiercely, but Tulpen wasn't looking at him. Her expression, part smile, part frown, she was examining closely Trumper's new prick.

Bogus felt pleasantly embarrassed. Maybe they should get dressed, he suggested, since Ralph and what's-her-name, Matje, were coming over. Then he bent down quickly and kissed her lightly on her stubble. She seemed about to . . . but declined to follow up this timid beginning. She kissed his neck.

Okay, thought Bogus Trumper. Scar tissue take a little getting used to, but I want to learn.

38: The Old Friends Assemble for Throgsgafen Day

In the kingdom of Thak, they really knew how to throw a Throgsafen Day. For weeks before the fest, wild boars lay about in marinades and great elk were hung to ripen on the trees; barrels of eels crowded the smokehouse; cauldrons of rabbits, rubbed with sea salt and apples, were simmered in the fat of a rendered bear; a caribou—of a now-extinct species—was stewed, whole, in a vat stirred with an oar. The fall fruits, particularly the blessed grape, were harvested, mashed, allowed to ferment, strained and sauced, and last year's long-aging brews were rolled out of the cellars, tapped and tasted, distilled and tasted again and again. (The common drink in the kingdom of Thak was a urine-sour, murky beer, a little like our own American beer when flat, mixed with cider vinegar. The special drink in Thak was a distilled brandy made from plums and root vegetables; it tasted like a mixture of slivowitz and anti-freeze.)

Of course, Throgsafen Day actually took more than a day. There was the day before Throgsafen when everyone had to sample everything, and the night before Throgsafen when everyone had to prepare to make merry. On the morning of Throgsafen, small parties were held to compare hangovers, and these flowed right into the main event itself—a continuous meal, lasting some six hours. Then vigorous physical exercise was recommended for the men, whose terrible athletic verve needed some release. This took the form of combative sports and sex.

371

The women took part in the latter event; they also danced and made half-hearted attempts to de-gunk the castle.

On Throgsgafen night, all the lords and ladies carried great troughs of food and left-over debris through the villages, throwing out scraps to the wretched little peasant children. This was a sobering part of the evening, but the party returned to the castle at midnight to toast all the dead friends of Throgsgafens past; this went on until dawn, when a special court of the Council of Elders was traditionally held to determine penalties for all the murders, rapes and other petty crimes which had occurred in abundance over the exhausting holiday.

Our own tame, dry-turkey version of Throgsgafen is indeed an embarrassing substitute, so Bogus Trumper and his old friends were determined to inject the spirit of *Akthelt and Gunnel* into the affair. A bold gathering was planned. Despite the unpredictable qualities of Maine in November, it was decided that Couth and Biggie had the only castle worthy of housing such a bash.

The presence of large dogs lent an original Throgsgafen flavor to the outing. One of the dogs was Ralph's. He'd bought it in celebration of Matje's growing pregnancy, and also for her protection on the New York streets. An uncategorizable beast named Loom, it made the trip to Maine from New York a bit trying. Trumper drove his Volkswagen with Tulpen beside him holding baby Merrill in her lap; in the crammed back seat, Ralph and his pregnant Matje fought with Loom. A burdened roof rack on top of the car held Merrill's crib, warm clothes, baskets of wine, booze, and such oddities as rare cheese and smoked meats which Biggie and Couth couldn't get in Maine. Biggie was handling the main dishes.

The other dog—Trumper's birthday present to Colm— was already in Maine. A Chesapeake Bay retriever with a thick, oily coat like a used doormat—Couth called it The Great Dog Gob.

Trumper and Tulpen didn't have a dog. "A baby, forty fish and ten turtles are enough," Bogus said.

"But you should get a dog, Thump-Thump," Ralph said. "You're just not a family without a dog."

"And you should get a car, Ralph," Trumper said, aiming his stuffed Volkswagen up the Maine Turnpike. "A

372

great big car, Ralph," Trumper said. Loom, the back-seat beast, was salivating down his neck.

"Maybe even a bus, Ralph," said Tulpen.

By Boston there was no room left in the tiny glove compartment for any more of Merrill's awful diapers, and Matje had to stop to pee eight times because she was pregnant. Trumper drove furiously, his dull gaze riveted straight ahead; he ignored the wails of Merrill, Ralph's endless complaints about the leg room and the ominous breathing of Loom. What was I ever thinking of? Bogus wondered. It seemed to him a miracle when they finally arrived at the fog-shrouded sea-house glazed with falling sleet.

Gob and Loom hit it off right away; they romped themselves into a slaver of slush and mudflat muck, and Colm went wild trying to contain the brutes.

This day before Throgsgafen was an indoor day, and the menfolk organized pool games and bantered about who had brought what.

"Where is the bourbon?" Bogus asked.

"Where is the pot?" said Ralph.

"We're out of butter," Biggie told Couth.

"Where is the bathroom?" Matje asked.

Biggie and Tulpen had a discussion about the smallness of Matje's belly. She was a wrenlike creature whose degree of pregnancy, which was almost term, resembled a small cantaloupe.

"God, I was much bigger," Biggie said.

"Well, you *are* much bigger, Big," Bogus said.

"You were bigger too," Ralph told Tulpen. She looked at Bogus and saw that he might feel shitty about having no memory of his second wife's pregnancy with his second son. She went over and goosed him quietly.

Then all the men gathered around Matje and felt her tummy, under the pretense of assessing the child's sex. "I hate to tell you this, Ralph," Bogus said. "But I think Matje's going to have a grape."

The women arranged baby Anna and baby Merrill in a side-by-side display on the dining-room sideboard. Anna was older, but both of them were still in the phase where all that's required is to sleep them, slurp them and wash their bottoms.

Sightseeing in such foul weather was limited to the two nursing mothers' breasts and Matje's swelling grape, so there was much bad pool and good drinking. Ralph was the first one to feel the effect. "I must tell you," he said solemnly to Couth and Bogus. "I like *all* our ladies."

Outside, in the rolling fog and sleet flakes, The Great Dog Gob and the uncategorizable Loom wrestled in the slush.

Only Colm was in a rotten mood. For one thing, he was simply not used to so many guests; for another, the babies were placid, boring, unplayful creatures and the dogs in their excited condition seemed dangerous. Also, usually when Colm saw his father, Bogus gave him undivided attention. Now there were just a lot of silly adults talking. It was foul out, but it was better out than in, so to demonstrate his boredom, Colm would track lots of slush into the house and schemingly allow the wild dogs in, almost urging them to break rare Pillsbury vases.

The grownups were finally sensitive to Colm's problem and took turns taking walks with him in the terrible outdoors. Colm would bring back one sodden grownup after another "*Now* who wants to come with me?" he'd ask.

Finally it was time to do something in the way of preparing a minor warm-up feast for the evening—not to compare, of course, with tomorrow's major event.

Tulpen had brought some meat from New York.

"Ah, New York meat!" said Ralph, pinching Tulpen. Matje gouged Ralph with a corkscrew.

After dinner, it was almost peaceful; the babies were in bed and the men were stuffed and woozy. But Colm was overtired, and irritable about having to go upstairs. Biggie tried to coax him, but he refused to budge from the table. Then Bogus offered to carry him upstairs, since he was so tired.

"I'm *not* tired," Colm said disagreeably.

"How about some *Moby Dick?*" Bogus asked him. "Come on."

"I want Couth to put me to bed," Colm said.

It was obvious that he was simply in a mood, so Couth lifted him up and started off upstairs with him. "I'll put you to bed if you want," he told Colm, "but I don't know
374

Moby Dick and I can't tell stories the way Bogus can . . ."
But Colm was already asleep.

Sitting at the table between Biggie and Tulpen, Bogus felt Biggie put her hand under the table and lay it on his knee; almost simultaneously Tulpen touched the other knee. They were both thinking he might feel hurt, so he said reassuringly, "Colm's just in a snit. It hasn't been such a hot day for him."

Across the strewn dinner table, Ralph sat with his hand on Matje's grape. "You know, Thump-Thump," he said. "We could do the movie right here in Maine. After all, this is sort of a castle . . ."

He was talking about his next film project: *Akthelt and Gunnel.* The movie was pretty well planned. They were going to Europe when Trumper finished the script; a production company in Munich was committed to backing it. They were going to take their wives and babies too, though Trumper had urged Ralph to consider leaving Loom behind. They had even thought of trying to include Couth in it as the cameraman. But Couth wasn't interested. "I'm a *still* photographer," he'd pointed out. "And I live in Maine."

In a passing, ungenerous moment, Trumper thought that the real reason Couth wasn't interested in the movie was because of Biggie. Bogus felt vaguely that Biggie still disapproved of him, but when he'd mentioned this once to Tulpen, he'd been confused by her response. "Frankly," Tulpen told him, "I'm glad Couth and Biggie won't be coming."

"You don't like Biggie?" Bogus asked.

"It's not that," Tulpen said. "Sure, I like Biggie."

Now this old confusion passed again over Bogus like a drunk's flush.

It was time to sleep. People groggily faced the unfamiliar upstairs of the great Pillsbury mansion, losing themselves in halls and stumbling into the wrong bedrooms.

"Where do I sleep?" Ralph kept asking. "Ah God, take me there . . ."

"To think that it's only the day *before* Throgsgafen," Couth said plaintively.

Biggie was having a quiet pee in her bathroom when Bogus walked in on her. As usual, he left the door open.

"What in hell are you doing, Bogus?" she asked him, trying to cover herself.

"I think I'll just brush my teeth, Big," Bogus said. He didn't seem to realize he wasn't married to her any more.

Couth peered in the open doorway, mildly surprised. "What's he doing?" he asked his wife.

"He's brushing his teeth, I guess," Biggie said. "For God's sake, at least shut the door!"

Just when everyone seemed to be straightened out and settled in their proper rooms, Ralph Packer appeared naked in the hall. Through the open bedroom door behind him, Matje could be heard inquiring what he thought he was doing. "I am *not* going to pee out the window," he shouted. "There are bathrooms all over this bloody castle, and I intend to find one!"

Biggie sweetly led the nude Ralph to the right place.

"I'm sorry, Biggie," Matje said, hurrying after Ralph with his pants.

"Es ist mir Wurst," Biggie said, and touched Matje's tummy fondly. If Trumper had been there, he would have understood Biggie's Austrian dialect. "It doesn't matter" was what it meant, but the literal translation was, "It is sausage to me."

Trumper wasn't where he could have heard her. He was having delicious love made to him by Tulpen; he was too drunk to appreciate such loving, really, but it did have a startling aftereffect: he found himself wide-awake and sitting up very sober. Tulpen was deeply asleep beside him, but when he kissed her feet to thank her, she smiled.

He couldn't sleep, though. He kissed Tulpen all over, but she couldn't be aroused.

Wide, wide awake, Trumper got up and dressed himself warmly; he wished it were morning. Tiptoeing to Colm's room, he kissed the boy and tucked him in. He went to look at the babies, and then listened to the other adults sleeping, but it wasn't enough. He tiptoed into Biggie and Couth's room and watched them sleeping in a warm tangle. Couth woke up. "It's next door, down the hall," he said, thinking that Bogus was looking for the bathroom.

Wandering around, Trumper found Ralph and Matje's room and looked in on them too. Ralph lay splayed out on his stomach, his hands and feet dangling off the bed.

Across his broad, hairy back, tiny Matje lay sleeping like a flower on a compost heap.

Downstairs, Bogus opened the French doors to the pool room and let in the air. It was very cold, and the fog was moving out of the bay. Trumper knew that there was a barren rock island in the center of the bay, and that this was what he saw, revealed and concealed by the shifting fog. But if he stared hard, the island actually seemed to roll, to rise and fall, and if he stared *very* hard, he could see a broad, flat tail arch up and smack the sea so hard that the dogs whined in their sleep. "Hello, Moby Dick," Trumper whispered. Gob growled and Loom staggered to his feet and then collapsed.

In the kitchen, Bogus found some paper and sat down and began writing. His first sentence was one he'd written before: "Her gynecologist recommended him to me." Others followed and formed a paragraph. "Ironic: the best urologist in New York is French. Dr. Jean Claude Vigneron: ONLY BY APPOINTMENT. So I made one."

What have I begun? he wondered. He didn't know. He put the paper with these crude beginnings in his pocket to save for a time when he had more to say.

He wished he understood what made him feel so restless. Then it occurred to him that he was actually at peace with himself for the first time in his life. He realized how much he'd been anticipating peace someday, but the feeling was not what he'd expected. He used to think that peace was a state he would achieve, but the peace he was feeling was like a force he'd submitted to. God, why should peace depress me? he thought. But he wasn't depressed, exactly. Nothing was exact.

He was chalking up his pool cue, thinking how he wanted the balls to break, when he became aware that he wasn't the only one who was up and awake in the sleeping house. "That you, Big?" he said quietly, without turning around. (Later, he would lose another night's sleep wondering how he knew it was her.)

Biggie was careful; she only skirted the borders of her subject—the phase Colm was going through, how he was at the age when boys turn more naturally to a father than to a mother. "I know it's going to be painful for you," she told Bogus, "but Colm's turning more and more to Couth. When you're here, I can tell the child is confused."

"I'm going to Europe soon," Trumper said bitterly. "Then I won't be around to confuse him for a good long time."

"I'm sorry," Biggie said. "I really like seeing you. I just don't like how it makes me feel, sometimes, when you're around."

Trumper felt a strange meanness come over him; he wanted to tell Biggie that she simply resented being confronted with how happy he was with Tulpen. But that was insane; he wanted to tell her no such thing. He didn't even believe it. "I get confused too," he told her, and she nodded, agreeing with such sudden vigor that he felt embarrassed. Then she left him alone again, fleeing upstairs so quickly that he thought she must be trying not to cry in front of him. Or not to laugh?

He was thinking that he actually agreed with how Biggie felt—that he liked to see her, but didn't like the way he felt around her—when he thought he heard her coming back downstairs.

But this time it was Tulpen, and Trumper saw at a glance that she'd been awake for a while herself and that she'd probably just passed Biggie in the upstairs hall.

"Oh, shit," he said. "It's so complicated sometimes." He went quickly over to her and hugged her; she seemed in need of some reassurance.

"I want to leave tomorrow," Tulpen said.

"But it's Throgsgafen."

"After the meal, then," she said. "I don't want to spend another night."

"Okay, okay," he told her. "I know, I know." His voice went on comforting her without much meaning to his words. He knew that back in New York there'd be a week of trying to understand this, but it didn't pay to think too hard about what came after the holiday, about the often lonely business of living with someone. Surviving a relationship with any other human being sometimes seemed impossible to him. But so what? he thought.

"I love you," he whispered to Tulpen.

"I know," she said.

He took her back upstairs to bed, and just before she

378

fell asleep, she asked him groggily, "Why can't you just fall asleep next to me after we make love? Why does it wake you up? It puts me to sleep, but it wakes you up. That's not fair, because I wake up later and the bed's empty and I find you staring at the fish or watching the baby sleep or playing pool with your old wife . . ."

He lay awake until dawn, trying to figure all that out. Tulpen was sleeping soundly and didn't wake up when Colm appeared at their bedside in layers of sweaters over his pajamas, wading boots and a wool hat. "I know, I know," Trumper whispered. "If *I* come down to the dock, you can go down too."

It was cold, but they were wearing lots of clothes; the slush had turned to ice and they slid on their bottoms down the steep flagstone path. The sun was hazy, but the air was clear inland and across the bay. Out to sea, a dense fog was slowly rolling in; it would take a while to reach them, though, and they had the clearest part of the coming day to themselves.

They shared an apple. They heard the babies waking up in the house above them: brief cries, then a renewed silence on receiving their respective breasts. Colm and Bogus agreed on the dullness of babies.

"I saw Moby Dick last night," Bogus decided to tell Colm, who looked a little suspicious. "It may have been just the old island," Trumper confessed, "but I heard a great *slap*, like his tail hitting the water."

"You're making that up," Colm said. "That's not real."

"Not *real?*" said Trumper. He'd never heard Colm use the word before.

"Right," said Colm, but the boy's attention was wandering—he was bored by his father—and Bogus wanted desperately for things to be lively between them.

"What kind of books do you like best?" he asked Colm. As soon as he spoke, he thought, God, I am reduced to making small talk with my son.

"Well, I still like *Moby Dick*," Colm said. Was he just being kind? ("Be kind to your father," Bogus heard Couth telling Colm, shortly before they had all arrived.) "I mean, I like the story," Colm said. "But it's just a story."

On the dock beside his son, Trumper fought back sudden tears.

The great houseful of flesh above them would wake soon, almost like one giant person—perform its ablutions, feed itself, try to be helpful and kind. In this pleasant confusion a keen sense of things would be lost, but out on the dock, watching the sun slowly losing to the fog, Trumper felt bright and crisp. By now the fog covered the mouth of the bay and was bound to roll in on them; it was so thick that you couldn't tell what was behind it. But in his momentary piece of clear light, Trumper felt he could see through his brain.

Bogus and Colm heard a toilet flush, and then Ralph shouted from the house, "Oh, that goddamn dog!"

Upstairs, a window opened; Biggie was framed in it, Anna in her arms. "Good morning!" she called down to them.

"Happy Throgsgafen Day!" Bogus yelled, and Colm took up the cry.

Another window opened and Matje poked her head out like a parakeet from its cage. Downstairs, Tulpen opened the French doors of the pool room and held Merrill in the air above her head. Couth appeared in Biggie's window. Everyone was getting a last feel of the morning before the fog came in.

The kitchen door flew open, ejecting Gob, Loom and Ralph. He yelled, "Those goddamn dogs threw up in the laundry room!"

"It was *your* dog, Ralph!" Couth called from his window. "My dog never throws up!"

"It was *Trumper!*" Tulpen yelled from the pool room. "He was up all night! He was up to something! Trumper puked in the laundry room!"

Bogus protested his innocence, but everyone chanted his guilt. Colm seemed delighted by this weird adult performance. The dogs began the day's cavorting, falling heavily on the ice. Bogus took his son's hand and they made their careful, slippery way up to the house.

Heavy traffic conditions ruled the kitchen. The dogs fought furiously outside the door while Colm, seeking to increase the chaos, blew a shrill whistle. Ralph announced that Matje's grape had grown. The women demanded that all but the children fast instead of having breakfast; they were already at work on the midday feast. Biggie and

Tulpen each flaunted a breast which lolled free, a nipple-glued child riding on each busy hip. Matje fixed breakfast for Colm and scolded Ralph for not cleaning up after the dogs.

Ralph and Couth and Bogus hung around, with their slightly off-putting morning smells and a certain prickliness of appearance. Matje and Biggie and Tulpen were blowzy, wearing not quite clothes: bathrobes and soft slept-in stuff—a warm rumpled sensuousness about them.

Bogus wondered what he could have thought he wanted. But the kitchen was far too flurried for thinking; bodies were everywhere. So what if dog puke still lurked unseen in the laundry room! In good company we can be brave.

Mindful of his scars, his old harpoons and things, Bogus Trumper smiled cautiously at all the good flesh around him.

Bestselling Novels from

#1 POCKET BOOKS